UNHOLY
TERRORS

PRAISE FOR
UNHOLY TERRORS

"A whirlwind journey, filled with heart-wrenching tension and sinister twists. This is the kind of dark romance you thirst for!"
—**ALEXANDRA CHRISTO**, internationally bestselling author of *To Kill a Kingdom*

"Bloody and lovely at once, *Unholy Terrors* is a moody meditation on desire and duty, fate and free will, and the bonds we are born to and the ones we choose for ourselves."
—**ERICA WATERS**, Bram Stoker Award–winning author of *The River Has Teeth*

"A stunning fantasy romance with claws—literally—Clipstone once again proves herself a veritable force of a storyteller. With evocative, lyrical prose and a deftly woven atmosphere, *Unholy Terrors* coaxes beauty from the monstrous and suggests that, just maybe, the two aren't so different after all. A must-read that begs to be devoured, but is certainly worth savoring."
—**M. K. LOBB**, internationally bestselling author of *Seven Faceless Saints*

"*Unholy Terrors* is a lush, immersive read that sinks its claws in deep and doesn't let go until the very last page. As romantic as it is gruesome, this heart-stopping gothic fantasy explores what it truly means to be a monster."
—**KELLY ANDREW**, author of *The Whispering Dark* and *Your Blood, My Bones*

"Lyndall Clipstone has woven a dark dream that ensnares all five senses. Fanged yet delicate, with its windswept moors, blood moons, and aching romance, *Unholy Terrors* is utterly spellbinding."
—**RACHEL GILLIG**, author of The Shepherd King duology

"Like a beautiful nightmare, *Unholy Terrors* sinks its claws into you and refuses to let go. This is the enemies-to-lovers gothic fantasy you've been waiting for."
—**MARA RUTHERFORD**, author of *The Poison Season*

"Deliciously addictive! *Unholy Terrors* simply dazzles as Clipstone entraps us yet again in a rich, blood-soaked redesigned fairy tale, drenched in lush lyrical prose. The story brims with gothic romance and shrouded mystery. Prepare yourself for what awaits in the Thousandfold."
—**DANA SWIFT**, author of *Cast in Firelight* and bookseller at Books & Books

"*Unholy Terrors* is a darkly adventurous delight from first to last, one that gives new meaning to 'spellbound' as it explores a landscape of evocative romance and gothic magic and weaves a mystery as unshakable as a nightmare and infinitely more stunning."
—**MONICA ROBINSON**, author of *Peeling The Yellow Wallpaper* and bookseller at The Spiral Bookcase

"*Unholy Terrors* cradles you with clawed fingers that no scissors can clip. It folds you into a feather-soft story that's lined with thorns. Make one move, and it draws blood."
—**KEL RUSSELL**, lead bookseller at Main Street Books / Second Flight Books

ALSO BY
LYNDALL CLIPSTONE

Forestfall

Lakesedge

UNHOLY TERRORS

LYNDALL CLIPSTONE

HENRY HOLT AND COMPANY

NEW YORK

Henry Holt and Company, *Publishers since 1866*
Henry Holt® is a registered trademark of Macmillan Publishing Group, LLC
120 Broadway, New York, NY 10271 • fiercereads.com

Our books may be purchased in bulk for promotional, educational, or business use. Please
contact your local bookseller or the Macmillan Corporate and Premium Sales Department
at (800) 221-7945 ext. 5442 or by email at MacmillanSpecialMarkets@macmillan.com.

Library of Congress Control Number: 2023020128

First edition, 2023
Book design by Rich Deas
Printed in the United States of America

ISBN 978-1-250-88773-3
10 9 8 7 6 5 4 3 2 1

For all the sharp-toothed monster girls
who sought a bright place in a shadowed world.

He's mad that trusts in the tameness of a wolf

—William Shakespeare, *King Lear*

PART ONE

No vespertine shall

cross the wall, even in death.

—First commandment of Saint Lenore

CHAPTER ONE

IN THE MONTH BEFORE THE GATHERING, THE WALL WEEPS blood.

We stand in its shadow, Lux and I, as the day turns to windswept dusk. The wall is built of bones and magic, held together by a spell that wanes throughout the year. Moon by moon, it turns more fragile. And these nights, the bloodied nights where the magic of the wall is like an unraveling thread, are when the vespertine come.

It's early storm season, and the days are still long enough that there's light to see by as I check Lux's armor, running my chipped-polish fingers from buckle to buckle. She's dressed the same as all the wardens. The same as me. A white linen dress with collar and sleeves buttoned close, a leather belt with a strand of bone shards clipped to one side, a sickle-curved knife sheathed on the other.

Out beyond the wall, the moorland is hazed by dimming sunset. The holy wards, stuck in the earth at regular intervals, look like the sharp-pointed wrought iron fence that encircles our chapel yard.

Lux raises her arms obediently as I tighten the straps that hold her armor in place. We've worked as a team since she joined the wardens when we were both children. She's my best friend—my only friend—and the movements between us have been repeated so often that now our preparations feel like a ritual. Lux standing straight-backed, her hazel-gray eyes focused on the slice of moorland visible through the barred gateway. Me, with my head bowed like a penitent as I carefully check each knot and stitch.

This armor is a new creation, one I've just finished. Wolfspine bracers, each vertebra sharpened to a brutal point, and a rib cage strengthened at the joints with silver chain. Tonight, if we encounter a vespertine, it will be the first time the armor has been tested. And that makes me nervous.

I fasten and refasten the buckles three times over. Then Lux huffs a sigh between her black-painted lips and shifts her weight from one foot to the other. "We're good, Everline. Stop worrying."

I scrunch my hands into my pale skirts to still my restlessness. My own armor and weaponry are a modified version of what the other wardens wear—twin knives, no shards, none of the carefully sewn pockets to hold chips of bone or vials of honey required for casting magic. It takes no time at all to check the clasp on my belt and straighten the strands of bone-and-chain lariat that drape from my collar to my waist, clinking against the rib-cage bodice fastened over my linen dress.

Lux gathers up her hair and begins to braid it back, tying the ends with two white ribbons. Both of us share similar coloring—olive skin and treacle-dark hair—but there's a glow to her I've always coveted. Her hair is shot with strands of umber that catch the sunlight, and her cheeks have a petaled flush that intensifies when she's pleased, or angry.

Finished with her braids, Lux takes another ribbon from her pocket and motions for me to turn. I turn. She combs her fingers through the length of my hair, then starts to weave it into a braid.

Facing away from the moorland, I look toward the enclave. I can see the chapel with its iron fence and real glass windows. The entrance to the catacombs is beside it, framed by the citrus trees that pass for our orchard. A few orange fruits still persist on the highest branches.

"There," Lux says. "All done."

She winds the braid up into her hand. Holding it away from my neck, she traces a zigzag pattern over the freckles that mark my nape in a constellated pattern. The last step in our familiar routine.

A sound echoes across the yard, footsteps crushed over the graveled path. Lux lets go of my hair. My stomach sinks at the sight of Briar Linden—my half sister—walking toward us with an unhurried stride.

She's a year my elder, and we look nothing alike. She's clear-eyed and fair, the same as our father, their features so similar that no one would ever doubt she belongs to him. She even wears her armor the same way he does, with her white linen sleeves pulled down beneath wristlets of bone and a single, polished clavicle hooked on her shoulder as a pauldron. Neither was made by me.

Even from here, beneath the low susurrus of wind, I can hear the *clink-clink-clink* of bone on bone as endless shards clatter together in her overfilled pockets and on the strand at her waist. She carries a single knife on her belt with a ribbon tied to the hilt, as though it's some kind of stickpin you might use to hold a chignon in place. I've only ever seen her draw it once.

Briar comes to a lazy stop when she reaches us. Her wheat-gold hair is shaved on one side, the rest pulled over her opposite shoulder in a loose braid. Her lip is pierced at the center with a silver barbell, and she chews at it when she looks at me, her pale brows knotting into a frown.

"Oh, good," she says, sounding not at all pleased. "You're still here."

"Have you come to deliver our farewell? I hope you've brought a lace handkerchief to wave."

She brushes an invisible speck of dust from her sleeve. "I'm going with you."

"No, you're not."

"I wasn't asking your permission, Everline. While Father is away, I'm in charge." Raising one finger, she deliberately taps at the insignia pinned to her chest—the branch-and-bone symbol usually worn by our father, Fenn Linden, commander of the Vale wardens.

"Fenn," I say, "doesn't attach his insignia with a tailor's pin."

Ignoring me, Briar goes on. "*I'm* in charge. And I'm assigning myself to your patrol."

"I could always stitch the insignia on for you. I have a needle and thread in my pocket."

There's a flicker between us, one of those dizzying moments where I can almost feel the balance tilt in my direction. Then she quirks her mouth into a smile. Her lips are painted black, the same as Lux's; her smile a sharp line etched across her delicate face. "I suppose you do have more room in your pockets, since you don't need to carry anything to cast spells."

My hand goes to my knife hilt, the motion more instinctive than anything with real heat. Briar tilts her head, eyes on my blade. The air between us carries a haze of barely perceptible tension, as her fingers twitch toward the strand of bone beads at her hip.

Lux steps between us. She lifts her chin in the direction of the gate. "Shall we go before the wards are entirely out of power?"

Briar moves lightly past us and presses her hand against the lock. There's a click as the magic that holds it closed shifts. The gate swings open. She walks out onto the moor, her index finger pressed to her mouth as she licks away the blood claimed by the unlocking spell.

I bite down hard on the inside of my cheek, trying to ignore the sting of her earlier words. Briar Linden is the best caster at the enclave. Better than anyone—including Fenn, who has commanded the wardens since he was only a little older than I am now. But all wardens have an aptitude for magic. Even those without Briar's skill can manipulate the blood-and-bone spellwork used to maintain the wall and fight back the vespertine when they try to break through.

All wardens have an aptitude for magic—except me.

Lux turns to the wall, scrapes her thumb through one of the freshly oozing drips of blood. She smears it across the bridge of her nose in a crimson streak. I echo her gesture. Briar does the same, avoiding my gaze as she catches some of the blood on her finger

7

and paints it elegantly onto her face. The magic-infused blood from the wall has an icy tang to it, like something just unfrozen. It crackles on my skin as we walk out onto the moorland.

The ground here is flat, deceptively so. From where we stand, beside the wall with our blushed shadows flung up against the closing gate, the world appears to end abruptly; gorse and heather cut off in a line. Beyond is only darkening sky, colored by slants of early sunset.

It's a wild place of thorn and weed and jagged stones. All threat and fable, a graveyard and a battlefield. Where the first wardens fought the first vespertine, then dragged their bones to the edge of the moor to build our wall.

We have the battle scene immortalized in our chapel. A single arching stained glass window set high above the altar, filling the entire apse. It shows Saint Lenore with her bone armor and glimmering sword, all lit up as brilliant as a sunrise. Nyx Severin—creator of the vespertine, a monster who was once thought of as a god—is laid out at her feet, his body displayed in shards of violet and obsidian glass that not even the midday light can pass through.

Lux and I fall into step as we cross the open fields between wall and ward line. We've worked together like this since we were recruits. Patrolling the moorland and setting wards to reinforce the wall as its magic fades throughout the year. I know her movements like they're my own. Her quiet progress forward, the way she tilts her head to listen to the night.

By contrast, the sound of Briar's footsteps behind me is jarring and discordant. Her presence is as prickly as a stuck burr, no matter how hard I try to ignore it.

We reach the apiary, framed by sprawling tangles of wolf roses and lavender blooms. I put my hand against the nearest hive, its whitewashed wood still sun-warm. Bees hum beneath my palm as they work in the nectar-laced depths. No flowers will grow in the enclave, so we tend the bees here.

It was Saint Lenore who first discovered that honey from the bees she kept could sweeten the blood spells cast by Nyx Severin. The spells he used on his worshippers, trying to draw power from their bodies as he sought a way to transcend the Thousandfold, where he was bound.

Lenore changed these spells, used the honey to turn the magic against Nyx and his vespertine when she and the first wardens fought him, putting an end to his monstrous reign.

Now, just as Saint Lenore did, all wardens carry a stoppered fiola alongside their bone shards and silver chains. Made of annealed glass, these vials are our weapons against the vespertine. And a drop of honey is added to each newly made fiola before it's sealed.

Lux pauses beside me, her eyes narrowed to the distance. A wayward tendril of hair has escaped from one of her braids. It marks a curlicue against her cheek as she examines the moorland ahead. "There," she says, voice softened. "Can you see them?"

Our holy wards are made from spike-sharp pieces of bone, split to shards and polished smooth. A length of silver chain, held in place by iron stakes, is strung between them, forming a barrier across the moorland. Beneath each ward, where they are pierced into the ground, the earth should glow—but there's a blotch of darkness where one of the wards has failed.

We slip past the hives. Briar falls in beside me, winding her stranded bone beads around her knuckles. As we make our way to the burned-out ward, the scent of faded, dying flowers in our wake, the end of the world cleaves the horizon. The landscape is a bruise, all spiny gorse leaves and pallid heather, the darker charcoal of lichen stones.

I follow Lux along the barrier to where bones circle the base of each stake. Small shards and chipped vertebrae stained with dried blood. The ground inside each circle flickers with an otherworldly light—the holy fire of consecration, one of the first spells all wardens learn, where they spill their blood on honey-slicked bones and set them into the earth with a whispered incantation.

As we walk, I cast a sidelong glance at Briar. She's never patrolled with other wardens before, and I can't help but wonder what compelled her to join us tonight. It sets a queasy foreboding in the pit of my stomach. I'm tensed, anxious, as I turn to look at the darkening moorland beyond the wards. The painted shadows *seem* empty, but that stillness is deceptive.

Vespertine live for the night. They're wolflike, eldritch creatures; silent and swift, quick to strike, quicker to vanish. And even though Saint Lenore gave her life to destroy Nyx—their leader, their creator—the vespertine continue to deliver determined assaults against the wall. Like a tide, crashing against the shore until it crumbles away.

But the wardens hold them back. We gather each year to reinforce the power of the wall. Between times, as the magic weakens, we set our wards. And when the shadows lengthen and night falls, we come here to the barrier and fight whatever gets spat out of the darkness beyond.

Only once have the vespertine breached the wall. It happened just before I was born, but Fenn has told me countless times how the creatures spilled through the shattered bones. They fought past the enclave and slaughtered their way into the Hallowed Lands, where both the citizens and the wardens who fell were dragged back to the vespertine stronghold beyond the moorland.

He's told the story so often that it's turned vivid, as though I were there. I am out in the night amid the chaos and the terror. I am watching the monsters swarm and watching them devour. The air is sharp with screams, with howls. The earth turns dark with blood.

It's marked on me, this not-quite-memory spun from Fenn's words, a warning as indelible as a scar.

Because in the heart of that battle, my mother deserted the wardens.

As we reach the burned-out ward, I draw my blade. Keep my eyes fixed on the shadowy distance while Lux kneels down to tend the barrier. Briar paces back and forth behind me. Her bead-wrapped hand is at the hilt of her blade, which she draws just far enough to bare a slash of polished steel.

Lux pulls the bones from the ground, dismantling the expired ward. She slips the old shards into one pocket—ready to be cleaned and used again—and takes new ones from the other, setting them carefully into the earth. She uncaps a vial of honey and lets it drip over the bones, then, using another shard, she pierces her finger and daubs a thumbprint of blood in the center of the ward. Her magic ignites. The consecration gleams up, shimmering silver.

I hold out a hand, help Lux back to her feet. Her palm is gritty with dirt, blood and honey smear her cut fingertip. We stand together at the mended barricade. It stretches away from us in both directions, an unbroken line of wards flickering like stars against the dusk.

Then one of the lights goes out. Fast. Much faster than a burned-down bone ward.

Lux tightens her grasp on my hand, pulls me close to her side. A tremor passes through the air, like something alive that's twitching its skin, irritated by an unwelcome touch. As the temperature begins to change, a rapid drop to frostbitten cold, a shiver tracks down my spine. I want to flinch, but I force myself to be still.

"It's all right," I tell Lux, sliding my hand free from hers. "You can let me go."

She nods, lip pinned between her teeth. She lost a sibling to the vespertine when they attacked the Hallowed Lands. A sister, one year her elder, the same as the distance in age between us. Lux is ever-cautious, always protective of me. But as we draw our weapons, I'm not afraid.

I am bone and blade and armor. I am vital, alive. Soft flesh guarded by spear-sharp spines. When I blink, I see red-petaled flowers behind my closed lids.

In the enclave, I am Everline Blackthorn—a warden without magic, there only by the grace of my father, the commander. But out here, with Lux, it doesn't matter that I'll never cast a spell, that Fenn treats me more like a recruit than a daughter, that the fiola I wear around my neck is empty glass.

Even the treachery of my mother—and my questions about her that Fenn will never answer—feels softer, a faded hurt rather than a persistent ache.

The vespertine emerges from the pooled shadows beyond the line of wards, an indeterminate shape cloaked in darkness. I drop to a crouch, my blade already at my palm. The point cuts my skin. My blood lacks the power of warden magic, but it's a bad omen to fight monsters with an unmarked weapon.

Briar flexes her snared fist, her knuckles crackling beneath the strands of silver and bone. Lux twists a shard between her fingers. The sharpened end is already bloodied, consecration glimmering around her hands. She murmurs a spell and the light grows brighter, washing over the ground.

When it hits the vespertine, we fall into sudden silence.

The monsters we fight are familiar horrors with pelted fur the color of midnights and mist; onyx eyes and spike-sharp teeth. They hunch over the ground, four-legged; their shoulders mantled with bone.

I know vespertine, more than any warden. I'm the one who strips them apart once they're dead, taking the fur and teeth and bones that I'll forge into armor. It's the only magic I have, one I taught myself when I realized I could never work the holy power of other wardens.

And this creature has the same feel as the others we've fought. The same ice-laced change to the air as it approaches. The same sharp, coppery stench of tarnished magic and old blood.

But this vespertine is like a *girl*, moving upright as she picks a delicate path toward us through the tangled gorse. She raises one pale, clawed hand and flicks back a sheaf of long, inky hair from her face, revealing narrow, fine-boned features that are decorated by paint. Swaths of grayish-white paste mark her cheeks, and grim skeleton-toothed stripes of black cover her mouth. Her dress is pale, ragged lace, smeared with mud like she's crawled out of a ruin. When she sights us, her lips draw back, baring a row of crowded fangs. Her narrowed eyes shimmer like oil over water.

She is terrible and beautiful in equal measures.

Lux and I exchange a glance, though everyone knows you should never look away from a vespertine. "What . . . ?" Lux begins, but before she can finish, Briar unsheathes her weapon.

Her naked blade sings with a sharp, steely sound as it comes free. The ribbon on the hilt snaps and flutters as she charges forward.

"Briar, wait!" I grab for her arm, but my fingers close on empty air. She casts me a single, disgusted look over her shoulder as she lunges at the creature. Then the world turns blurred, all claw and blade and motion. "Oh, *hells*."

Lux and I rush into the fight. At any other time, the two of us together—her magic, my armor, our strength—feels like a dance. Practiced and familiar as a ritual or a courtship. But now, as we fight alongside Briar, all sense of rhythm and control is lost to this disastrous mess.

Briar attacks with heedless fury; all her attention directed at the creature. Used to fighting alone, she doesn't wait for us or accommodate our movements. We fall into a chaos of sharp elbows and undone hair, wards stuttering at our feet as consecration sparks and the undone barrier chains wrap the vespertine's ankles.

I dart forward, my weapon raised, but Briar turns at the same time, and the hilt of her blade catches my ribs. I stumble back, my breath loosed into a sharp *huff*, a stinging ache when I try to inhale. The vespertine collides with me, snarling, and we fall down together in the dirt. Up close, she looks even more grotesquely human, with a fragile softness to the curve of her cheek, the bow of her lips. Beneath the iron scent of bitter blood, her skin smells like honey. My stomach tightens at the wrongness of it. The horror of a monster wearing a girl's face.

Her bared teeth snap inches from my neck. I twist away, but her claws rake my throat. She clutches at me, her gaze narrowed, and her claws press deeper; piercing, relentless. A terrible heat rises up from my skin, as though her very touch has burned me. I choke out a cry, sharp hurt winding me into a coiled, animal panic. I suck in a breath, trying to gather myself. I'm better than this, even without magic. I'm not some cringing village girl afraid of creatures in the dark.

I've never allowed myself to be.

I twist against the ground, moor grass crunched beneath me as I get my knees up, my boots between myself and the vespertine. I kick her—hard—and she falters back. Lux drags her away from me, catching hold of the creature by the scruff of her neck, still moving like the vespertine is a wolf-shaped thing.

Distantly, I can hear Briar yelling at me, "Everline, *move!*"

She casts aside her blade as she rushes forward, her fists are all chains and bone-beads and dripping blood. I roll aside, barely avoiding the brutal crush of her boots. The air burns with consecration. Briar slams her hand against the creature's sternum, and the vespertine chokes out a guttural cry.

Lux slips quickly behind the vespertine, twists the length of her silken hair into a rope, and drags back her head. With one swipe, she cuts the vespertine's throat. Silence floods in, thickening the air with a quiet that's broken only by the sound of our ragged breathing. Lux steps back, hands raised as though in surrender. The creature, dead, crumples at our feet.

We stand in a half-circle around the body. Everything feels distant, like I've woken from a nightmare. The ones I'd have as a child. As though this is nothing but a fable told to me by someone else, instead of a truth played out right before me.

A heated sting blooms at my throat. Confused, I press my fingers to the ache, and they come away stained with blood. I remember the claws, my skin, the girl with her teeth at my neck.

Wordlessly, Lux drops her weapon, not even pausing to clean the blade. She reaches for her field kit and passes me a folded square of gauze. I press it to the wound.

"What," I say, slow and tentative, "was that?"

Briar paces a rough circle around the body, a bone shard twisted against her palm. "Oh, I don't know, Everline. Maybe it's the resurrection of Saint Lenore."

Her teeth are set in a sardonic grimace, but there's a waver in her voice that echoes my own unsteady fear. She kicks at the ground; tugs the ribbon from her hair, unraveling the length of her braid.

Usually, this moment would feel like a triumph. One less monster to fight back from the wall. One less chance for the vespertine to break through our defenses where the magic has waned. Normally, this is when I'd strip the beast back to fur and bone; then we'd burn the corpse.

But I can't bring myself to move. Even to put my hands on this creature feels wrong.

I stare at the dead vespertine, and the stillness of the night presses down on me. "We need to show this to Fenn."

Briar cuts me an irritated look. "He has a title, Everline."

Scowling at her, I amend: "We need to show this to the *commander*."

Her insistence on Fenn's title is not about duty. It's her way to claim him, in a way I never will. Other wardens are raised in the Hallowed Lands, coming to the wall when they're called to join the enclave at the gathering. But I've lived here my entire life, ever since Fenn returned from the brutally failed mission that left my mother dead and me, his newborn daughter, in his arms.

I was raised in the shadow of the wall. But even that wasn't enough to eclipse the truth of my birth. That my mother broke her vows and betrayed the wardens, deserted her watch and fled to the moors as the vespertine tore through the Hallowed Lands.

Even before Briar came to the enclave, Fenn kept me at a careful distance. He's never wanted me to call him *father*, a fact that Briar seized upon. Irritated at my use of his given name, wanting me to be only another recruit rather than what I really am—her illegitimate sister.

I turn my back on Briar, focusing instead on the fallen vespertine. Lux and I are strong enough to carry a body between us; we've done so before, with vespertine struck down on other nights. But when I reach toward the creature, a shudder crosses my skin. My mouth tastes bile-bitter. I start to search through my pocket, where I keep my sewing kit in place of bone shards, and take out a pair of tailor's shears.

My skirts are made from layers of linen, folded around and attached at the waistband. I cut the stitches from the topmost layer and pull loose a swath of pale cloth. The piece of fabric is large enough for a makeshift shroud.

"Here," I say, passing one end to Lux, "help me with this."

Awkwardly, with cloth folded over our hands, we fold the linen around the vespertine. Briar watches us for a moment; then, with a sigh, she takes out a stick of incense, lights it, and lets the clove-scented smoke drift above our heads. The spiced scent laces through the air around me as I kneel down to tie the shroud closed.

"Wait," Briar says. She retrieves her own blade, then, carefully, picks up Lux's bloodied weapon from the ground. The stains on the steel shimmer blackly in the moonlight. She cleans it against the trampled moor grass, hands it hilt-first to Lux, who nods and sheathes the blade.

I gather up the shrouded creature, swallowing back nausea at the wrongness of this, the feel of her so unlike the shape of any other vespertine, folded inside the thin layer of cloth. Her body is still warm. It's like I'm carrying another warden, battle-fallen. I press my lips together, let out a sharp breath through my nose.

"I can do it on my own," Lux says, reaching.

I want to argue, but she's already taken the weight from me. My panic subsides, becoming a throb at my temples and an ache in my chest, a faint dizziness that I can almost ignore.

On our return to the enclave, Briar walks a few paces behind, her fists wrapped with stands of bone beads, her gaze pinned to the dark. We cross the moorland in silence until the wall takes shape in the distance.

The pearlescent bones are woven together, echoing a trefoil arch. From this distance, the wall glimmers with an ethereal light that fills the horizon—a full moon, a necromantic cathedral. High above, a single lantern shines from the watchtower like a tiny, far-off star.

On any other night when we return, and I see the bones and the wall and that celestial brightness, I feel elation, relief. But right now, there's only a cold, tired resignation.

An unshakable feeling that after tonight, nothing is ever going to be the same.

CHAPTER TWO

THE ENCLAVE IS DESOLATE WHEN WE REACH THE WALL, everything layered in a silence that spills past the iron bars of the entranceway. I move toward the closed gates with my sleeve pushed back, my hand outstretched. Lux and I take turns to feed the gate spell when we walk the wards together, her on the way out, me at the return. But before I can touch the lock, Briar steps forward, into my path.

I falter. My feet drag loose a scatter of earth; I come to an awkward stop. She regards me unyieldingly, her expression latched as tight as the magic-sealed gate. We stare at one another, my hand caught in the empty space between us. I draw back and curl my fingers against my mantle, clutching a worn-smooth rib-cage bone. I feel as though I reached too close to a fire and singed my wayward knuckles on the flames.

When I try to walk past, Briar matches my steps, refusing to allow me through. Her pale gaze slices toward the vespertine, still in Lux's arms. "You can't bring that in here."

Incredulously, I look between them. My fingers tighten around the bones of my mantle until my nails bite against my palm. Lux hesitates, the streaked blood flaking off her cheeks and her braids unraveling.

She carefully lowers the shrouded form to the ground and says to Briar, "We already decided not to burn her."

Briar shakes her head; a golden wisp of hair comes free from its ribbon, sticking to her sweat-damp cheek. "'No vespertine shall cross the wall, even in death.' You know this."

"So what do you suggest?" I snap. "Leave the body outside, unburned, let her blood scent draw every monster in the moorlands? Hells, Briar, let me past."

With a frustrated huff, she plants her feet wide apart and stands, unmoving. "You swore to our father that you would obey the warden vows. You can't ignore the rules when it suits you, Everline."

"Oh, so now Fenn is *our* father? Whatever happened to *he has a title*?"

"You may be a warden in name only, but even you should realize—"

I catch my braid up into my fist and drag it away from my neck, showing her my warden mark—the moonlike crescent at the top of my spine. "I'm a warden," I say, the words forced out between my clenched teeth. "Marked as any other."

Each year, in the months before the gathering, a lunar marking appears on all those called to join the wardens: raised blackly on their neck. Briar's is just beneath her left ear; Lux bears hers in the hollow of her throat. And every marked warden can use magic, can feed the wall, can fight against the vespertine.

21

Briar's *in name only* is a sharp blow, since I've had my mark since birth, unlike the other wardens. I can give my blood to the gate spell. I was taught alongside the other recruits to wield blade and bone against the vespertine. But when Fenn performed the ritual to awaken my magic—cutting my hand, mixing my blood with honey for the fiola—it failed.

Every attempt to awaken my magic has failed.

Briar tugs my braid loose from my hand. My hair falls down to cover my bared nape. "I've seen your mark, Everline. And like I said, even you should realize bringing that creature inside the enclave would be a sin."

I round on her, feeling dizzy—the way I always do when I'm about to do something I shouldn't. Like my body is trying to warn me to stop. But all I can see is Briar, with her armor that I didn't make and the pinned-on sigil that belongs to Fenn, and suddenly the fear and fatigue of this night coalesce, and it's *all her fault*.

I step forward, my boots heavy on the bare earth of the walkway. "You think you're better than me because Fenn favors you. But do you really believe after what you did at the wards tonight, you'd make a good commander?"

Briar huffs, defensive. "You got in my way. If you'd just listened—"

"If you'd just waited—"

A flare of lantern light casts from the enclave. There's a slam of the chapel door flung open, then a crush of footsteps across the graveled path that surrounds the training yard.

"What," comes a voice, "is the meaning of this?"

We fall silent, like we're bespelled, as Commander Fenn storms toward us from the chapel. He's still dressed in travel clothes from his visit to the Hallowed Lands, thick gloves and a heavy cloak knotted around his broad shoulders. His hair is the same golden shade as Briar's. He wears it tied back, but a few errant strands have escaped, framing the patch that covers his left eye.

Scowling deeply, he hangs his lantern on an iron hook beside the entrance, then drags off one glove and shoves his hand against the gate, pressing his fingers to the lock. We shift hurriedly into a line as his gaze marks over us, cataloging each piece of disarray. My wounded throat. Briar's tense, stark anger. Lux, with the shrouded vespertine at her feet.

Finally, Briar steps forward. "Father. I'm just reminding Warden Blackthorn of our commandments. She wants to bring a vespertine into the enclave."

My face goes hot; pricking with embarrassment and irritation. I glare at Briar. "Don't pretend you care about rules when you wouldn't even follow a simple instruction out there."

"I don't need your instructions, Everline. I outrank you."

Roughly, I gesture to my throat, still bloodied. "And now I have this token to remember your excellent leadership."

Fenn holds up his ungloved hand, cutting off Briar before she can speak. "Enough!" His fingertips are smeared with blood from the gate spell. He takes out a folded cloth from the depths of his cloak and wipes them clean as he turns toward me. "I'm ashamed of you, Everline. You're a warden, not a *child*. Whatever disagreement you have with your sister, it should not get in the way of your holy tasks. I thought we'd moved past this disobedience."

The disappointment in his tone clouds the air like a billowed haze of incense smoke; when I draw a breath, it pours into the depths of my lungs, harsh and acrid, choking me.

I stare up at him as heated shame burns across my cheeks. And even in this wholly wretched moment, I can't help searching his face for the similarities between us. The way his mouth slants like mine when he's displeased. The sharp angle of his chin. The hue of our eyes—a blue so dark, it's almost black.

I pull at my fiola, sliding the empty glass back and forth along its silver chain. "This *is* a holy task."

His expression turns steely, warning. "There is nothing holy in dragging an unburned vespertine to the wall, especially now when the magic of the bones is so fragile. Or perhaps you wish for a repeat of the past?"

He means my mother. The way that she abandoned the wardens when the wall failed, severing her vows like a silken thread cut with the sharpest tailor's shears. This is the only way he'll speak of her: a cautionary tale, a lesson to be learned.

Each time Fenn mentions my mother, it's like a key has been turned, a door cracked open to reveal the barest sliver of the room locked away on the other side. Eagerness spirals wretchedly through me, the hunger of a wolf for a wounded hare. My pulse turns quick, and my throat goes dry, all of me pulled wire-taut with desperation to know *more*.

Why did she break her vows and abandon the wall that keeps us safe, the place we're all sworn to protect?

But each time I've tried to press him for answers, that door slams closed, and I'm left as I always am—shut out in the dark, full of longing for impossible things.

I bite my questions back, feel them knotted in my stomach. I can't even argue with him, tell him that Briar was the one who forced her way into our patrol, that she rushed forward when the vespertine appeared. I'll only confirm Fenn's accusation that I'm childish; unable to put my vows above my feelings.

I let out a breath and square my shoulders. "I apologize, Commander."

This is all I can offer him, the proof I can be a true warden, a dutiful daughter; that I'm more than a wayward girl set to repeat the mistakes of a mother I never even knew. I long for my apology to change things between us. But he only nods curtly, folding up my words and tucking them away like a letter he's finished reading.

He puts his glove back on, fastening it tightly at his wrist before he turns to Lux. "Now, would you care to explain why you've brought a vespertine to the gates instead of burning it?"

Lux wavers a little beneath his stare. She drops to one knee, supplicant, as she folds back a corner of the shroud. "Because of this."

In death, the vespertine looks even more like a girl. Her eyelashes are fanned against her painted cheeks as though in slumber. Her mouth is curved into a rictus that seems almost pouting, fangs dimpling her lower lip.

Everything goes still, the moment laid out like pieces of a pattern spread on a tailor's board. The vespertine with her girlish death mask. Lux, her head still bowed. Briar, with her hand pressed to the pinned insignia.

And Fenn—his gaze turned hard, marked by the same stern

grief as when we go down to the catacombs to tend the dead. It disorients me, the way he's so *sad* rather than shocked. He takes a breath, as though to steady himself. Then, to Briar, he says, "Take it back to the moorland and burn it."

"Please, Fenn," I persist. "Why does this vespertine look so—"

I cut off, unable to voice it. *Human.*

He turns to me; then, carefully, he touches my throat, his gloved fingers casting over the blood. "You're hurt."

I'm overtaken by the treacherous urge to throw my arms around him and press my face into his chest. I clench my fists until I feel the indent of my nails on my palms, force myself to remain still.

"I-it isn't deep."

He watches me for a beat; then his gaze softens, the barest flicker. And it's almost like a reward when his voice gentles, when he pats my shoulder and says, "Go with Warden Harwood and see to your cut."

His kindness carves all the fight from me. I'm suddenly aware of the ache in my throat and the fading adrenaline that's left my whole body ragged and sore. I can't trust myself to speak. I give him a terse nod, then step through the gate.

Lux follows me, and the gate closes behind us. I glance back to see Briar holding the lantern and Fenn with the vespertine in his arms. They walk out to the apiary field, the circle of light around them growing smaller and smaller as they move farther from the wall. Tears sting my eyes. I blink them away.

"Come on," Lux says, sliding her arm around my waist, "let's patch you up."

As we walk through the enclave to the infirmary, watered light filters from beneath the closed chapel doors. Shadows of movement against the glassed windows show the wardens at work inside, lighting incense and tending to the ossuary shrine beneath the image of Saint Lenore.

I feel restless, desperate. Wardens don't frighten easily. We live beside a wall built from bones, watch it weep bloodied tears. We go into the dark to face monsters. *I* face monsters with nothing but my armor and my two curved blades.

Fear is for girls who live in the Hallowed Lands, with their tender worries and fingers unmarked by steel or spells. But now, unease fills the air, ominous as a prophecy. All the events of the night—the changed vespertine, the unsurprised sorrow in Fenn's eyes as he looked down at her—are like a handful of broken shards that I'm desperate to gather up and fit together. Yet as I clutch them, I only draw blood as the razored edges scrape my palms.

I think of him out on the moorland with Briar, gone to burn the monster we killed. If I were his trueborn daughter, if my mother had not betrayed her vows, would he have told me what it was that made him look so unshocked, so mournful, at the sight of the vespertine girl?

The infirmary is tucked behind the entrance to the catacombs, down a shallow flight of stairs. Clementine trees blot leafy outlines across the doorway, and inside, the mingled scent of decaying citrus and bone dust filters through the louvered window. I light the lantern. It flares reluctantly with a dying insect noise, all flicker and buzz.

A battered rosewood dresser is shoved against one wall, an

enamelware sink against the other. The sink is patterned with a worn-out design that might be flowers, and there's a rusted stain beneath the dripping tap, streaked down the inside of the basin like old blood.

Lux turns on the tap. Steam clouds up from the heated water, hazing the room before it drifts toward the open window. Sighing, I lean back against the dresser and unhook the lariat chains from my collar, setting them aside onto the countertop.

Blood has soaked the front of my dress in ribbonlike streaks. I think of the vespertine and the spreading stain from her cut throat. Picture her laid out on the moorland, Briar standing over her with a lit torch.

"None of this feels right," I tell Lux, knowing how I sound, like some fable witch delivering an omen. "Did you see the way Fenn looked when you drew back the shroud? It was as though . . . he's seen a changed vespertine before."

Frowning, she rubs at her cheek, wiping away the crimson stripe. "Whatever it is—whatever is wrong—it will be better once the gathering has passed. When the wall isn't bleeding and the magic is restored."

I press my lips together, wanting to believe her. But I can't let go of the wrongness that has permeated the evening, the way Fenn avoided my questions, and the longing that drags insistently against me, like there are ribbons tied on each of my limbs. "What if this is about my mother and the way she disappeared?"

Lux picks at a scrap of her chipping nail varnish, then shuts off the water and leans back against the sink. She regards me for a moment, her mouth softening, her brows knit together in tender concern.

"Evie," she says, a gentle lilt to her voice. "What your mother did—you're not bound to that path. She broke her vows, but you are here."

As wardens, we swear three oaths: to come to the enclave when marked and called, to keep our watch and take no prisoners, and—as Briar so irritatingly pointed out—to never willfully allow a vespertine to cross the wall.

My mother broke all these vows before her death.

All I've ever wanted was to free myself of her treacherous legacy. But though it should feel right, feel *holy*, to burn the dead vespertine out on the moor, when I think of Fenn standing over her with a torch in his hand, a sick, panicked shudder runs through my whole body.

Burning that creature—that girl—feels worse than breaking the rules to bring her inside the enclave. Once she's gone, the proof of what we saw will vanish, and I'll be left doubting myself, wondering if that look on his face was nothing more than a fevered dream.

From outside, the scents of ash and smoke drift through the window. They're faint enough I could pretend I'm imagining them, but I'm not. I shut the louvers, but that only serves to make it worse—the stink of sacrifice now trapped inside the room with us.

Lux takes my hands between her own. I stare down at her scarred knuckles, the healed-over marks, countless nicks from bone shards and gate tithes. She drags her thumb against my palm, and the rasp of her calloused skin against my own settles me, draws some of the tension from my shoulders.

I lean back against the dresser as she reaches for a cloth, wets it in the sink. As she tends to me, I catch a glimpse of my face in the oval mirror that's fixed to the wall. My rounded cheeks, my dark freckles. My unruly hair and the new, blunt line of the bangs I just cut. I wanted to look more severe, but at this moment, with my worried eyes and bitten lips, I look like a child who played with scissors.

Lux presses the cloth to my throat, cleans away the blood. I scrunch my nose at the sharp ache from the wound. "How does it look?"

She tilts her head, considering. "It's not so bad," she says, the corner of her mouth lifted into a half-smile. "You'll have an impressive scar when it heals."

"Just what I've always wanted. Truly, Briar did me a favor."

Laughing, she touches beneath my chin, tilts back my head to smear stinging antiseptic over the cut. There's a ritual in this, too. Coming to the infirmary after our nights on the moors. Tending cut palms and bruised knuckles and split lips.

"There," Lux says, stepping back. "You're done."

I take a strip of linen from the open field kit on the dresser and tie it around my throat. A macabre choker necklace.

I press my fingers to my neck, feeling the throb of the claw marks. My mother's death has always trailed me like an unwelcome shadow, her demise on the moorland an ever-present reminder of how easily I could break. And now, I'm annoyed at my carelessness.

How I let Briar rile me enough to slip like this and put myself—
and Lux—at risk.

Lux unstoppers the sink and lets the water drain free. Her own
throat looks suddenly too bare, soft and vulnerable.

I pull a measuring tape from my pocket, hold it up against her.
She arches a brow, then lets out a congenial laugh, standing duti-
fully still as I stretch the tape across her neck, mentally piecing
out a collar. Silver strung ribbon, woven with bone chips sharp
enough to turn back claws.

A sound comes from outside. Boots on the stairs, then a brusque
knock at the door. Before either of us can respond, Briar steps into
the room. She goes to the sink, runs a washcloth under the tap,
and starts to wipe the paint from her lips.

"You're wanted on the wall," she tells me. "Father has called
you to the watch."

She wrings out the cloth, the spatter of paint-grayed water in
the sink like a punctuation mark. It's not a punishment to be called
to the watch, but the way Briar announces Fenn's order makes it
seem so. Lux casts a sympathetic look at me as she gathers up the
stained linen and scraps of gauze. "I'll leave the lamp on for you in
our room," she says.

I fold up my measuring tape, slipping it into my pocket as I
climb the stairs to the enclave. My boots crunch over the ground
as I cross the graveled path to where a steep wooden staircase leads
to the watchtower. I tug the ribbon from my braid, let the night
wind pull at my loosened hair. "Hells, what a *mess*."

Up close, the wall is dewed with blood, trails seeping out from
every space between the latticed bones. I can feel how the magic

31

that strings the bones together is dwindling, like the sputter of a lampflame almost out of oil.

The wind is stronger at the top of the wall, cold against my cheeks. Fenn stands near the tower railing, his gaze fixed to the distance. I go to stand beside him. Laid out beneath us, the moorland is a woven cloth, all dark threads: the apiary with its pale hives like a row of stitches, the tangled gorse and faded heather deepening to shadows past the end of the world.

The only scrap of light comes from just beyond the hives, where the pyred remains of the vespertine smolder with a sickly orange glow.

Fenn sighs. For the briefest moment, a strange flash of regret casts over his face as he stares down at the flames. But when he realizes I'm watching him, he steps back from the edge of the tower and schools his expression into a neutral frown.

He takes off his gloves and slips them into his pocket. His nails are varnished with the same black paint that Lux uses. There's a strip of leather cord tied around one wrist, which he's worn as long as I can remember. He's never said, but I'm certain it belonged to my mother.

He tugs at the cord, once, then shakes his head. "When you came back from your hunt, what would you have done with the body if I hadn't been here to stop you?"

"I—" I hesitate, unable to lie—because he *caught* me—but not wanting to tell the truth.

"It's against your vows to bring a vespertine past the wall, Everline."

Longing winds through my body; a thread that's tied around

my heart, tangled in the curve of my ribs. I think again of Fenn's reaction when he saw the dead vespertine beneath her shroud. He wasn't surprised . . . he was *sad*.

"Fenn." My voice sounds too small, too soft, up here above the bones. I swallow, trying again. "Have you ever known a vespertine to be changed like that before?"

He remains determinedly silent. Up here on the watchtower is all stars and silence, a pallid drift of pyre smoke, the night-dimmed enclave far below us like a separate world. I curl my hands to fists, imagining the closed door, the scrape of a key from the other side of the lock.

I want nothing more than that lock undone, that sliver of light to spill into the darkness where I stand. "In all the fables, there's never been a vespertine like this. Like a *girl*. A human."

Finally, I've spoken it aloud, and I wonder if this is how it feels to cast a spell, to murmur holy words and watch a flare of consecration ignite from bone and blood. Fenn looks at me in a way that I can't read. His voice is low, serious, when he says, "Imagine yourself a commander. The fate of the wardens and the wall and the Hallowed Lands resting solely on *you*. The vows we swear are what keep us—and everyone—safe."

My hand drifts to my nape, fingers pressed to my mark. I try to push aside the unintended hurt of Fenn's words. Who would have a commander without magic? Let alone the illegitimate daughter of a warden who deserted her duties. The ache I feel—for this *belonging* I will never have—is wretched; I'm even more pathetic than Briar with her pinned-on sigil.

I am so far from who Fenn wishes me to be. Never have I felt so keenly as though I've been made double, split into two girls. One a dutiful warden, who strives to keep her vows. The other a wayward child who carries the inheritance of her mother's heresy. The dutiful girl would be silent, stand in the tower, and keep her watch.

But I have jagged shards in my hands, and I'm desperate to piece them together even at the risk of bloodshed. "Something is out on the moorland, and it changed the vespertine we fought tonight. Is that what you saw when you went there, when I was born? When my mother died?"

Fenn sighs into the dark, his breath thorned with anger. "Every choice your mother made, every vow she broke, only led to destruction. When the vespertine attacked the Hallowed Lands, she deserted the wall and left us to fight—and die—while she fled. And when I finally found her at the border to the Thousandfold, it was too late for me to save her."

A cold shiver tracks down my spine. The Thousandfold. This, then, is the secret that's lain between us, caged by every veiled warning, every laden silence. My mother died in a land many thought myth, where Nyx Severin first arose in our world. Filled with perilous magic, it's a place where all wardens are forbidden to go.

It spills from my mouth in a scatter of breathless words. "If she died in the Thousandfold, that means . . . I was *born there.*"

Fenn gives me a warning look. "Everline."

The Thousandfold is a place of horrors, where the cathedrals built in Nyx's honor now lie in ruins, destroyed when Saint Lenore made her final stand. I can hardly imagine it—that my life began where so much blood was spilled, where a monster was once wor-shipped as a god. "Why was she there? Why did my mother go to the Thousandfold?"

For so long, I've hungered for answers, and now the truth is an acerbic tincture that I'll swallow down, greedy and desperate.

Fenn crosses the space between us with funereal slowness. His expression is stricken, raw with grief. He puts his hands on my shoulders. Crouches slightly so our faces are even.

"Your mother broke her vows, and it cost her life—and almost yours, too." His thumbs press against my clavicles, both gentle and stern. "You did well tonight. You kept the wards lit. You stopped the vespertine. You did well. Leave it at that."

The care in his gaze turns my bones milk-soft. His concern for me feels so *personal*. The same way he'd be worried about Briar. Unwelcome tears brim my eyes, and I hate how much this moment—this rare tenderness—has made me feel like a child again.

I look up at Fenn, the familiar angles of his face. His eye, the patch, the scar across his cheek. The way his warden mark curves around the side of his neck, the point of the crescent ending just beneath his ear. He taught me everything I know. How to fight, how to tend wounds, how to cleanly kill the vespertine.

He *gave* this to me—my whole life at the enclave. The past owes me nothing, that world beyond the wall, the mother I don't remember. I shouldn't need it—need her—while I have Fenn and the wardens. Even if I have no magic. Even if he will never claim me as his true daughter.

But the night is full of ghosts. The blurred image I have of my mother, built from my own guesswork—a young woman with the same freckled skin and treacle-dark hair as me—is overlaid by a vision of the slaughtered vespertine, all corpsepaint and blood-stained lace.

"Tell me," I demand. "Tell me why she was out there. Tell me what she did, what all of this means."

Fenn draws a breath, and my heart goes still. But then he falls to silence. Turning instead to stare at the expanse of sky that stretches over the moorland.

The clouds pare back, unveiling a pomegranate-round moon.

And above us, the sky burns red.

CHAPTER THREE

THE CRIMSON MOON, UNVEILED, GLARES DOWN, PAINTING the enclave in bloodied hues. As the clouds peel farther back, the reddened light seeps across the ground below the watchtower, spills through the windows of the chapel. There's stillness, then the sound of voices raised and hurried footsteps.

The chapel doors fling open and the wardens who were inside—two siblings, who were recruited at the last gathering—rush out. They were tending the altar, and the smaller of the two still clutches an unlit ossuary candle as they look around nervously, searching for Fenn.

When Lux and Briar come from the infirmary, their upturned faces are colored by the changed light, as though they've been washed in gore.

"*Hells,*" Fenn swears beneath his breath. He moves toward the stairwell at the edge of the tower. "Wait here, Everline."

I follow him with quick, dogged steps, catching his arm to make him stop. The truth I sought from him—so close only a moment before—is slipping away from me; the shards I'd almost set together are back in jagged pieces, an indecipherable mess of razored edges.

I clutch Fenn's sleeve, my fingers twisted in the woolen fabric of his cloak. "Tell me what this means."

His mouth thins into a taut line, and I feel him tense—as though he wants to push me away but is forcing himself to be still. Slowly, he turns to face me. "It's an eclipse. That's all."

I've seen the moon eclipsed before, the bone-pale orb washed black, enclosing the entire world in darkness until the light slowly reappears, slice by slice. *This* is not the same. I know it isn't—and so does Fenn.

I can read the truth in each sharp line of his stance, the way his arm has begun to tremble beneath my grasping hand. As he looks from the enclave below to the red-drenched distance, his face is scored by the same grief as when he saw the changed vespertine.

"It's a blood moon," I say. "Like the night the wall was breached. And like the night when I was—"

He curls his hand around my own and starts to unknot my fingers from his sleeve. "Nothing is going to breach the wall. The magic will hold until the gathering; I promise you." Freed from my grasp, Fenn steps away from me.

The crimson moon burns across my vision, spots of red dancing through the dark when I blink. There have been only two other times when an eclipse bled across the sky like this. The night when the vespertine breached the wall, when my mother deserted the wardens.

And the night when I was born.

Now, as the light turns to blood, I'm overcome by a terrible thought—one that I cannot force away. The changed vespertine, my mother, myself . . . we're all connected in a way I want to deny, yet cannot help grasping for.

I reach toward Fenn, my hand outstretched in the empty air just like when Briar interrupted me as I tried to unlock the gate. "Father," I whisper, "*please.*"

Fenn's gaze snaps to mine. The word—*father*—hangs between us like a broken vow. I can't remember the last time I spoke it aloud. Everything goes still. I've cast a spell with this transgression—even the night wind has fallen to a shocked silence. An apology rises like instinct, but I hold it back. My mouth goes sour, my palms sweat-slick, my pulse a rapid *thump, thump, thump* against my ribs.

Fenn takes a deep breath. He reaches to his waist, to the hilt of his sheathed blade. He draws it slowly and holds it out, laid flat across his palms. I stare at him, pinned in place, unable to move or even look down at the weapon he offers me. "Everline," he says gently. "Give me your hand."

I give him my hand, wishing I could hide the way I've started to tremble. Carefully, he presses the blade into my grip. We stand together, his calloused palms encouraging my fingers tighter around the hilt. We look at each other for a drawn-out moment. His eye on me, his iris that deep ink-blue, the only distinctive feature we share. Beneath the tower, the sounds of wardens' anxious voices echo through the red-painted night.

Questions sit like poison berries between my teeth, ready to burst and spill their bitter juice when I bite down. Why did my mother abandon her watch—her vows—and go to the

Thousandfold? What did Fenn see on the border of that forbidden place when he went after her?

I open my mouth, about to speak, but Fenn turns away, the moment broken. "I have to see to the wardens. Stay at your watch, Everline."

I let my gaze drop, forcing back all the things I cannot say. With a sigh, I manage, "Yes, Commander."

He releases me, then unclasps his blade belt, the sheath now empty of his blade. He places the whole of it—the bone-and-chain straps, the pouch of shards—into my hands. As he makes his way down the stairs to the graveled yard in front of the chapel, wardens gather around him. The newly recruited siblings, still with their unlit candle, straighten their shoulders, trying to look brave. One of the older wardens, her dark hair caught up in a chignon and a row of silver rings glinting in her ears, stands poised beside the chapel entrance as she waits for Fenn's instruction.

Briar slips through the crowd, rushing to Fenn's side. Together, they guide the others back through the still-opened doors, with Lux falling in at the end of their line.

When she reaches the entranceway, Fenn draws her back. He bends to murmur something in her ear. Her gaze darts toward the watchtower, to me. Fenn's brows lower, and he shakes his head. Lux looks quickly away. With a terse nod, she waits until he's followed the other wardens into the chapel, then she closes the doors.

She stands, attentive, her hand on the hilt of her blade and her eyes pinned to the dark. The picture of a dutiful warden, except for the troubled slant of her mouth, the way her fingers twist anxiously as she holds her weapon.

I wave to her, trying to get her attention, but she determinedly avoids looking in my direction again.

With a sigh, I wrap Fenn's belt around my waist and buckle it with unsteady fingers. I don't sheathe the blade he gave me but instead clutch it tight, until the leather-wrapped hilt is pressed hard against my sweating palm. It's heavier than my own weapons, setting my stance off-balance as I walk to the other side of the tower.

When I glance down at the new blade, it is as though I'm seeing it for the first time. The grip of the weapon is wrapped in plain cloth, not trailing ribbon. And the blade isn't metal forged like the ones I wield, like the one Lux used to cut the vespertine's throat tonight. This is bone.

This is the Vale Scythe. Fenn's relic blade.

Crafted from the bones of dead vespertine, this was the weapon used by Saint Lenore when she fought Nyx Severin at the heart of the Thousandfold; when she sacrificed herself to destroy him. After that final battle, the remaining wardens retreated to the enclave, and Saint Lenore was laid to rest in the catacombs beneath what became our chapel. And the first commander took up her blade, sanctifying it with a holy name.

Although I make armor from vespertine bones, our weapons are forged from steel or iron. Only a commander uses the relic blade. But Fenn—he gave this to *me*. The Vale Scythe is our duty forged in holy bone, a weapon laden with the weight of vows. And I know, with certainty that feels like a wound, why he has set it in my hands.

This is his answer to everything I've asked about my mother.

Why she deserted her watch for the moorland. What happened before she died that left him so haunted, that carved such distance between us. No matter how much I press him, this is the only truth he will give me: that I should stay silent and unquestioning, that I should remember my vows, my duty.

I gaze out at the moor, where the changed vespertine still smolders on her pyre. Overhead, the blood-bright moon hangs in the sky like a cut fruit oozing juice over clotted clouds. Beneath, the land unfolds to the end of the world like a rippling sea of reddened ink. But the pooled shadows between the gorse and heather are thickly dark, and when I look into their depths, the shadows seem to slip and slither, playing tricks.

For the barest moment, I am certain there's a shape crouched near the low-burning pyre flames.

Desperately, I stare into the night. A figure is kneeling beside the ashen remains of the vespertine's pyre, head bowed low. The wind rises, and something flutters—a cloak, a silken fall of dark hair. I bite my lip so hard that I taste blood.

Clouds shift; a slash of moonlight cuts down. I can make out details now. The creature is tall, masculine; with broad shoulders mantled in something bonelike, sharp. His pale, angular features are half-hidden by swaths of corpsepaint. His face tilts upward and I catch sight of the intent, oil-slick glimmer of his gaze.

I start to shiver. Even from here, I can sense the same ice-laced change in the wind. The same stench of copper and death. There is another humanlike vespertine—on his knees, as though in mourning—at the pyre of the one we killed earlier tonight.

I take a faltering step toward the stairs, looking from the moor to the enclave. From the kneeling vespertine to the chapel where Lux stands watch. I can feel it, the visceral, triplicate link binding the monsters and my mother and my own wretched self. Fenn knows—I'm certain of it—just as I'm certain that he will never, ever reveal those secrets to me. This creature below, couched in bloodied night, could be my only chance at the truth.

I was thirteen when Fenn first tried to make my fiola. I'd shown no magic, told myself with increasing desperation that I was just late to bloom. A wilted flower trying to rise from an errant seed blown in from the moorland. Never mind that nothing like that can grow on the enclave side of the wall.

Fenn cut my hand and pressed my finger to the vial, and then—

I shake my head, forcing down the memory. *No. Not now.*

I was born with a warden mark, raised in the shadow of a wall built from blood and bones. I'm not like Briar, who stayed with her mother until her mark arose, or Lux, whose parents sent her gratefully to join the wardens, seeing it as a chance to avenge their first, fallen daughter. The enclave is all I have.

But though Fenn claimed me—admitting his liaison with my mother, and the betrayal of his vowsworn wife who lived with newborn Briar in the Hallowed Lands—he has never treated me as anything more than his duty, his burden. And no matter how hard I try to please him, I can't escape the pull that lies beyond the wall. Even with the weight of his relic blade in my hand.

Somewhere past the edge of the world, across the moorland, lies the answer of why tonight has become a troubling fever dream. With the appearance of these omens—the new, changed monster we killed; the one come to mourn her; and the blood-ripe moon—I can no longer ignore the desire I've tried so hard to bury. I want to follow this creature back to the Thousandfold and see what it is that Fenn has kept from me through my entire life.

The truth is out there, tangled up with the secrets of my origin. Death and birth, my mother's broken vows. My absent magic, the ever-widening distance that spans between Fenn and me.

I sheathe the Vale Scythe in the belt Fenn gave me as I move toward the stairs, eyes fixed ahead, not giving myself a chance to waver. I take the stairs two at a time, then cross the graveled yard in long strides.

Lux is a silhouette in front of the closed chapel doors, outlined in profile by the illuminated glass. The warden chapel is built of bones, and the entranceway is inlaid with polished teeth, set into the black-oiled wood in patterns like flowers. Lantern light filters through the arched windows on either side of the bone-studded door.

I grab Lux's sleeve and pull her close. With my lips beside her ear, I whisper, "There is another one. Another vespertine like the girl we killed. I saw him from the tower."

She draws back to look at me, wide-eyed, one hand on her blade hilt. "You have to tell Fenn."

"No. I can't."

Lux regards me warily. "What," she asks, worry in her voice, "are you planning to do?"

Incense smoke snakes out from beneath the closed chapel doors, tracing the air with scents of clove and ash. I can hear the low hum of Fenn's voice inside, catch pieces of his words—"eclipse"—"the wall will hold"—"the gathering"—as he speaks to the wardens in a reassuring tone.

"If I tell Fenn, he'll kill the creature and burn him. Just like before. But I need to know—I need to find out—" I take a breath, square my shoulders as I swallow down the rising panic of my disobedience. "I'm going to follow the vespertine to the Thousandfold."

Lux pales. "Evie, you *can't*. Fenn will never forgive you if you break your vows like that. And I—"

I reach for her hand, still clutched around the hilt of her blade, and uncurl her grip. My fingers weave through hers; I feel desperate with tenderness. "I didn't want to go without saying goodbye to you."

My voice wavers, and my throat goes tight, an ache deeper than the bandaged wound. Before I can start to cry, I tug her close and wrap my arms around her. With my face buried against Lux's shoulder, I let out a single, shuddering breath.

She runs her hand down the length of my hair, her fingers trembling as she touches me. "Everline," she says, choked. "Please—"

I pull away before she can finish, and run toward the narrow laneway that leads to the barracks. They're empty now, and unlit. Lux calls my name again, but I don't look back. I can't break the spell that has filled me with enough senselessness to see this through.

The entrance to the barracks is a single door, undecorated except for the ornate handle—a carved femur, worn pearlescent through years of use. The handle is sleek against my palm when I pull the door open, the feel of it as familiar as my own skin.

I climb the stairs quickly, the new weight of the relic blade jolting against my thigh. The room Lux and I share was once an attic, used to store jars of honey and folded linen. It still has a dust-and-beeswax smell imbued into the wooden walls. I'd shared with the other recruits on the lower floor at first, but when I kept waking from nightmares, Fenn moved me to where I wouldn't disturb anyone else.

As I enter the room, moonlight shines mutedly through the single louvered window. My unmade bed, and the scattered worktable covered in scraps of bone and fabric, are lit by wavery crimson. Ignoring the oil lantern that hangs from the ceiling, I go to the trunk in the corner and start to pack supplies into my canvas satchel.

Footsteps echo from the stairwell, and Lux appears in the doorway. She stands with her arms folded, one hip leaning against the lintel, and gives me a mournful look. "You're really determined to do this, aren't you?"

I take out a field kit with bandages and antiseptic, tuck it into my satchel beside a pair of folded woolen stockings. "I have to."

"The gathering is only a month away."

"I'll be back before then. And even if I'm not, they don't need me." I pause, hold out a hand, my palm upturned. A bitter laugh catches in my throat. "It's not like I have any magic to give the wall."

Lux crosses the room and takes hold of my hand. "We do need you. *I* need you."

I look at her. Pale and worried in the faded light, her face picked out in rose hues from the bloodstained moon. Quietly, I say, "My mother was in the Thousandfold when she died. Fenn told me tonight."

Lux stares at me, wide-eyed, as she takes this in. Her mouth, still rouged with dark lip stain, opens with a shocked gasp. "And that means . . . you were born there?"

I glance toward the louvered window. "The last time there was an eclipse like this was the night I was born. It's all connected. The creatures, the magic, what happened out there when she died. Fenn is never going to tell me what he saw. I have to go; I have to find the answers about the changed vespertine. And about myself."

Lux squeezes my fingers, runs her calloused thumb against my palm. She hesitates for a moment, then goes to the shelves beneath the window and takes down the rolled travel tent that we use when we check the wards more than a day's walk from the enclave. "The storm season is about to begin. Once the moorland is flooded, there's only one path to cross the river. We'll have to be quick."

I stare at her, my satchel still hanging loosely from my arm. "You can't come with me, Lux. You have too much—"

She turns on me sharply; her glare cuts me to silence. "*You have too much to lose.* That's what you're going to say, right?" Wordlessly, I nod. Lux sighs, expression softening. "Maybe I do have too much to lose. My place here, my honor as a warden. I have that. But I also have you, Evie. And losing *you* would be worse than being disavowed or sent back to the Hallowed Lands."

"Lux, I'd never ask this of you."

She picks up her satchel from where it's hung in the corner, fixes the strap over her shoulder. "Well," she says, mouth crooked in a grin that doesn't quite reach her eyes. "I'm not waiting to be invited. I'm coming with you, Evie. There's nothing to discuss."

Gently, she presses her hand to my cheek. Her hazel-gray eyes are luminous in the shallow dark. I shiver as memories rise of the two of us, how we stood together and waited for Fenn to make our fiolae. His blade, the splatter of blood into a waiting vial. And the terrible, knife-twist moment that came after, when everything went wrong.

The way she moved into the attic room on her first night here. And when I had a nightmare and called out into the dark, she'd curled beside me in my bed, the two of us in a nest of blankets. She held my hand until I fell back asleep. She chased the terrors away.

The way I love her more than anything—and how fiercely glad I am, at the same time I'm hopelessly sorry, that I won't have to face this alone.

CHAPTER FOUR

THE ENCLAVE IS CAUGHT IN MIDNIGHT STILLNESS AS WE slip through the gateway. At the wall, the bones bleed crimson tears, a steady *drip-drip-drip* that gathers in gory pools against the earth. The air stinks of rust, of salt, of death. Above, the moon burns red.

Everything is burnished dark, but I imagine the path to the pyre marked beneath our feet, my boots pressing the ghostlike traces of where Fenn walked with the dead vespertine in his arms. We move quiet and quick, our shoulders drawn up and our heads lowered.

I can't escape the feeling of being watched. There's a prickle against my nape that doesn't fade, no matter how often I glance behind me, and I'm certain I can hear footsteps. But when I look back, there's no lights from the enclave, and the gate remains closed. The empty watchtower is like an accusation above the bloodied bones of the wall, my absence framed in the stretch of sky between the wooden railings and the tower roof.

The ground slopes low as we reach the apiary field, and for a moment, the view behind us is covered by swells of lavender and wolf-rose vines—flowers planted for the bees. When I take a deep breath, the lingering scent of ash is mixed with pollen and petals. We're close to the pyre where I saw the creature kneeling. The watched feeling prickles my skin again. I put my hand on Lux's arm and draw to a stop. "Did you hear something?"

She glances at me, then peers—watchful, listening—into the night.

There's a rustle from the grass, the sound of leaves crushed under boots. Lux steps closer to me, a shard in her hand, as I draw the Vale Scythe. It drags at my wrist, heavier than my lighter iron blade. I'm tensed, spun tight. My mouth gone dry; my heart so loud it overtakes all other noise.

A figure emerges from the darkness. I raise the Scythe. But it's not a vespertine—not the creature I saw by the dimming funereal flames. It's Briar. She glares at me, her cheeks flushed, her eyes bright. Her unbraided hair is in disarray, and she wears a travel cloak knotted roughly around her shoulders. "What do you think you're doing out here?"

I put my hands on my hips and glare back at her. "Going for a moonlit walk. We wanted a clearer view of the eclipse."

Her mouth twists. "Really, you are the worst kind of pest." Then, her attention tracks to my hand, still clutched around the relic, and she draws in a sharp, horrified breath. "Everline Blackthorn. It wasn't enough to break your vows and drag Lux away from her post—"

"I didn't drag her anywhere."

"That wasn't enough, you had to *steal* Father's relic? What exactly are you trying to prove?"

The space between us turns storm-heavy, the air crackling. I sheathe the blade with deliberate slowness. "I didn't steal it. He *gave* it to me."

She gnaws at her lip, and a cruel, pleased feeling starts to uncurl from the pit of my stomach. I tighten my fingers against the blade hilt, think of Fenn—stern, solemn—as he pressed the weapon into my hand. I know he gave me the relic as a reminder of the vows I swore to uphold; a token in exchange for my dutiful silence. Still, I'm so meanly *glad* at how unsettled Briar looks.

The flush on her cheeks deepens; she glowers at me incredulously. "You're such a liar."

"You're right. Actually, I ambushed him in the watchtower and stole his entire blade belt. Then he went calmly into the chapel without even realizing."

I draw aside my cloak, showing her Fenn's belt fastened around my waist. She blanches; the truth scouring the flush from her cheeks, weighting the angles of her shoulders. I'm dizzy with the feel of it, the balance finally tilted in my favor.

With effort, Briar gathers herself. She takes a ribbon from the pocket of her cloak, twists her hair back into a chignon, and ties it in place. "Listen," she says, all bared-teeth fierceness, "he may have let you play at being a real warden, let you hold his relic blade while you sat in the watchtower. But I *know* he didn't give you permission to sneak out here."

I take a step toward her, my boots crushing a wayward sprawl of lavender. The scent of heady perfume thickens the air. "So you volunteered to chase me down? You needn't try so hard to ingratiate yourself with Fenn. You're his trueborn daughter, remember."

"I didn't volunteer. I just—" Briar hesitates; then, with a sigh, she turns toward Lux. Her expression softens, and the sharpness is gone from her voice. "I came out of the chapel and saw you had left your post. I knew Everline must have dragged you away to do something foolish, and I wanted to give you a chance to return before the commander noticed."

Lux bows her head. Her mouth tilts into a faint smile. "So you've come to bring us back?"

I'm disoriented, thrown queasily off-center as the advantage I thought I had slides rapidly away. "I'm not going anywhere with you, Briar Linden."

I turn my back on her and walk toward the apiary fields, trailed by the scent of perfume from the late-season flowers that line my path. In the distance, I can hear a low hum—a drone that resonates through the night, peculiar and discordant. Slowing my steps, I narrow my eyes toward the distance.

The hives are ghosts in the dark, their wooden sides blushed pink beneath the eclipse-stained moon. Beyond is a veil of smoky shadow that drifts past the edge of the world, stippled with tiny lights from the distant line of wards. When I blink, the lights blur and change, and for a moment, there are *eyes* peering through the mist. A creature, haze-hidden, staring at me with a fixed, fervid gaze. The watched feeling that prickled my skin before rises again. I shiver, rubbing my hands along my arms.

Lux is behind me, her footsteps slow and careful as she traces my path through the field. The droning sound grows louder, and I wonder if the creature I saw earlier, that other humanlike vespertine, is nearby. Somewhere out in the dark. I picture him, washed by the bloody eclipse, crouched low in the grass with his eyes narrowed and fangs bared as he tracks us, as we come toward him.

I keep hold of my blade, reach out my free hand to Lux. With our fingers twined, we edge forward, deeper into the apiary field. I hear Briar sigh in exasperation, the crunch of her boots as she follows us. Clouds cover the moon, and everything turns dim, the shadows in the distance sweep over us, a fearsome night bird with sprawling, ink-black wings.

I glance toward Lux. The feel of her hand in mine is reassuringly familiar. I tell myself I am not afraid. If there are monsters in the dark, let them come.

At the center of the fields, the drone and hum rises to a fever pitch, filling the air as sharp and sudden as the shattering of glass. Lux presses close beside me, and our steps falter, stirring up plumes of ash.

We're at the pyre. And beside the burned remains of the vespertine we killed, one of the hives has been knocked down. Destroyed. The pale wood is torn open, with ragged claw marks left in the splintered remains. Inside, honey glints like a wound—stuck with debris and flakes of ash and squirming, dying bees. The rest of the bees swarm in angry chaos above the hive, circling desperately into the air before they dip into the ruins to catch at scraps of honey.

I watch them, stricken, feeling as if all the blood has suddenly drained from my body. Bees swoop past my face, close enough that

I feel their wingbeats on my skin, the scrape of their legs as they tangle in my hair. Briar, rushing breathlessly toward us, catches hold of my arm and drags me from the swarm. "Don't just stand here, you *baby*," she snaps. "You're going to get stung."

I stumble after her, tripping over my feet as we run past the pyre and through the other side of the apiary fields. Here, a sea of wild grass replaces the flowers. I take a deep, grateful breath of air that no longer smells of ash or spoiled honey. Lux comes to a halt beside me. Carefully, she shakes loose the bees that are tangled in my braid, helps me brush them from my skirts. They fly back to rejoin their swarm.

"A vespertine ruined the hive," Lux says, pressing a hand to her chest, touching the notches of her rib-cage armor. She traces the bones, runs her nails across a length of ribbon. "They've never done that before. Did you see anything when you were in the tower?"

Bees are holy to the wardens. The colonies in these fields are descendants of the original apiary tended by Saint Lenore, the bees whose honey was mixed with blood in the first fiola ritual to create the sanctified magic used against Nyx Severin.

I look back to where the pyre and the ruined hive are laid out in a scatter of ash. The field is empty save for the three of us and the swarming bees. But I can picture that creature who knelt by the dead vespertine so vividly, as though his presence has left a stain on the ground. I hesitate, reluctant to voice the words. "I think it was a vengeance."

Lux knots the end of a braid anxiously around her fist. "You think the vespertine you saw did this to take revenge?"

The wolflike monsters we guard against would never do anything so human as mourn. Those vespertine are all instinct, bloodthirsty and unstoppable.

But the creature I saw from the tower was not a wolf.

"Yes. I do."

Briar peers at me, her eyes narrowing. "What are you talking about?"

"When I was in the tower, I saw another vespertine, changed. Like the one we killed tonight." I sound delirious, as though I am recounting a feverish hallucination. But the clawed-up hive is more proof than my fractured words could ever be.

Briar looks between Lux and me, a flicker of something unreadable passing over her face. "You saw another of those creatures?" She arches a brow, waits until I nod in confirmation. "Is that why you came out here—to kill it? You *know* you should have called for Father right away."

With accusation in each line of her body, she looks so like Fenn that I can feel the weight of his disapproval, by proxy. I press my lips together; a hot flush of shame creeps up my neck. The truth—that I don't want to kill the creature but trail him to the Thousandfold—is so much worse than Briar's assumption.

And even more impossible to admit is my buried hope that I'll find traces of my mother in those forbidden ruins. That by following her ghost into the depths of the Thousandfold, I will finally know the truth. Why she was there. What happened on the night I was born.

Defensively, I turn toward the distance, where the bloodied

moonlight shimmers, a garish beacon. "I am a warden. Is it so unthinkable for me to want to protect the wall from this threat?"

It isn't a lie—not wholly. The truth I seek, and the threat of this new creature are one and the same, intertwined like tight-spun threads. But Briar narrows her eyes, suspicion marked clear on her features. "Breaking your vows is not the way to protect the wall. *You* should know that."

Her veiled reference to my mother makes my shame burn even hotter. I hate the way Briar sees me so clearly. I want to hide myself from her more than anyone; instead, she cuts me down with words wielded as sharply as a warden's blade.

Lux steps between us. She puts her hand on Briar's shoulder, the one not covered by armor, and squeezes gently—a warning touch. "Leave her alone. If the vespertine ruined the hive, he must be close. We need to find him before the trail is lost. All you're doing now is wasting time."

Gratitude pools through me, soft beneath the bruised-bone tightness of my ribs. Lux has kept my secret, reinforced the half-truth that we are only here to hunt the vespertine. She offers me a careful smile. Her hand is still on Briar's shoulder.

The air seems to still for a moment. Even the distant hum of the bees goes quiet. Briar and Lux exchange a peculiar, heated look, then Lux glances down at her hand. At her fingers, pressed into the fabric of Briar's cloak. Flustered, she steps quickly back, as though she's been burned, and shoves her hands in her pockets.

Briar tugs at the buckle on her blade belt, hitching it tighter around her waist. "Fine, then. Let's go."

I stare at her, incredulous. "*You* aren't invited."

"Well then, I suppose my only choice is to go back to the enclave and tell Father exactly where you are and what you're doing."

"Go on, then," I say. "Run back to the commander and tell him I wouldn't let you break vows with me."

Lux twists the hilt of her blade between her hands. With a sigh, her gaze tilts sidelong toward my wretched sister. "You don't need to threaten us, Briar. You can stay."

"No, she can't," I snap, hating how childish I sound.

Lux flashes me a stubborn look. "I want her to come with us, Evie."

Her shoulders are squared, determined. I've seen her like this often enough to know she won't back down. Angry words rise through me in a tangled rush, but I keep silent. If I try to say anything, I'll start to cry. And besides—I don't want to argue with her. Especially not in front of Briar. I shouldn't *have* to argue. Lux is supposed to take my side, the same way I always take hers: without question. That's how it's always been. At least, until this moment.

I pull the strap of my satchel higher on my shoulder and start to walk, not bothering to look back. After a beat of silence, Lux and Briar begin to follow, moving at a slower pace so they keep a measured step behind me, rather than walking at my side. Everything is tense and wretched. I stare ahead, trying to ignore them. There's a trail of flattened marks through the grass, roughly in the shape of footprints. The path of the vespertine, leading out onto the wider moors.

He's crushed through a thicket of wild lavender, which has

spread from the apiary field. As I walk alongside the creature's blurred footprints, careful not to disturb the marks, the air turns sickly sweet; the same scent of torn petals that surrounded me earlier, in the other part of the field. Except here, the sweetness of bruised flowerheads and broken stems is overlaid with decay.

The vespertine's trail leads right to the barrier at the edge of the world. When I reach the line of wards, I pause—remembering the watchful glimmer of light that I saw, the way the consecration changed and became a keen-eyed glare. A few paces away from where I've stopped, one of the wards leers toothlessly. I stare at the absent space in the line of lights. Apprehension catches against my ribs, gnawing me with sharpened teeth.

When Lux and Briar reach the barrier, they stand for a moment, unmoving. Then Briar kneels down to inspect the scattered bones. "You didn't notice the light burn out when you were in the tower, Everline?"

I shake my head, irritated by her accusation. I *should* have seen it. But everything has melted away except for the image of the vespertine on his knees by the pyre as I stared down at him.

I look more closely at the broken ward. Hooked to the top of the stake is a rusted lantern tied on with a length of ribbon. It looks strange. *Antique.* The tin font is spotted with rust, the handle worn smooth as the femur bone on the barracks door. The glass chimney and the wick are both soot-smudged. The flame burned out so recently that the leftover heat is vivid enough to warm my skin.

There's only a thin layer of grimy oil left in the font, but it must have been enough to burn for a while, to replicate the glow of a ward. I stare at it, fear sinking over me, through me. A leaden, barbed thing that carves a shuddering ache down the length of my sternum. I clutch at my fiola. The vespertine I saw must have done this—destroyed a ward and replaced it with a lantern light.

"He *tricked* us," I say, holding out the lantern to Lux so she can feel its warmth.

She touches the smudged side of the glass, her face turned pale with worry. "What kind of vespertine would destroy the hives for revenge or mimic a ward light?"

The moorland is quiet, washed in the glow of the bloodied eclipse. Beneath the silence lies the heaviness of secrets, an unfolding horror I can barely put words to. "The vespertine have changed—and Fenn, he *knew*, long before tonight."

Lux glances toward Briar. "Did he say anything when you went back to burn the one we . . ." She falters, looking in the direction of the hive field. "The one we killed?"

Briar shakes her head. Even she looks troubled by the gravity of this moment, our discovery. I watch her, intent, waiting for her response. But all she says is, "We need to reset the ward."

Frowning, Lux unclasps her shard pouch from her belt and tips out a handful of new bones. She sets them in place at the base of the stake while Briar uncaps a vial of honey and drips it over the shards. Then Lux pricks her finger and lets her blood fall onto the earth, murmuring softly in holy speech. Pale light gleams from the earth as the new consecration ignites. Briar tucks the spent ward into her pocket.

The unison of their magic is so different from how Lux and I

59

tend the wards. Their power is solemn and beautiful as it weaves together. It stings to see them working like this, in such careful rhythm. I turn away, searching the landscape beyond the barrier for signs of where the vespertine's trail continues.

"There," Lux says once the ward is alight. Getting to her feet, she holds out a hand to Briar, then falters when she notices the fresh cut on her finger. Briar stands up, unassisted, with studied indifference. Lux steps aside, her bloodied finger in her mouth.

I point past the silver chain and the wavering consecration light, to where a line of blurred footprints marks the wind-tangled grass. "He went this way."

We gather up our skirts and cross the barrier of the wards. There's a tightness in my chest, a tangled thread pulled around each rib. We've crossed the ward line before, but never so close to the gathering when the magic at the wall is this fragile. And never with the intention of going this far or to this fate.

The enclave is a smudge on the horizon, a pale scrollwork of bones and the sharp-pointed watchtower outlined against the sky. Lux takes my hand again as we make our way down onto the wilder fields, offering me a tentative smile. When I next look back, the enclave has vanished, swallowed up by the rising slopes at the edge of the world.

We move warily forward. Each sound becomes magnified; every rustle of grass or shift of wind sends my pulse fluttering. I feel as startled and restless as the bees that swarmed above their ruined hive. The moonlight dims and brightens, made changeable by the movement of clouds. I'm certain the vespertine is right there, past the edge of the shadows, watching us with his eyes that shimmered like wards.

His trail is laid out in sparse clues across the moorland. A footprint. A broken branch. A scrap of dark fabric torn from a cloak, caught on a thicket of brambles. We follow the path as the land wends farther down, flattening out into the undulant stretches of marshy plains. The grass rises taller around us, reaching our knees, then our waists. We walk where the vespertine did, stepping on the trampled leaves and broken stems left from where he forged his way through.

Our steps turn cautious, our voices hushed. Each breath of wind makes me jump, the crackle of grass beneath my boots sends my pulse into racing staccato. We're so far from the enclave now—and though we're armored and have our blades and our bones, it's hard not to feel small beneath the expanse of blood-colored sky, at the center of the ominous night.

Finally, the tall grass gives way to a barren stretch of ground. There's another footprint in the earth, a scrape of moss torn from the trunk of a wind-bowed tree. Water shimmers in the distance, darker red beneath the blood-bright clouds. The Blackthorn River.

We make our way toward the riverbank, where a line of stones forms a makeshift bridge across the water. The river winds all through the moorland, curving around like a question mark. There's only one remaining bridge—the Moongate—which is out to the west, near the mountains. When the storm season begins and the river floods, these stones will be covered, and that far-off bridge will be our only way back.

It feels so strange to stand at the edge of the landmark that shares my name. The river is all I have of my mother—Ila Blackthorn—whose family mapped it when they lived here before the vespertine and the wall, a time so long ago that it feels like a fable. I never asked Fenn if there were other Blackthorns still alive somewhere in the Hallowed Lands who might know my mother—or me. I was afraid to mention the possibility of distant relatives in case he sent me to them.

But after my fiola ritual failed for the third time, Briar pulled me aside and whispered what I'd already begun to fear. "You're not a true warden. They're going to make you leave."

I slapped her, and we fell down to a scrabbling, inelegant fight at the center of the training yard. She bloodied my nose, and I split her lip; I shoved her onto her back and got my knees on her chest. Overcome with rage, I was wild as a wolf, my hurt turned to a hunger that wanted blood. Briar had drawn her blade—the only time I've seen her bare the curved steel of it—before Fenn dragged us apart.

As I skulked away with a crumpled scrap of field-kit linen pressed to my face, I heard him tell her, "Everline belongs at the wall. She has nowhere else to go." Perhaps he'd meant to shame Briar into tolerating me. No matter what his reasons, it *hurt*. I knew then what I'd always suspected: He'd made me a warden because he had to, rather than because he wanted me at his side.

At the edge of the river, there's a lone footprint smeared in the mud—the place where the vespertine crossed. We take off our boots, tying the laces together so they can hang from our satchels.

The nearest stepping stone is carved into a patterned arch like the window frames in the enclave barracks. It must be part of the ruins left behind from the buildings destroyed in the fight against Nyx. We're crossing the river on pieces of a chapel built by his enthralled worshippers.

Halfway across, Lux and I pause on a large, flat stone as we try to choose the best path forward. Glancing at Briar, who is farther ahead, I ask Lux quietly, "Why didn't you take my side before?"

She hesitates, looking around as though searching for an escape. But there's only the slow-moving water, the makeshift bridge. "I thought it would be helpful to have her with us."

"I don't need—or want—her *help*."

"I know you don't. But—" Lux's voice lowers. She sounds troubled. Sad. "This is so dangerous, Evie, what we're doing. And you don't have the same . . . protection . . . as the other wardens."

A startled laugh spills loose from me, loud enough that Briar looks back at us with a scowl. "You think I can't protect myself without magic?"

Lux puts her hand on my arm. She's trembling as she strokes her thumb against my wrist. "I want you to be safe."

It's like a slap, this betrayal. I've always known the other wardens considered me *less*, but I never thought to count Lux among them. I clutch at the hilt of the relic blade and give her a pointed look. "Even Fenn didn't think I was so weak."

"Everline, that's not what I meant."

I turn away, avoiding her outstretched hand, and step quickly from stone to stone, until I land heavily on the opposite bank, my bare feet sinking into the mud. Everything wavers and blurs, and it takes all I have to hold back the hot, shameful rise of tears as I stride away into the dark.

CHAPTER FIVE

THE FARTHER WE GO PAST THE RIVER, THE MORE SIGNS OF Nyx we find. The moorland is an inland sea, with islands of decaying shrines and crumbled ruins that still hold memories of their former shape. An arched window framing empty sky, a flight of stairs that leads to nothing, a wrought iron fence around a clutch of thorns. It's as though the moment we crossed the water, our familiar life fell away, and everything we knew from the enclave is strewn behind us like petals torn from handfuls of flowers.

We've entered a different world, one I've only glimpsed on our nights tending the wards, when the vespertine come from the dark. This is a land of monsters, where moonlight spills like pools of blood, and secrets are tucked into crevices between the tumbled stones of buildings once raised in worship of Nyx Severin.

It's like a nightmare that has woken me, breathless and dizzy, certain the terrors of my dream have been pulled through to haunt me still.

The vespertine's trail leads past the riverbank mud and into the grass. We move from mark to mark as the trail grows colder and the night draws out. There's another torn scrap of cloth caught on a broken branch, a thicket of gorse that's been trampled down. But then . . . nothing.

Clouds fill the sky, covering the bloodstained moon. It starts to rain in a slow, steady drizzle that veils our hair and turns everything to a blur. I draw up the hood of my cloak and wrap my arms around my waist, feeling miserable. Lux and Briar stand ahead of me, huddled and shivering, their eyes to the ground as they search for the next piece of the trail.

We pace back and forth in a widening arc. The rain grows heavier. A slender tributary of the river cuts over the moorland, turning the ground to heavy mud that drags at our boots with every step. We tuck up our skirts and tiptoe across the rare pieces of solid ground among the damp.

The water in the tributary is dark as spilled ink; rippling against the reed-knotted banks with a hollow hiss. Everything is cast in shadow, but the bloodstained eclipse leaks down through gathered clouds. And I can make out enough to see that the rain and the river have washed away the creature's trail as thoroughly as an antiseptic-doused cloth cleans blood from a wound.

Briar glares at me from beneath her dripping hood. "Are we going to circle around in the dark until we're completely lost?"

I sheathe my blade and wring the water from my hair. "You were the one who insisted on following us. If you've changed your mind, then you're quite welcome to leave. In fact—I'd prefer it."

"Hells, Everline—"

Lux steps between us, holding up a conciliatory hand. "Maybe we can shelter in one of the ruins until the weather eases."

As though in answer, lightning blooms behind the clouds, illuminating the moorland with a red-tinged flush. Thunder echoes balefully from the distance, rolling toward us in slow, deep notes. At the crest of a nearby hill, a solid form takes shape, spired and tall, the most undamaged of all the ruins we've passed.

We hurry toward it, chased by the rain. The wind cuts like a knife with its cold edge pressed right against my ribs, and it fills the air with sounds: a high wail, a somber growl. And then— howling, howling—the familiar wolflike call that echoes so often beyond the ward lines as the gathering draws near. I can't escape the feeling of eyes in the dark, that there are vespertine hidden by the moorland shadows, tracking us with watchful hunger.

I shiver and shiver, clutch hold of the Vale Scythe and bow my head beneath the rain. Lux and I fall into a protective stance, pressed close to each other. The same as when we're beside the wall, setting wards to chase away the monsters. Briar stays behind us, her eyes wary, hand on her blade.

The ruin rises higher and higher as we draw close, as though it was a half-imagined thing about to slip from reality and we have tethered it with our eager gazes. When we finally reach the entrance, a dizzy relief runs through me, unknotting like a thread pulled free from a stitch. The solid lines of the building close out the moonlight, painting us all in shadow as we approach.

The walls stretch outward across the waves of heather, and a sharp-tipped spire spears up from the roof, a dark arrow against the layered clouds. It's like a chapel, but to compare it to the one in the enclave—a bone-wrought room with a single stained glass window and a narrow altar to Saint Lenore—is like comparing the sharpness in a sewing needle to that in a warden knife and calling them both blades.

This ruin is twice as large as the enclave chapel, with ornate scrollwork carved into the stones framing the line of windows. Each window is filled by paneled glass that shows intricate, leadlight scenes. I can make out the vague depiction of a cloaked figure standing above a line of penitents shrouded in pale robes; only a silhouette. But something in the figure's outspread arms and looming height sets me on edge, drags a renewed shiver across my wind-chilled skin as I remember where we are—and who the chapels here were built in devotion to.

We crowd together at the arched front door; decorated with bones in a pattern as intricate as knitted lace. The handles are vertebrosternal ribs, worn smooth with touch and time. A queasy shudder goes through me, a fierce, irascible panic. I bite the inside of my cheek. I'm not squeamish about *bones*. And whatever this chapel was before, it's empty now, only a ruin.

Ignoring the tightness in my stomach, I wrap a fold of my cloak around my hand and step toward the door, a sour, panicked taste on my tongue. I turn the latch. The chapel opens itself to us with a sound like a sigh.

Inside is thickly dark. The air smells of incense and honey, the same scent of worship and magic familiar to home, but here it reminds me of the burned-down pyre near the apiary field, the way the syrupy insides of the wrecked hive mixed with the ashes on the ground like a spell gone wrong.

As we enter the cavernous space, I feel, inexplicably, that we're being swallowed up, and while the enclave chapel has always felt like the heart of the wardens, this sepulchral space is a *stomach*.

My hand goes out by instinct, searching for Lux, but she isn't beside me. Instead, she and Briar stand close together, framed by the door as they look uncertainly into the darkened room. Their hands are clasped. My chest twinges with a sudden hurt, an echoing reminder of how I felt before when Lux spoke up for Briar and insisted she come with us. I'm struck by a sudden, childish urge to cry. Ashamed, I fight back the rise of my wretched tears.

Another flash of lightning pierces through the sky. Brightness washes through the open door, making a path from entrance to altar. At the apex of the chapel, the largest stained glass window blazes like a newly lit lantern. Each panel of the design is revealed in clear, hideous illumination.

Nyx Severin stands with his arms outspread; his fists are full of bone shards. Blood drips down, a hail of gleaming droplets as brilliant as rubies, as he casts his powerful, enthralling spell. Beneath him kneels a row of penitents, their heads bowed and their hands clasped to their hearts as blood pours on them like rain.

The stories told of Nyx—the way he was worshipped—have become a hideous legend, a terrible caution. He fell to the earth like a dying star, a being of such power that people couldn't help but believe him to be a god. He would call worshippers aside to attend him in illicit, secretive ceremonies where he promised to grant them power, given by the touch of his divinity.

And here is a shrine they built in his honor, this whole chapel a monument to the time before his wonder evolved into horror. Before the truth of him came clear: that he used blood and bones and magic to bend the worshippers to his will, to drain their lives and use them in his quest for greater strength. For the power to unbind himself from the Thousandfold.

We fall to stillness; I'm held in place as though I've been pinned. The light vanishes, sending the room back into shadows. But the image might as well be printed across the dark. The horror of it isn't something that can be blinked away or lost beneath the rise of clouds.

"No," says Briar, her voice gone thick. "I am absolutely not staying in here."

"We have the tent," Lux offers. "Maybe we can find a place to shelter beneath, outside."

She turns toward the other side of the hall, where a narrow door leads to a small side room. They go through in single file, Briar striding ahead with her blade fully drawn, Lux trailing behind her more cautiously.

Before I join them, I linger for a moment. Spare a final look toward the window. My fear has become a cloying, hungry feeling—the way my mouth would water at the sight of glossy nightshade berries or a cluster of amanita mushrooms—the inescapable lure of a deadly, beautiful thing.

Through the door is a space that must have once been a kitchen. An enormous brick hearth fills the remaining wall, but the rest of the room is tumbled stones, consumed by a greedy tangle of ivy with stems as thick as coiled snakes. Beyond, there's an overgrown garden, where rows of self-seeded herbs have turned wild against a backdrop of spindly citrus trees studded with late-season clementines. Past that, a wrought iron fence divides the chapel grounds from the rest of the moorland.

I start to unpack the tent, laying out the rolled canvas and the length of rope tied around a bundle of pitch pins. Briar examines it with a scowl. "Where's the other one?"

"What other one?"

"Are we supposed to *share*?"

Lux glances at Briar, then quickly looks away. "Evie and I always share."

I unwind the tent rope. Until now, when Lux and I would go out together onto the moors, it never seemed worth carrying an extra tent when the space in our satchels could be used for other things. But now, with a sharp despair, I realize what this means— all three of us spending the night together inside a single enclosed space. Briar, who I can't stand. And Lux, who thinks I'm unable to protect myself against the dangers of the moors.

The rope comes loose from its knot in a sudden unraveling, the pitch pins clatter onto the ground at my feet. I scowl at Briar as I kneel to gather them up. "Should we have brought the entire enclave with us?"

She sidesteps me as I collect the pins. Dragging her hood back over her rain-wet hair, she stalks out into the garden and starts to pace along the line of the iron fence. Lux watches her go, then picks up the tent ropes to untangle them.

We make camp in silence, tension palpable between us. The tent is small, and it doesn't take long. I feel Lux's eyes on me as I check the knots, hammer the pins into the softened earth at the edge of the ruined kitchen floor.

Out in the garden, Briar sets her wards. She walks beneath the clementine trees with a length of silver chain, pulling shards from the pouch at her waist to plant in the earth every few steps. I watch as she pricks her finger, smears a daub of honey on the bone, then pierces the ward through a loop of chain, anchoring it to the ground. Consecration glows behind her like a trail of luminescence left by a firefly.

Lux bumps her shoulder against mine, her mouth tilted into a soft, uncertain smile. "She's not bad," she says, nodding toward Briar. Then, conciliatorily, "But the ones you make are better."

Though I can't wield magic, Lux taught me how to build wards using a handful of bloodied shards that she had already consecrated. I press my fingers to my palms, remembering her hands over mine as she showed me how to place the bones, the light from her power glimmering in a halo around us. "Only because I had such a good teacher."

Lux huffs out a quiet, fond laugh. Then, tightening the knot at the shoulder of her cloak, she goes to help Briar finish the final segment of the ward line. When Briar drops one of the shards, Lux bends to pick it up. Their fingers touch, their heads bow close, then they both draw back quickly.

I turn away, feeling as though I've intruded on a moment that wasn't meant for me. Brushing the dirt from my palms, I get to my feet and go to the opposite wall, where the thickened ivy weaves around a glassless window. With my elbows leaning against the vine-covered sill, I stare into the night, caught in confusion.

The closeness I have with Lux is as deep as a sworn vow. I'm not jealous of whatever lies between her and Briar. *I'm not.* But still, there's something in the way they steal sidelong glances at each other that pulls a strange hurt from my chest—and makes me angry with myself for feeling it.

Beyond the ruin, the heavy rain is lit by panes of crimson moonlight, the sparkling, bloodied hue of the droplets reminding me of the image of Nyx Severin in the chapel window. We've been raised on stories of Nyx, but standing inside a space built to honor him—with that ill-fated deference immortalized forever in paneled glass—makes the truth of him so much more vivid.

He may be gone, destroyed by the sacrifice of Saint Lenore, but his hideous legacy persists in the vespertine he made. We'd always believed their bloodlust was an instinct, a hunger bred into them by their monstrous creator. They were a threat to be guarded against with our wall built of magic-laced bones, our holy wards strung across the line that divides safety from danger.

But all of that has changed with the appearance of these new creatures. These vespertine—what could they mean?

A fresh shiver drags across my skin. I wrap my arms around my waist, feeling feverish despite the cold scrape of the rain-flecked wind against my cheeks. Out beyond the chapel lies more ruins, stones driven deep into the ground as though they tumbled from a great height—perhaps torn from the stories above. The shadows between them are deep and shifting, with the rippling, changeable look of the Blackthorn River when it reflected the bloodied moonlight.

Then . . . the shadows *move*, slipping out from between the stones, knitting together into a solid form. The way the chapel rose from the moorland as we walked toward it. A shape appears—cloaked and dark—accompanied by the crush of footsteps against the ground.

The vespertine.

He's tall, with a heavy fur draped around his shoulders. His mouth is painted with a cruel smear of black, and skeletal lines are carved against his cheeks. But the rest of his face is hidden by a moon-pale mask tipped by horns that jut upward against the clouded sky like a spire.

There's a beetle-wing glint in the depths of the mask, and I know that his eyes are on me. Wrongness radiates from him, the same way it did when I saw him from the tower. It passes over me in a sickly shudder, lighting up my whole body in a wave of heat, like a putrid fever.

Inside the hollows of the mask, his pupils catch the light, mirrored like a wolf's. Beneath the bandage on my throat, my wound gives an aching pulse.

And—he speaks.

"Which of you was the one who killed her?" His voice is strange and muffled, the consonants sharp at the edges, like they sit unfamiliar on his tongue. He paces closer, the words bitten out, hemmed by a guttural snarl. "Which of you *burned* her?"

I stare at him as my heart goes wild, terror lacing right down to my bones. He spoke. *He spoke.* We've heard the vespertine make sounds before—screams and growls, cries spat between sharp-tipped teeth—but nothing we could understand. Nothing that sounded *human.*

Lightning splits through the sky like a ripped seam, a sudden brightness that turns the whole world brilliant. Thunder chases close at the heels of it, so loud that my ears are left ringing long after the sound has rolled into silence.

I unsheathe the Vale Scythe. The honed edge of the relic is sharper than my iron blade, and it sings in the air, as though it senses the unholiness before me. Breathing heavily, I clutch my weapon and stare out into the dark, waiting for my eyes to adjust. Blink by blink, the shapes of the stones and the moor and the sky come into focus—and the space beside the ruin is filled with nothing but rain that has pooled like floodwater across the ground.

The vespertine—if he was there, if he was *real*—has vanished.

I take a faltering step back, feeling sick and dizzy. Lux and Briar are sitting outside the tent. They each have a dampened cloth, and the bones they collected from the burned-out ward are on the ground between them. I watch as they meticulously clean the dirt and honey and dried blood from the shards, making them ready to use again.

"Did you hear . . . ?" I begin. Lux looks up, her face as open as an unfurled flower, colored only by weariness and confusion, none of the urgent terror that has set a fire in my blood and made my heart beat as wildly as the wings of a trapped bird.

"It's all right, Evie," she says, misreading my expression. "We'll be safe here. The wards will ignite if anything comes close."

I glance toward the line of wards strung around the campsite, all of them still lit, as unfailing as lanterns freshly filled with oil. Outside the window, the stones are still vacant, the deepening spread of water beneath them marred only by stippling rainfall. I press my hand to my face and let out a shaky breath.

I've not felt this way since Lux joined me in our attic room at the barracks and held my hand through my last, fear-drenched nightmare. The darkness outside the ruins is just like those terrible dreams that pulled me from sleep as a child. The dragging fear is so familiar that I don't know what to believe. Nightmares are so much realer than a vespertine *speaking* to me.

Shivering and feverish, I take off my armor and my boots, then slip free of my outer layers, leaving my cloak and skirts and blouse draped beside the hearth in hopes that some of the rain will dry from them by morning. In my linen underdress, I go into the tent and curl beneath my share of the blankets with the relic blade tucked close to my chest, the hilt pressed to my ribs.

When Lux comes in, she sits beside me for a while. She's brought her weapon, just as I did, and she sharpens the blade with a whetstone—the scrape of the stone along the sickled metal a rhythmic *snick, snick, snick*. She sets it down in easy reach, alongside a pouch of shards and a vial of honey.

Her hand trails over my hair. She starts to untie the ribbons and loosen my braid. Finally, she says, her voice quiet, "I'm afraid."

I turn to look at her, confused. Of all the things she could have told me, this wasn't what I expected. Carefully, I ask, "Are you thinking of your sister?"

Lux's elder sister was killed by the vespertine when they breached the wall, when my mother deserted the wardens. It's something she speaks about only in whispers, during these secretive moments when we're alone and just before sleep.

She presses her lips together and ducks her head. "Yes. And no. I'm worried about *you*, Everline. When we fought near the wall, I could keep you safe. It didn't matter that you had no magic. But this is so uncharted. I'm afraid something will happen, and I won't be able to stop it."

"Lux, I'm not defenseless. I have armor and blades—I have everything except for magic." I hate the way my voice sounds so unsteady, like I'm about to cry. "And that is why I'm here. I need to know what happened—to my mother, what happened to *me*—to make me so changed. What Fenn is hiding about the vespertine and the Thousandfold. This is my only chance to discover why—Why I am like this."

She stares at me with dark-eyed helplessness. There's a softened throb at the heart of my palm, the echoed memory of Fenn's blade pressed down in the ritual that should have wakened my magic. Before either of us can speak, the tent rustles as the canvas parts and Briar slips inside. Her face is studiedly neutral, and I wonder if she overheard when Lux and I were talking.

I close my eyes and feign sleep as Briar gathers her share of the blankets and lies down as far from me as possible, on the opposite side of the tent. Lux cards her fingers through my hair, working loose the final segments of my braid. I let myself soften against her. Neither of us apologizes. Not yet.

With her fingers tangled gently in my hair, she falls soundly asleep. But despite my own fatigue, sleep eludes me. Awake and restless, I stare at the side of the tent, straining to hear past the sound of the rain for whispers or footsteps or the telltale spark of ignited wards. When I turn to my other side, I notice Lux and Briar have drifted together—Lux's arm curled over Briar's waist. In sleep, Briar looks so different with her perpetual scowl smoothed out and her mouth turned soft.

I bury my face in my folded arms, letting out a sigh that catches in my throat. With my tongue laced by the salted burn of held-back tears, I fall finally, truly asleep. The sound of the rain drifts into my dreams, and I'm lost to imagined tides, an endless black ocean, the howl of wolves. And a monster speaking to me with an incongruously human voice, sharpened by furious accusation.

Which of you burned her?

Then his voice changes, anger softening to sweetness, the sharpness now a lulling tone. As I listen, all my fear is washed away, and I feel so safe, so soothed. I am floating above the ground with petals of heather and wild lavender tracing gently against the soles of my bare feet.

When I surface, opening my eyes, the rain has stopped. The night draws out in unnatural stillness, without even the rustle of leaves or the stir of wind. I reach out a hand to Lux, but find only the indent left where she lay on the blankets—the space still warm—then the ribbon-wrapped hilt of her newly sharp-ened blade. Pushing myself up onto my elbow, I try to see clearly through the dark.

On the far side of the tent, Briar sleeps peacefully.

And Lux—Lux is gone.

CHAPTER SIX

I LEAVE THE TENT AND SLIP INTO THE DARKNESS, HOLDING THE Vale Scythe in my arms like a stolen secret. I'm still half-lost in my dream of blackened water and luring voices, and as I move past the broken wall and into the overgrown garden, I feel as though I am swimming through the flooded river—my breath held, my limbs heavy—as I struggle against the rising current.

The wards are still alight beneath the clementine trees, shimmering neatly in an unbroken row where Lux and Briar strung them along the wrought iron fence. Rain has left the ground damp, and my bare feet sink into the mud as I walk to the edge of the wards. The sky is still heavy with clouds, but the tangled sprawl of plants is limned diffusely in shades of lilac and silver, the color of early dawn. The bloodstained light that painted the sky in gory hues has waned alongside the setting moon.

Fearful, strung tight by apprehension, I edge past a cluster of black nightshade that has sprung up in the beds of mint and lavender. Leftover rain drips from its glossy berries and heart-shaped leaves. When I reach the fence, I curl my hand around an iron paling. Cold seeps through my skin, travels up the length of my arm in a slow tremor. I hold my breath and hear the sound of the river, the water like a whisper.

The moorland beyond the ruins is a stretch of rain-jeweled grass blanketed by trailing mist, the dark shapes of far-off trees curved grimly against the sky. Then, painted like a delicate rise of incense smoke against the darker shades of gorse and heather, I see Lux.

In her linen underdress, with her hair unbound, she moves like a ghost—a figure slipping in and out of the early light. Her skirts trail heedlessly on the ground, catching against the wet strands of grass as she walks.

I call out to her. "Lux!"

My voice is high and thin, carried across the dawn-lit stillness like the cry of a bird. I hold my breath, my heartbeat quavering, imagine all the eyes of the creatures I pictured hidden in shadows last night, now fixed to me. But the sound of my call melts into the mist. Like I dropped a stone into the river and it fell beneath the surface without even a single ripple.

Lux doesn't turn.

There's a narrow gate in the iron fence, a snare of ivy woven around the rust-flecked hinges. It opens soundlessly when I raise the latch. Clutching my sheathed blade to my chest, I step over the line of wards. Fear traces over me, creeping from the nape of my neck to the dip of my spine; this is the second time I've gone past the protection of warden magic—first at the end of the world and now here, outside the decayed remnants of Nyx Severin's chapel.

But I don't look back toward the tent, framed against the dilapidated kitchen, or the ruin, shadowed against the clouded sky. I only go forward, following Lux out into the moors.

I call her name again but she's far ahead, moving somnambulantly. Her pale dress is soaked with dew from hem to knee, her hair tousled by the invisible fingers of the wind. I buckle my blade belt over my linen slip, then gather up my skirts and hurry toward her. My breath held, my feet noiseless over the damp grass. I've almost reached her when a shadow peels away from the mist; sharp and angular, it carries the same shape as the distant trees, carved by weather into sinuous outlines.

Then it takes form—familiar, sickeningly familiar, though I don't want it to be. The trailing fall of a long cloak, jutting horns that pierce the mist-draped sky. The vespertine, his features still hidden by daubed corpsepaint and the honed edges of his pale mask that cut like knives down the sides of his jaw.

He places his hand at the small of Lux's back, gentle as a lover, his onyx claws dimpling the gossamer fabric of her underdress. The sight of her with this creature—unarmored, with no protective gauntlets around her wrists or strengthened rib cage on her chest— stirs me to a desperate panic. I bite back the frightened cry that rises to my lips and force myself to be silent, to be still.

Finger by finger, I curl my hand tighter around the Vale Scythe.

The vespertine bends to Lux, hand still pressed to her spine, his paint-darkened mouth beside her ear. I see his lips move, the stirring motion of his breath against her hair as he speaks.

As he speaks to her.

He whispers to her, and she goes loose and soft, bowed toward him like a sapling drawn into a gentle curve by the persistent brush of the wind.

I think of the voice in my dreams and the voice in the dark—the bitten-back anger as he spoke of *murder*, the way that voice was transformed in the alchemy of sleep until his words became alluring, seductive.

He called to me, and I did not go. Now he's come for Lux, drawn her from the safety of wards and blades and the darkened ruins; he's called her, and she has gone to him as though pulled by an invisible thread.

I draw my blade. As the Vale Scythe sings through the air, the vespertine's head snaps up. He turns from Lux and looks right at me. Beneath the weight of his gaze, I go wretchedly still, a mouse crouched beneath a bramble thicket when the shadow of a hawk passes overhead.

I can see him clearly now, and he's a creature from a nightmare. From worse than a nightmare.

His mask is gruesome, snarling—a skeletal wolf with fanged teeth and a jagged, open jaw. His cheeks are planed by sharply painted bones, his lips a smudge of onyx cut by grayish stripes: a rictus grin. The fur of his mantle shimmers, silver-tipped in the early light.

I stare at him, my bones turned soft, captured by the feral shimmer of his eyes. It's as though the distance between us has closed and he's right beside me. When he touches Lux, I feel the pinprick of his claws against my own spine. Feel his mouth against my ear, his words burning with a heated shudder. I can feel *him*—an unholiness that slithers over me until I'm sickened, the taste of dirt and death and defilement pasted on my tongue.

There's a sudden sound of footsteps; I'm pulled free of the vespertine's gaze. Briar rushes up beside me, her hair streaming loose, and her weapon clutched in a white-knuckled grip, the ribbon tied to the blade hilt spilling down from her fist. She grabs my arm tight enough to bruise, her fingers pressing sharply through the gauzy fabric of my sleeve.

"What are you *doing*?" She shakes me, hard enough that my teeth bump together, and I taste blood. Then, with a disgusted exhalation, she lets me go and runs toward Lux, calling her name, harsh and desperate. Briar's voice echoes across the flatlands around us, a panicked, animalistic cry. *"Lux, Lux, Lux."*

I start to run, too. We run together across the moorland, our bare feet sinking into the mud beneath the rain-wet grass, our hair flying loose behind us, our weapons drawn.

And there's something in this moment—the two of us, side by side, filled with terror and adrenaline—that eclipses our division; all the bitterness and hurt and envy are shrouded by the breadth of this present, urgent horror. It doesn't matter that Fenn will never be my true father, that Briar doesn't trust me, that Lux has softened toward her . . . All that matters is we are wardens, sworn to hunt the unholy terror who has emerged from the night.

The vespertine turns toward us sinuously, liquid as a pooled shadow. His mouth tilts into a cold smile, baring sharpened eyeteeth. He raises a hand, his fingers splayed against the sky. A weeping line cuts across his palm, oozing and blood-slick. Briar grabs for me again with the same fierceness as before—except this time, her touch is trembling with fear, not anger.

"Lux!" I call. "Lux, *please*—"

Lux regards me blankly, her gaze unfocused, a dreamy flush painted across her cheeks. The vespertine plucks something from the depths of his cloak. A piece of bone as thin and sharp as one of my keenest sewing needles. He clasps it tenderly between his index finger and thumb. His smile widens. Then he curls his fingers into a sudden fist, with the bone trapped at the center. The same gesture I've seen Lux make countless times when she casts a spell.

He's using magic. The vespertine can use *magic*.

There's a split-second moment for Briar and me to exchange a glance, her wide eyes and paled cheeks a reflection of my own terror. Then his power hits us, brutal as a sudden storm. Smokelike clouds gather, a swift, heavy dark. The crackling scent of ozone fills the air. I fall to my knees, gasping. My weapon thuds to the earth. I try to cry out, but my voice is swept away, all sound lost to an intense, high-pitched static.

My vision blurs and twists. The light flickers, painted with impossible, terrible things. An enormous ruin with arched windows. A carved iron panel that frames a bone-studded door, the hollowed-out carapace of a cathedral. Creatures with too many eyes and too many limbs. Horns and claws and bared teeth. I can feel them, feel their hunger.

Briar collapses beside me. I scrabble in the mud, trying to reach her, but the vespertine's magic is coiled tight, snaring me in unbreakable knots. It slithers over me, a nauseous, horrifying *wrongness*—the unholy power that Nyx Severin used, that he *made*—born of blood and bones and death.

Lux is just before me, but the space between us is unbreachable. Her wrists look so fragile without the protection of her bracers, bird-boned and delicate, her skin as translucent as parchment. I call to her, my voice lost to the howl of the wind. She regards me again with the same vague, dreamy expression, lashes veiling her gaze in a slow blink.

The vespertine extends his hand to her. She steps into his arms.

He's still for a heartbeat, and again I feel the burn of his gaze. Somewhere beside me, I can hear Briar, her choking cries. We press together, fighting against the magic, trying to push ourselves back to our feet. My nose starts to bleed. The air howls. My bones are lit with unbearable, searing pain. I fight, I fight—then all of it, the noise and the power and the terror, rushes over me.

The vespertine cradles Lux against his chest. She curls into him, her eyes closed and her head against his shoulder, her bare feet dangling elegantly over his arm. Blood drips from his cut hand and stains the side of her dress. Droplets fall to the ground, bright and brilliant, and I see him transposed against the stained glass window in the chapel. Nyx Severin with his clenched fists and his blood raining over the penitents.

I fall to my knees, powerless to move, to scream, to do anything except watch the monster walk away with Lux cradled against him, carrying her the same way we carried the wrapped corpse of the slaughtered vespertine.

CHAPTER SEVEN

THE ONLY STORY FENN HAS EVER TOLD ABOUT MY MOTHER is this: She broke her vows on the day the vespertine attacked the Hallowed Lands.

At the gathering, the wall failed. Even though I wasn't there, I can picture each detail of that night. The wardens in a line against the barrier, their cut hands pressed to the bloodied bones, the air bright with holy magic. Then the glass-shard shatter as the wall broke apart. The air filled with howls as the monsters rushed into the breach.

The moon turned red, a blood eclipse just like the one that would spill across the sky on the night of my birth and again on the night when we killed the changed vespertine. Beneath that crimson light, my mother ran from her duty.

The wardens fought as they were trained to do, sweeping through the monsters with their blades and bones. It was a brutal fight, hard-won, and when it was over, there were countless new dead laid down in the catacombs beneath the enclave chapel and in burial grounds across the Hallowed Lands. Among them was Lux's elder sister, slain before the wardens arrived.

It haunted her, that night. She confessed to me once when we whispered about it, curled together beneath the window in our attic room. How her parents looked at her and saw only the daughter they'd lost, how their grief made them afraid to love her like they had her sister. How she'd wished each year to be marked, to be called to the wardens.

I've tried so hard to escape the legacy of Ila Blackthorn. To distance myself from her treachery, the way she abandoned the enclave when she was needed most. I wanted the truth of what drove her to break her vows, to flee to the Thousandfold. But all I've done is repeat her mistakes. As though my path across the moors was an instinctive motion, built into my blood, the way a natal homing creature will migrate back to its place of birth, following a ley line mapped out long before it ever drew breath.

I come awake to a quiet world, everything draped in cold daylight. The sun is overhead, and our shadows crawl beneath us in a blur. Everything returns in pieces. The ache in my chest. The taste of death against my tongue. The blank space on the ground where a third shadow should fall.

The fear is last—and worst.

Briar has her arm around my waist, her hand knotted in the fabric of my dress, her fist pressed hard against my ribs. There's no tenderness in the way she holds me, dragging me bodily along as I stumble and stagger. In the distance, the chapel comes into view, the line of wards still glimmering with a cruel hopefulness beneath the shadows of the citrus trees.

"Wait!" I twist against Briar, trying to turn back. "Lux! She's—she's—we can't *leave* her with him."

Briar wrenches me against her. We're so close, I feel the fierce exhale of her sigh. In the fragile daylight, she looks raw, her features sharpened by fear and despair. Her eyes are bloodshot, her cheeks slicked with tears, a dark bruise at the edge of her mouth.

She scrubs at her lip, as though to wipe away the bruise. "Do you think getting yourself captured, too, will solve things?"

I shove at her again, my ears still throbbing with echoes of the terrible sounds that overwhelmed us when the vespertine used his magic. I close my eyes and see the images that writhed in the mist behind him—there and not there, as though he had slit open the belly of the hells and let all the worst horrors pour out into the waking world. I start to cry, my breath choking on a sob.

"This is my fault." Grief pulls loose the truth from me like threads ripped from an unstitched seam. "We weren't just hunting the vespertine. We were following him to the Thousandfold. To where my mother died."

Briar's mouth thins, and her teeth scrape her lower lip, catching against her piercing. "How do you know that's where she died?"

"Fenn told me." It sounds so simple, now, here in the daytime rather than in the crimson-lit night when we stood on the watchtower. "But when I pressed him for more, he refused. So I came here to find out for myself. It's my fault that Lux was caught. I have to go back. I have to find her."

My voice catches, I'm lost to wracking sobs. I press my fist against my mouth, trying to quiet myself. Briar regards me for a moment. Then, wordlessly, her fingers unlace from my wrist. She raises her hand, strokes back a wayward piece of hair from my cheek. It's the first time—that I can remember—that she's touched me without violence.

Our eyes meet, and for the barest moment, there's only our shared grief. The ache. The loss. Slowly, I let myself sink forward until my head rests on her shoulder. Her arms go around me with a tentative motion, and I turn my face against her collarbone—this is an uncertain dance, neither of us sure of the steps. Briar lets out a ragged sob against my hair. Tears leak out between my clenched-closed lashes, dampening the collar of her linen underdress.

We cling together; wretched, desperate. Two girls trapped by their shared sorrow. In the scoured-clear light of daybreak, Lux's absence is an open wound. The harsh, plain truth of it sinks over me, through me, turns my skin sweat-slick and my heartbeat frantic. I wanted answers, but I led my dearest friend into danger.

Now I am sure of only one thing: I have to make this right.

Briar and I step apart, tears drying on our cheeks. She extends her hand, her fingers trembling. "Come with me, Everline. We need to get back behind the wards."

I step toward her, let her draw me close. She slides her arm around my waist, clutching another fistful of my dress like she's still afraid I will turn and run in the other direction. We walk in silence back to the chapel. In the overgrown garden, insects hum around the dying flowers. The black nightshade leaves trace against our skirts as we pass. We step across the line of chain and bone, the wards flickering in our shadows.

Briar leads me to the tent, and I sit down. Shivering and numb, I stare toward the glassless window, framed by strands of ivy. The moor beyond lies undisturbed, any sign of the vespertine or Lux or those monsters he painted in the mist all swallowed up by the lowering swells of the landscape.

I'm distant, drifting far outside myself. All my earlier adrenaline has been replaced by leaden shock. My fingers are too clumsy to work the buckles when I try to unfasten my blade belt. Briar watches me struggle for a moment, then pushes my hands impatiently aside.

I sit, compliant, while she takes off my belt. She holds it in her lap, traces a finger over the hilt of Fenn's blade. A flush paints her cheeks, and she bites her lip as she stares down at the weapon. "Why did he give this to you?"

Her expression, the tone of her voice, is so achingly familiar to me. I've lost count of the times I've felt the same envy now marked clear on her face. The sinking hurt, the unavoidable longing— when I saw Fenn walk beside Briar with a hand on her shoulder or heard him introduce her as *my daughter*. The way he offered her so much easy praise, then, in the same breath, reminded me of my failings.

At any other time, it would please me, the way her eyes shimmer with jealous tears. How she looks at me like I'm a cuckoo bird who has pushed her from her rightful place in a well-tended nest. But now, Lux is gone, and all that's left is the two of us—Briar and myself—and I want to lay everything bare. The creature we killed beside the wall. The sky washed in blood as the moon turned red. The Vale Scythe, weighted against my hip. Why I was compelled to break my vows, to run away and search for my past like a girl caught by a fable witch's trail of bread crumbs.

"I wanted to know what happened on the night I was born. Because I think whatever Fenn saw—and whatever he knows about Ila Blackthorn's death in the Thousandfold—is connected to what's happening now. The changed vespertine. The blood eclipse. He's hiding the truth. You know he is."

Briar sets aside my blades with the belt coiled neatly around them. Dark-eyed, she looks from me to the shrouded moorland beyond the ruins. "There could be a dozen reasons that your mother died near the Thousandfold."

"You saw the way Fenn looked when we brought the dead vespertine to the wall. Maybe my mother was nothing more than a traitor who broke her vows and abandoned her watch." I falter, wincing at the sound of my words. "But that still doesn't explain everything else we've seen."

She shakes her head, tugging a hand through her unraveling braid. Her knuckles are scraped bloody, and crescents of moorland dirt are stuck blackly beneath her fingernails. "What did Father say, then, when you questioned him?"

"When I asked for the truth, the relic weapon was the answer he gave. He won't tell me anything more. All he wants from me is silence, is duty."

Briar laughs tiredly. "Father is well versed in the language of duty. But if you hoped to make him love you more, to please him, then running away is not the answer."

She says it gently, less an insult than a reluctant truth. And I wonder, for the first time, if the closeness Briar has with Fenn is more hard-won than it appears.

"I didn't come here to try and make him love me. I just— If there's a reason why I'm like this," I spread my hands, as though to indicate my lack of magic, "why he doesn't trust me—then I need to know. I can't let the truth come so close and stay at the wall like nothing has changed."

Briar looks at me, her expression unreadable. Then, with a sigh, she reaches for her satchel, which is beside the tent, and takes out her field kit. She pulls it open and upends it at our feet, scattering folded gauze and amber glass bottles.

"Here," she says, uncapping one of the bottles of tincture and splashing it liberally on some gauze. "Wipe the blood from your nose."

I press the cloth to my face, flinching at the cold sting of the herbal liquid. Briar wets another square of gauze and starts to daub the blood from her scraped knuckles. I watch her as she works, the drying scabs that mark her fingers where she pricked herself to light the wards she made, the deepening bruise on her swollen cheek.

"The vespertine spoke," I say to Briar, my voice muffled behind the folded cloth. "You heard him—didn't you?"

"Yes," she admits grudgingly. "I did."

Her hair, worked loose from her braid, falls down to hide her face, but I can tell by the hitch of her breath that she's still crying. I put my hand on her knee, feeling uncertain. She stares down at it for a moment, then sits back on her heels and pinches her fingers against the bridge of her nose. Sniffling back her tears, she takes my hand and places it into my lap, as though my touch is a gift she's politely returning.

She nods toward the tent. "You should lie down. I'll pack our things while you rest."

I watch her as she gets to her feet, brushing down her rumpled skirts to smooth out the creases. "We're going after them."

It isn't a question, but Briar shakes her head at me slowly. "I'm taking you back to the enclave."

I laugh, incredulous. "I'm not some unruly child to be dragged home in disgrace. We can't just *leave*. Not when Lux is—"

Briar stiffens—her jaw clenched and a bright flush coloring her cheeks. "What do you think we can do, alone, against that monster? Shall we offer ourselves to the vespertine like a plated sacrifice, let ourselves be captured just like Lux was?" Her fingers go to her throat, curling around her fiola. "I'm taking you back to the enclave, and then Father and I, and some *proper* wardens, will take care of this."

Her veiled insult—*proper wardens*—is like a slap, a wounding reminder of Lux's concern that I was too unskilled, too defenseless, to face the moorland without magic. But I swallow down my hurt, set the ache aside.

"We don't have *time*! Once the river floods, we'll be cut off from the moors until the end of the season. By then, Lux could be—" I bite my lip, refusing to speak it aloud. "We have to find the vespertine now. I know it's hard for you to accept, but I'm not completely helpless."

Briar glares down at me. The raw-eyed girl who I held as we cried and shared our grief is gone. There's not a shred left of her now. She's made such an irrevocable return to her old self that her softness, her vulnerability, feels like a hallucination. A fever dream.

"Being a warden is about more than just power. You couldn't even stay at your watch, Everline. How can you think to face a threat like that . . . *creature*? You said it yourself—this is all your fault. So let me make the choice that is best for Lux."

Without waiting for my response, Briar goes over to the iron fence, her ribbon-hilted blade clutched tight in one hand. I watch as she starts to pull apart the line of wards, picking loose each shard and coiling the chain into a neat spool. She keeps her back to me, and the angle of her drawn-up shoulders is like a slammed door. The fleeting softness that rose between us when we cried together has completely dissolved.

I stand up slowly, scrubbing my sleeve against my face. With my hair unbound and my feet still bare, I make my way across the ruined kitchen and go inside the chapel.

The stained glass depiction of Nyx Severin is lit up like a sunrise, daylight marking clear each line of him—his spread arms, his clenched fists, the brilliant droplets of his blood. I stare at the pane of obsidian glass where his face would be, daring myself not to be afraid. Then, the image of the vespertine with his skeletal mask overtakes the depiction of Nyx. The row of penitents becomes Lux—vague-eyed and compliant, stepping into the vespertine's arms.

Nyx is long dead, but that creature used the same unholy magic. I feel like a child again, woken from a nightmare and staring helplessly into the dark. Briar is right; what hope do I have against this threat? But I can't turn back. When I think of returning to the enclave, leaving Lux among the monsters, it feels as though I've been asked to carve out a piece of myself. My heart, my lungs—to be set down like an offering at a shrine.

Restlessly, I cross the room and go toward the stairwell. The flight of stairs—a carved banister, wooden steps worn at the center with the footsteps of long-dead worshippers—leads to a narrow hall above. It's reminiscent of the enclave barracks, with a row of beds stripped down to bare mattresses and a dresser with a splotchy mirror that reflects the pale blur of my face as I pass.

A second flight of stairs leads to an attic. It's locked, but a large iron key is still in the door, and the latch opens easily when I turn it. Inside, the corners of the room are crowded with remnants of furniture—a chair that must have belonged to the kitchen, a rusted lantern filled with grimy oil, a straw-tick mattress tipped on its side against the wall. A narrow alcove holds a rust-streaked sink, a circular mirror tacked to the wall above.

The air up here has a peculiar scent to it, like the clove incense we burn at our ossuary. But gone bitter, stale. I push open the window. The frame scrapes a protest, and a sharp breath of wind rushes in, sweeping away the collected dust. Tears bead at the corners of my eyes, drawn by the sudden change in temperature. The cold is welcome against my feverish cheeks.

There must be another way, another choice. This can't be all—to abandon Lux to the mercies of the vespertine and give up any hope of finding the truth about my origins. I hate how I feel so helpless.

Below the chapel, the moorland is laid out like a draped cloak. The curves of the Blackthorn River, swollen from the storm, the faded purple of the heather flowers that are starting to wither. More of the ivy from the storeys below has clambered up the side of the building, trailing in glossy tendrils across the sill.

All the window frames in the enclave are carved with neat rows of crosses: *x, x, x*, like you would mark a missive to a secret lover. A remnant of the rules made when the vespertine still ran wild, rules that came into favor again after the wall was breached. In the last days of the attack, when the swarm of monsters had dwindled but the wardens hadn't yet won, creatures would slither out from the night, feral and desperate. Warnings were passed among the citizens: Keep your windows closed and score the sill with crosses; never let yourself bleed beneath the moonlight.

I press my fingers into the marks. My thoughts stir; a reckless curiosity. What might happen if the rules were made inverse, if I flung my window wide and spread my blood across the sill, if I let the scent of my willingness be caught by the night wind?

All this time, I've thought our only hope lay in the pursuit of monsters, but what if, instead, I drew the monsters to me, called them out of the dark?

My blood feels like ice, my bones are lead. But my mind is made up. I turn and go back down the stairs, leaving the window wide and a swirl of clove-scented air trailing me as I walk back through the chapel and out into the kitchen.

Briar has lit the stove, but the small fire does little to cut through the chill filtering in through the glassless window, rustling the ivy with invisible fingers. She sits near the flames with her face turned from me, her hair pulled over one shoulder as she weaves it back into a braid.

The tent has been taken down, and our satchels are tidily packed. Briar is fastened up just as neatly—her collar buttoned to her chin, armor buckled tight, blade sheathed at her hip. Here is the dutiful choice: to follow her back to the enclave and commit myself to the wardens. The girl I once ached to be, the true daughter of Fenn Linden, would do that without hesitation. But right now, I am Everline Blackthorn, who abandoned her watch and broke her vows. And the *duty* I owe, above all else, is to Lux—captured, at the mercies of this new, changed vespertine.

She isn't dead. I am certain of this. He called to her, seduced her, lifted her so tenderly into his arms. He could have torn her apart while we watched. Instead, he carried her away. And I am going to save her, even if I have to break every tenant I swore when I became a warden.

"We could bring him to us," I whisper. "We could let him think we're being lured. Then we could trap him instead. We could make him talk. We could make him give her back."

Briar looks hard at me, her gaze the same merciless blue of a scoured-clear sky. She lets the silence draw out as she holds me in place with her stare. Her fingers are still working down the length of her braid, weaving in the final strands. She ties the end with a piece of ribbon, a sturdy double knot. "Really, Everline. It's unnatural how much you delight in breaking your vows."

"He *spoke*, Briar. He spoke to me."

"Do you think you can reason with him, ask him politely to

let Lux go?" Briar tugs at the ribbon on the end of her braid. "We need to go back to the enclave. It's the only way to save her."

"No," I insist. "It's *not*. I'll call the vespertine back. Make him tell us who he is and where he's come from; what is happening in the Thousandfold. Then, we will save Lux."

"You can't do anything if you're dead. And the moment you get close to him, he'll attack with his wretched magic."

I twist my hands together in my lap, rumpling the stained fabric of my linen underdress. A thought tugs at me—glossy berries dewed with leftover rain. I get to my feet and go into the garden. The iron fence is bare without the line of wards, like bones of a creature that have been picked clean by scavengers. The black nightshade sprawls elegantly in tangled beds, clusters of berries framed against velvety leaves.

Slowly, I reach out and pluck the fruit. The berries are dark as the vespertine's claws. It's surreal to see them cupped in my palm; black nightshade is a thing we've all been taught to never touch, the same as the amanita mushrooms that grow in the marshlands beside our flower fields. They're a dangerous remnant of when Nyx Severin ruled as a god, when people, desperate to show their fealty, would consume slivers of mushroom and squeeze drips of berry juice onto their tongues to induce visions.

I walk back to Briar and set the plucked stem with its dangerous berries on the ground between us. She pales, her eyes fixed on it like a snake has slithered out from the ruins and now sits, hissing and coiled, ready to strike. "Everline," she says guardedly, "what are you planning to do with *that*?"

"I'll call him to us tonight; I'll wait by the open window and spill my blood beneath the moon. When he comes, I'll let him think he's lured me the way he did to Lux. And when he tries to use his magic, I'll poison him. Then . . . I'll take him captive."

"Father will exile you. Even if you save Lux. He won't have a choice."

There's a softened edge to her voice that surprises me. For the barest moment, Briar looks almost sorry. So many times, I've had the unwelcome thought that in another place, another world, we might have been true sisters. The divide has been impossible to cross . . . but now, in the ruined chapel of Nyx Severin, the distance feels narrower.

I bow my head, thinking of how I knelt at the ossuary when I became a full-fledged warden and swore my allegiance to the effigy of Saint Lenore.

To suffer a vespertine to live, especially one this dangerous, is a terrible sin, worse than my attempt to bring the still-warm corpse of the creature we slaughtered through the gate into the enclave. If I do this, I'll save Lux and damn myself, prove to Fenn that all he's feared of me is the truth: I am my mother's daughter, a girl incapable of keeping vows.

It hurts, and I hate myself for it—for how much I dread what he'll do to me. I picture myself stripped of my armor and exiled to the Hallowed Lands.

But there's no other choice. No one else can save Lux. No one else can give me the answers I seek.

I put my hand on Briar's arm. "When we go back, I'll tell Fenn it was my idea. I'll take the blame for all of it."

She doesn't respond. I lean closer, and she lets out a helpless sigh. Solemn as a vow, she murmurs, "You're not the only one who cares for her, Everline."

"Then help me. Stay with me and help me capture the vespertine. We can save Lux together."

Briar catches hold of my chin, tilting my face so I am forced to look right at her, unable to turn away. The tiny flicker of softness I thought I glimpsed before is gone. "We'll do this together," she echoes. "But it's for Lux—not you—that I'm staying."

I jerk away from her touch. "You really will take any chance to be insufferable."

Ignoring me, she stalks over to our satchels and picks up my belt and blades. Dropping them unceremoniously into my lap, she glares out through the window frame to where a fresh line of storm clouds has begun to gather at the horizon. "Capture him, Everline—if you can. Capture him, make him talk, and once you have your answers . . . I will cut his throat. That vespertine will not live beyond tonight."

I get to my feet, blades in my arms. The hilt of the Vale Scythe presses against my ribs as I bite the inside of my cheek, tasting blood. I stare to the distance, where an invisible path on the moorland marks where we ran last night in our desperate attempt to save Lux from a monster. I think of holy fire, of blood and claws. I think of redemption. I think of sacrifice.

Slowly, I draw the Scythe. My bared teeth feel as sharp as the sickled edge of my blade. "Don't worry, Briar. I know how this has to end."

CHAPTER EIGHT

IN THE BARRACKS ROOM, I PREPARE MYSELF FOR SACRIFICE. I'M dressed and armored, with spined bracers around each wrist and my empty glass fiola strung from its chain, clinking delicately against my rib-cage bodice. But beneath the layers of bone and lace, beneath the tightly fastened straps and knotted ribbons, I feel immaterial. Like a wisp of incense smoke. I'm endlessly aware of how dangerous this is, to face a monster with only my whetted blade and a fistful of poison berries to protect me from his ruinous power.

Briar watches me from the opposite side of the room. I braid my hair, thinking of Lux and the way we'd tend to each other before we left the enclave. The absence of her hands makes my fingers feel clumsy, pieces of my hair slipping from my grasp. The loneliness of tonight, of this preparation, hurts. But it feels deserved, too—like the strike of a wooden blade against my knuckles when I've fumbled in the training yard.

I find a pot of black rouge in my travel kit. Line my eyes with swoops of ink, then slowly paint my lips. My face in the mirror glass is funereal, my freckled skin too pale beneath the blunt line of my bangs, my lips a grim, ashen heart. The knotted ache in my stomach that's pulled at me all through the day draws tighter and tighter.

Outside, the heavy clouds darken with the final threads of sunset. As thunder rumbles, low and ominous, I picture Lux curled and shivering somewhere out on the moors—trapped in a far-off ruin with the vespertine as he watches her the way he watched the burned-down pyre.

"I think tonight will work better if I'm alone," I tell Briar, looking at her from the reflection of the dresser mirror. "So he'll truly believe me defenseless."

Her mouth quirks into a hard, mirthless smile. "That won't be a stretch of the imagination."

"Your confidence in me is truly heartwarming."

I check my armor, testing the sharpness of the bones at my wrists. Then, with a sigh, I push myself up from the dresser and cross the room to collect my blade belt from where I've left it, laid out on the unmade bed. I buckle it around my waist, the weight of the Vale Scythe more familiar, now, as it sinks against my hip. I touch the hilt, then check my second blade. I take a length of silver chain and drape it from my belt, the way Lux would wear a strand of bone beads.

My stomach clenches again, a drawn-out cramp from low in my belly. I press my palm to the ache of it and then realize what it means. With a sinking feeling, I gather up the hems of my skirts. A telltale streak of fresh, bright blood has blotched the lace hem of my underwear. "Oh, *hells*."

I start to dig around in my satchel for a cloth. Briar heaves out an exhausted sigh. "Really, Everline. Did you forget the tincture?"

Whenever we venture beyond the wall for longer than a single night, we take an herbal concoction—brewed with sharp-tasting flowers and spoonfuls of honey—to stop our cycles and spare the inconvenience of dealing with cramps and cloths.

But now, though the ache of cramps is already bothersome, I can't help but see this as a welcome accident, yet another rule broken alongside all the others. When I picture myself going out to face the vespertine all tender and raw, I feel full-moon ripe and belly-soft. Like a red-petaled flower torn up and scattered into a trail, an invitation to bloodlust.

"I was a little preoccupied," I mutter as I fold the cloth and set it in place.

Briar takes an amber glass vial from her field kit, unscrews the stoppered lid. She moves toward me with the stopper in one hand, filled with the colorless tincture, the glass winking in the last scraps of daylight. "Open your mouth," she orders.

I lean obediently against the sill and open my mouth, tilting back my head to let her drip the tincture onto my tongue. It's sweet as the honey wine served in the enclave chapel on the coldest nights, a flavor that is out of place here. Briar puts the lid back on the vial and places it on the dresser next to my comb and pot of lip paint. She frowns at me. Then, like an afterthought, she pulls a crimson hair ribbon from her pocket and ties it around the end of my braid.

My hands scrunch restlessly in my skirts, unsure what to do—I want to reach to her and run my fingers over the buckles on her armor, smooth down the strands of her braid, the way I might with Lux. But I'm afraid to break the spell of this moment, our new closeness. So I crush handfuls of my dress to keep myself from touching her until she turns back toward the window.

She stands, framed by the lowering night, her hand on her blade hilt and her eyes on the moorland below, like she's at watch in the tower on the enclave wall. "Good luck," she says. "Try not to do anything *completely* foolish out there."

As I walk down the stairs, I put my hand into my pocket. The nightshade berries, plucked from their stem, roll silkily against my fingertips. The chapel hall is laid out in gloom, the stained glass window of Nyx Severin only a faint, rose-hued glow that drips in fleeting colors across the floor as I pass beneath it.

Out in the kitchen, the air is cold as it rushes in from the garden, sibilant through the branches of the citrus trees. Everything smells of smoke and early rain. The wards have been put out, and the only illumination left is from the remnants of the fire—tired orange flutters through the open drafts of the stove door—and a lantern on the brick mantelpiece above.

I take the lantern over to the window. Place it on the sill. Oil draws up the wick and feeds the flame with a crackling stutter. Dappled light spills over the ivy, like false fireflies stippled through the leaves. The sun has set, and handfuls of early stars are pinpricked across the narrow sliver of indigo sky visible between the storm clouds.

Beneath this sky, the windswept moorland looks undisturbed,

as though the grass and flowers have woven themselves back together to hide the evidence of all that happened last night. It's a relief when I pick out the place where Briar and I faced the vespertine, to see the ground churned and cut with the remnants of our bare footprints and the tracks of the vespertine's boots. The choreography of our violence is marked out on the ground like a pattern to be tailored.

I light a stick of incense and set it beside the lantern. Clove-scented smoke drifts out into the night. If I closed my eyes, I could pretend I'm standing at the ossuary in the enclave chapel, ready to make a vow.

I draw my smaller blade, press it against the tip of my index finger. Blood wells up. I drape my hand over the windowsill, past the lacework of ivy. My fingers crook against the air, beckoning. Blood falls on the leaves with a slow *drip, drip, drip.*

Cramps pinch low in my belly, and I feel vital, sanguine, human. I'm warm flesh; I'm the beat of my pulse in the divots of my wrists. When I press my lips together, they're sticky with dregs of the tincture's bitter honey. The air traces across my bloodied hand, and a shiver goes right to the pit of my stomach as I imagine the rust-and-copper scent of me taken across the moor, through the night, and into the depths of the shadows where the vespertine waits.

I stare into the darkness outside, imagining the shape of him, the sharp outline of horns and the flutter of a tattered cloak as it snaps back and forth in the wind like a battle banner. I touch the hilt of the Vale Scythe, then slip my hand into my pocket and gently stir my fingers through the nightshade berries, picturing the events of last night like a dropped thread wound back onto a spool, then unfurled again.

This time, the vespertine will lie at my feet while I stand above him, as stalwart as the depiction of Saint Lenore in the enclave chapel. My lips move soundlessly as I rehearse what I'll say, how my voice will turn brutal and fierce as I hold my blade to his throat and demand him to answer me.

Time draws out, marked by the waver of the lamp and the gathering storm. It starts to rain. Foreboding crawls over me, slippery as a snake. I try to breathe past the tightness in my chest, plane back my sharp edges. Let my body turn soft and pliant, playacting as a fragile girl about to be caught unawares.

Lightning blooms in the depths of the sky. The clouds are flooded with brief, veiled brilliance before a low tremble of thunder runs across the ground. The air has a bladed cold, keen as frost. Spitting rain drifts through the open window. With Briar in the room upstairs and the horizon covered by the storm, I could believe myself wholly alone out here, the only creature alive on the moorland except for a single raven that circles overhead, filling the silence with its harsh call.

Another peal of thunder echoes from the distance. Then another, more muted sound. The heavy press of footsteps, boots over windswept grass.

The vespertine walks toward me, slow, slow, slow.

There's a regal grace to his unhurried movement, the way he steps across the rain-drenched ground with deliberate care, the path of his hand—his fingers long and pale, banded with inky tattoos—as he reaches to push back his hood. I hold my breath as his face comes clear in the light from my lantern. He's still masked, vicious bones curved sharply along his cheeks. He smiles at me, his mouth smeared with blackened paint, the bared edge of his teeth fanged and feral.

"Warden." His voice is quiet, but I hear it as though he is right next to me. "Come outside."

I gasp, the sound clear even beneath the whine of the wind and the hush of the rain. He tilts his head, the motion wolfish—so reminiscent of the monsters I've fought near the wall. It's so *wrong*, this boy with his sharpened horns and low-pitched words, the way his eyes gleam as he watches me. My heartbeat rises until I feel it throbbing at the hollow of my throat. I'm endlessly aware of how soft I am beneath the spines of my armor, how breakable.

"Come outside," he says again, and all the hair at the nape of my neck rises up, the way a small animal would raise their hackles when they've been cornered by a larger, hungrier creature. I clutch hold of the sill, tight, to hide how my hands have begun to shake. With my skirts rucked up, I climb through the window, past the burned-out remnants of the incense and over the rustling, glossy ivy leaves.

The vespertine moves closer. Even in the dim lantern light, he casts a heavy shadow. It slithers before him, oozing over the ground, thickly dark. He extends a hand toward me, all deference, like I am a cottager girl being helped down from a carriage. I reach for him, and this is *wrong*, this is nothing but *danger*, but he takes hold of me, his fingers closing around mine. His skin is heated, and I think of the glass in the lamp he used to mimic our ward, how the residual warmth cast against our cheeks as we bent close to examine it.

I step through the window and down onto the ground. His thumb drags over my knuckles before he lets me go. His fingers are rough with tiny scars, just like a warden's hands, and I feel sickened, remembering the way he clutched the bone shard in his bloodied fist. I can't stop staring at his claws.

A bitter rise of panic coats my tongue, tasting of the unholy magic he cast. My fingers are left hot, as though I was scalded when he touched me.

There's a shallow cut on his throat, thin as a stitched seam, and he rubs his hand against it, smearing his skin with crimson. He bends to me, his eyes turned mirrored when they catch the lantern flame. He tucks back a strand of hair that's come loose from my braid and puts his mouth right against my ear. His breath scrapes the line of my neck. My pulse rises to a wild, desperate staccato. I'm certain he can hear it.

"Tell me," he murmurs, "which of you was the one who slit her throat?"

His magic rises over me like a tide. At the lulling sound of his voice, my limbs turn heavy, my panicked heartbeat begins to slow. The pliant girl I pretended to be earlier is rapidly becoming truth; I'm ready to roll on my back and bare my jugular vein to his claws. A hungering growl echoes from the depths of his chest.

Slowly, slowly, fighting against the pull of his magic, I ease my hand into my pocket and take a berry, holding it between my finger and thumb. The way he held the shard when he cast his spell.

I put my other hand against his cheek, near the edge of his mask. Wariness flickers in his gaze as I look up at him. I shift closer until the curve of my rib-cage armor is flush to his chest. Let him think I've turned yielding, mild.

Beneath his cloak, he wears something thin, close-fitting, and beneath that, he's all warm leanness. The unnatural heat of him burns over me; I'm overcome with fear and disgust. His lips part, and he breathes a sharp "what—" Then I slip my fingers into his mouth, feeling the scrape of his fangs against my knuckles as I let go of the berry and quickly draw back.

My hand is still on his cheek. I press, hard, against his jaw to force his mouth closed. Startled, he bites down—trying to bite my fingers—and I hear the *crunch* of the berry between his teeth.

He snarls and coughs, choking on the bitterness and trying to spit out the juice, but it's too late; I can see his pupils already dilating behind the hollowed depths of his mask. Poison-struck, the vespertine sinks to his knees. His eyes are wide and liquid-dark, a choleric flush making its way down the sides of his throat. He lashes out, but I step out of reach, my fist snared white-knuckle-tight with the chain that's strung from my belt.

Thrown off-balance, he slumps forward on hands and knees, still coughing, his claws carving at the dirt as he struggles to right himself. I clutch the chain and stare at him, the curve of his horns like knives over the loose fall of his dark hair. Everything slows to a dreamlike blur. The world around us trickles away, and all that's left is the vespertine at my feet, the taste of his magic fading from my tongue as the spell he used to enthrall me dies away, pulled loose like a thread from an unfinished hem.

I unhook the chain from my belt. Twist one end into a loop. Moving quickly, I slip it around the vespertine's wrist and draw it tight. He hisses, fighting against me as the silver digs into his arm, cutting a line against the tattered sleeve of his cloak.

"I don't want to hurt you," I tell him.

He fixes me with a furious glare, eyes sharp even through the poison haze. "You've a strange way of showing it."

"I want to talk."

"Talk," he echoes, mouth twisted. "And what would you like to *talk* about?"

"You captured one of my wardens. I want her returned to me. Bring her back safely and I will not harm you."

The vespertine lets out a bark of laughter. "I don't bargain with murderers."

Anger rises through me, and I welcome it—the tightening of my jaw, the heat that flushes my skin—because it's easier to feel than the memory of that other, too-human vespertine, her throat parted by Lux's blade. The cooling weight of her inside the makeshift shroud as we carried her back to the wall.

I think instead of all the bodies in the enclave catacombs, of Lux's sister, of bloodied sky and bloodied earth and howls in the night. Of the ruins around us, remnants of a fallen world. The image of Nyx Severin spilling his blood over the bowed heads of his worshippers who were soon to become his victims. "All of *you* are murderers."

The vespertine snarls, his teeth painted black with streaks of poison. His breath turns labored. His hands clutch fistfuls of earth. I should be pleased at the sight of him on his knees in the dirt, but

111

all I can think of is Lux, stolen away to where I can't reach her. I knot the chain, ready to snare his other hand, but he launches himself up from the ground. Throws his full force against me.

He shoves me back against the wall of the ruin. All my breath tears from my lungs in a stuttered gasp. The lantern falls with a shatter of glass; the flame goes out, a rush of acrid smoke. I fight for air, tasting the astringent sap from crushed strands of ivy, as I struggle to keep hold of the chain. It trails at our feet, tangling our ankles.

With my free hand, I draw the Vale Scythe. I slash out, aiming to wound the vespertine, but the angle is wrong; he feints past the swipe of my blade, then grabs hold of my dress, the pale fabric crumpled to nothing inside his fist. He drags me against him.

Splinters of broken glass crush beneath our boots. I collide with his chest. This new closeness sends a cold slick of terror through me; my body is lead; my veins are ice. The vespertine is clumsy from the poison, and his claws tear my dress, tangle in the ribbon at the end of my braid. I'm lost to the hitch of his breath, the rhythm of his heart that I can feel echoing through the bones of my armor. My vision starts to blacken. Darkness crowds in like the storm-clouded sky has swept right down on top of us.

Through the haze, I stare at him—the wolfish outline of his mask, the spired points of his horns, the feral, furious gleam of his narrowed eyes. I stare at him and think of Saint Lenore in the chapel window. I think of my mother, dead and buried somewhere out here on the moors. The looming danger, Lux lost in the night, the secrets Fenn kept about my birth in the Thousandfold. The answers I'll lose if I let this creature escape, if I let him kill me.

I bite down hard on the inside of my cheek—the sharp pain and bitter wash of blood enough to shake me loose. I cast aside my blade and grab a whole handful of berries from my pocket, squashing them in my fist before I force them into the vespertine's mouth. His teeth catch my knuckles with a stinging scrape, and he starts to gag.

I snatch up the chain, try to loop it around his other wrist. He shoves his elbow, sharp, against my stomach, and I buckle forward. He snarls against the crook of my shoulder. I feel the press of his fangs against my throat.

Then the chain goes taut between us. A bright rush of consecration lights the air, sudden as a flame on lamp oil. The vespertine falters back with a rasped, choking sound. Briar is behind him, her blade drawn and the steel blazing with magic. She has the vespertine by the back of his collar.

She looks from him to me. "I thought I told you not to do anything foolish?"

Ignoring her, I turn to the vespertine. He struggles against Briar's grasp as she drags his collar tight his throat. He bows forward, mouth open as he fights to breathe. His lip is bloody, he's bitten his tongue.

"Look at me," I order. His eyes meet mine—glazed with pain and poison but still lucid. "I'm offering you an exchange: your life for my warden."

The vespertine stares me down for a heartbeat. Then his eyes narrow to a hot fury, and he spits a disgusting mouthful of blackened blood at my feet. I flinch back just in time: it splatters across the ground rather than my boots.

I draw myself up and backhand him, hard, across the face. The bone of my gauntlet leaves a raised red welt across his cheek; fresh blood oozes from his split lip. I move to hit him again, but Briar catches my arm. "Honestly! This isn't some training-yard fistfight."

She kicks sharply at the backs of the vespertine's knees. He crumples, and she draws her blade, presses it to his throat. The vespertine snarls through his clenched teeth.

"No!" I cry out. "Briar, wait!"

She stills, glaring at me incredulously. "You've had your chance to question him. This creature is not going to give us any answers."

"He knows where Lux is. We have to keep him alive."

Her eyes narrow. "You mean to take him as your *prisoner*?"

The warden commandments are clear—no vespertine should be suffered to live. Faced in close quarters, we're to give them a swift, clean death. It's against our vows to hold one captive. It's a truth I learned before all others, as familiar as my own name. And now, everything wavers, as if I've shaken the very world around me with the sin of what I'm going to do.

I put my hand over Briar's and guide her blade away from the vespertine's throat. Lowering my voice, I remind her, "You said he won't live beyond tonight."

She scowls. "I know what I said."

The vespertine starts to laugh, a gurgle of blood and spit. "Go ahead, kill me. You can warm yourselves on the ashes of my funeral pyre—I know how you wardens love to watch things burn."

"Be quiet," Briar snaps. "Nobody asked your opinion."

"Until tomorrow, he is mine," I say. Briar shakes her head. My hand is still over hers, and I clutch onto her so she can't raise her weapon. "Until sunrise."

She looks down at our hands, fingers woven around the hilt of her blade. With a rough sigh, she pulls away from me. "Fine. *Fine*. You have until sunrise tomorrow. After that, I'll cut his throat and we'll go back to the enclave to deal with this in the *right* way."

I turn back to the vespertine. My chain is still tangled around his wrists. I pull it sharply, and he gets to his feet. He stands unsteadily before me, his chest shuddering, a slick of blood and poison smeared across his painted mouth.

I feel dizzy with the truth of this, that I've taken him prisoner. My cheeks are fever-flushed; cold sweat trickles down my spine beneath the press of my armor. With effort, I gather myself and pick up the Vale Scythe from where I cast it to the ground earlier. I wind the chain around my free hand; then I press my blade beneath the vespertine's cloak, the curve of the Scythe sharp against his ribs.

"Walk," I tell him. "You belong to me now."

CHAPTER NINE

W E LEAD THE VESPERTINE THROUGH THE OVERGROWN garden where the citrus trees are bowed against the wind, their leaves dripping rain. He follows me with obstinate slowness, letting the chain drag out between us until I have to wrench him forward. Briar watches him closely, her hand clutched tight around her bone beads. Fury simmers clearly in each line of her body—the flash of her eyes, the tightness of her jaw. She looks at him the way you would a venomous snake slithering across your feet—stilled and poised, caught in the space between *flee* and *strike*.

As we open the iron gate and move into the ruins, she presses something into my hand. A ribbon-tied bundle of bone shards, tinged with smears of blood and lit by the glow of consecration. Lux has occasionally given me her own lit shards to use, but for other wardens, it's a rarely done thing, as intimate as a sworn vow.

An incredulous laugh bubbles out of my mouth. "Are you *that* worried about me?"

"Everline, anyone with a pulse would be worried about you.

This creature would have torn your throat out if I hadn't shown up." Briar puts her hand over mine, folding my fingers closed around the shards. "Take him to the attic and lock the door."

I tuck the shards into my pocket. Pull at the chain again, urging the vespertine forward. The nightshade has sunk over him, and he's caught in a daze, thickly snared by the flush of poison inside his veins. His eyes are half-closed, and his breath is stilted, rasped through his blood-smeared teeth.

As we reach the chapel hall, Briar calls after us. "Remember—you have one night. Then we're done. I'm not breaking any more vows for that creature."

Her voice—cold and resolute—echoes after me as I lead the vespertine through the darkened chamber. This is the trueborn daughter of Commander Fenn, the girl who hunts alone, with all the aspirations of her pinned-on insignia and her refusal to back down on any principle she holds close.

The rain grows louder as the vespertine and I climb the stairs. The sound of it against the slate-tiled roof tugs loose a sense memory of storm-swept nights in my attic bedroom, a thought too tender for here, in the ruins where Nyx Severin was once worshipped.

The vespertine falters when we reach the attic door. He snarls at me, I press my blade against his ribs. Haltingly, he steps into the room. I close the door behind us and turn the key, feel the snick of the lock as it slides home. When I place the key in my pocket, it clinks against the ribbon-tied shards.

The attic is dark, the wooden floor and paneled walls consuming the faint light that comes through the single window. I pull a chair from the tangle of furniture in the corner. Its legs scrape against the floor with a hideous sound like nails on glass as I drag it to the center of the room.

I shove the vespertine forward, my blade still raised. "Sit down."

He slouches into the chair. He's trembling all over, hands curled to fists, claws sharp at his palms. Rivulets of sweat trail over his cheeks, smudging the paint as they trickle past his jaw, down his throat, beneath the collar of his shirt. Glaring up at me through the wayward strands of his inky hair, he pulls at the chains circling his wrists, testing the strength of the knots.

I slip behind him, winding up the slackened length of chain. I pull his hands to his back, then wrap the chain around them again. He snarls and struggles as I bind him. The chair legs grate in protest against the floor. His claws flex, scrabbling as he tries to catch my wrists.

I put my hand flat against the back of his neck in warning. "Stop it."

Sensation hums between us, electric-bright. It travels sharply through my fingers and up the length of my arm, as though all my veins have been hit with consecration. The vespertine lets out a ragged gasp; I falter back like I've been burned. I stare at my palm, expecting to see a raised blister, but there is only my skin, marred by the same sword callouses and healed-over cuts as always.

My stomach clenches with a twinging cramp. I press my hand to my abdomen until it settles, the memory of the vespertine's touch and its aftermath marked on me like a sinister kiss.

His head bows forward, the grim features of his mask hidden by the spill of his hair. On the nape of his neck is a strange, inky smudge. I can't make it out clearly, but there's an unpleasant familiarity to the shape of it.

I go to the window, where a lantern is on the sill. The font sloshes with oil, and there's a crumpled box of matches tucked into the drawer at its base. It lights, slow, oil hissing as it draws up the wick, the flame smoky and smelling of ash and dust. The room brightens. Our shadows stretch to jagged silhouettes against the wall.

Slowly, I peel aside the collar of the vespertine's cloak. He jolts at my touch, the chains clattering as his hands strain inside the loops. Marked at the top of his spine is a moonlike crescent, painted as though with ink. My hand drifts to the back of my neck, fingers curling beneath my hair to press where my skin is marked in exactly the same place. "Why do you have a warden mark?"

"Oh, am I *marked*? Are you here to escort me to the enclave? Shall I lend my magic to your wall?"

I crouch in front of him so our faces are even. He glares at me with poison-dark eyes. I've felt the scrape of his claws on my cheek and the brush of his lips against my ear, felt him struggle against me as we fought. Yet somehow, at this moment, I feel more vulnerable than I did when I faced him out on the moorland—even with him in chains, even with my blade at my hip and the threat of the shards hidden in my pocket.

In the shifting lamplight, he's more fearsome than ever. His paint-smeared mouth is swollen, wet with blood where I split his lip, sticky with blackened dregs of nightshade juice. Beneath the hollowed bones of his mask, he's as eldritch as the creatures drawn out of the mist by his terrible magic.

"Tell me," I say, my voice turned solemn as a vow. "Where is my warden?"

He stares me down, unflinching, his gaze broken only by one slow blink. A hitch of anger curls sharp inside my chest. I reach to him; he twists away from me—but he has nowhere to go. I grab hold of the mask and tear it from his face. A hiss escapes his blood-slicked mouth, and he closes his eyes, as though, unmasked, the world is too bright.

Without the horns, without the skeletal grimace of sharp, sharp teeth, he looks entirely different. Even his eyes—when they open—have changed, the depthless hollows now a vivid green. Beneath the sweat-smeared corpsepaint, his skin is smooth, the split in his lip the only blemish on him. His dark brows are arched like the marks on a moth's wings.

He looks so young—perhaps only a handful of years older than me. Just like the girl we killed near the wall, he's so different than the monsters I've spent my life guarding against, those wolf-like creatures that rise from the moorland night with their wild ruthlessness.

He could almost be human—but tiny details mark him as clearly *other*. His mouth, twisted into an open scowl, bares twin canines that are too long and too sharp. There's a keen, preternatural watchfulness in his virulent eyes.

Unbidden, I draw closer, as though caught by the same lure as when he bespelled me. My fingers trace his cheek, following the line of the skeletal design painted across his jaw. He pulls away with a disgusted grimace.

I set his mask aside. Tighten my hold on the Vale Scythe, let the feel of it steady me. "Where is my warden?"

He holds my gaze, and I see a flash of something in his eyes—there and gone, a fleeting emotion reined back before I can decipher it. "Your *warden*," he says, drawing the word out slowly, mockingly, "is in the Thousandfold."

I stare at him, horrified. My mind floods red, washed by the remembered light of the blood eclipse. The Thousandfold. The place where my mother died and where I was born. Where Fenn saw terrors and secrets beneath the reddened sky, secrets that have carved between us for my entire life.

"If you've harmed her, then—"

"She is alive," the vespertine snaps. "No one has cut her throat or burned her on a pyre."

I think of the girl we killed—her blood on Lux's blade, the weight of her in the makeshift shroud—and my cheeks flush with a sudden heat. I curl my hands to fists until my nails sting my palms, trying to push aside the unwelcome rise of guilt. "Don't act as though you aren't capable of cruelty. The enclave catacombs are filled with the dead—wardens and citizens—cut down when the vespertine last broke through the wall."

"Nevertheless, *your* warden is unharmed."

I lean forward, hands pressed to my knees, narrowing the distance between us. Teeth clenched, I force myself to be calm, to keep my voice measured. "What do you want with her?"

The vespertine arches a brow, his mouth twists into a sneer. "What did you want with my vespertine when you fought her on the moorland outside your wretched enclave? Let me guess. You were following orders. It was your duty to protect against the *monsters*." He looses a sigh and his expression turns wholly serious. "Perhaps that's all I wanted. To remove the threat of one who would seek to hunt us down."

I pass a hand across my face, swiping away the tangling strands of hair that have escaped my braid. "Then let's end this here. It was against my vows to take you as a prisoner. To keep you alive is a sin. But I want to make a trade—your life for my warden. Return her to me and I'll let you go."

"I told you already—I'll not bargain with a murderer."

I move closer to the vespertine. I can feel the heat of his skin and smell the tense, blood-and-sweat scent that's radiating off him, see the bruises on his mouth and my wavering reflection in his eyes. "Briar will execute you at sunrise. I'm your only hope. Help me—set Lux free—and I'll spare your life."

"Your *Lux*," he says acidly, "will remain in the Thousandfold. And now you know how it feels to lose someone you love."

He starts to laugh. I'm overcome with visions raised by his words—a lifetime ahead where Lux is absent from my side, cleaved away from her place in the wardens. All because of my fault, my failure.

I draw the Vale Scythe, shove the curved blade against his neck. "I will cut your miserable throat."

His smile turns hard. "Do it, then. Show me your tender mercy.

Cut my throat. Burn me to ash. No matter what you do, you'll never reach her. If you thought the magic I used on you last night hurt—it was *nothing* compared to the power of the Thousandfold. Try to cross the border and it will tear you apart."

I press closer; the vespertine makes a sharp, choked sound. His throat is reddened where I hold the blade. He bares his teeth, fangs sticky with traces of blackened berries. Then—with another stilted breath—he slumps forward, landing hard against me with his face in the crook of my neck and shoulder. I flinch, sickened, and shove him away.

His eyes are rolled back into pallid moons, his mouth slackened in a bloodied grimace. I stare at him—poison-ravaged, the imprint of my blade still blushed against the skin of his throat. I want, so badly, to meet his challenge. To kill him and burn him until he's nothing but scattered ash. But under the heat of my rage is unavoidable truth. If he dies, then Lux dies with him.

He is my path to the Thousandfold. I'm so close, standing here on the wild moors with the Thousandfold stretching its shadows toward me, and Lux alive somewhere within. This creature is my best hope of saving her, of going not just to the borderland but *inside*. To the place where the truth lies buried.

I can't let Briar kill this creature and drag me back to the enclave in disgrace. I need him to save Lux. I need him to uncover the secrets of my past.

I need him to bend to me.

This boy with his fanged smile and skeletal mask, the incongruous warden mark on his nape—when I look at him, I feel a pull, a calling, like a bird drawn north when the season changes. Once again, I'm struck by the unshakable belief that we are all connected: the monsters, my mother, and me.

I sheathe my blade with a muttered curse. Swallowing down a shudder, I untie the chains and drag the vespertine to his feet. He stirs, struggling against me, then falls to a fit of ragged coughing as I guide him across the room to where the straw-tick mattress is propped against the wall. I pull it down, then lower him to the makeshift bed.

He curls on his side, fist pressed hard to his bloodied mouth. Thickly, he asks, "What did you give me?"

"Black nightshade. You're going to feel wretched until it wears off."

"Black nightshade," he repeats. "How *rustic*."

He slackens again, eyes sunk closed. His cloak is filthy with mud and soaked from the rain. I have a sudden fear of him caught by a chill, too lost beneath the delirium of fever to be any use to me. Steeling myself, I reach to the clasp at his shoulder, trying to ignore the heat of his skin when my knuckles brush against his collarbone, the way that undressing him feels like a blade at my own throat.

Beneath the cloak, he's dressed simply—a pair of high-waisted black trousers and a thin knit shirt. But over that is . . . armor. A chain and leather harness covers his chest, the straps fastened with tarnished steel buckles. At his wrists are bracers made from knotted leather straps and chips of worn-down bone.

I touch one of the chains, trying to comprehend. The construction of his armor—the layered bones and leather, even the way the knots are tied—is identical to the methods I use. I taught myself, piecing out patterns from designs of armor worn by the wardens who fought alongside Saint Lenore.

"What *are* you?"

He glares at me, gaze veiled by inky lashes. "Don't act coy, Warden. You know exactly what I am."

As though for emphasis, he reaches to his throat and hooks his tattoo-banded fingers beneath the collar of his shirt. There's a glint as lamplight catches on a flicker of metal. He draws out a chain, strung heavily with glass vials that chime together. He has warden fiolae, dozens of them, the blood inside their glass gleaming like tarnished rubies.

I close my hand around the vials and pull, hard as I can. The chain snaps, tiny silver links spilling free. The broken ends hang down between us as they twist back and forth in spirals of silver. His gaze flashes over the necklace; then he grabs for my wrist.

Caught off-guard, I falter back as his fingers slide beneath my sleeve and past my bracers. His claws slice my forearm; a sharp, piercing hurt. I think of Lux and my mother. The tangle of vials trapped in the hot clutch of my hand is like a terrible omen, a fated prophecy that spells only ruin.

All my anger that's seethed and seethed—my helplessness when my magic never came, the hurt I've swallowed down with each slight from Briar, the way Fenn drew back when I called him *Father*, the legacy of my birth that I can't escape. It all crashes down on me, and I'm lost to fury, caught halfway across a flooded river, dragged into the merciless current.

I cast aside the stolen vials and strike the vespertine, catching him in the ribs with my closed fist. He chokes out a stunned breath. I twist my arm free of his grasp, then shove him down—my knees on his shoulders—holding him pinned as he lies beneath me. A trickle of blood drips from my wrist where his claws slashed me.

"I've broken so many vows to bring you here," I tell him. "All I want is your help."

He snarls, his lip freshly bleeding. "My answer won't change, Warden. No matter how prettily you ask."

He spits the words like venom, syrup-slick. I think of him on the moor with Lux, his hand on her back, claws tracing her spine, his mouth against her ear. The slow, languid way he lifted her into his arms. The other vespertine look like monsters. This one looks like a monster wearing a boy's face.

Yet he's a monster all the same.

I touch my wrist again, feeling the sting of the fresh wound. I stare at his hands, the inky marks tattooed on his fingers. The brutal sharpness of his claws. He has taken and taken and taken from me, and now I want to even the field between us, to narrow the imbalance of our power.

Inside my pocket, next to the bundled shards and the iron key, is my set of tailor's shears. They're whetted sharp enough to cut through hardened leather and slivers of bone. I take them out; they gleam in the lantern light as I hold them over the vespertine. I tell him, "Give me your hands."

A painful stalemate drags out between us. Then his gaze darkens, all challenge, and he shoves his hands toward me. I take hold of one, pin it tight between my elbow and my hip. I set the blades against his thumbnail and start to cut his claws.

He doesn't struggle, only glares at me, the challenge still set. Like he doesn't believe I have the resolve to follow through. His teeth clench together, and he makes no sound. But by the third finger, he starts to gasp raggedly. The clipped pieces scatter onto the floor like gruesome raindrops. I finish the first hand, move on to the second. He makes a sound, a bitten-back cry. When I hesitate, he sneers, fangs sharp against his swollen lower lip. "Finish it, Warden."

I cut the rest of his claws in silence. When I'm done, I look down at his newly blunted fingertips. I've cut too close, and some of his fingers are bleeding, blood smeared beside the inky tattoos.

My stomach clenches. I cast the shears aside, horrified at myself, at my cruelty. At how quickly I've moved from the girl who knelt at the ossuary in the enclave chapel and swore to keep her vows.

There's no holiness in this.

I get to my feet and go into the narrow bathing alcove, lean against the sink with my eyes scrunched closed and my ribs heaving. Nausea drags over me. I feel like a knot unpicked with the edge of a pin, dug loose in frayed sections, ragged and raveled. I turn on the tap; pipes groan and clatter deep inside the wall as a torrent of water pours out. It's red—from rust—and the sight of it sends a fresh wave of queasiness over me.

I scrub my hands until they're raw, stifling a sob. There's a cloth beside the sink, and I soak it with clean water, then take it back to the vespertine. He lies curled on his side with his eyes closed; his chest rises and falls in slow, poison-stilted breaths. The cloth drips a cold trail onto the floor at my feet as I stand there, watching him.

Tiredly, I pick up the stolen fiolae and slip them into my

pocket, then go over to the locked door and sit down with my back against the wood. I set aside the cloth. Pull the ribbon from my braid and unweave the strands, letting my hair fall loose. Then I wrap my cloak around myself and rest my cheek against my drawn-up knees. In my pocket, the fiolae chime together quietly.

Beneath the rain-hushed stillness of the room, I hear Fenn's voice—the way he sounded when he told me the stories of how the vespertine broke through the wall, stories of the carnage and my mother's treachery that followed. He gave them to me in place of the fables other children would be read before they went to sleep. Those veiled warnings that I should forget my past and devote myself, entirely, to the wardens.

But my mother and her secrets were always there, woven through each moment of my life. And now, it aches to realize how close I am to those answers. Yet, at the same time, how hopelessly far. Unless I can convince this monstrous creature to help me, I'll be left with nothing but broken vows and a betrayal that has cost the life of my best friend.

I glare at the vespertine. At the inky spill of his hair, the sharp angle of his shoulders, the pale bones and knotted leather that brace his forearms. The space of floor between us is like an accusation. I think of all the ways I could hurt him, worse than I already have.

But in the end, it wouldn't matter. He'd be dead, and Lux would still be lost.

CHAPTER TEN

The rolling sound of far-off thunder stirs me from my reverie. I don't know how much time has passed, but the attic is dim, the lantern extinguished, though the font was filled with enough oil to keep it burning. I've let my time with the vespertine fall away like thread from a dropped spool. Wasted these scarce moments on tears and fatigue instead of convincing him to help me.

I get to my feet, one hand against the door as I peer into the shadows, waiting for my eyes to adjust. Everything comes into coherence blink by blink. The empty chair, the trailing chain, the makeshift bed where I'd left the vespertine in his fitful, poison-laced sleep.

The bed—it is empty.

I spin toward the corner of the room where the shadows are deepest, catch sight of a figure—tall, broad shoulders, a gleam of eyes—before the vespertine closes the distance between us in two swift steps. He shoves me back against the door. Cages me, his hands on my shoulders. I feel his blunted claws. His thumbs digging bruise-hard into my collarbones.

I twist against him, reaching for the Vale Scythe. Before I can draw it, he presses a blade to my throat. Our eyes meet. I let out a shuddering breath. The heavy, blunted edge of the blade is straight, not the sickled curve of a warden's weapon. He has the shears—the bloodied shears, which I left on the floor.

"Please—" I whisper, feeling the bite of the shears against my throat as I speak. "It doesn't have to end like this."

The vespertine glares at me, his eyes the sole brightness in the room. There's nothing left of the pallid, bleeding ruin I made of him. Unmasked, without his cloak, he's a pared-down image of the creature who appeared through the moorland night. But despite the bareness of his too-human face, he is unmistakably a monster. The way his features shift into hard anger is just as fearsome as the mask he wore—those sharpened horns, those jagged bones.

His mouth carves to a feral grin, all hate and hunger. With deliberation—the blade still pressed to my throat—his other hand slides to my waist, fingers curled around the lowermost bone of my armored bodice. There's a snap, and he wrenches a piece from the rib cage, dragging it loose from the chains that hold it in place. He brandishes the bone between us, the same way I held up the stolen fiola chain. His thumb marks the broken point of the rib; then his clawless fingers close to a fist with the bone at the center.

His magic cascades over me. I gasp, curl forward. Desperately, I reach into my pocket and tear a shard from the ribboned bundle. It's tacky with Briar's blood, gleaming palely from the consecration

130

she cast. I twist the shard in my palm, my vision washed dark by the vespertine's power. I wish, helplessly, there was another way out of this.

With a swift, wretched motion, I stab the shard into his chest, past the draped chains of his armor, through the thin fabric of his shirt. I strike him hard, in the side of his ribs, the same place he broke my armor.

The blade falls away from my throat. The vespertine breathes out a corrosive snarl, one hand pressed to the wound. The shard is stuck between his ribs. He scrapes at it, trying to pull it loose. I reach for the Vale Scythe. His gaze snaps to me, and he utters a stream of tangled words—like holy speech, but turned discordant, spun backward.

Hideous visions crawl into my mind: a bloodied moon, a cathedral casting its solid shadow over the moorland. I see a creature at the altar—too tall to be human, horns jutting from his head like a ruinous crown. The vespertine's magic is a wave, a flood, completely unstoppable. *It's not real; it's not real.* I force my shaking hand to draw my blade.

The Vale Scythe gleams like a crescent moon against the haze of the vespertine's power. I slash at him; he turns at the last moment—my relic blade strikes his armor, biting into the bones knotted around his wrists. A *crack* splits the air, and we spiral apart, engulfed by a rush of wild magic that rises swift as a storm. We're lost in a cloud of soot-thick, bitter-scented mist that flickers with bursts of brightness. I taste rot and rust, followed by the unbearable bittersweetness of burned honey.

Figures flicker against the dark, there and not there. The cathedral falls to a pile of ruined stones beneath the bloodied moon. Framed in the hollowed arch of the doorway stands a figure. Her hair is loose, pluming in treacle-dark waves that are tangled by the wind. She wears a pale dress stained with something clotted and dark.

And in her arms, held like an offering, is a child.

The Vale Scythe is still in my hand. I clutch at the hilt, let the bite of leather and bone against my palm force me back into coherence. The haze clears. Behind me, the attic door hangs open like a gaped mouth, the lock broken loose and the wood around it all scarred. The destroyed shears have been cast aside onto the threshold.

The vespertine is gone.

Footsteps echo from the stairwell, and Briar appears outside the door—chest heaving, her hair unfurled from its braid. On anyone else, the expression she wears would be tender concern, if not for the anger in her eyes. "Are you hurt?" I shake my head. She lets out a fractious breath. "What happened to the shards I gave you?"

I start to laugh—fizzy, hysterical giggles. My voice is rasped, like I've been screaming, yet I don't remember making a sound. Briar glares at me with deepening fury. I wave a hand, trying to catch my breath. "He— I—I've warded him."

"What you do mean, you *warded* him?"

"He attacked me, and I fought back with one of the shards." I explain. Briar raises a brow, and I go on, recounting the events of the night, how the vespertine stole the shears I'd used to cut his claws, then caught me by surprise when I'd thought him soundly lost beneath the snare of poison.

She shakes her head in exasperation. "Hells, Everline. You are truly hopeless."

I want to ask what she would have done in my place, but I know the answer: She would never have gotten into such trouble as this. "They were your wards. Marked with your blood. Could you use them to find him?"

Briar glances briefly toward the window, where the fogged glass has begun to glimmer with early daylight. "Find him? No. We're going *home*, back to the enclave. We need help. Proper help, not your ridiculous playacting."

Turning toward the stairs, she gathers up her skirts, ready to descend. "Wait!" I call after her. "We can't let him go. He told me where he's taken Lux. She's in the Thousandfold."

Briar falters to a stop, her hand going out to clutch hold of the banister. "Then we don't need him at all."

"No," I say. "We do. The Thousandfold is protected by magic. The same magic the vespertine used on Lux—on me. We can't go inside without his help."

Her face turns horror-pale. Her teeth press sharply into her lip as she deliberates over my words. Silence draws out between us, interrupted only by the howl of the wind against the walls. Briar has been raised on stories of the Thousandfold, just as I have. All wardens are taught about that place of heretical chapels and poisonous magic, where the ashen remains of Nyx Severin have polluted the ground. The power the vespertine used against us only reinforces this truth—it's a place forbidden to wardens, a graveyard landscape that is all threat and ruin.

Briar swallows heavily. Then, with a defeated sigh, she goes into the barracks room to retrieve her blade belt. Buckling it around her waist, she brushes past me and crosses the landing.

"Come on," she snaps from over her shoulder as she hurries down the stairs into the darkness below. "Let's get moving before we completely lose his trail."

I follow her out through the chapel, past the kitchen with its cross-scored windowsill and my blood dripped onto the ivy leaves. A wind rushes in from the gardens, frostbitten cold against my cheeks. Too late, I think of my cloak, still upstairs. Shivering, I walk behind Briar as we go beneath the dripping trees and onto the moor, where the landscape is blanketed in heavy mist.

As the rain beats down, Briar wrenches a handful of shards from her pocket. She pricks her finger, smears her blood over the bones. She drops to one knee, and with a vicious shove, she stabs the shards into the ground.

Brightness sparks and crackles at our feet like a fresh-lit flame. An echoing charge comes from the distance, the way lightning blooms within a storm cloud. The trail flickers like a ward line— blood from the vespertine's wounds, tinged by the magic Briar has cast, a connection of holiness and power that I could never hope to replicate.

We track the vespertine doggedly through the rain, through the shrouding mist. The ground is marshy. Rivulets of water spill between thickets of gorse. Our boots slosh through the deepening mud, and soon my skirts are soaked to the knee.

My cheeks and ears are scoured raw with cold, my thoughts

empty of everything but shame and guilt and the image of Lux, lost to the Thousandfold. I follow Briar through snares of brambles, past jagged, moss-hemmed stones. I can hear the river—swollen from the storm—as it lashes against the banks nearby. The land slopes into a thicket of spindly citrus trees that are circled by fallen fruit. We pause, both of us breathing heavily as we narrow our eyes at the ground.

The trail has split, a forked path of bloodied prints that glimmer in two directions on either side of the trees. Briar draws another shard, pricks her finger, sets it to the earth. Both the trails flare bright, equally lit by her magic.

Sighing roughly, she sits back on her heels and licks the blood from her thumb. Her skirts are muddied around the hem, and straggles of baby-fine hair have plastered themselves to her cheeks. The haze of rain-drenched mist spreads across the moors behind her like a silken veil.

I drag in a breath, tasting the rotted citrus that has flavored the air beside the tree. With my fingers curled against my palm, I look from one flare of pale light to the other. "We'll have to separate."

Briar rakes a hand over her hair, pushing the loosened strands back from her face. "Fine. I'll take this path. You follow the other. If he isn't there, double back and meet me here. And if you *do* find him, act like a true warden for once in your foolish life."

Her words paint a vivid picture of the vespertine laid out at my feet, my blade spiked through his heart. That is what a true warden would do, unquestioningly. I think of him dead, the light extinguished from his green, green eyes, his body reduced to ashes on a funeral pyre. I think of Lux, lost forever, her bones beside the remnants of my mother in the Thousandfold, the two of them laid together beneath the earth.

I shake my head in vehement refusal. "You can't kill him, Briar."

She clutches her pouch of bone shards and stares at me, long and hard, as the ribbon tied to the hilt of her blade snaps and thrashes in the wild wind. "You know what needs to be done."

I tilt my face upward in desperation, stare at the sky where clouds roil as another storm gathers. A scatter of raindrops falls through the branches and lands on my cheeks. "You saw Fenn— how he reacted when we brought the dead girl to the gates. There's something out here, something hidden, and he is keeping it from us. We need the vespertine's help—to find Lux and to find those answers. We can't kill him. He isn't the same as a monster we'd fight near the enclave, trying to break through our walls."

Briar presses her lips together in a tight, bloodless line. Her eyes shimmer wetly, and for a disconcerting moment, I think she's about to cry. Then she blinks, and her face turns steely. "If Lux were here, she'd be ashamed of you."

I open my mouth to argue—how dare she claim to know how Lux would feel *at all*—but I'm struck silent. In spite of everything, there's truth in Briar's words. I said it myself. This has all been my fault. I drew Lux into this dangerous place, put her at the mercy of these terrible creatures.

Heat burns across my cheeks, bright and fervent, as though I've been slapped. I turn my back on Briar without response, letting the sting of her words wash away with the rain that spills over me as I move out from the trees. Dimly, I hear the sound of Briar's footsteps retreating heavily as she goes in the opposite direction, following the other trail.

The trail I've chosen is as luminous as moonlight, as though someone took the blood eclipse and broke it to pieces, spilled it in silver and crimson across the earth. As I trace the path of magic and blood, I start to murmur under my breath, like I am making a wish or trying to conjure a miracle. *Let me find him. Let the trail I follow be the right one.*

There's nothing and nothing and nothing, only endless stretches of moorland, colored in hues of sable and gray as the sun edges higher behind the clouds. The rain drips through my hair and down the nape of my neck, tracing a shivering path along my spine.

In the distance, I see the Blackthorn River with its white-capped waters gnawing hungrily at the banks. The sound of the water fights the sound of the rain, and for a breath-caught moment, it reminds me of the vespertine's magic—the terrible hiss and spin that made my nose bleed and raised monstrous visions from the empty air.

And then, as though I've summoned him, I catch sight of a figure at the very edge of the flooded riverbank. The vespertine, draped beside the tributary we crossed on our way to the chapel—now flooded and frantic—churning with a rapid, hungry current. He's half-in, half-out of the water. He's got ahold of a thick handful of reeds, clutching it like a tether line. His shirt is hitched up, and holy light glimmers from a lurid wound at the curve of his ribs where the bone shard is still pierced through his skin.

I stride toward him with my hand tight around the Vale Scythe. I put my mud-caked boot on his chest, feeling the buoyancy of the water beneath him. The eager river. "Twice now," I tell him, holding up my fingers for emphasis. "Twice I've had your life in my hands."

He glowers at me, his swollen lips still stained by dregs of poison. His hair swirls in the water, drawn into snarls by the current. "Damn you, Warden. *Damn* you."

Even now, half-dead and pinned beneath my boot, he's unyielding. "Do you still think I won't kill you? After all, you've made it clear that you'll be of no use to me alive."

The water foams around him. His eyes are dark, his fangs bared—the picture of abject fury. "I've seen the mercy wardens give to monsters."

I look down at him. The sin of what I'm about to do comes over me with a dizzying rush. Broken vows upon broken vows. But I need a way to keep this boy—this monster—safe from harm and loyal to me. And right now, chilled from the rain and fatigued from the events of the night—his capture, our struggle, this reckless chase—there's only one solution I can think of.

"I'll guarantee your safety if you come with me. I will—" The words catch, tasting bitter as incense smoke. "I will make you my vowsworn."

Even to speak it aloud feels like the worst heresy. All wardens promise themselves to Saint Lenore. But some wardens will also swear a vow to another, sealing their lives together. It's the deepest fealty, a binding and holy connection that can only be undone with powerful magic.

The vespertine gives me a scathing look, with all the helpless fury of a cornered wolf—ears flattened, teeth bared. "Why would I ever want your vow?"

"Because any other warden would have already cut your throat. If we're sworn, you'll be under my protection. You'll not be able to harm me, or I you. If I'm to save your life, then I want that certainty."

He turns his face away. As if in denial of what he's about to do, the way I'd cover my eyes when I awoke after a nightmare and could still see haunting shapes against the dark. Then his lashes dip, fluttering blackly against his paint-smeared cheeks; he thrusts his hand toward me.

"What a delight it will be," he says, words laced by disgust, "being bound to you."

I clutch at his wrist, feeling the leather edge of his bracers. We're both rain-slick, and I can't keep hold of him; I twist my sodden sleeve over my hand and try again, leaning back to pull with all my strength to drag him free of the water. We teeter on the bank for a moment, then tumble to the ground. I land heavily, draped across his chest with my undone hair spilling around us. Our eyes meet, and we're so *close*. His gasping breath burns like fever against my skin. I can feel the rapid beat of his heart.

His face, for a fleeting moment, is all unguarded shock. "You saved me."

"I could push you back in if you'd prefer."

He shoves me away and rolls to his side, starting to cough. His chest heaves as he struggles to gather himself. I feel just as ragged and ruined. I lie back on the ground as the wind whisks over us, staring up at the clouds. The rain falls onto my cheeks like icy tears.

The vespertine starts to laugh, his eyes scrunched closed in a grimace. "You do realize how these types of vows are made, don't you?"

When I swore my vows to the wardens, it was at the ossuary in the chapel. I remember Fenn's hand beneath my elbow as I approached the altar, where the centermost skull—the effigy of Saint Lenore—was wreathed in gold. How I stood on tiptoe and pressed my lips to unyielding bone, sealing my promise with a kiss.

"Of course I know." Unbidden, my gaze traces the curve of the vespertine's mouth. Heat crawls over me beneath the chill of the rain, a flush that prickles my nape where my warden mark lies hidden. "Do *you*?"

He sits up slowly, wincing as the shard beneath his skin gives another twinge of magic. He smiles, baring his fanged teeth. "Yes. I do. We have our own version of your holy vows." The way he says it, the word *holy* sounds like a curse. "I don't trust you—or your promises, Warden. If you want me to swear fealty to you, then you'll take my vow as well. So our truce will be doubly bound."

My stomach tightens with an endless knot of apprehension as I remember the feel of his magic, the way it writhed around me. But I need him. I need to be able to trust him. And if this is what it takes to secure his help, then so be it. "Fine."

"Fine," he echoes. "You can go first."

I push myself onto my knees, narrowing the distance between us. Slowly, I raise my hand and place it flat against his chest. His breath catches, and his fingers clench. Then, with effort, he forces himself to relax, and he reaches to me. Lays his own hand against my chest in an echo of my gesture. His skin is warm, even after being draped in the river; I can feel the heat through all the wet layers of my clothes. We sit unmoving, listening to the rush of water beside us, the rising violence of the wind as it casts across the moorland beyond.

Then I start to speak. "I, Everline Blackthorn, swear on the catacombs of the enclave chapel, on the ashen heart of Saint Lenore, that you will have my trust. I will never harm you. You are mine and will be protected with all in my power."

Until this moment, I tried not to think of it, what these words would mean. Now it travels over me in a bone-aching shudder. We are bound. We will belong to each other.

The vespertine swallows audibly, and his hand gives a small *twitch* before pressing firmly against my heart. "I, Ravel, swear by the blood and power of the Sanguine Saint that you'll have my trust. I will never harm you. You are mine and will be protected with all in my power."

My eyes snap open, and I look at him, shocked. The air shimmers with the weight of it, this secret shared. This creature is no longer just *vespertine*; he has given me his name. "Ravel?" I repeat, the taste of it strange and syrupy against my tongue.

He stares past my shoulder, features schooled into determined indifference. "Finish the vows, Warden."

I shiver, cold from the wind and the horror of what I'm doing. Sin after sin after sin. But what does it matter, this unholy pact, if I can save Lux and secure our safe passage into the Thousandfold?

I edge closer to the vespertine—*Ravel*—and slide my hand up to cradle his jaw. I'm trembling. He touches my cheek, then drags his thumb across my lips. I bite back a gasp at his touch. I'm struck by the same feeling as when I first cut myself to mark my blade before a fight—the way I held my breath, the anticipation of pain that overlaid an undeniable thrill.

I've been kissed before: once, by a girl who'd accompanied her new-marked warden sister to the gathering, who hadn't known me or my treasonous bloodline. As I slipped away with her, I'd thought it a harmless moment of sweetness I could steal, like licking the spoon after filling a vial with honey. But afterward, I'd felt only anger at myself for hoping it would be so easy. I was still Everline Blackthorn, magicless and baseborn. No fleeting kiss would transform me like a maiden in a fable.

Or so I'd thought. But now, as I lean toward Ravel, it feels as though I'm in the darkness, falling, falling, and I hope that whatever is beneath me when I land will be soft, not sharp.

I close my eyes and pull him toward me, fierceness surging through my veins like a rise of wildfire. His lips meet mine, and he makes a soft, peculiar sound. A shimmering current paints the air, and I open my mouth—a gasp finally escaping me—and his mouth opens, too. He clutches at my hip and drags me closer. His tongue sweeps mine, and I taste something bitter and dark, coffee left too long on the stove, the alluring decay of fruit beneath the clementine tree, the rust and ash flavor of his magic.

I clench my eyes tightly closed as images stream through my mind, one after another. But there's no cathedral ruins bathed in crimson moonlight. No horned monster staring down at me from a pulpit, no treacle-haired woman in her stained gown. There's only a boy atop a sweeping flight of stairs, the crumbled shape of an arched window behind him. A girl stands at his side, swathed in a woolen cloak that hides her face and hair. She holds his hand with desperate tenderness, her childish fingers laced through his in an unbreakable grip.

Ravel pulls back, his hands at my shoulders, forcing distance between us. He's wide-eyed and shocked, the expression so incongruously human.

"I saw . . . ," I begin, but his brows knit together, and he turns away, glaring at the river, the waves that lash the banks. I fall to silence, swallowing down my questions like a handful of poisoned berries.

Ravel licks at the edge of his thumb. There's a wound there. That's what he put on my lips. His blood. I scrub my mouth against the back of my hand, trying to wipe away the memory of our kiss.

He gives me a hard-edged smile that doesn't reach his eyes. "Well, we've made our vows, Warden. Shall we call truce?"

CHAPTER ELEVEN

Halfway between river and ruin, the storm dies around us, rain clouds turned to streaks of mist, closing out the rest of the world. A shadow darkens that clouded distance as Briar appears, her blade drawn and consecration haloing her clenched, bloodied fist.

We meet in the same copse of trees where the trail split. Beneath the dripping arch of branches, the ground is littered with rotten fruit, and the overripe scent drags a rise of sickly hunger from the depths of my stomach. The feel of the vespertine's kiss is printed over my lips like a brand, and lingering traces of blood lie metallic against my tongue.

"This is Ravel," I say to Briar. His name is unfamiliar in my mouth, the syllables tasting of burned coffee, bittersweet and ruinous. "He is going to help us."

She gives me a look that carves to my heart, laden with the same disappointment I've seen so often from Fenn. The way he looks when he catches me at my worst moments. All the times

I've cried, or pushed him for answers about my birth, or slipped and called him *Father*.

Briar draws her blade. I put myself between her and Ravel, and she grits her teeth. "Get out of my way, Everline. I've had enough of this."

We fall into a grim dance—to one side, then the other, Briar trying to shove past me as I match her steps—a reenactment of the way she barred my path back to the enclave, refusing to allow the shrouded body of the vespertine inside. It would be comical if the stakes weren't so high, if my heart wasn't pounding so fast. I can feel the rapid *thud, thud, thud* of my pulse against my throat.

In all the urgency of my foolish planning, I've not thought of how to tell Briar the decision I've made, the depth of my sin. Desperately, I shake my head. "You can't."

She raises her blade, the keen edge bright against the storm-washed sky. "I *said* get out of my way."

Ravel snarls at her. His bloodied fingers curl in a memory of claws; he bares his fangs. Instinct takes over, and I'm moving before I realize what I mean to do—I reach for his hand and pull him close against me. "He's mine," I blurt out. "We're vowsworn."

The confession tears itself loose, an unbidden thing. My fingers lace through his, and our palms press together like a promise. Ravel makes a sound of muted shock. A crackle of sudden heat tremors between us. His fingers press reflexively against mine; then he pulls himself free of my grasp with a noise of disgust. With a scowl, he takes a step back, keeping a wary distance between himself and Briar.

She ignores him. Turning instead to stare at me with utter

horror. I meet her gaze, my cheeks hot, a queasy ache of despair in the pit of my stomach. Until this moment, I've kept the gravity of my choice at a distance, refusing to acknowledge what my bond with Ravel will truly mean. But now, faced by Briar's shock, I can no longer avoid it; as though she's held up a mirror and my ruin has been reflected back at me, stark and inescapable. "It was for Lux," I say. "He'll have to lead us to her—and protect us against the vespertine—now."

Briar's mouth opens; then she shakes her head, setting her teeth against whatever she intended to say. Sheathing her blade, she drags her attention from me to Ravel. "Tell me the truth. You will return our warden safely?"

He lifts one hand with slow deliberation, takes hold of his rain-drenched hair. Twisting it around his ink-banded fingers, he wrings the water from the tangled strands. Angrily, I catch his wrist. He tries to pull away, but I tighten my grasp, refusing to let him go. "And," I press, "you will guide us to the Thousandfold."

"Yes," he snaps, his tone laced with acid. "I'll guide you there. She'll be returned to you."

His words feel like a baited trap I'm willingly stepping into—as though with a single wrong movement, I'll be caught. Ravel gives another tug at my hand, breaking my grip. He moves away, rubbing the feel of my touch from his wrist. Briar glares at him; then her eyes narrow at the blood soaked through his shirt, where I pierced him with the shard. "He'll be no use to us if that turns septic. We'll need to go back to the chapel and see to the wound."

She turns on her heel and strides out from the sheltering trees, onto the moorland, her head bowed against the fading rain. Ravel glances at me, one brow raised. Irritated, I gesture for him to follow her. We walk in the path left by Briar's boots, and Ravel trails sullenly behind, measuring his steps so we aren't near each other.

The chapel spears up from the windswept landscape, a tower of splintery stone. My stomach unknots as we move toward it, as though my body has already begun to recognize this place as *home*. I hate myself for that undeniable thought.

We pass beneath the dripping orchard branches and go through the gate, into the ruined kitchen. Ravel stalks over to the opposite side of the room, where the glassless window lets in a fierce, cold draft. He folds his arms, leans one shoulder against the ivy-laced stone wall. The silence laid among us is as sharp as newly whetted steel.

I take off my mud-caked boots. Briar adds more wood to the dying fire burning in the brick hearth. "Bring my field kit from upstairs," she orders. "I'll heat some water."

In the barracks room, I quickly strip off my sodden clothes and scrub my hair with a towel before putting on a clean dress and a pair of warm, dry socks. I remove my mantle and my weapon, but I keep the bone bracers around my wrists; I can't bear the thought of being entirely unarmored.

Briar's field kit is on the dresser where she left it. I slip it into my pocket, then, as an afterthought, unbuckle the straps of Lux's satchel and take out the oversize woolen sweater that she brought.

The lilac-and-elderflower scent of her surrounds me; I hold the sweater close and take a deep, wistful breath. Keeping it tight against my chest, I go back down the stairs.

Briar has found a chair—twin to the one from the attic—and dragged it close to the hearth. On the stove, steam plumes from a tarnished copper kettle. I pass her the field kit, and she gestures toward the stillroom door. "See if you can find a bowl." Then, to Ravel, "You. Sit there."

He moves petulantly toward the hearth. Before he sits, he looks at me, and his mouth ticks into a hard smile. "Are you going to bind me this time, Warden?"

An unwanted blush heats my face. "I'd rather not."

Briar scowls down at Ravel's hands—his blunted claws, the places where I cut him accidentally with my shears. Then she pinches the hem of his shirt between her fingers and lifts it to peer beneath at the bloodied wound. I think of Lux, our closeness in the infirmary, the tender way she blotted the wound at my throat. I graze my thumb over my neck, trace the remnants of the cut still marking my skin.

There's none of that intimacy in the way Briar touches Ravel; she examines him clinically, her eyes narrowed in concentration. A peculiar emotion twists my stomach when I notice the way she's so *unaffected*, with none of the crackling heat I feel each time he comes near to me.

With a sigh, I turn away from them and go into the stillroom. The small, windowless space is mostly empty, with dust on the shelves and a faded scent of herbs in the air. But in a cupboard, I find a mismatched stack of enamelware bowls, perhaps once used to prepare tinctures for the chapel. I carry the largest one to the kitchen and rinse it from the kettle, before filling it with water. When I offer the bowl to Briar, she folds her arms, refusing to take it from me. Nodding toward the field kit, she says, "The cut won't need stitches. Pull out the shard and clean his wounds."

I stare at her incredulously. "But I thought you were going to—"

"This is *your* mess, Everline." She crosses to the doorway that leads into the chapel, her pale hair a ghostly smudge against the darkened hall behind her. Wayward strands have fallen loose from her windswept braid; a trail of muddy water drips from her skirts. She glances at me over her shoulder as she leaves, her expression stern, and lets out an irritated sigh. "I want to change out of these wet clothes. Try not to cause any more disasters while I'm gone."

Her heavy footsteps retreat into the space overhead, followed by the slam of the door in the barracks room above.

Ravel ignores me determinedly. A sliver of light cants through the glassless window frame, picking out the lines of his face. Most of the paint has smudged away now, but grayish remnants stain his cheekbones, and his mouth is blotted dark as a bruise. I stare at him a beat too long, noticing without wanting to notice his sharpened jaw, the haughty angle of his aquiline nose.

The last thing I want to do is tend this creature. I start to unpack the field kit, telling myself this is no different from the countless nights I've gone with Lux to the infirmary, where I held a cloth to the pulse points of her wrists or wrapped bandages around her bruised ribs. But with Lux, my hands never shook; my stomach never felt so knotted up.

I set out a roll of linen bandages and a vial of antiseptic salve, then a stack of folded gauze cloths. Ravel is still ignoring me, his face turned toward the window. The room seems so echoing and empty with only the two of us in here. Yet in spite of that, I'm unavoidably aware of him; our closeness. When I swallow, my throat feels tight. "You should take off your armor."

Slowly, he unbuckles the harness from his shoulders, removing the armor with the muted slide of leather, the clink of tarnished chains. He sets it aside; then his gaze drifts toward me with marked deliberation. He pauses, mouth tilting; then he grabs hold of his collar and drags off his shirt in a single motion.

I falter to a stunned silence. All I can do is stare. His skin is the pale gold of new honey. Beneath the wound on his ribs, there's a wicked, toothy scar—long-healed, printed on him like a faded crescent moon. And I can see now, so clearly, the strength I felt when we clashed out on the moor. Lean muscles and a planed-flat chest. There's a line of dark hair on his stomach that arrows toward his waistband, and once I notice *that*, an incandescent heat floods across my face.

Ravel starts to laugh. "I don't know why you're blushing like a vestal nun after that kiss. We're *vowsworn*, remember?"

He speaks the words with a mocking tone, but fresh heat kindles in my cheeks as I think of the thoroughness of our vow-kiss, the bittersweet taste of his opened mouth and the strangely helpless noise that escaped me when he drew me close.

I hate that he's so easily unsettled me. I bite down on the feeling, imagining it crushed between my teeth. "There's nothing in our vows that require being undressed."

"A shame, really. I've been wondering how many knives you have hidden beneath all those bones and lace."

I wet a cloth with antiseptic and use it to clean my hands. Then, collecting the bowl and a handful of gauze, I go over to stand beside him. "What I may or may not have hidden is none of your concern. Now hold still."

He closes his eyes and tilts back his head, sprawling loosely in the chair as I lean over him. I set the bowl at his feet and dampen a square of gauze. His bare skin is hot against the palm of my hand. It feels wrong—to be this close to him, to heal his wounds when I should never have let him stay alive.

The shard protrudes grotesquely from his skin, but Briar was right—it's a clean cut; it won't need to be stitched. Carefully, I take hold of the shard and pull it loose. Ravel hisses, blunted claws flexing against his thighs. I take a fresh square of gauze and press it to his ribs, cleaning away the blood.

My heart is still pounding; flushed and flustered, I smear antiseptic on the wound and dress it with another square of gauze. I pick up the bandages. The only reason to put my hands on a creature like Ravel should be to destroy him. Instead, here I am winding a strip of linen around his chest, the same way I would for Lux when she was hurt.

Ravel leans forward so I can better reach to pass the bandage behind his back. This close, I can't help noticing how his dark lashes fan against his cheeks. The way he smells—bitter and ashen—the same scent as his magic. This close, I can hide nothing from him—the blush that burns over my cheeks, the nervous tremor of my touch.

His head dips forward, and I stare at the darkened lines of his warden mark. Again, the undeniable certainty comes over me—of a connection between myself and the Thousandfold, evidence printed on this creature with his warden mark in the exact same place as my own. I have a sudden, disquieting urge to take Ravel's face between my hands and rub away the smears of paint, as though unmasked and unveiled I might finally be able to see the truth of him.

My fingers trail slowly to his nape, press against the curved, blackened lines. He jolts away from me, glaring, and I step back, an incandescent blush risen all over my skin. The ends of the bandage hang down loosely; Ravel ties them into a knot.

With shaking hands, I pick up Lux's sweater and hold it out to him, laid flat on my palms like a holy offering. He puts it on begrudgingly, then collects his armor and stalks over to the fireplace. Standing with his gaze pinned to the flames, he rebuckles the bracers firmly at his wrists. Clasps the chains into a silvered harness pinned at his shoulders.

I don't know how to parse the unwanted intimacy of this moment. All I can do is turn my back on him, lift the weight of my hair from my neck as I tug loose the ribbon that ties my collar closed. "We have the same mark. In the same place. See?"

I stand with my nape bared to him like an apology, holding very still. Slowly, he comes toward me, then moves aside my collar to examine the mark. His blunted claws scrape, gently, against my skin. I have to bite my lip to stop myself from making a sound. Ravel presses at the mark; then he pulls away. "I'm no warden," he says flatly. "That should be obvious."

"What are you, then?"

He turns away without answering and goes toward the entrance to the chapel, gesturing for me to follow. "Come with me. I have something to show you."

I hesitate a moment, then walk behind him into the hall. The back of my neck prickles with the remembered feel of his touch. Inside the chapel, the stained glass window is lit by afternoon sunlight. Nyx Severin gleams in obsidian, the drops of his blood a garish ruby. I look at Ravel, wait for his reaction to the image—a hint of shame, or pride, or even recognition. But he doesn't spare it a glance as he walks toward the stairs.

We pass the barracks room, and Briar emerges, drawn by the sound of our footsteps. She's put on a clean white dress and tied her hair into a chignon. Ravel brushes past her, headed toward the attic. She falls in beside me with an irritated huff, her newly polished boots loud against the floor in contrast to my woolen socks.

The attic door hangs on its hinges. The lock is a mess of scars; my tailor's shears lie discarded on the floor where Ravel cast them aside. I pick them up and run my thumb, mournfully, against the blunted blade—notched from where he jammed it in the latch—before tucking the shears into my pocket. Inside the room, it's fogged and gloomy, the window glass blotted with condensation.

Ravel crosses to the window and shoves it open. Freezing

wind gusts inside the room, and the light washes over us, gray and watery, speckled by remnants of the rain. I wrap my arms around myself and exhale a plume of breath as I go over to stand beside Ravel. "What did you want to show me?"

He indicates the landscape below, the same view I looked upon when I first came to the attic. As the moor spreads out beneath us, it reminds me of being on the watchtower, that same heady feel of being *above*. The trees look like figurines I could hold inside my cupped palms; the Blackthorn River trails over the ground like a dropped ribbon.

And beyond, at the horizon, a barely visible stretch of shadow marks the earth like a low, banked cloud. "There," says Ravel, "is the Thousandfold. Your warden is inside, at the very heart. She's a prisoner in the chapel of the Sanguine Saint."

Briar and I fall silent; the room is filled with only the noise of the wind. It sends a bolt of tension through me to hear that name—the title Nyx Severin gave himself when he pretended to be a god. It's the second time now I've heard Ravel speak it so casually, with such familiarity. It seems a thing that should be whispered, in hushed and fearful tones. A shiver crosses the back of my neck, and I slide my fingers beneath my collar to press against my warden mark.

"You'll take us there," Briar says to Ravel, no question in her tone. "And release our warden."

He gives her a tired look. "I will take you to the border. You can wait there, and I'll bring your warden to meet you."

"No," I tell him. "I want to go with you, all the way into the heart of the Thousandfold."

"What's the matter?" He turns to me, brows raised, a mocking lilt in his voice. "Don't you trust me, even though we're vowsworn?"

"I want to go inside. You must know a way to protect against the magic." I put my hand on his arm, fighting back my desperation. I can't let him see how badly I need this—his help, a safe passage into that forbidden enclave. Grasping for an excuse, I go on. "I owe it to my warden to ensure her safety."

Ravel smirks. "So you *don't* trust me."

"Your vow is wasted on him, Everline," Briar says irritably. "He has no stake in this, nothing at risk. He'll turn on you—on both of us—the instant he has a chance."

Ravel snarls at her, the sound rising from low in his throat. His eyes turn sharp, alight with leashed-back fury. "You have no idea what I've risked to be here with you."

My hand is still on his arm. I tighten my hold, give him a warning look. "Enough."

Rain-washed air spills through the window, casting trails of cold against my cheeks and tangling the strands of Ravel's hair. I look at the column of his throat, the wingbeat of his pulse, the tarnished lariat chains strung across his chest.

The bones in his armor are timeworn, ancient as relics—strands of knotted metacarpals tied in place by strips of leather at his wrists, twin ribs on either of his shoulders, stitched to the harness. Slowly, I slide my hand down his arm, run my fingers over his bracers. I press against the bones. A shimmer of magic lights up, too dark to be consecration. A sour taste floods my tongue, and my ears hum with the low drone of a remembered noise.

It's the same as the power he used against us, the power of the Thousandfold. "There's magic in your armor," I say, more to myself than to him. Ravel nods. I wrap my fingers around his wrist, feel the magic throbbing against my hand. "*You* made this?"

"You needn't look so shocked."

The oily feel of his power clings to me, sending a cascade of shudders down my spine. I scrub my hand against my skirts, trying to wipe away the unpleasantness. Then a thought rises, one that feels laced with heresy. My stomach knots as I dredge up the words. "If I were to armor myself with this magic, would I be able to enter the Thousandfold?"

Ravel considers this for a moment, laughing ruefully. "What is inside the Thousandfold that you want so badly, Warden?"

"Just tell me if it would work. This magic, could you do it again—with another set of armor?"

He levels me with a skeptical look, then, mouth twisted in distaste, he takes hold of my wrists, circling his hands over my bracers. An echo of the way I held him only moments before. He traces the bones, tests the points of the vertebrae with his thumb. He's unguarded, strangely boyish as he concentrates—lips parted, gaze intently focused. There's no shimmer of magic or memory of ruinous power when he touches me. But still, a current of heat passes between us, stirring new warmth across my skin.

Briar watches us both, her arms folded, eyes narrowed distrustfully as she tracks the movements of Ravel's hands. He leans closer. His fingers fit into the space between the knotted ribbons of my bracers and my bare wrists. I feel so exposed—and more abashed than before, even, when I saw him half-unclothed as I tended his wounds.

He draws back, shaking his head. "It won't work. These bones aren't the same as the kind I've used."

"What do you mean?"

He makes an exasperated noise. Then, with a rough sigh, he starts to take off his armor, laying the pieces into my hands. "It's just *different*," he says emphatically. "You figure it out, Warden, since you know so much."

Chains drape my forearms, then a tangle of buckles and leather, interspersed with the sharpness of bone. The whole mess of his armor is hot against my wind-chilled skin, and I'm caught by the hateful memory of Ravel—his bared chest, the scar tucked into the curve of his ribs. Unbidden, my hands clench, my fingers pressed painfully into the bones. A renewed, dizzying rush of magic spills over me.

Familiarity hits me with a sudden, breath-stealing blow. I'm back in the watchtower as Fenn places the Vale Scythe in my hands. This is the same, the same unmistakable feel of holiness that I felt when I drew the blade and saw the hallowed bones shine in the moonlight. The bones in Ravel's armor . . .

"They're relics?" My hands start to shake at the feel of his armor in my hands, the wrongness of it. Something made by monsters can't possibly be holy. "Where did you find these bones?"

He steps back from the window and spreads his arms wide to me in supplication. "There are catacombs on the moorland." He falls into a deliberate silence, biting at his lip as though struggling with a difficult decision, his face all mock seriousness. "I suppose I could take you there if you ask politely."

"And when I replicate this"—I nod to the armor—"then you'll provide the magic to enchant it."

"You still haven't said *please*. Don't they teach you to use manners at the enclave?"

I swallow down an irritated noise. "Please," I say, not bothering to hide the acid in my tone. "My *darling vowsworn*. Take me into the catacombs and help me enchant the armor."

Briar cuts a glare between the two of us. "Can you just . . . *not*?"

Ravel smiles at her deferentially. "Forgive me, Warden."

Then he turns back to me. His eyes are as green as poison, his fangs are bared. And I'm nervous in spite of the fact that Briar is here, watching us both with her hand on her blade. In spite of the fact that we're vowsworn, that with my promise and his bloodied kiss, we've sealed our truce. I still don't know if I can trust him.

But I don't have another choice. If I want to pass beyond the border of the Thousandfold, then I need his help. "Please," I say again.

He's silent for a moment longer. Then, finally, he says, "I'll help with the enchantment. And if you're determined to follow me to the heart of the Thousandfold, I'll lead you there. Perhaps you'll remember my hospitality next time a vespertine shows up at your wall."

Briar steps forward, still clasping her blade, and takes hold of my arm. Her fingers curl over the tarnished chains and leather straps, Ravel's armor that is still clutched in my hands. "For both of us," she says to him. "You'll provide magic for both of us."

I glance at her, indecision like a weight on my chest. She meets my gaze, her expression cold and unrelenting, an utter refusal of any protectiveness I might spare her. I swallow down my intended denial and turn back to Ravel. "Take us to the catacombs, then."

PART TWO

A warden takes no prisoners;
all captured vespertine must be destroyed.

—SECOND COMMANDMENT OF SAINT LENORE

CHAPTER TWELVE

W E SET OUT AT DAYBREAK AFTER SPENDING A TENSE, uncomfortable night in the ruined chapel. Briar and I were both too anxious, too wary, to sleep in the barracks room—to allow ourselves to settle in the heart of this place built to honor Nyx Severin. So instead, we added more wood to the kitchen fire and spread our blankets beside the hearth, trading watch shifts while Ravel slept in the farthermost corner.

He lay with his face turned pointedly toward the wall, as though he could barely stand to be in the same room as us. The firelight threw his shadows against the coiled ivy vines, transfigured him into a blurred, abstract shape. In my fatigue, his outline became the jagged silhouette of the creatures I'd watched for in the darkness beyond the enclave—those four-legged, monstrous vespertine that howled through the night, that hunted us with their feral hunger.

Unsettled, I drew my weapon and went to stand by the glassless window. The moorland surrounding the chapel was impenetrable, storm-swept and lightless, all wailing wind and the torrential sound of the rising river. But I couldn't escape the sense there was something—or someone—out there, beneath the layered night. Monsters crouched and hidden, their eyes narrowed, their claws curled sharp into the shadows.

When I woke Briar to take her turn at watch, I kept my blade drawn and lay with it pressed to my ribs, my hand tight on the hilt. The heat from the fire traced across me when I closed my eyes, turned my dreams to amber and orange. In half-sleep, I imagined the weight of an arm draped over my ribs, the curve of a chest against my spine. I woke with my hand outstretched, breathing the elderflower scent of Lux's tangled hair, to find only dust and the faintly glowing coals of the burned-down fire.

By morning, the sky is heavy with a gathering storm, filled by clouds the color of nightshade berries. Ravel leads us through a world that's veiled by mist, where droplets of dew are strung like jewels on every leaf and grass stem. When the faint light catches them, they glint with the cold shimmer of broken glass.

We pass through a copse of dripping trees, then the ruins of another chapel—this one smaller and more decayed, just a vacant window arch and a scatter of lichen-laced stones. Pale shadows crowd close against the broken walls where a thicket of wolf roses has pushed through the foundations.

The back of my neck prickles, and tense sweat breaks out across my palms. I feel it again—the certainty of another presence, that we are being watched. As we move past the ruin, we cross a trail of heavy prints crushed over the heather, the blooms smeared to a ruin of petals by the weight of heavy feet. I pause beside the track, and Briar comes to stand beside me.

There's a torn weft of fur caught on one of the heather branches, a gray so dark it's the color of smoke on lantern glass. I pick it loose, shivering at the feel of it—silken—how it reminds me of when I touched Ravel's hair. "The vespertine are here."

Briar drags the toe of her boot alongside the prints. "Of course they're here. We're in the domain of monsters."

"But they don't hunt during the daytime," I say, swallowing down the note of question that creeps into my voice.

She gestures sharply at Ravel, farther along the path. He's outlined against the sky—his cloak and hair wind-whipped, his shoulders squared as he forges determinedly through the rustling grass. "How do you know he isn't leading us into a trap?"

I pull at the ribbon tied to my braid. "I don't. But he's our best chance—our only chance—at saving Lux."

"Just don't let your guard down." Still glaring at Ravel, she reaches into her pocket and draws out a bundle of freshly bloodied shards. "Here. Make sure you *use* them when you're in trouble next time."

"Don't you mean *if* I'm in trouble?"

"You shouldn't have broken your vows for that creature. We never should have come here." She drags in a breath, then lets out a slow exhale. Quietly, in reluctant confession, she admits, "When Father burned the vespertine we killed, he acted . . . resigned. As though he'd known she would appear." She pauses. Sighs again. "You're right, Everline. He *is* hiding something; I want to know what's there in the Thousandfold. And I want—I want Lux safe, too."

She blushes, and her gaze slides away from me. I slip my hand into my pocket, holding the ribbon-tied shards like a protective charm. Unbidden, the image rises of Lux and Briar asleep beside me on the final night we were all together. The easy comfort of their entwined limbs. The way it hurt to see the softness between them, even though I didn't want to let it hurt me.

Suddenly, my words are tangled up on my tongue, and all I can do is dip my head in an awkward nod. "We're going to find her. I promise."

Briar smiles, rare and unguarded—her mouth tilted up at one side, her front teeth crooked—a detail I always forget, and always find inescapably charming. I'm so used to having her as a rival; this new softness between us is disorienting. It draws out all the emotions I've tried so hard to keep buried, the way in my weakest, most wanting times I look at Briar, and Fenn, and wonder how it might have been if we were an uncomplicated family. True sisters who could share a father without envy.

We fall into step, our shoulders close enough to brush as we make our way across the dew-drenched moor. We're armored and cloaked, our blades polished and our pockets filled with clinking bones. Ravel is ahead, waiting for us beside a sharp outcropping of granite and gorse that falls away to a lower valley beneath.

He leans against a ruined wall, his arms folded and his foot tapping impatiently as we move toward him. He hasn't bothered to wash the paint from his face, and smudges still mark his cheeks, blotches of grayish rouge. The chains of his lariat gleam dully beneath the tarnish when they're touched by the sunlight.

My fingers flex with the remembered weight of those chains laid across my hands. I've never added magic to my armor. I never wanted to. Though I could have asked Lux to consecrate the bones in the pieces I'd forged, it would only have been temporary. My armor has always been a solidly physical thing, a creation of leather and steel and bone that I could make from my own hands. I fell in love with it, this strength that was mine without magic, a way for me to offer something to the wardens in place of my absent power.

Ravel leads us to where the land dips into a lowering swell. I keep my hand on my blade, examining the shadows pooled at the depths of the hollow. The air is eerily still, as though we've fallen into some liminal, held-breath place. A thicket of asphodel flowers spreads around our feet like fallen stars, their colorless petals held motionless.

Ahead, there's a plinth of stone woven thickly with glossy coils of ivy. Beside it, under a curtain of sharp-tipped leaves, a flight of stairs leads down. The opening gapes like a mouth, bordered by broken stones that have the look of fanged teeth ready to snap closed. It's so different from the catacombs beneath the enclave chapel, all dust and gentle candle flames, where the dead are laid in their hallowed alcoves. This place feels alive. It doesn't want us to enter.

Tendrils of shadow creep out from the stones, weaving sinuously among the motionless asphodel flowers. There's no sound but the faint susurrus of wind above the hollow. Somehow, the stillness is even worse than the howls that echoed through the storm outside the chapel ruins.

Vespertine are creatures of the night, hunting beneath a watchful moon. But I can't shake the image of fanged horrors following us down into the catacombs, spilling out of the funereal dark with teeth and claws. A cold shudder scrapes down my spine, and I draw Briar aside. Voice low, I tell her, "I think you should wait here. It will be . . . safer."

She bites her lip, teeth clinking over her piercing, and narrows her eyes to where Ravel has already begun to descend the stairs. "He didn't even bother to wait for us," she huffs. Then, begrudgingly, "I'll stay here and keep watch. And *you*— Be careful, Everline."

"I'm always careful."

Briar rolls her eyes. Then, after a beat of hesitation, she reaches out and tucks back a loose strand of hair behind my ear, and reties the ribbon at the end of my braid into a double knot.

"Listen," she says, voice low. "*Ravel*, that creature—no matter what vow or truce you've sworn, you can't trust him."

"I don't trust him. I *need* him. That isn't the same." I sigh, then take her hand, give her fingers a brief squeeze, feeling the rasp of her sword-calloused palm against my own. "I'll be back as soon as I can."

Tersely, she nods. She takes the lantern from her satchel and passes it to me. I click it alight, then I follow Ravel into the dark.

His cloak billows out behind him, caught by an underground draft. The stairs lead down and down. The heaviness of earth rises over our heads, and I feel swallowed up, devoured. I falter, my hand pressed to the wall, thinking of the stones above, the way they looked like a mouth, all hunger. Ravel continues ahead, and I'm left on my own for a heartbeat of time before I catch up; he turns to me, annoyed, blinking against the sudden light from my raised lantern.

He tilts his head, listening for the sound of Briar's absent foot-steps. "Where's the other one of you?"

"She's keeping watch."

There's a flicker of confusion on his face; then he lets out a rough, amused laugh. "Do you think I mean to trap you down here?" Slowly, he lifts his hand, presses a blunted claw to my lips. "We're vowsworn, Warden. I couldn't harm you even if I wanted to."

My throat goes tight at the feel of his fingers against my mouth. The coppery taste of blood—the memory of his kiss—seeps over my tongue. I swallow thickly and take a step back; his hand falls away. "You're not the only monster out here."

"No, I'm not." He laughs again; then his gaze turns serious. "But I am, possibly, the worst of them. And I've vowed to keep you safe."

His words draw a flush to my skin, a peculiar heat that prickles through my body. I reach into my pocket and clasp the shards, let them press reassuringly against my palm. "I'm not entirely defenseless."

"I've noticed." Ravel gives me a wry look, touching his ribs where I wounded him. Then he turns back to the stairs. "We're almost there."

I follow him the rest of the way down in silence. We pass through a low, carved archway; I bend, ducking beneath the lintel of stone. The floor levels out, and we emerge into a wider space; a single corridor beneath a ceiling of bare wooden struts. I hold up my lantern; the small flame highlights the line of alcoves on either side of us. Each contains a carved stone gravesite.

These are the remains of Nyx Severin's victims, who fell in the violent times before Saint Lenore and her wardens rose against him. When the Thousandfold was not a ruin but a hallowed settlement, built in worship of a monster who everyone believed to be a god. *The Sanguine Saint.*

The catacomb is filled with cobwebs, the gravestones blanketed thickly with dust. As I walk among the tombs, an aching tension knots fast in my chest. In his desperation to unbind himself from the Thousandfold, Nyx Severin devoured his worshippers like a plague through a hive field. It was supposed to be an honor to be called to him, to be granted his divinity. Instead, he carved the faithful up; he cut flesh and pulled teeth, used their blood and bones in his unholy experiments. And when they tried to run, he made the vespertine to capture them and drag them back.

This is why we are wardens. This is why we keep our vows. Yet I—just like my mother—have gone against all the protection afforded us by Saint Lenore and her sacrifice.

Ravel notes my horror-struck expression with unconcealed amusement. "Surely you're not afraid of the dead, Warden, when you wear them so close to your heart? Or do you only feel safe when the dead are monsters?" He looks pointedly at my ribcage bodice, where I've bound a silken ribbon around the broken end of the bone he snapped. His smile sharpens, his voice turning bitter. "Do you carve them up yourself or just pick their bones from the ashes after you burn them?"

I think of all the nights I've spent on the moor with the bodies of vespertine we'd killed, with whetted blades and bloodied hands, as I pared back fur and cut through flesh to unveil bones. Whenever I did this, I'd feel grim and holy—like an undertaker preparing the dead to be interred. We killed the vespertine to keep everyone safe, and the armor I forged from their remains extended that safety, protecting the wardens who guarded the wall.

But it was a solemn, ritualistic task. Not one that felt joyful.

And now, when I picture the vespertine girl—the way she looked when her throat was cut, the weight of her body as I wrapped her with the makeshift shroud—I imagine her blood printed forever on my hands, a stain that can't be scrubbed away. I think of the vision I saw when Ravel and I swore our vow: two children on the moorland, their hands joined as monsters writhed and snarled at their feet.

"Who was she?" I ask quietly. "The girl we killed?"

He stares at me a moment, a muscle feathering in his jaw as he holds my gaze. Then the silence fractures, and he exhales a slow, aching breath. "She was my sister."

"Oh." I falter, all of me as tangled as the snare I set to call him from the dark, to make him my prisoner. "Ravel, I—"

He holds up a hand, cutting me off. "Don't, Warden. I've no wish to speak of her with you."

Before I can respond, he takes the lantern from me and turns away, moving farther down the corridor. The light drags our shadows past the alcoves in grotesque silhouettes as we walk toward the back of the catacombs. Strands of cobwebs drape the corners of the ceiling like bridal lace, and there's a faded hint of clove incense in the air that reminds me of the enclave chapel.

The corridor ends at an alcove that's larger than all the others. It isn't sealed closed. Instead, the bones are laid out in a careful formation, demilune ribs and delicate clavicles, sharp-tipped vertebrae like the ones on the bracers circling my wrists.

Ravel hangs the lantern from an iron hook in the wall and steps back, leaving me alone. At the center of the bone formation is a slender notched shard, once part of a spine. I reach toward it with trembling fingers.

A disorienting familiarity closes over me with the slow creep of a tide. Power creeps from the insides of my wrists, to the hollow of my throat, to the shell of my ears. I feel a holiness that is not holiness, a hideous sense of *right*. Crushed herbs, dripped wax, bitter honey, blackened altars.

I think of my mother, dead at the border of the Thousandfold, her flesh rotted away and her bones strewn through the grass, asphodels wreathing her skull and a tangle of gorse through her ribs. I think of the stolen vision of Ravel and his sister, the way she held his hand so protectively.

Carefully, I take the relic. Untying the ribbon from the end of my braid, I wrap the bone to keep it safe, then place it inside my satchel. "We'll need another," I say. My voice is too loud against the solemn, dust-moted silence. "For Briar."

Ravel reaches past me to unhook the lantern. For a moment,

I'm braced by his arms, the two of us pressed uncomfortably close. He looks at me, eyes gleaming, wolflike. "There are more cata-combs a few days' journey to the north."

I stare up at him, still caught by the feel of the relic's power tracing through my veins like spooned-out honey. The remnants of that magic and Ravel's closeness work a strange kind of spell, and I find myself speaking before I realize what I intend to confess. "I have a sister, too. Briar and I share a father."

Ravel's mouth twitches into an almost-smile. "I guessed as much. You fight like siblings."

"We are, and we aren't. I was raised at the enclave, and she grew up with her mother in the Hallowed Lands. But even when she joined the wardens, our father never treated us like siblings."

"Families are complicated," he says, voice soft with strange understanding.

"She is trueborn and I— Our father broke vows to be with my mother. And I don't think he's ever forgiven me." My heart starts to beat terribly fast. I slip beneath Ravel's arm, needing to get away from this dizzying closeness.

I can't help but wonder if this is some arcane part of the promise we've made, that all my secrets will be laid bare to him. Because in this moment, I want to tell him everything. How I broke my vows and abandoned my watch to search for the Thousandfold. How I want to know the truth about my mother—and myself—as badly as I want to find Lux, to keep her safe.

"It's hardly your fault," Ravel says to my retreating back. "Or is that a warden custom, for a child to wear a father's sin?"

My face burns hot, but somehow there's a relief in speaking

about this with him, like poison cut from a wound. "Not his sin. Perhaps just his guilt. As you said, families are complicated."

The lantern light spills over us, a wash of gold. In this flame-bright glow, Ravel's features are carved out intensely, like he is a statue made for these catacombs: an eldritch funeral guardian. He lets out a breath, pulls a hand through the length of his hair. "Warden," he says, lashes veiling his gaze. "There's something I have to tell you about the magic you want for your armor."

"What is it?"

He sets aside the lantern on a small shelf above one of the alcoves. Slowly, he takes a step toward me. My stomach tightens, and I'm filled with unreadable emotion, a quaver of fear chased by a more fervent sensation that I don't want to look at too closely. "To make the armor . . . I'll need blood."

I touch my pocket, feeling the weight of the shards. I look at him, confused, wary, as I think of Briar with her fingers all pinpricked, sucking a cut on the edge of her thumb. Ravel with his fist clenched around a bone as blood dripped through his tattooed fingers. "Do you not have enough blood to spare for the spell?"

"I could ask you the same question." Ravel's eyes narrow, tracing over my hands. My fingers are calloused, my palms mapped by the thin scars left from whetting my blade, but there's none of the marks that would be on another warden. "You don't have magic, do you?"

"Of course I do."

"No," he says with rising certainty. "You don't. That's why you make your armor; that's why you fought me with chains and

174

blades. Because you have no magic; you have nothing but your own brutality."

I'm stunned into silence for a beat, then anger spirals up to replace my shock. "If I've been *brutal*, it's because you forced my hand when you captured my warden and refused to return her. I've tried to treat you gently—"

"There has been nothing gentle about you, Warden."

"Don't you dare try and claim moral higher ground when you hold Lux captive! When you wore stolen fiolae like *jewels*. If you need blood for a spell, use your own."

"I can't." He's flushed with anger, color bright across his cheeks beneath the smears of paint. Breathing heavily, raggedly, he curls his fingers against his palms in frustration. "Listen. The power I need to enchant a relic—to protect you from the Thousandfold— will take more than a cut finger. It demands a price. If you want my help making your armor, then I need blood that is not my own."

I turn cold, piece by piece, as I stare at Ravel, remembering the way his teeth snapped inches from my throat when we fought. Remembering all the stories Fenn told me—in warning—about Nyx Severin and his cruelty, how he consumed the bodies and blood of his worshippers to gain relentless power.

I feel as though I've been wrapped in a shroud, lost beneath a final, suffocating dark. This is a sin worse than any I've committed. There can be no absolution from this. "You want to feed from me."

Ravel makes a low noise, a muted laugh. He spreads his hands in supplication. "*Want* is a strong word for it."

I trace my fingers against my throat, feel the scabbed remnants of the healing wound left from the other vespertine. *His sister.* Beneath the wound, my pulse beats rapidly. I look toward the door, the stairs that ascend back into the daylight. I could end this right now. I could walk out of the catacombs, back to the asphodel field, and tell Briar to cut his throat. We'd burn him to ash and return to the enclave; I'd confess my treachery to Fenn and hope he didn't exile me to the Hallowed Lands.

And Lux would be lost forever in the Thousandfold—along with all the secrets hidden there. The words she spoke on the night she chose to break her vows with me, when we ran away, come to my mind. Vivid, as though she has whispered in my ear. *Losing* you *would be worse than being disavowed.*

My fingers slide down past my collarbones, curl around my empty glass fiola. Lux's absence runs through me, a depthless ache. To let her go—to lose her forever—would be the worst sin; I love her so much, her life weighs more than all my broken vows.

I take a step toward Ravel, my body turned slow and leaden with the horror of what I'm about to offer. I'm an insect caught in oozing sap, my wings trapped forever beneath hardening amber. "Warden magic doesn't need this type of . . . bloodletting."

"No." His eyes shimmer in the dark, the lines of his face elegant and remote as the carved marble edifices in the alcoves that surround us. "It doesn't. But I am not a warden."

My voice dampens to a hush. "If I agree to this, you can't tell Briar."

"Don't worry. I can keep a secret."

He shifts toward me. Tension is coiled between us like strands of wire. I turn away, staring hard at the nearest alcove as I picture the dead inside the closed tomb, a hollow-eyed skull, femur bones arranged in a reverent arc. These victims of a monster once known as the Sanguine Saint.

I start to fidget with the buckles on one of my bracers. I can't believe I'm truly considering this. When I next speak, the words feel like they've come from somewhere else, certainly not *my* mouth. "How often would you . . . need me?"

Ravel moves a step closer so there's only the barest space between us. The heat of him radiates against my own skin like a fever. "And what if I said I needed you every night?"

"Then I would come to you every night."

My hand is still at my wrist. I slip the first buckle free. Ravel tracks the movements of my fingers with an all-consuming focus. "While your sister sleeps, you'd come with me out into the dark and you would—"

"I *would*. For Lux, I would do anything."

The second buckle is undone. I take off my bracer, feeling the sharpness of the bones against my palm as I put it carefully into my pocket. It clinks against the bundled shards, and for a moment, I think of Briar, the way she looked when she gave them to me, when she warned me not to trust Ravel.

I don't trust him. I need him. He needs me. And it is different. It is worse.

I push back my sleeve. Unarmored, uncovered, my skin feels

as transparent as pattern paper; I am laid bare. Ravel takes my hand. He presses his fingers to the tender inside of my arm, and my breath catches sharply. The way he looks at me makes me feel the same way I did when I held a knife to his throat.

He shifts closer. His voice turns low. *"Everline."*

The sound of my name from his lips carves through me like a blade whetted to a silver-sharp edge. I close my eyes and picture myself on top of the watchtower, seeing a wave of vespertine swarm toward the wall. The bones are blood-slicked, shattered apart. The magic that holds them together has waned to nothingness. This is the moment when my mother ran; she deserted her watch and slipped into the moorland beyond. But I don't run. I kneel down and press my hands to the bones at the very top of the wall. I feel the power dragged from me into the barrier until it is strong enough to force the monsters back.

I start to speak, my words drawn out like I am possessed. Layering sin upon sin, another terrible promise added to the vows I've sworn to this unholy creature. "You will guide me through the catacombs. You will lend your magic to the armor I've made. You will lead me safely into the Thousandfold. And in return, I will feed you."

As soon as I've said it—*feed*—Ravel closes the final distance between us. I stumble back, my spine against the hard stone wall. He catches hold of my wrist, fingers pressed over my pulse. My heart is beating so fast that I'm sure it's about to stop. He looks down at me, his eyes as green as emeralds, and there's nothing boyish about him, not now.

He is only hunger.

He brings my wrist to his mouth and looses a single, heated sigh against my skin. I'm strung tight with anticipation, a fierce, despairing heat uncoiling through me. "Just get on with it, Ravel; for the love of all the Saints, just—"

He bites down.

His fangs are sharp; the swift pain reminds me of the first time I slipped with my thickest needle and pierced my finger. Nothing, then *hurt*. I make a small, whimpering sound and try to move back, but the wall is behind me and Ravel has hold of me, one hand clasped at my hip while the other encircles my wrist.

At first, he holds me tightly, his blunted claws pressing in. Then his touch loosens, and he slides his hand to my waist, stroking my ribs in small, idle circles. His head rests against my shoulder, the spill of his hair mercifully shielding me from the expression on his face. The hurt of his bite starts to fade, replaced by a warmth that spreads up my arm and down through my fingers. It's . . . *pleasant*. I try to push that thought away, but it's no use. I clench my eyes shut, but that doesn't help, either, because now I can feel everything. The rasp of his tongue, the shape of his mouth, the blunted half-moon of his teeth pressed into my skin beneath the sharpness of his fangs.

I hear him swallow and my stomach twists, but it's not with disgust. *He's a monster. He's a monster.* I tell it to myself, over and over, but soon the words become as pleasant as the spike of his teeth in my vein. It's as though I'm delirious with fever, the whole world gone languid and dreamlike and slow.

Finally, finally, he works his bite free. Draws back with a shuddering breath. He's flushed with a look of benediction, otherworldly as holy fire. It's because of me, that glow. My blood is in his veins. My stomach twists again, and I try to shove my thoughts aside. I can't let it in, this realization that I've sinned, that I've fed him.

And that I've promised to do it again and again.

CHAPTER THIRTEEN

EARLY SUNLIGHT COMES THROUGH THE BARRACKS WINDOW, illuminating the faded corners of the room as Briar fixes my hair. A dull, fatigued headache throbs at my temples, in time with the strokes of the brush. I barely slept once we returned from the catacombs, lying restless in my makeshift bed even while Briar kept watch along the newly lit line of wards outside the ruin.

A storm threw itself against the chapel walls, and beneath the wind I heard voices in the dark, cries and howls, formless words that drew an ache from my chest. But when I went to the window and looked outside, there was nothing but the empty moorland, the falling rain, the inescapable feeling of being watched.

Briar finishes with my braids, ties them with a satin ribbon. She leans her chin against my shoulder for a moment, and our faces are reflected side by side in the wavery mirror glass. Our eyes smudged with remnants of black rouge, our lips still paint-stained, our features marked by fear and fatigue. I manage a wan smile at her, then get to my feet and go to finish dressing.

Beside the window, washed in pale light, I put on my armor, fastening the rib-cage bodice tightly around my chest. When I slide my bracers over my wrists, the place marked by Ravel's bite throbs against the pressure of the buckled straps. My skin feels tender beneath the linen bandage I've tied there to hide the mark.

The relic bone is inside my satchel, along with my tailor's shears—the blades resharpened—and my sewing kit. I've kept the bone wrapped in ribbon, but I can still feel the power that clings to it, a distant pulse like a hollowed heartbeat.

Ravel comes to the doorway, dressed for the journey with his cloak fastened over his borrowed sweater and his hair scraped back into a messy knot, tied with a strip of cord. I notice for the first time the tiny steel rings in each of his ears, made of the same tarnished metal as the chains on his armor. He looks at us briefly, adjusting the strap of the satchel he has slung over his shoulder. "Let's go," he says. "Before the storm catches up with us."

We collect our own satchels and follow him down the stairs. It's more than a day's travel to the second catacomb; we will have to spend at least one night on the moors. Outside of the chapel ruins, the sky is leaden, the clouds ominously low. Ravel waits by the iron fence for Briar to take down the wards so he can pass. I stare fixedly ahead, refusing to look at him, though I can feel the heat of his gaze on me.

Once we set off, I slow my steps and let him draw into the lead, staying close beside Briar as we bow our heads against the rising wind. As though if I refuse to walk near him or meet his eyes, the awful truth of what I've promised—my vows, my trust, my *blood*—will vanish.

The sky presses down, a sweep of inky clouds close out the daylight. We're just outside of dawn, the sun hidden behind deep swaths of gray, shadows gathered thickly beneath the ruins that we pass. Overhead, a flock of dark-winged birds flies in a sharply arrowed formation, as if they, too, are desperate to outpace the promised violence of the storm. Their high, wailing cries fill the air and set my teeth on edge.

We follow a narrow track of dry earth that weaves between opaque pools of water. Thickets of heather line the path, all their flowers dropped from the cold and their spindly branches clutched at nothing like desperate, reaching hands. The shadows lie liquid-dark. A velvet cloth, a spill of ink. I catch glimpses of shifting shapes—a sharp, twitching ear, a glinting eye—but when I turn to look, there's only the water, rippling. Only the moor grass, stirred by the wind.

We make our way past a tumbled ruin—an ivy-wrapped wall, a hollowed arch of stone that frames a view of the Blackthorn River. Between wall and arch, something moves, uncoiling like a tendril of ivy dragged loose. Caught by the wind, it reaches farther, higher, until it takes on the jagged outline of a mantled shoulder, an outstretched hand with delicate, elongated fingers.

I falter, my boots sloshing into a quagmire of mud as I stumble away from the path. The hand carves the air with a beckoning motion. My throat goes tight, and I swallow, tasting honey and ash and blood. Then all the fear drains from my limbs and my heartbeat slows, a peculiar calm flooding through my body. I take another step forward. River water seeps over my feet, wicking through my woolen socks.

"Everline?" Briar calls from ahead, and I turn, still feeling slowed and leaden. Every instinct tells me to go into the ruin, let the rest of the world sink away, be swallowed up by the mist. Briar strides toward me, skirting the muddied ground. "What are you doing?"

"The ruin—" I manage. "Something was there."

She frowns, biting worriedly at her lip until her piercing clinks against her teeth. With her hand on her blade, she examines the vacant archway, bordered by rustling ivy, the backdrop of the storm-swollen river. Beyond the leaves and stone, there is . . . nothing. Only the rush of water and the cloud-dimmed light that paints over the moorland in grayish hues. Yet the feeling persists, the undeniable *pull*—the same way I feel when I am close to the relics, to Ravel or his magic.

Slowly, Briar shakes her head, loosening her grip from the blade's hilt. She slips her hand through the crook of my arm and draws me back to the path. I follow her, feeling dazed and uncertain as we continue onward. We fall in behind Ravel, who has his hood drawn up against the worsening rain. Briar keeps hold of me, and when her fingers press against my elbow, I can feel that she is trembling.

We continue on in watchful silence. Whenever we pass a ruin or a windswept copse of trees, I can't help but scan the spaces beneath them, beside them, in search of more pooling shadows, more darkness that will coalesce into a solid shape. Gradually, the ruins and trees become sparser. Everything turns quiet beneath the rain, washed in faded shades of torpor—gray grass, gray clouds, gray light. When we finally sight a derelict, spired building, it seems like a mirage painted on the horizon. With each blink, I'm surprised when it hasn't vanished.

We reach the ruin as the sun sets, the light gone with a softened sigh behind the banked-up clouds. There are two tumbled walls and a ramshackle slate roof that keeps out most of the rain. Briar places a line of wards outside while I set up our tent. There's a small hearth in one corner; Ravel piles up kindling, then waits for me to set the fire with the matches I've kept from the attic lantern.

The wood burns slow and smoky, with more light than actual warmth. We sit beside the flames, and Briar divides up a loaf of black bread. Shivering, we crouch together by the fire to eat like wary, starveling creatures that have hidden from the night.

Briar takes first watch, and Ravel goes to sleep just as he had in the chapel ruins—as far from us as possible, close to the wall, with his face buried in his folded arms. I go inside the tent and lie awake, listening to the sound of Briar's footsteps as she paces back and forth to check the wards. It feels like no time at all has passed before she slips in through the canvas with a rush of cold air.

"Your turn for watch," she murmurs sleepily.

I get up slowly as she unbuckles her armor and takes off her boots. She curls into the warm place I leave behind, pulling the blankets up around her shoulders, and falls asleep so rapidly, it's like watching a heavy stone cast into the deepest part of the river.

I tie the collar of my cloak tighter against my throat, then go out into the ruins.

The fire has dwindled down. I stretch my hands above the remnants of the coals. Around the campsite, the wards make a lighted border, tiny flares of brightness where the shards are stuck in the earth, haloed by the glimmer of consecration. As I watch them, one of the wards flickers, then dims.

I draw the Vale Scythe and move closer to the darkened ward—breath held, heartbeat rising. I take one step, then another, and there's a crackle, a hiss, like the sound of a struck match. The ward starts to glimmer again. I stand over it, thinking of the lantern tied to our barrier near the enclave. But this is just a shard, sticky with blood and honey and tied to a length of silver chain, identical to all the others Briar placed here.

Beyond the ward line, the landscape is impenetrably dark, but for the barest moment, I am sure there are eyes, virulent green, staring back at me from the depths of the night. I can feel the fixed weight of a hungering gaze, a certainty that something solid and real stands just within the shadows.

Then I blink, and it is gone.

Footsteps crunch over the ground; Ravel, stirred awake, comes to stand beside me. He looks out into the darkness. I remember what he said: that he's the worst of the monsters. He has vowed to keep me safe. Whatever creatures lie beyond our wards, we are not defenseless. I tighten my hold on my blade hilt, trying to reassure myself. But I can't shake the feeling of those eyes, that gaze. The way I felt like whatever watched from the darkness *knew* me.

"What did you see?" Ravel asks, his voice soft.

"I don't—" I hesitate, scanning the dark again. Beyond the wards, everything is motionless. "I don't know."

He stays beside me for another moment, eyes narrowed guardedly toward the moorland. A cold rise of wind drags over us; I start to shiver. Ravel glances at me. "You're cold. Come back closer to the fire."

I follow him slowly to the hearth. Everything is hazed, lit palely orange by the dying flames. It feels like we have been shrunk down and put inside the soot-smeared glass of a lantern. We stand together, neither of us speaking, a careful space between us. Then Ravel takes a step toward me. He puts his hand on my arm, above the sharpness of my bracers.

I hesitate, cast a nervous look toward the tent where Briar sleeps. But she hasn't stirred. Ravel and I are alone, with the night stretched out around us, all hushed and shadowed. I loosen the buckles on my armor. I fold back my sleeve. As I offer my wrist to him, I pretend I'm still inside the tent, that I've fallen asleep. This is a dream, one of my childhood nightmares returned. Ravel closes his eyes as he bends to my wrist, and I wonder if he, too, is convincing himself this isn't real.

When his fangs pierce my vein, I swallow back a gasp. I don't want to make a sound.

His thumb strokes my hand; he touches me with such unexpected gentleness. As he swallows down my blood, I'm filled with a longing for something I can't set words to. Beneath the howl of the storm, I imagine that I can hear Ravel's heart, and it's beating in rhythm with my own.

He draws away from me, keeping hold of my hand. Hesitantly,

he takes a scrap of clean linen from his pocket, starts to bind it around my wrist. His cheeks are flushed, mouth dark, as though he has swallowed a draught of holy wine. I pull from his grasp and turn back toward the tent, the untied ends of the bandage trailing down like the ribbon on Briar's blade hilt. All I want to do is flee into the dark, but I force myself to walk slowly.

"Warden—" he calls, voice lowered.

I don't turn. He doesn't try to speak to me again. I sit down next to the tent and listen to Briar's quiet breathing until it's time to wake her for watch. Then I crawl back into the still-warm blankets. I tie the trailing length of linen around the bite, then clamp my fingers over my cloth-wrapped wrist.

Ravel left the barest mark on me; if it were a cut, it wouldn't have even needed stitches. Maybe if I think of it like that—a minor scrape, a training-yard bruise—then it won't feel like such a sin. Exhaustion finally overtakes me, and I start to drift into sleep. But in my last moments of wakefulness, my mind turns treacherous. I think of Ravel lying out near the fire, the taste of my blood still on his tongue.

The hateful longing that overcame me while he fed rises again. Turns me shivering and feverish. I picture time spun back, that I'm out in the encroaching night beside him again, and his mouth is at my wrist. That he holds me close, pulls the ribbon from my braid, trails his blunted claws through my hair. That when he is finished taking my blood, he licks the bite closed, kisses the wound as it heals.

My hand dips between my thighs. I feel ashamed to think

of him this way, to place the vivid image of such a monstrous, unholy creature against the usual faceless daydreams of these tender moments. Yet it's impossible to picture anyone else. I close my eyes, as if I can hide from the truth of my own thoughts. I bite my lip bloody to keep from whispering his name.

CHAPTER FOURTEEN

W E REACH THE SECOND CATACOMB AT SUNSET ON THE
following day. The entrance is set in a cliffside, pressed
against a curve of the Blackthorn River. An arched doorway looms
above the moorland like a hungering mouth, and all around it the
stone is carved as intricately as a scene from a chapel window.

A horde of fearsome creatures; vespertine, with bared teeth
and needle-sharp claws, their shoulders mantled by shards of bone.
Behind them stands a taller figure, the pointed profile of his face
scarcely visible beneath a flowing, wolf-headed cloak. His hand is
raised, his elegant, elongated fingers crooked into a sickled curve,
beckoning to the monsters that surround him.

Nyx Severin, shown in triumph rather than defeat.

I'm struck wordless, caught by inescapable horror. As we make
our way beneath the carved arch that leads into the cliffside, I try
to ignore the way my heartbeat spikes. The cold tremor of nervous sweat that trails down my spine. Nyx Severin is dead, burned

to ashes at the heart of the Thousandfold. This is only a faded memorial, ancient violence written out in stone.

We enter the stone corridor that slants down to the catacombs. I brace for a rush of cold. Instead, unexpected heat rises around us with a steam-and-salt smell that reminds me of the baths at the enclave.

Ravel, noting my expression, tips his chin toward the space ahead. "There's a saltspring in the cavern."

Briar and I exchange a look. We're both filthy, with wind-snarled hair and damp, stained skirts; mud embedded beneath our fingernails. This morning when I awoke, I didn't even put on the clean dress I'd packed in my satchel. I couldn't stand to put fresh clothes over my grime-marked skin.

I turn to Ravel, who looks just as disheveled—his cheeks still gritted with flaking remnants of paint, his inky hair bound back in a tangled knot. "You didn't think to mention this earlier?"

"Should I have?"

"Maybe *you* prefer to be disgusting, but I like to take a proper bath more than once every full moon."

He rolls his eyes, pushing past me to lead the way down. He mutters sullenly, "The full moon wasn't *that* long ago."

Briar clicks our lantern alight. The dance of brightness over the walls paints shapes that look like more of the carvings: wolves and bones and bared, fanged teeth, many-jointed hands with grasping claws. But then my eyes adjust, and I realize the stone here is worn smooth, unbroken except for the occasional clutch of luminous mushrooms or slender, trailing ferns.

A steady *drip, drip, drip* accompanies our footsteps as the path slopes down. The corridor grows summer-warm, perspiration beading at my temples. I run my tongue across my lips and taste salt. The rhythmic sound of water comes from the distance. I imagine a curled-up creature asleep beneath the surface of the moors, their breath sighing back and forth with insidious slowness.

A shimmering cavern is unveiled beneath our lantern light. It's vaulted like a chapel, and spirals of stone hang like icicles from the ceiling. Beneath them is a shallow pool ringed with pale sand. A haze of steam drifts above the opaque water.

We follow the pathway around the pool to another vaulted space. It's narrower than the first catacombs we visited, with two alcoves framing a single, open ossuary. Briar hesitates at the doorway, looking at the gravesites solemnly. She drags her fiola back and forth on its chain as she takes in the reality of this space; the victims of Nyx Severin.

Ravel arches a brow at her. "Feeling squeamish, Warden?"

She glares at him. "No more squeamish than when I look at your face."

I take the lantern from her, and go on ahead, into the depths of the catacombs. In the farthermost alcove, a set of bones has been laid out in a spiraled pattern, like a many-chambered heart. Briar comes to stand beside me. We look at the display in silence, both of us overcome by intermingled awe and horror.

At the very center gleams a spindly length of metacarpal. Even before I've pressed my hand to the relic, I can feel the ooze of power. I draw a length of ribbon from my pocket and wrap the bone, then place it deep inside my satchel. It settles against the other relic. They nestle together, and their magic drones with a steady, lulling hum.

It reminds me of the apiary fields, the prickly, discordant sound of wingbeats. The knowledge that if we weren't careful when we poured the smoke and lifted apart the hives, then the bees would sacrifice their lives to fill our veins with their stinging venom.

I pull my hand from my satchel as a wave of dizzying nausea closes over me. The magic presses down, inescapable though I'm not touching the relics, and my ribbons are tied fast around the bones. I clench my teeth, letting out a panicked breath.

Briar takes the lantern from my trembling hand, and slides her arm around my waist. "It's all right," she says, gently, though her gaze is sharp. "Come away from the gravestones."

My head slumps onto her shoulder. She leads me out of the alcove, back into the warmth of the saltspring cavern. Carefully, she lowers me down onto an outcrop of stone beside the rippling pool. I sigh, raggedly. The satchel falls from my shoulder.

"I just— I need a moment." I lean forward, my elbows against my knees, trying to steady myself. Briar sits down beside me.

Ravel watches us, standing with his arms folded and his back against the wall. He shakes his head, gives me a wearying look. "You know, all this would be much simpler if you didn't *insist* on following me into the Thousandfold."

Briar glares at him, then points toward a corridor that leads deeper into the saltspring cavern. "Why don't you go and take a bath. Everline is right—you're filthy."

With a dry smile, he starts to remove the cord holding back his hair. He cards his fingers through the tangled strands, shaking them loose. As he moves past us, he says to me, "Tip your head back rather than forward. It will help."

I glance sidelong at him, my head still bowed. He reaches out and taps his finger beneath my chin, encouraging me to look up. Then, lazily, he walks away, slipping his arms from his cloak as he vanishes into the second, smaller cavern.

"We should leave that creature behind," Briar says once Ravel has gone. "And go back to the wardens. Surely there must be another way into the Thousandfold that doesn't involve using his wretched magic."

"I'm fine," I murmur, a hand pressed to my face. "Really, I can do this."

With a sigh, Briar puts the lantern down and gets to her feet. I tip my head back like Ravel suggested, irritated to notice that it does help. I'm hopelessly caught between two equally unpleasant choices. To give up, or forge ahead. I hate to rely on Ravel and his *help*, but I refuse to turn back when we've already come this far. When Lux—and the Thousandfold—are so close.

Briar starts to unbuckle her armor, then takes off her boots and her dress and the layers of linen undergarments, leaving everything in a neat pile. She wades into the pool until the water reaches her waist, then takes a deep breath and ducks fully beneath the surface, coming up with her hair loose and streaming. She's brought a comb from her satchel, and she leans back against the edge of the saltspring as she combs her hair, ethereal as a rusalka bride.

Slowly, I start to undress. It feels strange to take off my clothes, knowing Ravel is only on the other side of the wall. As I untie the knot on my sash and set aside my armor, I feel as though I've shed more than layers of lace and ribbon. When I take off my bracers, there's a dark, petaled bruise on my wrist, pinpricked by two smaller marks—left from Ravel's fangs. I keep my arm against my side as I step into the pool, thankful the clouded water hides the damning mark.

Briar holds up her comb. "Let me fix your hair."

I turn my back to her, and she takes hold of the knotted remnants of my braid. She's careful as she unweaves it. The gentle touch of her hands sets an ache in me. As my hair falls around my shoulders, freed from the braid, I tell her, "Lux always did this."

My confession fills the rippling quiet, solemn as a vow. Briar divides my hair into sections, and starts to comb out the knots. She laughs softly, sounding a little embarrassed. "I've always been so envious of you both. For a long time, I was certain you had a secret romance. I asked her about it, the night before she was . . . captured."

I turn to look at her. "You asked Lux about me?"

"I wanted to be sure I wasn't overstepping. With how I feel about her." Briar pauses, casting me a guarded look, her cheeks flushed. Shyly, she goes on. "But she told me you'd never—"

It's such a tenderly delicate gesture, that she would ask Lux what lay between us before she pursued a romance. A part of Briar I'd never thought to see. "No," I say, my voice turned soft. "We never did."

Her comb moves slowly through my hair, still working at the

tangles. "I don't want to replace you. I'd hoped she might have space in her heart for the both of us."

I think of the way Briar and Lux had lain asleep together on that last night in the ruins. "I do love her." My words draw loose, as if a spell has been cast by this place of salt and stone. Secrets strewn like petals on the surface of the pool. "But she was all I had at the enclave. My mother was always lost to me. And Fenn—I never had him at all, not even from the very start. I was so afraid I would ruin what I'd found with Lux, that I would lose her, too. The way things settled between us, I loved her; it was . . . different. It was enough."

Briar stills her combing. "Evie," she murmurs. "We're going to find her. I promise."

I nod, my eyes blurred with tears. "I know."

We finish bathing in silence, then climb out of the water and dry ourselves. In the steam-warmed air beside the pool, we put on clean clothes. My new dress is ivory linen, patterned with a pale running stitch. I'm grateful for the long sleeves that hide my bitten wrist. I refasten my armor, tightening the buckles on my bracers as much as possible. As though the straps of leather can hide my promise to Ravel, hold it in place.

Briar scrunches the water from her hair, then twists it up into a chignon as she moves toward the entrance to the second chamber. "We're done," she calls to Ravel. "You can come out whenever you're ready."

When he walks back through the corridor, the light from our lantern paints over him and, for the first time, I can see him truly unmasked. He's washed away the last traces of paint, revealing the dew-damp flush of his golden skin. His proud nose and the elegant lines of his jaw, the way his lashes fan against his cheeks. We stare at each other for a drawn-out moment; then he takes the lantern and goes toward the exit. Briar and I follow him, my loose hair dripping down my back. I take a cloth from my satchel, scrunch out the water from the strands as we walk.

Outside, the moorland is flooded in dimming orange sunset light. The air feels raw as it scours over my bath-flushed cheeks. Shivering, I go to sit on a flat stretch of stone inside the wards of our makeshift camp. Briar adds more wood to the banked-up fire, and I sit close to the building flames, letting the heat thaw my skin and dry the last of the water from my hair.

Once I'm warmed, I unbuckle my satchel and take out the relics, still wrapped in their ribbons. I brace myself for the dizzying feel of their power. But away from the catacombs, the throb of their magic is less insistent. More a faded hurt than the unbearable sensation of before.

I don't have the supplies for a full set of armor. But I've brought some strips of leather and a short length of chain, enough for a pair of bracers. Briar sits beside me and watches me work with open curiosity. She's never seen me make armor before. I lean back to allow her a clearer view, feeling shyly proud. I measure my wrist—the one unmarked by Ravel—to be sure of the fit, then start piecing out the leather and the chains.

Ravel paces back and forth inside the line of wards, staring moodily at the distance where the river gleams golden, reflecting the sunset. I start to stitch the chain and leather, then find a length of ribbon to use at the closures. The sun melts slowly toward the horizon, and by the time I've made the final stitch on the bracers, early dark has crept up behind the scant clouds.

"There," I say, laying out the armor in my lap. "I'm done."

The bracers are a simple, spare construction—a neat band of leather reinforced with silver chain, ribbons instead of buckles, and a relic at the center of each piece. The different shapes give the armor a wayward, capricious look: The bone I gleaned from the first catacombs is curved like a slender moon; the other piece we just found is sharp, like a captured star.

Briar smiles at me as she traces her finger down the lengths of ribbon. "What a pity you'll have to ruin such beautiful work with vespertine magic."

Ravel comes back from the wards. "My vespertine magic is all that will keep you alive once we're in the Thousandfold, Warden."

"Honestly, I can't wait until we're done with you," Briar tells him, her smile turning to a sharpened grimace. "I'm marking down the hours."

He snorts back a laugh, then crouches beside me. The firelight pools his shadow liquid-dark against the ground and turns his skin to vialed honey, his eyes to emeralds. He's painfully lovely in the same way as a coiled snake or a nightshade plant full of bright, deadly berries. A loveliness that will lure you close so it can poison you.

He takes the bracers from my lap. A still-damp strand of hair is ribboned across his throat. My fingers curl against my palms, itching with the desire to stroke it away from his neck, to let it trace against my skin.

When he goes to return the bracers to me, I shake my head. "I want your magic on them now."

His mouth tilts into a mocking smile. "Don't you trust me, Warden?"

This is the second time the question has fallen between us. *Trust.* "Before we go any further, I want proof that your magic will work."

"Fine. May I use your blade?"

He nods toward the Vale Scythe, still sheathed in my belt. I draw it slowly. My hands are shaking as I pass it to him. His thumb casts against my knuckles as he takes it from me.

Briar watches us, her fingers clenched tight around the hilt of her own blade. It feels like a hallucination, to see the holy weapon once wielded by Saint Lenore in the hands of a monster. Ravel tests the blade before drawing it across his palm, letting it cut him. His blood wells up from the neat slice. Briar gasps.

But I can't make a sound. I'm pinned in place by the sight of him daubing his blood in sticky smears across the relic. Our secret lies between us like a snare of silver chain, the hidden truth that the power he's using is not just *his* blood but mine as well.

When he's finished, Ravel crooks one tattoo-banded finger in my direction. "Give me your hands. Unless, of course, you still don't trust me."

Scowling, I hold out my hands to him. He slides the bracers onto my wrists. As he ties the ribbons, his fingers brush against the sleeve of my dress, over the secret, bruised mark of his bite. I suck in a breath, my eyes shuttering closed.

Ravel leans nearer, his hands clasped around the bracers. I can feel his breath feathering against my cheeks, smell the salt from the baths in his drying hair. He starts to speak in a low murmur. As he casts the spell, his voice has the same inflection as holy speech, like a grim perversion of the vows we speak at our altars.

Slowly, his magic curls around me. Briar puts her hand reassuringly on my nape, her fingers soft against my warden mark. Her touch drags loose a memory. I bite down on it, try to force it away, but I'm lost to Briar's new tenderness, to the dizzying rise of Ravel's power. All I can do is watch the memory unfold.

I'm lined up with the recruited wardens beside the wall. Fenn takes my hand, presses his blade to my honey-smeared palm. The lip of the fiola is cold as it scrapes across my skin, collecting a bead of blood. Consecration glows around us, shimmering like the swarms of fireflies that dance above the apiary fields in summer twilight.

Fenn seals the vial. His hand—clasped around mine—is warm. He's touched every other warden in the same way, but I pretend this closeness is different. I wait for my magic to rise, wondering if this will be the moment when he is finally, finally proud of me. My heart beats so loud that it echoes in my ears. I can hear the *whoosh* of my blood through my veins, like the sound of a flooding river.

But nothing happens. Where all the other wardens felt heat and zeal and strength, for me there is only silence.

When my magic failed, Fenn turned away from me without comment, gaze shuttered, his features as remote as the wall that loomed above us. He went on to the next warden, and I stood clutching my useless fiola as tears spilled down my cheeks. And now, as the memory finally loosens its hold on me, I start to cry again. Hot with shame, I struggle against Ravel, whose hands are still circled around my armored wrists.

"Let me go," I sob, pushing at him. "Let me go, let me go."

I wrench myself free of his grasp. And now there is only power, still on me, still *part* of me, flowing from the blood-smeared bracers and over my body, beneath my skin. It hums with a lulling rhythm. I'm in the center of a hive, slicked with honey, lost in the sugared dark. But this time, it doesn't hurt. In fact, it feels more *right* than any of those disastrous attempts Fenn made trying to awaken magic in me.

And that, somehow, is worse.

CHAPTER FIFTEEN

I PULL THE RIBBONS KNOTTED AT MY WRISTS, STRUGGLING TO untie them. Unfastened, the bracers fall to my lap, the leather still curved in the remembered shape of my arms. I drag my sleeves down to hide the mark of Ravel's bite, then slump against Briar with my forehead pressed to her shoulder. She strokes my hair. Gradually, my heartbeat slows. The magic subsides like blood drawn from a vein.

I sit back, draw a steadying breath. "Well," I manage, "at least we know that it works."

"Really, Everline," Briar huffs, exasperated. "I'll never understand how you so delight in courting danger."

"I promised you I wouldn't do anything foolish. You never said anything about *risk*."

She rolls her eyes. Then, carefully, she takes the bracers from my lap. Holding them warily, she examines the armor, winding the ribboned straps around her hand before she traces her fingers over the larger relic. Then she folds back her sleeves. Arms outstretched, she bows her head, waiting for me to fit the bracers on her wrists.

"Are you sure?"

"Yes," she says grimly. "I'm sure."

I smooth the leather cuffs over her arms. Tie the first ribbon, reach for the second. She catches hold of my hand, her face alight with fierce, determined tenderness.

"I'm sorry," she says. "For the way I hurt you. Fenn pushed you away and wouldn't let you stand at his side, and I hurt you to please him. It wasn't right, the way he's acted, and it wasn't fair. And for my part in it—I'm sorry."

I stroke my thumbs against her calloused palms, feeling the shard scars and the places worn rough from the grip of her blade. "No, Briar. I don't want you to be sorry. It wasn't right and it wasn't fair . . . for either of us."

Tearfully, she nods. I finish putting the bracers on her wrists, drawing the ribbons into a final knot, smoothing down the silver chains. I picture the two of us—my sister and me—armored with relics and vespertine power as we go into the Thousandfold. We'll fight our way past magic and monsters to rescue Lux. We'll look upon the very heart of the place where Nyx Severin rose and fell, where my mother died, the chapel where he was worshipped as the Sanguine Saint.

And when it's all over, the three of us will go back, go *home*.

But then the magic uncoils around Briar in a thickened haze. Like incense smoke. Like noxious poison. Her eyes widen as it washes over her skin.

She starts to scream.

I clutch her against me as she fights to breathe. There's a cry, a howl—the same piercing sound as when Ravel cast his magic over us at the chapel ruins. Briar presses her face to my shoulder as I grasp for her armored wrists. Her nose is bleeding, thick rimes of blood that stream down over her lips and chin. And the sound—the howls and the piercing, inhuman cries—comes again, louder, closer, and *real*.

Frantically, I look to Ravel. He presses in beside me; tensed, alert. Above the swollen river, the clouds have torn apart, baring a stretch of inky sky and a gleaming moon that announces the night. And on the banks below, shapes spill out of the moorland, colored in the same shades of indigo and silver as the lowering dark. Vespertine—dozens of them—clustered together in a starveling swarm, their claws dug sharply into the mud, their tails lashing, their hackles raised.

I turn back to Briar, catch hold of her wrists, fighting desperately to untie the bracers. But my hands are sweat-slick, shaking so much that I can't loosen the knots. The sounds chase one another until they're all woven up and there's no distinguishable voice, only a singular, terrible *howl*. The vespertine surge closer, their teeth bared, and the air is alive with their hideous, feral song.

I'm trembling all over, my heart gone wild—trapped by a heightened, desperate fear. Briar is screaming and the world is hazed with magic, and we are lost, lost to the horror of the dark. I think of teeth and claws, the carving on the cliffside of Nyx Severin as he looms above the swarm of monsters. All I can hear are screams.

I clutch Ravel's arm, pull him close. He turns on me with his teeth bared, a snarl caught low in his throat as he looks between the monsters and me, his gaze made feral, a flush across his cheeks.

"Stop them," I tell him. "Please."

He shakes off my hand and reaches for the Vale Scythe, the blade still stained where he cut himself to draw blood for the spell. "I need bones," he snaps, gesturing to Briar's sword belt, where a strand of beads is tied. "Then break the wards so I can get across."

Gently as I can, I lower Briar to the ground, then unclasp the strand of bone beads from her belt. Forcing it into Ravel's hands, I rush to the ward line, grab for the chain, and drag loose the nearest ward, creating a breach in the consecration so he can pass. He strides through the barrier and toward the creatures with the beads snared around his fist, the relic blade clutched in his other hand. As I run back toward Briar, we exchange a glance—his eyes narrowed, his mouth set—and he gives me a terse nod before tightening the strand of beads across his knuckles.

I kneel beside Briar and start trying, again, to untie the knotted ribbons so I can pull the bracers from her wrists. Ravel cuts his fingers and drags the bone beads through his grip. The vespertine swarm closer. He calls out a stream of words that is lost beneath the howls and the screams and the ruinous magic. In the sky above, the sickled moon turns red, as red as the blood that falls from Ravel's cut hand. A new eclipse that colors the earth in garish light.

The vespertine surge toward him, crossing the river now, the flood-rough water foaming around them. Ravel raises the stained blade of the Vale Scythe. With his hair pulled loose and his cloak caught up by the wind, with his fist dripping a jeweled trail of blood, it's like the image from the chapel window come alive. Nyx Severin—obsidian and eternal—power spilling from him like waves.

The air turns cold. Another sound echoes across the blood-washed night. One I haven't heard before. An oozing, haunting note that sends a splintering ache to my temples, makes my heart pound. Behind the monsters, a translucent shape rises up, a silhouette painted ghostlike against the moors. Tall and spare and almost *human*—as though Ravel has been twinned and is being reflected from the distance. I hold Briar against me, caught by wretched horror. It can't be. It can't—

Ravel carves his blunted claws through the air. The clouds writhe and boil, then sweep over the moon in a sudden rush, blotting out the light.

The world goes dark, and everything falls to an aching silence.

When the clouds part again, the moon is clear, pale as pared bone. The sky is indigo and ink, scattered with tiny stars. The vespertine are gone, leaving the moorland as still and untouched as if they were never here.

Briar has stopped screaming. She lies still, her head in my lap. Her eyes are wide and dark, unseeing. A slick of heated blood streams from her nose.

Ravel comes toward us hurriedly, still clutching the Vale Scythe. He reaches for Briar, slices through the knots on the bracers in two swift movements. The torn ribbons flutter limply to the ground like wilted flowers. He pulls the bracers from her wrists and casts them aside.

"Hells," he spits, "are all wardens so perfect at causing trouble, or is it only you?"

Ignoring him, I unbutton Briar's collar, press my shaking fingers to her throat. Her pulse flutters, faint, in the curve of her neck. With my face bent close to hers, I feel her shallow breath against my skin. Her chest rises and falls in a movement so slight, that it's barely there.

Ravel opens our water flask and pours some into his cupped hand, then splashes it against Briar's wrists where the bracers have left black-veined welts, clambering in poisoned tendrils over her bloodless skin. He rubs at the marks, muttering beneath his breath. I watch helplessly as he tends to her, still seeing the monsters that surged out from the dark. The impossible hallucination that rose behind them.

Nyx—but he can't have been there. He is bound to the Thousandfold. He is dead.

"I saw—" I begin, then Briar chokes out a desperate breath. I slip my arm beneath her shoulders, hold her steady as Ravel closes his hands around her wrists, his tattooed fingers taking the place of armor.

Eyes closed, he bows forward. He's tensed, focused—a deep line cut between his lowered brows, beads of perspiration at his temples. He drags his thumbs over her pulse points, smearing his blood on her skin. Finally, he sits back with a ragged sigh. The welts on Briar's wrists have faded to softened bruises; the clambering tendrils are gone. But she's feverish, shivering at the kiss of the twilight wind on her cheeks. I stroke back her hair, lay her down gently onto the crushed moor grass.

Ravel glares at the river; the chaos of churned tracks the vespertine have left in the mud, the now-vacant horizon. "I can't take you into the Thousandfold if she reacts like this."

I stare up at him, incredulous. Anger winds through me like a fast-growing vine, spreading glossy leaves over all my fear until I'm flushed and furious. "That's all you have to say about what just happened?"

"What *should* I say, Warden?" He spreads his hands in a gesture of surrender, but his teeth are set, his expression fierce. "Did you think this would be easy?"

I get to my feet, my hands clenched to fists, my nails dug sharply into my skin. We stare at each other, and the air is crackling, electric, a lightning storm of emotions brewed in the space between us. With effort, I force my hands to unclench. Wipe my sweat-damp palms over my crumpled skirts.

Briar lies prone on the ground, her eyes still closed, lost in too-deep sleep. "I need you to carry her to the tent," I tell Ravel, and the words seem to come from someone else, somewhere far away.

Silently, he lifts Briar into his arms. He's gentle, and that should make me grateful. Instead, I hate him for it. I hate the sight of her curled against his chest. The soft flutter of her lashes and the way her legs drape over the crook of his elbow. All I can think of is Ravel carrying Lux away from me, his face impassive behind the skeletal bones of his mask.

The waning firelight draws our shadows across the ground as we walk toward the tent. My mind drifts far away. I have floated into the mist-draped clouds, alongside the crying birds, where I can see myself, my pale-threaded dress and my unbound hair. I see the jagged ruins and the storm-swollen river, the moorland with tangles of gorse and the dying heather blossoms. The curve of the cliff face carved with the image of Nyx Severin, so like that impossible vision I saw in the crimson-lit distance.

I open the tent, and Ravel lays Briar down—still gentle, still careful. The air is scented with the promise of rain as the dark creeps in. Overhead, layers of stars glint among the scraped-back clouds. He pauses beside her, his head bowed. And despite his gentleness, the sight of him so close to her prone body fills me with restless anger.

I push past him and squeeze into the tent beside Briar. "Go away," I snap, then pull the canvas closed. From the opposite side of the fabric, I hear him sigh with irritation. His footsteps crunch heavily over the ground as he retreats.

I unlace Briar's boots and take them off, then find a clean handkerchief and try to wipe the blood from her face. She stirs a little as I press the folded cloth beneath her nose, lashes fluttering wanly against her cheeks. Her brow creases, and she makes a hurt noise. I wonder if she is picturing the Thousandfold, filled with all the terrors that spilled onto the riverbank, set to devour us.

I put aside the cloth and take her hand. I've so rarely touched her this way—with kindness, to give comfort—yet it feels so right, so familiar. Her scarred fingers, the way her roughened palm is calloused from her blade hilt, just like mine. I want to say something, but when I search for the words to reassure her, to make everything right, all I can think is, *There's no other choice.*

When I come out of the tent, Ravel is beside the fire, staring moodily into the flames. I notice that he's made coffee; our metal moka pot sits over the coals at the center of the campfire. Tense silence draws out between us. Not the crackling fury of before, but a quiet like the space between storms when the clouds have passed. When another, darker front blooms in the distance.

The moka pot starts to bubble, the plume of steam from its top interrupting the stillness. Ravel reaches to the fire with a cloth around his hand, takes the pot from the coals, and pours fresh coffee in two waiting cups. "If you want to rest," he says, "I can take first watch."

I shake my head. "No. I'll stay up."

"The vespertine won't come back—not tonight." He looks at me, guarded, from beneath the fall of his hair. "I vowed to keep you safe, remember."

I think of his earlier question; when he asked if I trusted him. He's proved the strength of our promise, rushed unhesitatingly to fight the creatures that surged from the dark. His power was enough to wash the bloodied light from the moon. It's overwhelming. He truly is the worst of the monsters, the strongest. And right now, I know I'll be safe with him here. But I'm still wound tense from my earlier panic, my breath unsteady and my heartbeat blurred as the fear subsides into my body. I don't want to sleep, don't want to be alone.

I reach for one of the cups, take a sip of coffee. It's black and perfectly bitter, burning my throat as I swallow. Clutching the cup between my hands, I stare at the fire as the flames lick slowly over the scraps of wood.

"Oh, what a mess I've made," I sigh. "Sometimes, it seems I can't do anything right. At the enclave, Briar was always so capable; she made it look effortless to keep vows. All I've ever wanted was to be more like her so that Fenn—our father—would see *me*, rather than only seeing what I wasn't. Instead I've done the opposite."

It's as though I'm still caught in the spell of confession from the saltspring cavern where Briar and I whispered our secrets. Now, I'm laying myself bare to Ravel. He regards me for a moment, the silence changed to a deeper, more unreadable hue. Then he takes the cup from my shaking hands and sets it aside. He shifts closer, his knee pressed to mine.

"It was the same with my sister," he says, a wistful laugh in his voice. "She was the perfect monster; everything I wasn't. No matter how hard I tried; I couldn't match her. Our father loved her best. She was the mirror he held up, a reflection of what I'd have to become if he were to love me, too. The chain you took—those fiolae—were a gift from him. I think he wanted to remind me how I'd need to be ruthless to survive in this world."

It's all so familiar—rules and duty, a love that must be earned. Fenn placing the Vale Scythe in my hands by way of answer when I asked him about my mother. I curl forward, covering my face as my breath comes loose in a drawn-out, hopeless sigh. Tentatively, Ravel puts his hand on my back—moving slowly and carefully, as though I am a danger, a wild creature with teeth bared and claws unsheathed. And I feel that way—lost beneath this rise of emotion, ready to flee into the darkness, to hide beneath the barren stretch of the carved cliffside.

But there's something in the warmth of his hand between my

shoulders, the way he touches me, that keeps me still. I think of his sister, the fierceness with which she fought, the way she stared at me as Lux cut her throat. How her last sight was of my wide-eyed shock, how my neck will always bear the marks of her claws.

I look at Ravel, haloed golden by the firelight. The grief that lies between us is a shared, palpable ache. "What was her name— your sister?"

His fingers press against my spine, a memory of flexing claws. Quietly, he says, "Hazel."

Hazel. A girl, a perfect monster, a vespertine who was dead at our hands. Who burned to ash in the hive fields outside of the enclave while Lux tended the wounds she left on me.

Questions rise, cloying against my tongue, like a spoonful of golden honey that's been laced with poison. I remember the vision I had when Ravel and I sealed our vow—a boy with his sister, two children on the steps of a ruined chapel, surrounded by monsters. I want—more than anything—to know the whole truth of him. To draw him apart like a ruined seam, have his secrets revealed to me stitch by broken stitch.

But this moment feels so tenuous, with only the thinnest line of trust between us, a single thread drawn taut. I'm so afraid if I question him further, this trust will be broken.

"I'm sorry," I tell him. "I'm sorry we killed her."

Ravel glances at me, and I see his warring grief and hurt, anger tinged with sorrow. I take his hand, my fingers trembling. Wishing I could place us back on either side of the ward-line, retreating to a past where Lux is safe and Hazel alive. He reaches up—uncertainly—to touch my cheek. His thumb strokes a gentle arch against my jawline. My lashes flutter, my eyes dipping closed.

His voice turns quiet, and there's a softness to his words that reminds me of how it felt to see his face, unmasked, for the first time. "You're not alone in this, Warden."

Never has the vow we swore to each other seemed more real than in this moment. I swallow, tasting blood, the memory of the kiss that sealed our promise. "If I'm not alone, then . . . neither are you."

He runs his fingers along my spine, back and forth, back and forth. A motion as delicious and soothing as ripples across the surface of a still pool, spreading from a dropped stone. We breathe together, my own breath instinctively slowing down to match his. Even and rhythmic. The fire sparks and crackles beside us. My body feels weightless, somnambulant, as though I'm still back in the tent with Briar and this is nothing but another dream.

I slide my fingers into his hair, tangle them through the inky, silken strands. Ravel makes a helpless sound, his eyes sunk closed, his lips parted. For the first time, I notice that his sharp-tipped eyeteeth are uneven—crowded forward, like they grew in too soon. His hand slides to my waist, drawing me closer.

I expect him to take charge, for his blunted claws to scrape my skin or his fingers to knot in my hair, unrelenting—the way he was when we fought. I can feel the fierceness of his held-back strength, the same simmering heat and power I felt in the relics, in the armor, in his magic. Instead, he's leashed in how he touches me, with such hesitance that it stirs me to delirium, to the same feverish moment I had when I touched myself and imagined his mouth against my bitten wrist.

I press my face to his shoulder, my eyes shut tight. I want to run—but whether toward him or away, I don't know. Helplessly, I whisper against his throat, "This is a sin."

His mouth rasps my cheek, too brief to be a kiss. "I know sin, and this is nothing close to it."

I reach to my chest, curl my fingers around my fiola as I try to ignore my persistent thoughts of his fangs in my flesh. The shiver of longing that follows. "I didn't think your kind *had* sin."

By way of answer, his hand slides down my arm; then his fingers trace the buttons on my sleeve. With deliberate slowness, he unhooks them, easing them one by one from their silken loops. Slowly, he unwinds the linen bandage from my wrist. The bruise hidden beneath is shaded petals of deepest blue, an iris bloomed under my skin. Ravel stares at the mark, his teeth dragging over his lower lip. I wonder if he noticed it last night when we stood in the shadows, his eyes heavy-lidded, his mouth on my desperate pulse.

He raises my wrist to his mouth. A small, desperate sound escapes me, and I'm dizzy with emotion, overcome with a wanting that is equal parts desire and disgust. I tense, waiting for his bite, but he doesn't move. Instead, he sighs, casting a heated shudder across my skin. Then he draws back.

We look at each other, and something passes between us, unnameable and transient as the most arcane spell. The world turns still—even the flames beside us cease their motion.

Suddenly this—whatever *this* is—feels like a mistake. We made a truce, and the terms were clear. His life spared in exchange for safe passage into the Thousandfold. My blood given in exchange for his magic. The vows we swore did not involve this—fervent touches and stolen half-kisses, such illicit closeness.

As if in unspoken agreement, we both uncoil, pulling away. "You really should rest," Ravel says, turning back toward the fire. I'm so unused to seeing him this way—without a mask, or paint, or any artifice. But still so clearly a monster. "I can keep watch."

I fold my unfastened sleeve back down over my wrist, then get to my feet. I go toward the tent with my hands clutched in my skirts, fighting the urge to look back. Wretchedly, I think of how I felt when I set out from the enclave. That night, when I abandoned my post and ran into the moorland dark, I was so *certain*. Even the vows I'd broken—my disobedience to Fenn and betrayal of the wardens—was justifiable.

As I slip into the tent and curl up beside Briar, I wish that I could feel so sure again. No matter what uneasy truce I've made with Ravel or the promises we've sworn, there is only one way for this to end. Once Lux is safe and we've made our way out of the Thousandfold, I'll be Everline of the wardens—perhaps in disgrace or exile, but still bound in blood to the enclave and all it stands for. And Ravel will be a vespertine—remnant of the horrors wrought by the creature once known as the Sanguine Saint.

We'll be back on opposing sides of a line drawn across the ground.

Enemies, as we were before.

CHAPTER SIXTEEN

We return to the ruined chapel at nightfall, as dusk folds lilac mist over the moorland. Though it was always the plan to travel this way after our visit to the second catacomb, to replenish our supplies before we searched for the next relic, our return still feels like a retreat.

As we follow the same path, in reverse, I can't help but seek out landmarks. The first place we camped, where I stared at the fire as Ravel's teeth sunk into my wrist. The ruin with its hollowed arch and shrouding ivy vines, the memory of ominous darkness, an impossible shape, a hand beckoning to me.

All around us, where the trees cluster their windswept branches, where jagged stones rise from the moorland, the shadows are heavy. I keep the Vale Scythe drawn; Briar and Ravel hold bloodied shards. The dark feels watchful, laden with crouched and hidden things, monstrous eyes that track each step we take.

Finally, the chapel rises in the distance. We set a circle of freshly consecrated wards around the ruin, then Briar and I trail upstairs. For the first time, we spend the night in the barracks room. My last thought before I sink into dreamless sleep is of the wards below, gleaming like candles at an ossuary.

But even with the exhaustion of the journey, I still wake before dawn the next morning. The bed where Briar slept is empty. She's on the other side of the room, kneeling beside her satchel as she packs it sparely, with only the barest items—a clean dress, a field kit, a length of silver chain.

I sit up slowly; she turns at the sound of my rustling blankets. The room fills with drawn-out silence. Briar is dressed and armored, her lips freshly painted with black rouge. The only hint of the terror that overcame her at the second catacomb—her bloodied nose and blurred gaze, her endless screams as the vespertine surged from the dark—is in the faint shadows beneath her eyes, the mournful edge to her smile.

"I have to go back," she says, her voice turned soft. "Back to the enclave."

The early daylight turns everything veiled, surreal. I feel as though I'm still asleep. "What—what do you mean?"

"I can't use the vespertine magic. Not in the way you can. Maybe I could build resistance, with time, and wear the armor. But Lux needs us now. She needs *you*." Slowly, Briar gets to her feet and comes toward my bed. "You have to go on without me."

I stare at her, feeling helpless. When I left the enclave on the night of the blood eclipse, I intended to be on my own—I didn't want to put Lux, or anyone else, in danger. I was willing to risk my vows, my life, in search of the truth. But since then, everything has changed. And the picture I've held in my mind is of the three of us—Lux, Briar, myself—emerging triumphant from the Thousandfold.

"We can find another way," I murmur, but Briar is already shaking her head.

She picks up a ribbon from the dresser and starts to braid her hair. "This *is* another way. You'll find Lux; I'll go to Father and ask for reinforcements." A sigh escapes her painted lips, and she pulls the ribbon into a knot. "I hope he'll listen when I tell him what we've seen."

I think of the monsters that hunted us. Ravel facing them down at the edge of the flooded river, using his magic and my warden blade to drive them back. How Fenn tried to evade my questions, the resignation in his eyes when we brought the changed vespertine—Ravel's *sister*—back to the enclave.

"I have something you can use as proof." I get up, cross the room to where I left my clothes when I undressed last night. Searching through the pockets of my cloak, I take out the chain of stolen fiolae. The vials chime together when I hold it up, the chain shimmering silver through the tarnish as it drapes from my hand. "Ravel was wearing this when I captured him. Show it to Fenn, and he'll not be able to deny what's out here. He knows— I'm certain he does."

Briar looks at the fiolae, wide-eyed and silent. Carefully, she takes them from me, folds them inside a cloth before placing them into her satchel. Her chin trembles, her eyes are bright; her expression reminds me of all the times I've been hurt and fought hard not to cry because I wanted to look brave. "I should leave now," she says. "So I don't waste the daylight."

I blink back the blurring rise of my tears. Already it feels like another lifetime ago that we approached the cliffside, that we went into the luminous saltspring and sat like water nymphs with our hair loose, whispering secrets to each other. I want to pin Briar here, stitched close beside me, and refuse to let her go. I can't do this; I can't face this alone.

But there isn't another choice.

"Wait," I tell her. "I have something else for you."

I push aside my clothes and find my armor, the rib-cage bodice with a ribbon tied around its broken edge. Briar looks from the armor to me. Her mouth curls into a tremulous smile. She takes the bodice and slips it over her dress. We're both crying now, heated tears that drip slowly over our cheeks; neither of us moves to wipe them away.

As Briar puts on the armor, I think of Lux and me in the shadow of the wall, the rituals we performed each time we left the safety of the enclave. I reach for Briar in the same way, adjusting the ribbons and the buckles of the bodice until the fit is perfect. We look at each other for a brief moment; then I draw her into my arms.

She buries her face against my neck. I breathe in the scent of her hair—clove incense, flower petals, the lingering salt from the springs—and I imagine all the foolish and untroubled seasons we might have spent together if things were different.

Briar wipes her tears against her sleeve, then puts on her cloak, tying the ribbons tight at her collar. She picks up her satchel and, together, we walk out of the barracks room.

Our footsteps echo on the stairs with a hollow sound as we go down into the entrance hall, making our way to the arched front door with its panels of inlaid bone and its pearl-smooth handle made of polished femur.

We stand framed on the threshold as air sweeps past us into the ashen quiet of the chapel. Briar glances, waveringly, toward the path that leads toward the enclave. "I'll need to cross at the Moongate now that the river has flooded. But I will travel as quickly as I can."

"I'll wait for you here after I've found Lux. I'll bring her back safely for you, I promise."

She adjusts the strap of her satchel, then gives me a serious look. "Take care of yourself, Evie. And remember—whatever vows you've sworn to that creature, he's still a vespertine. Keep the shards I gave you close by. Don't let your guard down."

I take her hand, hold it tightly between my own. "Goodbye, Briar."

She presses her lips together, a fresh rise of tears welling in her eyes. Solemnly, she turns away, her cloak caught up by the wind, the early daylight casting streaks of gold in her hair. I watch her grow smaller and smaller, a single warden with only my armor and her magic against the terrors of the dark. And, as though I'm casting a spell, I send out a vehement hope that the monsters in the night will pass her by. Let them come for me and only me, and spit out my bitter blood, and choke on my sharpened bones.

The path slopes down, and Briar disappears behind the swells of undulant moorland. Everything lies motionless, as though the barrenness of the landscape means to emphasize her absence. Quietly, I close the doors and, with a finality that aches like mourning, I think to myself, *We had only just begun to feel like true sisters.*

Ravel is asleep beneath the stained glass window at the other end of the chapel hall. Light slants down through the glass in shades of onyx and crimson, a bloodied hue reminiscent of the eclipse, the way the world ran red. I stand above him, feeling querulous—he's curled on his side with his fist pressed against his mouth, his expression peculiarly innocent.

I put my hand on his shoulder. He stirs awake at my touch, regards me blearily from beneath his ink-dark lashes. "Briar has gone back to the enclave," I tell him. "You and I will go on together without her."

I turn to leave, but Ravel reaches for me. "You don't have to run away," he says, his voice roughened from sleep. He pauses; his mouth tilts into a faint smile. "Unless you want to."

Without Briar, the full truth of our bargain is laid out before us, and it frightens me. I'm as alone with him as I was on the night in the attic, but now there are no chains or locked doors. Only our promise, sealed in blood and holiness. "No. I don't want to run."

He sits up, dragging a hand through his hair as he smothers a yawn. Then he makes room for me on the bench. I lower myself down beside him. We're not touching, but the knife blade of space between us feels electric, ominous. I fold my hands in my lap—stare down at them, my chipped nail polish, the healing scrapes across my knuckles.

"She needn't have left," Ravel says. He considers me for a moment, pensive and curious. "Tell me, Warden. Why are you so determined to enter the Thousandfold?"

"Because it's where I was born." I start to tremble, feeling weightless and dizzy as my secret lifts from me. "And it's where my mother died. My father would never tell me why she was there or what happened when I was born. Only that she deserted her watch and that I should take care not to break my vows in the same way."

"Is that why your father is so set on you proving yourself as faithful?"

I start to laugh, the sound catching in my throat. "He was right to worry. Look at me." I spread my hands wide, my palms upturned. "All I've ever wanted was to be a true warden, but treachery is in my blood."

Ravel looks down at my outspread hands. For the barest moment, his face turns terribly sad—a tucked-away hurt that doesn't belong to me. "Do you believe we're all destined to repeat the mistakes of our parents, that we can't outrun the legacies we've inherited?"

"I—I don't know."

His mouth softens, his smile turning weary. "It's something I've wondered for a long time. My father, too, was certain I'd repeat the mistakes of my blood. My *human* blood."

Limned by the chapel shadows, all I can see of Ravel are the features that are decidedly other. His fangs, his ethereal loveliness, his blunted claws. Then the light shifts, and I note the softness in the curve of his cheek, in the silk of his hair.

I put my hand on him. A muscle in his forearm twitches beneath my touch. He stares determinedly ahead. I feel the same way I did the night I unmasked him, trying to piece together what I know of him with what I know of the vespertine.

And like then, all I can ask is the same question. "What *are* you?"

His jaw goes tight, and there's a flush across his cheeks, as though he's ashamed. "I'm exactly what you've always believed me to be: a monster." With a rough sigh, he gets to his feet and paces over to the ossuary beneath the stained glass windows. He lays his hands against the bones, his arms spread wide, head bowed like a suppliant. "Hazel and I were orphaned in the Hallowed Lands when the vespertine broke through the wall. They killed our parents and took us captive. And our father—our *new* father—did his best to raise us in his image."

I think of the figure beside the ruins on our way to the second catacomb. The image that shimmered translucently against the dark behind the hungering surge of vespertine. Familiar and impossible. The unshakable feeling I've had, that something has watched me the entire time I've been on the moors. Shuddering, I look up at the window, at the depiction of Nyx Severin—a bone shard clutched in his fist and power spilling, ruby-bright, from his hands. "You mean . . ."

Ravel turns to me, and the shape behind him transforms—no

longer obsidian glass and lead-light panels but a shadow cast by Ravel himself, twin to the silhouette of Nyx. Realization slams into me, sharp and brutal: why he wore the skeletal mask with the razored horns, the gruesome corpsepaint that disguised his boyish features. He wanted to look less human, more like a monster. More like . . .

"Yes," he says, solemn as a vow. "My father is the Sanguine Saint."

My hand goes to my waist—a reflex—but I'm unarmed, clad only in my underdress, my armor and blades upstairs in the barracks room. I go cold with dread, suddenly aware of how soft I am, how breakable—flesh and blood and *girl*. I want to flee, but terror holds me in place, caught like a rabbit in a snare.

"He's dead," I whisper—as though the lifeless image above us might be able to hear me. "Saint Lenore sacrificed herself to destroy him."

But even as I speak, I know this isn't true. That the blurred, haunting figure I saw out on the moorland among the shadows and the mist was not my imagination but undeniably, hideously *real*.

Ravel gives me a rueful smile. "It takes a lot to kill a god, and even a girl with aspirations of Sainthood is not that powerful. But she did leave him . . . changed." He takes a careful step forward, but when I flinch, he goes still. "Do you know why Nyx experimented on his worshippers?"

Haltingly, I nod. "We were taught that he could only exist fully inside the Thousandfold. He wanted to free himself, to gain enough power to leave the borders without losing his strength. So he took blood and bones from his worshippers, trying to craft the spell. But before he got close, they discovered the truth and revolted against him."

"Yes," Ravel says quietly. "And the final attack by Lenore left him weakened—not dead, as you've been led to believe. Afterward, he needed the help of someone more powerful than a vespertine, more loyal than a worshipper. And so—" Ravel smiles, rueful and bitter. "Nyx Severin became a father."

I stare at him—this monster, this boy—as he shatters the vital tenets that have been my entire existence. And all the whispers I've heard of Fenn's return to the enclave after my birth make hideous sense.

The way he walked into the chapel hollow-eyed and blood-stained, the way he refused to discuss what had happened. This is the truth couched in the silence he laid between us, the distance he refused to let me narrow. Whatever he saw that night in the Thousandfold when I was born and my mother died and the sky turned red—*he knew*. He knew that Nyx Severin was still alive.

"Nyx is still trying," I say, so overcome by dreadful certainty that it's not even a question. "He's still trying to release himself from the Thousandfold."

Ravel bows his head. Palings of light from the window gleam through his hair like rivulets of darkened blood. "He's tried for my entire lifetime—and Hazel's, as well—to perfect his new spell. We were vital to his process."

"He *experimented* on you?"

At my open shock, Ravel starts to laugh. There's a keen edge to the sound, his ire like a newly sharpened blade. "Did you think he raised us out of tenderness, Warden? He wanted children who were monsters, and as he refined his magic, we became just that."

Ravel and Hazel were once the children I saw in the vision when we made our vow, two children facing down a sea of monsters. They *became* those monsters, their humanity stripped away. Ravel's earlier comments about legacy and destiny now have a wretched second meaning.

I get to my feet and move toward him, my eyes fixed intently on his face. I think of the toothy scar nestled in the curve of his ribs, the way his fangs look as though they grew in unnaturally quick. He speaks of his origins with a mix of pride and shame, the same conflict that stirs within me when I face my own past.

I glance again at the image of Nyx in the window glass, the obsidian outline a clear echo of the figure I saw when the vespertine attacked our campsite. "Your father must know that you're helping me. I've seen him—he's watched us, followed us. What will happen when we enter the Thousandfold?"

"When we enter the Thousandfold, you will be under my protection. I will take you there in daylight, guarded by my magic. You will be safe with me, Warden. I promise." Ravel takes my hand and holds it gently. His thumb rasps over the center of my palm, tracing my heart line. "That was the vow we swore, bound in the power of my father's own blood. I won't let him hurt you."

Unbidden, my gaze drags over Ravel's mouth. The memory of his bloodied kiss is like the touch of a ghost. I start to recite the words of his promise, spoken at the edge of the Blackthorn River.

"'I swear by the blood and the power of the Sanguine Saint that you'll have my trust.'"

"Yes," he says, in barely a whisper. "You'll have my trust. And do I have yours?"

He's coiled so tight with tension that I can feel him tremble. I've confessed the truth of my past—of my birth—and he's offered his own secrets in return. We've laid ourselves bare to each other, and I'm struck anew by the way everything is undeniably connected—my mother, myself, Nyx Severin, all the secrets of the Thousandfold.

If I've any chance to rescue Lux and discover, once and for all, what lies buried in the heart of those ruins, then my only choice is to trust Ravel and the vows we've sworn.

Slowly, slowly, I reach toward him. He goes utterly, helplessly still as I trace my fingers across his throat. The place where he cut himself, to cast the spell that lured Lux, has now healed to the barest scar. He swallows, I feel the stilted motion. "Warden—" he says, tender and desperate.

My hand slides up to cradle his jaw. When I press my fingertips to the corner of his mouth, every piece of him draws tight—like a string set to snap. I trace my thumb across his lips, an echo of how he sealed our promise with a smear of blood.

Shakily, I start to unfasten the ribbons that lace my collar. I push my hair aside, letting it fall behind my shoulder. "Yes," I tell him. "You have my trust."

Ravel's gaze runs over my bared neck. He looses a ragged breath, realizing my intention. A hot rush of emotion crosses me, so conflicted that I can't parse it out. Shame and fear and beneath it all—*want*. I want this. To draw him close. To tuck back my unbound hair, to offer my throat to him.

For a moment, I think he means to refuse. Then it's like we're being pulled together by an otherworldly force, a connection that neither of us can resist. He takes my shoulders and guides me toward the ossuary so that we've traded places; he stands before me while my back is pressed to the ancient, layered bones. He leans close, I feel the heat of his exhale against my skin. The world condenses to the sound of his breath, the spill of his hair against my cheek. He smells like ash and incense, like an altar.

His teeth skim down the curve of my neck. The touch is so unsettlingly gentle. Then there's the pierce of his fangs, the sting of his bite, and all the gentleness is gone.

"Oh—" I gasp, unable to stop the sound. I curl my hands into fists, close my eyes, and try to go still. But it doesn't help. I knew what this meant when I offered. Yet I hadn't wanted to look too closely at the truth. Now, there's nowhere to hide from it—the heat of his tongue as he licks away the blood, the loud punctuations of his swallows. I'm shaking; I'm falling.

I reach out heedlessly; my hands tangle in the cloth of his shirt. I can feel the burning heat of his chest as though there's nothing between us. My knuckles are pressed hard against the rapid beat of his heart, the shudder of his ribs.

Ravel draws back for a moment, his mouth above my aching pulse. A trickle of blood seeps from the bite. He licks at it, his tongue rasping over my skin. I think of how wretchedly I wanted this, for him to kiss my healing wounds. "Don't stop," I murmur, delirious with heat and longing. "Please—"

My hands are still clutched in his shirt. I drag him closer, wanting to erase the last distance between us. He catches me by the waist and presses me back against the ossuary. He nudges his way between my thighs until his hips are pressed to mine. I curl toward him, my whole body a traitor, my heart gone wild as heated desire turns my bones to melted honey.

His bite goes deeper, becoming an intense, bright pain that edges on pleasant. It hurts and then it doesn't. My breath stutters out in panting gasps, a wanting, eager sound that I can't hold back. There's a hidden ache far down within my belly, in the very pit of me.

I press myself even closer against him, and my hand slides beneath the thin fabric of his shirt, my fingers tracing the scar nestled in the curve of his ribs. It's sharp-edged, like thorns stitched to his skin. I can feel the unsteady catch of his breath, the raised staccato of his heartbeat against my hand.

Ossuary bones press my spine, hard and cold. The knot inside my belly coils tighter and tighter. Stars dance behind my closed eyes. And as Ravel Severin profanes me beneath the image of his father, I don't know if this is a communion or rebellion, but either way—I'm lost.

Whatever vestiges of humanity he might have, he's still a monster. His very existence is unholy. And yet, right now, with his teeth in my throat and his body pressed to mine, trembling and feverish . . . everything feels so *right*.

I thread my fingers into his hair, the strands knotted through my grasp, and let out a ragged moan that turns to his name. *"Ravel."*

He works his teeth gently free of my throat. He sighs, then lifts a shaking hand and touches my cheek. His pupils are blown wide, his eyes full of a strange, dark hunger that has nothing—or everything—to do with my blood.

We stare at each other, both of us breathing heavily, as though we have been fighting. It's like the first time we clashed, except that was all sharp claws and his hands on my wrists, poisoned berries crushed between his teeth.

And this—this is soft, soft, soft.

His lashes cast umber shadows against his cheeks as he bends to me. Even his breath is soft as he sighs against my mouth. Then his hands shift from my waist to the altar, and he shoves himself back—holding himself braced with his arms on either side of me, as though to force himself to keep his distance. The space between us is a fragile thing—one wrong motion and the world will shatter.

"Tomorrow," I begin. My voice shakes, so much less resolute than I need to be. I swallow, try again. Firmer. "Tomorrow, you'll take me into the Thousandfold."

Ravel nods and steps back, away from the ossuary and away from me. He drags a hand over his hair—tangled from my clutching fingers—and starts to walk down the central aisle of the chapel, toward the stairs. Before he leaves the room, he glances back and gives me a wordless look, hopelessly honest.

His eyes are so sad; this is the boy who Nyx Severin wanted to carve out and replace with a monster. "You asked, once, if my kind has sin? Of course we do. Everline—you are my greatest transgression."

The sound of my name in his mouth is like holy wine, the syllables laid out on his tongue alongside the taste of my blood. Before I can respond, he turns and ascends the stairs, his footsteps echoing quietly past the second landing and into the attic room.

CHAPTER SEVENTEEN

I N THE PALLID HOURS BEFORE MORNING, I SHARPEN THE VALE
Scythe until it gleams. Put on a new dress, the color of asphodel
flowers, with trailing skirts and a high lace collar, cobweb-delicate,
that clings around my throat. It hides the bruised remnants of
Ravel's bite. Even now, the place above my pulse where his teeth
sank in—darkly petaled in a falcate mark—throbs in time with
my pulse.

It stormed all night, the lash of rain and wind as restless as my
thoughts. I lay in the barracks room with the shutters open and let
the moonlight cover me, my hand pressed to my bitten throat. I
couldn't sleep; though I ought to have stored my rest like rations
put aside for a hard season, I knew the moment that I closed my
eyes, I'd see hideous things. A ruin spread out beneath a shadowed
sky, vespertine spilling from the mist, the corrosive gaze of the
monstrous god we'd thought dead.

That monstrous god—Nyx Severin—is Ravel's father.

Now the storm has quieted. And I feel as though, instead, the relentless stir of wind and rain has shifted inside me. When I stand at the mirror to pin up my braided hair, my lantern-lit reflection is smooth and still. But underneath, I am all clash and torrent, a pelt of raindrops, each of them a tangled feeling, a close-kept secret.

Fear of the Thousandfold, and what I'll discover there. If the magic that Ravel has promised me—our blood-bound vow—will be enough to keep me guarded and hidden from his father once I've crossed the border into his lands.

Fear of what might happen if I fail.

What might happen if I don't.

I slip the final pin into my hair as Ravel appears in the doorway. He's dressed like he was on the night I first saw him, mantled with bones and silver fur, his face grimly painted—his mouth a smear of black, his eyes lined dark. He holds his mask in his hands and turns it over and over as he looks at me, not speaking.

Then he sets the mask down on the dresser and takes out a cloth-wrapped parcel from the inner pocket of his cloak. "Here. I mended these for you."

The parcel has been tied with a length of twine, a careful knot. I draw it loose, my hands starting to tremble. Inside are the bracers I made, the leather straps oiled to a dull shine, fresh daubs of blood painted over the relic bones. Ravel has stitched new silken ribbons through the fastenings in place of the ones he cut. They're crimson, made from the ribbon I wore in my braid on the night I captured him.

I look at him uncertainly through the veil of my lashes. "Thank you." Then, not sure if I am daring Ravel or daring myself, I stretch out my arms. "Will you put them on for me?"

He hesitates a moment, glancing down at his mask on the dresser. The grim visage watches us both with hollowed eyes, their gaze so deep, I could be lost within it. Then he takes the bracers from my hands. He's careful as he slides them onto my wrists, as he ties the ribbons, and I wonder if he is thinking of the bruised mark of his fangs beneath my sleeve. Or the twinned mark on my throat.

The power imbued in the relics begins to stir and shift. It pours through my veins with the syrupy languor of winter honey, shivering and slow. And, for the first time, the magic doesn't seem like a thing I have to fight against or suffer beneath. There's only a quiet drone that casts all through me, like the hum I'd feel when I laid my hand against a hive in the apiary field.

The rightness of this moment—this feeling—is a certainty, a confirmation. That the pull I've felt to the Thousandfold, the sense of connection that sparked on the night of the blood eclipse, is real.

Ravel looks me over: my pale dress, my buckled blade belt, my pinned hair. His mouth thins into a displeased frown. "You look like a warden."

"I *am* a warden."

He searches through my cosmetics, which are scattered on the dresser, choosing a jar of lip stain and a small brush. "May I?"

I turn toward him. He presses at my chin with his thumb and tilts my face upward. He brushes the paint across my mouth, his touch disconcertingly light. His eyes are narrowed in concentration, his lip caught by his teeth. Then he sets aside the brush and the rouge, starts to draw the pins from my hair.

Pin by pin, he places each one on the dresser with a softened *clink*. I shiver at the scrape of his blunted claws as he unweaves my braids. The bruise on my neck aches with a steady, painful throb. I tell myself this is no different from when I've had my hair combed or my lips inked by Lux or Briar. But all I can feel is closeness—the hem of his cloak brushing against my skirts, the uneven rhythm of his breath stirring over my skin.

And Ravel, he stares at me intently, the same way he looked when I saved him from the flooded river. A mix of unguarded shock and veiled sorrow. When he's finished, he runs his hand over my unbound hair very softly. A slow, hot ache uncoils through me, an ache that matches the pulse in my throat, the pulse of magic against my wrists. I think of his teeth at my neck, my blood in his veins.

I lift my hand, place it against his chest—the same as when we made our vow, feeling the rising pace of his heart. He sighs, a desperate shudder, like I have pulled the sound from him. I'm caught by a longing that both draws and frightens me. I know that everything between us is an impossible transgression, that I should go no further. Yet all I want is to pull him close.

"Hells." Ravel snarls the word quietly—as though he's speaking to himself. He moves back, widening the space between us, and collects his mask from the dresser. Slipping it into the satchel he wears slung across one shoulder, he turns toward the door. "I'll wait for you downstairs."

I listen to the fading sound of his boots as he leaves the room. When I look in the mirror above the dresser, I see the face of a stranger. With haunted eyes, a skeletal mouth, a wash

235

of treacle-dark hair spilled loose. I'm changed, eclipsed the way a storm cloud would blot out the moon. No longer Everline Blackthorn but some new creature with the mark of a vespertine's teeth printed on her throat and relics tied to her wrists with crimson ribbons.

I picture myself returned from the Thousandfold with Lux at my side. My face swathed by corpsepaint and pale lace wrapped around my bruised throat. When I come back to this chapel and reunite with Fenn, will he think me a girl who braved monsters in search of her destiny? Or that I am my mother remade, that I've repeated the mistakes that cost her life?

With a sigh, I pick up my satchel and tighten the knot of my cloak, then follow Ravel down the stairs. As I pass through the chapel, I dare a glance toward the window and the ossuary beneath, and it's a shock to find it unmarked. Those moments last night where I clung to Ravel and traced the curves of his ribs, where I bared my throat to him with the intimacy of *trust*—it feels like it should have left a scar upon the altar.

Ravel waits for me in the overgrown garden, where the ward lights gleam like pale stars. I unweave the length of silver chain and draw the nearest bone shards loose. We cross the barrier and go beneath the citrus trees with our heads bowed and the rain-wet leaves tracing over our hair. I still have the shards Briar gave me, but I don't remake the wards I broke—whatever happens now, I'll need more than a line of consecration to keep me safe.

We leave the chapel behind and move out onto the windswept moor. Ravel doesn't put on his mask but keeps it inside his satchel; I can see the sharpened horns curved up past the buckled fastening. It's dark enough that we need a lantern, though in the distance, early sunlight grazes the horizon. Everything around us is drenched from the storm; the droplets strung along the grass strands shimmer when the lantern light catches them. It's beautiful, and I'm surprised to find it so.

But the air is filled with a persistent whine that scours coldly against my cheeks and hums inside my ears. The shadows pooled beneath the windswept trees stretch closer as we pass. I try to reassure myself; it is dawn, long before the night when the vespertine come creeping in. We will be safe. At least until we reach the Thousandfold.

Still, I can't escape Nyx Severin; images of him—set in stained glass panels or carved in cliffside stone—paint themselves against the distance. When I raise the lantern to better see the path ahead, I imagine him there, outlined against the sky, translucent as a smear of incense smoke. Everywhere tastes of threat, of horror. The rising sound of the wind is the howl of the vespertine; the whipcrack rush of air through the moor grass is the bite of their sharpened teeth.

We pass the first catacombs, where the ground is stippled with pallid asphodels. I cast a lingering glance back toward the ruined entranceway. Remembering the scent of dust and ancient bones and promises sworn in the dark. The shadows beside the weatherworn stone ripple and stir, reaching out with tendrils that are gone when I blink.

I grasp the hilt of the Vale Scythe. Ravel keeps his attention fixed ahead, but when he feels me tense, he moves incrementally closer so that our shoulders brush. In the satchel at his hip, the planes of his mask turn silver as the sun crawls higher in the clouded sky.

The sound of the Blackthorn River rises ahead, louder and louder; it overwhelms all else. The water gnaws hungrily at the banks as broken branches are caught up by the current, dragged past us and out of sight. I think of the other stretch of this river, watched over by carved stone, where Ravel faced down the vespertine with his blood and my weapon. The same tenuous magic that I'll have to trust to protect me now.

It starts to rain more heavily as we follow the river, pelting drops that turn the water's surface to a fractured blur. The sky presses down, and we're immersed in fog, the whole world veiled gray. Time slips into meaninglessness. We're so far from the chapel, the enclave, from anywhere that is familiar or vaguely safe.

My lantern flame wavers uselessly, revealing only billows of shifting cloud. The mist is a false night where day is devoured piece by piece. I feel as though I've been drawn into a vivid waking dream that's all threat and terror. The river fractures into a meshwork of tributaries—surging and storm-swollen. And beneath the sound of the rain and the howl of the wind come other, darker notes.

I see shapes—heavier than shadows—trailing alongside us, like branches dragged through a stream, caught up in the wash of the storm. I blink; they flicker; they darken.

I draw my blade, the Vale Scythe a pale moon in the paler mist. I whisper, "Ravel," and he narrows his eyes warily toward the shadows. At first, everything is still; then a howl carves through the air like a sharpened knife. My heartbeat stutters. Ravel takes hold of my hand. His fingers are sticky, bloodied. There's a shard of bone pressed between our palms.

"This way," he says, a low hiss, and drags me forward.

We run toward a cluster of narrow trees that shields a ruined cottage. The slate-tiled roof is held together with moss and thorns; water pours from one corner of the gutters into a muddy pool beside the entranceway. We rush inside. Ravel slams the door behind us, shoving his bloodied hand to the latch. The air turns hazed, as though the mist has followed us into the room. He tightens his hold on the shard. His power rises around us.

The relics at my wrists begin to pulse; I shudder as the magic seeps further through my body, into my bloodstream. My mouth fills with the taste of rust, and ash, and clove incense. A howl splits the air, then another, then another. A sinister chorus of inhuman cries, the sounds of fury and hunger. On tiptoe, I creep to the window and clear a space in the dust that covers the glass.

The vespertine circle the cottage, crouched low against the earth like a grim ring of wards. They blur together as they move, their fur in shades of soot and smoke and silver, their eyes like embers. The largest one—with antlered horns and a snow-white coat—tilts its muzzle to the sky and howls.

I stare into the mist behind them, searching desperately for the figure, the shape that I glimpsed before, when they came for us at the catacombs. But the mist stays blank, unblemished by another presence.

Ravel draws out another shard. Blood drips from his hand onto the threshold of the room. He starts to chant, low, beneath his breath, words that have the shape of holy speech. But they are not holy. They are anything but that. I clutch the Vale Scythe so tightly that my knuckles turn white.

Outside the cottage, the vespertine coil and writhe. The mist starts to thin, the daylight breaking through. And as the darkness fades, they fade as well. Like a rise of smoke from a pyre, they drift apart, ashes scattered in the wind. Soon there is only the gray emptiness of the moorland. The hollow sound of the rain on the roof. The ever-present rush of the river.

Ravel sinks down with his back against the wall, letting the burned-out shards drop to the floor beside him. He stretches out his legs; then his head tilts back, releases a ragged sigh. I take a cloth from my satchel and pass it to him; he wraps it around his bloodied hand. "It's safe now," he says, voice roughened with fatigue.

Sunlight comes weakly into the room, shining through the space I cleared on the glass. I stare at Ravel, caught in undeniable awe of the power he just used. I can still feel it on my skin, still taste it on my tongue. It throbs alongside my pulse, as though the magic from the relic bracers is drawn to the lingering feel of his strength, casted in the air like a trail of shimmering motes.

This is the boy who the monsters fear, the son of an eldritch god.

I start to pace the room, feeling restless. Trying to shake the emotions that have flooded me—heat and longing, the alluring traces of Ravel's power. The cottage has a strange familiarity. I've never been here before, yet little details of the room snare me like scraps of forgotten memories.

There's an iron-grated hearth and a curtained alcove where a straw-tick bed lies scattered by handfuls of fallen leaves. I move from the hearth to the window to the sleeping alcove. The woolen blanket on the bed, chewed by moths, is the same color and weave as the ones in the enclave barracks. There is a bone-handled comb and a row of amber glass jars on the shelf beside the dust-smeared window, with dried remnants inside.

I open the smallest bottle and breathe in slowly. A sense memory rushes over me, sending my tongue curling against the roof of my mouth. The bitter, astringent traces of the antiseptic tincture we use to clean our wounds. The other jars hold black ink and rose-petal rouge; then there's a vial of crystallized honey.

"My mother was here," I say, my face to the window, my words caught up and whisked away beneath the noise of rain and river. "After she left the enclave, this must have been where she stayed."

Ravel comes slowly to stand beside me. He looks at the jars, the bed, my trembling hands that are knotted, anxiously, in my skirts. I start to laugh, shaking my head at how foolish I sound. A wistful, grief-struck girl who wants her mother so badly that she sees her face in the moon or believes her transformed into a bird. But he regards me solemnly, then dips his head in a slow nod.

"It might have been. The Thousandfold is just over there."

He points to a stretch of land beyond the window, unveiled by the dissipated clouds. The Thousandfold carves a swath along the skyline, huddled and ominous. We're close enough that I can make out the spired points of buildings against a backdrop of skeletal trees.

I picture the vespertine fleeing the daylight, gone back to that shadowed space to hide in hollows of stone, curl up in the foundations of ruined buildings. Then I think of my mother, here, in the days before she died. Staring from this window as I dreamed in her womb, she would have looked at the same view we're seeing now.

I imagine her draped in a cloak with her hair trailing down her back, as she left the cottage and walked toward the Thousandfold. As she crossed the border. Then the image shifts, transforms, and it becomes Ravel after he lured Lux from the chapel, the silhouette of him blended against the shadowed ground as he strode away with her curled in his arms—a ghostlike wisp drawn through the darkened night.

"When you came for Lux, whose idea was it to take her?" I ask, not looking at him. "Yours—or his?"

Ravel picks up his mask. He stares at it pensively, his mouth pulled into a taut scowl. "It was my choice." He casts a fleeting look in my direction, as though in challenge. Then, with a sigh, he turns his attention back to the mask. "Hazel and I were supposed to go together to the wall—to test our powers against the wards you'd set. But on the way there, we fought. She went on ahead, told me she didn't want my help and that I should stay behind. So I did. I stayed until I saw the smoke from the pyre and realized she was dead. That you had burned her."

"Ravel—" I begin, but he cuts me to silence with a look that's sharp as a whetted blade.

"My father blamed me for her death. And he was right. If I'd been better, been *more*—it would have ended differently. I should have been there, should have protected her."

"You mean . . . you would have killed us."

He'd held me so carefully after the vespertine attacked, when Briar was hurt from the relic armor, when I ached with guilt.

His cheeks had flushed when he told me about his past, his voice gravid with the weight of confession. These were tender gestures from the same creature who pinned me to the ruins as the razored edge of his teeth scraped my throat.

"Yes," he says bluntly. "I would have. And I intended to when I saw you on the moorland. That night, when I stood outside your window and you looked at me, all I could see was a hand on a knife; I thought of how when Hazel died, my father told me, *It should have been you*. I needed something more to give him. And I realized that to bring a warden back—alive—would be a truer proof of my fealty."

I turn cold, overcome by terror; I feel as though I've plunged into the flooded river and been swept beneath the current. The world is a blur of noise and shadow, with the magic from the relics snared around me like a thorn-studded vine that's cut through my flesh, my ribs, my heart.

"You *gave* her to him." My hands are shaking; I clench them to fists, to still their trembling. "You—"

"And *you* killed my sister." Ravel glares at me, his own hands clenched just as tight as mine, holding the mask in a grip that makes his knuckles blanch. The tattoos banded across his fingers turn starkly black in contrast. "But we're here—together—now, aren't we?"

The air sparks, tense and electric, between us. I think of him chained, think of him bloodied, think of his claws cut to pieces at my feet. Then I think of Hazel Severin—her eyes fixed to mine as Lux's blade dragged across her throat. When Ravel called us *murderers*, he spoke true. We were there to protect the wall, and they were there to destroy it—all of us certain our mission was righteous, all of us bound up in wretched duty. So desperate to fulfill roles laid out long before we were born.

"We might end this," I murmur, and it feels like heresy even though it's printed clearly across my heart. "You and I, we made a truce, and we might . . ."

Ravel dips his head, his hair falling forward to hide his expression. Solemnly, he echoes, "We might."

The small measure of distance between us seems both impossibly wide and all too narrow. I want to go to him, to draw him into my arms. Seek out a moment of comfort amid the chaos of both our worlds.

But as soon as I make the motion, he turns away from me, sets the mask over his face. The rain has eased, but he keeps his head bowed when he goes out of the room and back onto the open moor. His boots cut a path through the windswept grass. I follow it—follow him—as we leave behind my mother's cottage and continue toward the Thousandfold.

It seeps across the landscape as we draw closer, not a sudden shift but a gradual transformation, like a stain of blood that has soaked through a piece of cloth. First, the grass flattens; then the ground turns dark and mud begins to catch our boots. The trees loom taller and taller, still grimly shadowed even as the sun streaks across them. Beyond the trees is a barren stretch of earth, then scattered ruins, their stones laced by lichen and moss, groves of ferns at their foundations.

I keep my blade drawn as I peer through the trees, trying to pick out movement beyond. The branches above us are strung with bone shards hanging from delicate threads. They twist in the wind like ghostly, silent chimes. Everything is quiet, but I am poised, anxious, as I listen for those telltale howls. "Will they come for us?"

Ravel approaches the trees with his arms folded tight against his chest. He's nervous and tensed—even though his face is hidden behind the mask, I can make it out in the sharp angle of his shoulders, the way his boots scrape a restless trench through the mud and the moss.

"No. I'll be able to keep you hidden." He reaches overhead and plucks one of the shards. The snapped thread trails out between his fingers as he presses his thumb to the sharpened edge of the bone, piercing his skin. A bead of blood wells up, and he smears it across the shard. Then he extends his hand to me. "We'll have to be touching for it to work."

I inch across the mud-softened ground, my boots catching on the turned-up coil of a root until we're standing close to each other. Dressed like this, with silver fur mantled about his shoulders, with his skeletal mask and its arched horns, he's even more endlessly tall. Behind the hollowed eyes, his gaze glimmers like poison. His hair is an ink spill, tendrilled by the wind.

I take Ravel's hand. A light touch—my fingers loose around his. The magic imbued in the relics stirs against my skin. The power feels fine-edged here, as though it's been distilled, clarified by the ash-scented air and the monochrome light. "Is this . . . enough?"

He shakes his head. "Closer."

I glance to where the moorland unfolds behind us, sky and flowers and rain-damp earth. Beyond that, the cottage, then the chapel and, farther still, the ward line, the wall, the enclave. I think of all I've faced to reach this point. All that lies ahead.

And then I think of Ravel's mouth on mine, how he tasted of bitter coffee beneath the smear of blood that marked our vow. The sharp, bright rush of heat and *want* that overwhelmed me when his teeth first sank into my skin. I shouldn't be thinking of this, but the more I tell myself to stop, the more the visions rise.

My cheeks turn hot as I step closer to him. My fingers weave through his. My palm is pressed to his palm. I clasp his hand tighter, tighter, tighter. The shard is trapped between us, lifeless bone slowly warmed by our skin. "Go ahead," I tell him. "Show me what you can do."

"What we can do together," he corrects. "This will only work because you're here, Everline. Perhaps you don't have magic, but you have a mark; you made the armor; you've wielded a relic blade against the vespertine—there's power in that and power in your warden blood."

A shimmer of pride rises through me at his words. And in spite of my broken vows and the danger we face, I'm not ashamed of how I feel. I've been handed something fragile and precious, the knowledge that even without magic, I—as a warden—have played a vital part in this journey.

Ravel guides me forward. We slip past the line of trees. The air grows denser, and the magic is there, coiled between us, eager and wanting. A heartbeat, then it rises over me. It dances past my bones and into my blood, every part of me ratcheting tighter until my heart feels like it will peel open. A scream, a howl, a disorienting rush of power—the same unholy strength that Ravel cast on me outside the ruins. Except now, it's *for* me, not a thing to hurt but to help.

Power simmers beneath my skin, at my palms, along my fingertips. I close my eyes and draw in a deep breath laced with ash and mist and *Ravel* who, I realize, has carried the scent of the Thousandfold with him all this time.

All the light is stolen away. The world becomes leaden shades. My breath catches as I feel my skin *split*—my palms, my mouth, my wrists. I open, open, and the strength of Ravel's magic—of the Thousandfold—pours into me. Roots and rot and bones wrapped around us like a shroud.

Everything I've held familiar falls away. I catch flashes of things half-hidden in the dark. Scraps and scatters, one after the other, the images so tangled up that I can barely comprehend them.

I see the ocean far to the north, all mangrove mud and roots that arch to steal fresh water from above the tides. The air stinks of sour brine, of bloated, washed-up things. I see creatures that are half-ocean. Cuts at their throats that flutter as they draw in air. Tentacles that writhe and grasp. Circular mouths that gape open to reveal row after row of sharpened teeth.

I see the Thousandfold as it was before—towering walls and

stately trees, windows sharded with onyx glass. Alcoves lined with granite statues that watch the path beneath them with countless eyes. I see wolflike beasts with bloodstained fur, their shoulders mantled with bone-plated armor. They hunch over terrified penitents, teeth in their flesh, holding them pinned. Screams fill the air as the captives are dragged away into the catacombs' dark.

The acidic taste of horror, of queasy panic, floods my tongue. The magic claws through me. My veins are iron-tight; my blood burns. I know the vespertine are all around us, hidden beneath the shadows. I can feel them there. But we are shielded; we are safe. Ravel holds me fast, his grip unrelenting. He leans close. His words hiss over my ear. "Don't let go."

We go on, farther, farther. Branches above and shadows beneath, the gleam of feral eyes and the razored edge of bared, bloodied fangs. The ground is a pool of shallow, ice-cold water that seeps through my boots and numbs my toes. I see a frightened girl with treacle-dark hair all loose and tangled. She sinks to her knees in the mud, one hand pressed to her swollen belly as her eyes clench closed. In the distance, a familiar voice calls and calls, "*Ila, Ila, come back with me.*"

I see a wash of reddened moonlight as the darkness stretches toward her. It takes her hand with fingers that have claws . . . "*Ila,*" says a new voice, different from the one before. "*Ila, come here to me.*"

The voice scrapes my ears, my skull, my heart. It reaches into my chest, and it pulls. I falter. My hold on the power slips loose like a dropped spindle, unraveling, and everything goes still. There are trees and ruins and the endless grayscale dark. Then, through the branches and the stones, come snarls and howls. And the monsters are there, the creatures of the Thousandfold. They're stirring and blinking awake—they'll know we're here; they'll find us.

Ravel pulls me close against his chest. Our hands are still laced together. "Don't let go."

If I let the magic fail, if I lose my grasp on the slippery horror of this unholy protection, then we'll be caught by the vespertine. Visions and terror and power are set to tear me apart, but this is the only way through. The Thousandfold is going to devour me either way; it's just a choice between quick or slow.

Don't let go; don't let go.

I swallow down the fear and wrongness. I reach again to the power. Feel the burn and sting as my skin peels open fresh, as more roots and tendrils of magic spill around me. My nose starts to bleed, a stream of molten, coppery blood that paints my lips and my chin. The ground churns; bones bloom beneath our feet. I stand straighter. There's a rush of air, a stir of branches, and we're enclosed by the dark.

With Ravel's hand in mine, I walk toward the center of the Thousandfold.

CHAPTER EIGHTEEN

THE MAGIC SPITS US OUT IN A GROVE OF LEAFLESS TREES.
It's dark, the sky overhead—crosshatched with skeletal branches—speaking of midnights and hidden secrets. Still caught up by the snare of power, I tumble forward, my hand tearing loose from Ravel's as I fall to the ground. My skirts cascade around me. My satchel slips from my shoulder. I land heavily on my knees, and I'm tangled, wretched, helpless—the chain of my fiola drawn tight across my throat, my lungs straining to draw breath, my lips painted in blood.

"*Hells,*" I gasp, then fall to a fit of ragged coughing. My tongue is heavy with the taste of magic: ash and honey, cloying decay. The relics burn and shudder, twinned heartbeats of power against my wrists. My nose is still bleeding. I still have the Vale Scythe clutched in my hand.

Ravel untangles my fiola chain, then slides his arm around my waist and helps me to my feet. "We have to keep moving," he says quietly beside my ear. "This way."

I look frantically to the shadows around us, but they are vacant and still. A sigh escapes me—less relief and more a caught breath—as I let him guide me forward, my eyes sunk closed, my head against his shoulder. We reach a stone wall thickly covered in a snare of leafless, thorny vines. He drapes his cloak around his arm for protection and carefully lifts the thorns aside, revealing a hidden door. It's unassuming, plain wooden panels and a tarnished iron latch, none of the overwrought decoration that marked the chapel entrance.

Inside is a ruin that's more solidly built than the others we've passed, with a tiled hearth and two panes of louvered windows choked by more of the vines. It must have been a cottage once. Similar to the houses where Lux and Briar grew up in the Hallowed Lands. The wooden floor is carpeted by desiccated leaves; they crumple beneath me when I lower myself down.

Ravel latches the door, then kneels beside me. He presses a tin flask of water to my lips, his hand on my shoulder as he helps me drink. I swallow the water in large, aching pulls, rinsing the sour taste of magic from my mouth, then hand back the flask. He puts it away without drinking. He's still wearing his mask.

I look around the room, but shadows pool heavily in the corners, obfuscating the rest of the space. "Where are we?"

Ravel makes a wry sound, not quite a laugh. "Somewhere I come when I want to avoid my father. We'll be safe here for now."

His word echoes through me: *safe, safe, safe.* But all I can think of is the Thousandfold pressed against the outside of the ruin, the vespertine snarling at us from the dark. "How did you . . . ?" I gesture toward the vine-choked windows, the shadows beyond. "With Lux?"

Ravel passes a hand over his mask; at first, I think he means to remove it, but he only traces his fingers down the fanged edge of the jawbone. "She wasn't conscious."

I'm heated by a flare of anger, an aftershock that sparks, then gutters, overlaid by bleak, unending despair. I think of Lux, turned dreamy and pliant by the spell Ravel used to lure her from the ruins, how he must have carried her through the same trees that now arch above this cottage. I think of Nyx Severin— his real form and his form in the visions I saw when the vespertine chased us. The screams and the howls and the monsters and my mother—my mother and that eldritch voice that spoke her name.

"He knew her," I murmur, the truth so impossible I can hardly give it voice. "My mother was here, and Nyx—"

A sob shudders up from my chest. I clench my teeth together so hard that I taste blood, force myself not to cry. Ravel reaches to me, slow and tremulous; he lays his palm against my cheek. I flinch, startled by his touch. He makes a soft noise beneath his breath. "It's all right, Warden," he says, mouth closer to my ear than I realized. "It wasn't real. It was only a vision. You're safe now. Let me help you."

He has a cloth, taken from one of our satchels. Gently, he cleans the blood from my nose. I twist my hands together in my lap, digging my fingers hard into my knees. Ravel is little more than an outline against the dark—shadows on shadows—the angle of his shoulders and the sharp curve of the horns from his mask, but I'm endlessly aware of his nearness. The way his fingers tremble as he holds the cloth, the calloused rasp of his thumb pressed beneath my chin.

My entire being is spun into a thread, drawn out strand by strand until only a single fiber is left to hold me in place. Magic seeps from the relics on my wrists, coils through my body. The darkness of the room is bruising and heavy, so tight against my chest that I can breathe only in short, ragged gasps.

Suddenly, I feel as though I'm back in the enclave. When I still roomed in the barracks and I'd woken from a nightmare. And although we're hidden inside this ruin, the shadows around us are full of voices, of monsters. I blink and blink, willing my eyes to adjust, but everything stays lost beneath the dark.

I clench my hands tighter together. I'm certain that the shadows have pooled in my palms, gone beneath my skin. That all the darkness of the room has spilled inside me. A peculiar ache strikes my fingertips; the skin around my nails feels raw, my cuticles are damp with blood. I start to scrub at them, as though I can wipe away the pain, the shadows.

It's a hurt beyond a hurt. A pain that I feel inside my throat and on the back of my teeth. It can't—*I can't*—I press desperately at the marks with the edge of my thumb. They won't come away. The ache deepens, thrumming in time with my pulse. When my heart beats faster, when my fingers press harder at the stains— scraping now—the throb in my hands turns faster, too.

"Stop—" I whisper, sharp and choked. "Please—"

I shake myself free of Ravel's touch, and clasp my hands against my chest. My fingernails still itch and burn and ache. I scrape at them frantically, but the pain only worsens; fresh blood slicks at my cuticles. Between the memories and the magic, there's just too much to hold inside my skin. My nails feel loosened, and as I rub them, one shifts—there's something beneath. Harder and sharper and—

There's a soft *click*, followed by the flare of a match as Ravel lights a lamp. He turns the wick down low so the room is flooded with burnt-orange light, like a sunset behind gathered storm clouds. I dare a glance at my hands and see fresh, angry scrapes and welling blood and something shiny and dark beneath my thumbnail.

My heart twists against my ribs, a fist pounding on a heavy, locked door. *Thud, thud, thud.* I'm shuddering all over. My tongue tastes of ash, of rust, of the Thousandfold. I hold out my hands to Ravel, show him. "What's happening to me?"

He's sharp with tension—but he's trembling, as though he's wretchedly afraid. Slowly, he runs his fingers along mine, touches the edge of my nails and then . . . starts to *pick* at them. I hiss with the shock of it, the sharp, piercing sting, and try to pull away. But he holds me tightly, his blunted claws working at the edges of my cuticles where the skin burns and bleeds.

"*Hells*," he swears beneath his breath, leaning closer to my hands. "Everline, you—"

The frank shock in his voice is enough to still me. I fall into a numb surrender, stare at him wordlessly as he picks and peels at my fingertips, my nails. There's something in the look of our hands, together, that catches me. I've been here before. It's both familiar and unfamiliar at the same time. The lantern-lit room.

The vine-choked window. My nails with their chipped black polish. Ravel's hands on mine and—claws. *My claws.*

The magic from the relics strains hot and sharp through my veins, against my too-tight ribs. I shove Ravel away with a sob, the crimson ribbons on my bracers tangling between us. I feel berries crunched between my teeth, sour juice spilled down my throat. The unholy magic he used to enchant my armor and to take me safely inside the Thousandfold has twined and twisted through me like a poison. It's made me *changed.*

I shove him again. Hit him and hit him. "Why didn't you tell me this would happen?"

"I didn't know." He catches my hands, holds my fists tight against his chest. I can feel his heartbeat against my knuckles— just as frantic as my own. From beneath the mask, his voice comes out like a snarl. "I *didn't.*"

"You're such a liar." I wish we were back beside the river with him sprawled in the mud. I wish I'd pushed him under the water and let him drown. Another sob fights its way from my throat. My cheeks are wet, and my eyes burn, and I have claws—*claws*— growing from my fingertips. I can barely breathe. I gasp, fear and disgust choking me. "I hate you!"

"I didn't know," Ravel snaps, viciously. The sickly orange light from the lamp outlines the sharpness of his bared teeth. He drags in a breath, presses his hand again to the planed-smooth bones of his mask. "Hazel and I lived our entire lives in the Thousandfold, exposed to much stronger magic than I've ever used with you. It took us *years* to even begin to change. I never thought—"

He cuts off suddenly, his lips pressed tightly together, as though he's said more than he intended. I glare at him, clenching and unclenching my fists. Beneath the ache of the claws is a bruised-bone wrongness that I'm not sure I'll ever shake loose. I'd once thought I'd do anything to find Lux. I want to believe even this price is worth it.

I thrust out my hands toward Ravel, an echo of the gesture he'd made when I cut his claws. "Finish it."

Once again, he takes my hands between his own. The magic within me rises to where our fingers are entwined, and when he presses down, my skin turns cold. Frost on a winter morning. The cut of crisp air before the sun has warmed the sky. My breath hitches at the fresh sting as he picks and peels my fingertips, my nails.

Ravel pauses, looks down at our joined hands as though unsure of how to parse out this connection, this closeness. Then, methodically, he starts to work, gently coaxing through the new claws. "Hazel grew hers first. Father watched her unsheathe them—he was so proud of her, how she didn't even flinch. I used to fall asleep with my hands curled so tight that it would hurt, like I could force mine to appear." He laughs, then shakes his head ruefully. "In the end, my warden mark came before either fangs or claws. It seemed like proof that no matter how much vespertine magic my father poured into me, I was still human."

He says it—*human*—the same way he spoke of holy vows; the word carries a practiced bitterness in his mouth. I picture a boy with too-long hair and a gangly looseness of limbs, the shape of a body half-grown into something newer, older. He's curled at the base of a tree. His hands are clasped against his chest, one cupped within the other.

I see myself at thirteen, standing in a line of new recruits before the wall. I reach my hand to Fenn as he comes with the vial and the honey and the knife. As I wait, apprehensive, for the moment that will finally, finally mark me as someone who belongs.

"What happened when your claws grew?"

Ravel smiles softly, sadly. "My father was so proud. He marked my hands—to match his own. It was an honor." He glances down at his tattooed fingers. "And Hazel took me beyond the Thousandfold for the first time. We ran with a pack of vespertine until the moon set and they vanished back into the shadows, then went on by ourselves all the way past the river. I saw the warden sigils like a row of lanterns across the moor, and your wall made of bones, and I felt so very far away from the boy who had been born on the opposite side of it."

His voice is so wistful that it makes my chest hurt. "I wonder if I was on watch that night; maybe we both looked at those same sigil lights and that same setting moon."

"I was so far from the human boy who was born in the Hallowed Lands that I never told Hazel—or our father—how much it hurt to grow my claws. How much it frightened me, the sudden change, even though I'd longed for it. And how I'd wished for someone to hold me, and be gentle, while my claws came through."

I swallow, my lips pressed together on the memory of a bloodied kiss. "Is that why you're helping me now?"

Ravel looks at me steadily from the depths of his mask. "I'm sworn to help you." He traces a slow, methodical pattern over my skin. One by one, my nails dissolve to reveal the newly grown claws beneath. My stomach twists. And he says, with all the tenderness of a confession, "You would make a beautiful monster."

My whole body floods with a sudden, treacherous heat. I lean toward him with magic sharp against my bones, crimson ribbons trailed from my wrists like blood. I shouldn't want this, but I do, with the same doomed impulse that drove me back to the wall again and again to offer my hand to Fenn's blade. No true warden sworn to holy vows would react this way, turned to a feverish, syrup-boned *mess* by being named a monster.

Ravel presses his hands around my curled-tight fingers. Then, with all the care of a warden in the apiary field opening a new-smoked hive, he lifts my hands to his mouth. He kisses them—his lips pressed tenderly to each of my new claws.

A helpless, delirious sound escapes me. My gasp cuts through the quiet, and I feel as though I've been drawn through a veil, that suddenly everything has become more *real*. I look at Ravel, trying to read his expression. But his features are hidden by the planed bones of his mask and the skeletal paint on his skin. Haltingly, I take hold of the mask and slide it away from his face until it rests on his hair, the horns curved back into the loosened strands.

The lantern light paints him in shades of gold and burnished sunset: the curve of his mouth, the honeyed glow of his skin, the shape of his lashes when they flutter in a slow blink. A boy and a monster both, neither one nor the other, like a fanged snake devouring its tail. His life—torn from the Hallowed Lands and raised in the Thousandfold—is like my own existence in reverse.

We've fought so hard to slough off the trappings of our birth-rights, to prove our devotion to the worlds where we landed.

Everything was so simple before, when the vespertine were monsters to be guarded against, destroyed, and burned. When all I wanted was to find the truth about my mother and to rescue Lux from the Thousandfold. I still want those things. But right now, all my holiness is lost beneath the hum of the magic that's settled willingly into my bones. The inescapable heat of my desire, flaring bright as a rekindled ember.

Ravel gazes at me, apprehensive and uncertain. When I lay my hand against his paint-smeared cheek, he falters. The line of his throat shows the stilted motion when he swallows. "Warden—" His voice catches. Then, softer, he says, "Everline."

His hand is at my waist, fingers knitted to the curve of my hip. He drags it higher, following the outline of my ribs through the rumpled fabric of my dress. His palms are fever-hot, scalding, as he traces over me. I lean toward him slowly, as though at any moment, all of this will vanish. Whatever has drawn us together into melting softness at the heart of this hidden, thorn-snared cottage will be dispelled. We'll be back as we were: enemies, only enemies.

Every moment we've shared is laid out like the illustrated panes of a stained glass window. His sister's throat cut by a warden blade, the way he gazed at me across the dark outside the ruins, my helplessness when he carried Lux away into the mist. The delight I felt to see him chained and captured, the painstaking care with which he first bit me.

And the delicate moments. The things I didn't want to look

at too closely, that have remained the most persistent and unforgettable. The silk of his hair against my skin. The way his cheeks flushed and his voice turned softer, vulnerable, when he told me about his past.

The undeniable truth—I'm powerless to want anything except for Ravel Severin.

I curl my fingers into his hair, feel my new claws snag against the strands. I tilt my face upward. My lips brush his, tasting his ragged sigh. Our mouths meet, and the memory of our first kiss that sealed our promise unfolds from where it has lain within me, buried and burning. We fit together with an aching familiarity. My lips part on instinct; he still tastes of blood and bitter coffee.

There's a moment of tremulous stillness, like neither of us can quite believe this has happened. I draw back and open my eyes, and he opens his; we stare at each other, a wordless fright shivering through the air between us.

Then Ravel takes hold of the ribbon that fastens my dress. Winds it deliberately around his fingers until it spools his knuckles like a set of rings. He tugs me forward, a motion that sends my teeth together against a tattered breath. My eyes shutter closed. His claws—still blunted but sharper now, growing back—scrape at my hip, and he draws me toward him, under him, rolls us both, bodily, to the floor. There's a clatter as his mask falls aside. He presses me down into the bed of crumpled leaves. They rustle and whisper against my skin. His mouth is on mine, our kisses turned rough and desperate.

I slide my hands beneath his cloak, clutch at the fabric of his shirt, wanting to pull him even closer, to erase all borders between us. This is the *we might* of before, our fragile truce—all our risk and fury made into something else, something new. His knee presses between my parted thighs, dragging another gasp from me. He catches the sound, kissing me more deeply, his tongue hot as it sweeps against mine, his fangs a subtle sting against my lips.

I'm caught by the same mix of thrill and terror as when I walked onto the moorland the first time. When I held my first blade. When I woke on the first night in my attic room and saw Lux outlined against the moonlit window and realized I wasn't going to be alone.

Ravel kisses the side of my throat, the tender place above my pulse where he bit me. I wonder, frantically, if he will bite me again, how it might feel to kiss him and taste my own blood on his lips. But he only rasps at the bruise with his tongue, then moves lower, kissing a trail over the pale lace of my collar. His breath sears through the fabric of my dress, and the places where our bodies touch have a terrifying heat. The same unavoidable pull that I felt when I first laid my hands on his skin.

It's at once too much and not enough. I want to be closer to him, to have him bared and unguarded and to bare myself in return. I start to pull at the fastenings on my dress. He draws back, watches me for a moment; then makes a soft, yearning noise as he realizes my intention. He starts to help me. Our fingers jostle together as we pull at ribbons and buttons, and I'm unveiled, dressed only in my thin linen underdress with my clothes all crumpled beneath me.

He runs his knuckles down the line of my sleeve, his smile

hitched up in remembered amusement. His eyes keep skimming over the newly exposed stretch of skin above my collarbones. "This is what you wore the night you first chased after me."

"It seems a little unfair that you're so much more *clothed*."

He lets me undress him, turned careful and pliant as I unknot his cloak and slip his shirt over his head. Then we're both undraped, undone, my fingers curled searchingly beneath the waistband of his trousers, my skirts rucked up above my thighs and the ribboned fastenings of my underwear trailing loose. Our kisses turn slower, more tentative. Ravel presses his face against my neck. I can hear, more than see, the flush on him—like it's on his voice—when he says haltingly, "Will you show me . . . how you want me to touch you?"

I nod, leaves rustling against my hair. Thinking of the night when I curled beneath my blankets in the tent and imagined his mouth at my wrist, kissing away the hurt. How desire burned through me like a fever and when I touched myself, it felt so impossibly intimate, like he had been there beside me.

I take his hand, lay it on my thigh. This is the nearness I longed for when his teeth pierced my wrist in the catacombs. This is the conclusion I wished for the night at the altar when I offered my throat to him. My fingers circle his wrist, and I slide his hand higher, past the line of my underwear. He's careful as he touches me, mindful of his claws. I weave my fingers over his, showing him, then let my hand fall away as he starts to stroke at me. My teeth press my lip in a memory of when I fought the urge to whisper his name.

"Ravel." I breathe it against his throat, my tongue on his pulse, feeling the thin, raised line of the scar where he drew blood for a spell. His name tastes of smoke and herbs and altars. My fingers press at his ribs, his hip. I hesitate. "Will you—?"

He rasps a helpless noise of assent into my shoulder, then takes my hand and guides it lower. Just as I did, his fingers weave with mine, and he shows me how to touch him. He's hot against my palm, and I feel dizzy with it, the way he lays himself bare to me with such trust.

We're lost to ragged gasps and fractured kisses, his mouth on my ear, then my bared shoulder, while I breathe hot, helpless words into his hair. And it's not long before I'm shattering apart beneath him, before we're shattering together, my eyes shut and moonlight painted against my vision, a whole burst of stars; his formless, tender sounds; and my voice whispering Ravel's name over and over again like an incantation.

Afterward, we lie curled together like twin warden blades, his knees pressed into the backs of my bared thighs, his chin in the crook of my shoulder. I lift my hand to push a tendril of hair from my perspiration-damp cheek and feel the scrape of my claws. I'd almost forgotten. Now I watch the light glint over them, gleaming and onyx, as brutal as the shards of glass in a chapel window. I feel cold and strange, a prickly sting in my eyes like I want to cry.

Ravel puts his fingers to his mouth; he bites at his thumb, drawing loose a ruby-bright bead of blood. He offers it to me, eyes lowered, abashed, as though this is all the more intimate than the way we were just tangled and touching. "It will help you adjust to the magic," he says.

I roll to face him, let myself curl against his still-bare chest. I take his hand, my fingers trembling, and raise it to my lips. He slides his thumb past my teeth, I taste the sharpness of his blood. My eyes sink closed. And I think of a boy with newly grown claws, running all night with monsters to see a line of wards, gleaming, and a distant wall. Realizing how far he had come since his birth.

In this moment, I am there beside him, my claws unsheathed, my teeth sharp against the air as I throw back my head and howl in a dirge for the girl raised beyond that line of lights, on that wall of bones.

CHAPTER NINETEEN

As we leave the ruins behind, the taste of Ravel's blood stays thickly in my mouth, a rounded piece of copper laid against my tongue. He draws another of the plucked-down shards from his pocket and reaches for my hand. He's masked again, and he touched up the smudged paint on my face before we left; now my lips are a new black heart. There's almost no sign of what passed between us in the shadowed ruins.

Except for the current that tremors between our clasped hands. Except for the unspoken things barbing the quiet around us.

Outside, the world is stilled; the shadows beneath the spindly trees and between the ruined stones are empty. Ravel spikes the shard against his thumb, draws a bloodied stripe over the bone. His fingers lace through mine. Magic slithers around us, and he leads me forward.

I think of how it felt before and how I feel now. I'm still restless, remnants of panic draped across me like a netted veil. But the power doesn't carve through my body the way it did when we first crossed the border. Rather, it nestles in the depths of my lungs and curls alongside my bones. It holds me in a way that is . . . familiar.

And then—we reach the chapel at the center of the Thousandfold.

Made of blackened stone, it has a spired shape, taller than the trees, sharp-angled and unwelcoming. I can feel the secrets within it, hidden by those ancient walls. It's an oubliette—a place to keep things hidden, locked away, separated forever from the daylight. On the jutting roof, the gables are tipped by spiked iron whorls, as though a thorned creature has sprawled itself over the angles of the building.

We edge closer, slipping from the leafless trees to the towering ruin. The entranceway has the same arched shape as the enclave chapel, but instead of a door, the opening is choked by a spill of dark-leafed vines. There's a wrongness here, it seeps from every part of the ruin. It's mortared into the foundation stones. Somewhere inside is Lux, captive. We're so close to her now, she's so *near*, but the horrors of the Thousandfold are near as well.

There are vespertine beside the ruins, guarding the chapel entrance. I watch—still hidden—as the nearest one, with silvered fur and twin rows of onyx eyes—lets out a discordant howl. The other vespertine, one slender and sabled, another with a collar of sharded bone, join in the call; their heads tilted, eyes closed, fangs bared. The air fills with song and sound.

Ravel glances at me, then down at our joined hands. He strokes his thumb against my palm, drawing a gentle line with his blunted claw. Behind the mask, his gaze is solemn. "This way," he whispers, and he leads me down to the side of the chapel.

We bow our heads like penitents as we pass beneath rows of casement windows, covered by more dark vines. At the very end of the wall is another way in. Curtained by a tangle of thorns, just like the door to the ruin where Ravel took me to hide.

There is no door here, though. Just an open archway and a narrow flight of leaf-strewn stairs. When Ravel lifts the thorns aside, the stairs vanish into pooled shadows. Once again the feeling comes, that I am about to be devoured, that this archway is a gaped-open mouth.

I hesitate on the topmost stair, my boots scuffling in the leaves. But there are monsters outside; I can hear their footsteps crushed over the earth as they pace back and forth at the front of the chapel. I hear their hungering snarls, the bite of teeth against mist-draped air. Shivering, I go forward into the dark.

The ruin envelops us with a sound like a sigh, as though the Thousandfold has exhaled a slow breath. Ravel holds tight to my hand as we make our way down, and the ribbons from my bracers spill between us in tangling crimson strands. I can still taste his blood.

We descend into a narrow corridor. There's something about this space that draws my recognition, the way the air is scented with clove incense and grave dirt. The walls are built of bones, femurs and tibiae and ulnae and radials, packed with mud and tangled with vines to hold them in place. The entire foundation of this chapel is an ossuary.

Despite the harsh exterior, this ruin is so much like the enclave.

Like the funeral space beneath our chapel where the dead are laid in final rest, their hallowed remains woven into our walls. But *these* bones were stolen from penitents who were lured to their doom. Those same figures immortalized in stained glass with Nyx Severin's blood spilling over them like a scatter of rubies. The worshippers who came to him, who thought him a god, whose lives he consumed to make himself stronger.

I was right to feel devoured as I came down into this dark. And now, all I can see is my mother as she lay dying at the border of the Thousandfold, as Nyx called her name. Or Lux, woven into one of these walls, her mouth stopped by mud and thorns wrapped around her throat.

My breath is stuck and ragged; I'm shuddering with inescapable, feverish horror. I want to tear away the relics that are fastened to my wrists, tear away the slickly pooling magic that surrounds me. I try to speak, but all that comes out is a snared-animal sound. "*Lux*. Is she—"

"No," Ravel says, voice stilted. "She's not."

Then he cuts to urgent silence. Turns anxiously to the space above. I look up; the ceiling tremors with a vibration that loosens a trail of ashen dust. It spills over us, stippling my unbound hair and the shoulders of my cloak. There's a sound—footsteps—in the main room of the chapel. I hear the shuffle of padded feet, the click of claws. There are more vespertine above us, guarding the hall.

Their footsteps grow louder—they are right overhead—then slowly they dampen, turned softer as they pass. Ravel gestures for me to follow him; we slip through the corridor in silence. At the very end, in the place a relic would be housed if this were a catacomb, is a spiraled staircase. The banisters are inlaid with bone, worn smooth by the touch of countless hands.

More of the dark vines grow here, too, coiled around the banisters and cascading into the stairwell like a waterfall. Ravel tightens his hold on my hand, the bone pressing sharp between our palms. He stares at me, level and serious, from behind his mask. "I won't let them find you. I promise."

I nod, and lace my fingers more firmly through his. Ravel leads me up the stairs and out of the dark. Light from above filters down to catch on pieces of him—his sharp shoulders, the curve of his horns. Our boots crush leaves as we climb, and the air is thick with the scent of bruised foliage and bitter sap.

Halfway up the stairs, we pause. Ravel's head tilts as he tracks the sounds of the vespertine, as their footsteps grow louder again, scuffling and clinking, like a clawed hound pacing across a polished floor. The bloodied shard is still clutched between our palms, and with my other hand, I reach for the Vale Scythe.

The air grows colder, and there's a wash of sickly sweet decay, as though someone has lit a censer and let poisonous smoke drizzle down into the stairwell. The back of my neck prickles, and I feel a ghostly touch against my warden mark. The sinister twin to Briar's warm hand that pressed there when I first put on the relic armor. A shiver scrapes over my spine. I clutch my blade hilt tighter, feeling the unexpected sting of my new claws against the soft edge of my palm.

I swallow thickly and try to remember the taste of blood, the feel of kisses stolen in a darkened ruin. The vows Ravel and I swore to each other. His promises to keep me safe. But there is nothing except for death and shadows and Lux being devoured by the horror of this place—by Nyx Severin and his chapel built from death.

I let my head fall forward, bury my face in the back of Ravel's cloak. The swaths of prickly wool cover my fearful gaze, and in the muffling dark, I take a deep breath of him—the Thousandfold smell of ash and mist that's colored with his own burnt-coffee scent. His thumb rasps against my knuckles. Then the sounds from above recede again as the vespertine walk away from where we stand.

"Quickly," Ravel murmurs. "We won't have much time."

We climb the rest of the stairs, moving hushed and hurried. The hall above is nothing like I expected. There are no vaulted chambers or stained glass windows. Only a single, sepulchral corridor wreathed in more of those strange vines, lit intermittently by the stuttering flames of rust-spotted lanterns. It's overly bright after our time in the foundations, and it makes me nervous—but I'm glad that if the vespertine come, we won't fall across them unawares in the dark.

I follow Ravel through the hall, lined with doors. Doors and doors, each one with a slender bone handle and a latticework of iron that reveals a view inside. They're all empty except for a tangle of vines or a sluice of oily mud seeped across the floor. But then—I pause, press closer. My cheek against the cold screened iron. My heart sticks, and the magic in the relics burns against my wrists like a brand.

Inside the room, there is slick darkness and onyx tendrils and a face, a face, and a body . . . someone there, stretched and still. There are people here, knit into the chapel, held in place by those ever-present vines. Dead, they must be dead—but they haven't worn away to bone, not like the remains layered in the halls beneath. The people here are solid as carved granite, like the edifice on a tomb.

I push away from the door, go onward to the next, then the next. Each latticed screen reveals the same: a figure beneath a nest of vines, snared by the Thousandfold. Some are more uncovered, with bare arms and closed lashes against marble-smooth cheeks. Others are buried, no hint of who might be lost beneath. Some of the rooms have the look of altars, floors scattered with guttered candles and chips of bone, the scent of incense woven through the cloying, heavy stench of blood and decay.

At first I don't understand, and then—I do. These are the experiments Nyx made, the devoted worshippers who came to him with hopes of power and holiness. He bound them here and stole their lives, and now this chapel is a tomb.

All magic comes with a price. And how much would it cost for the power to revive a toppled god, for that creature to unbind himself from the Thousandfold?

These people—these rooms—this is how the creatures of the Thousandfold are born. How the vespertine come from the shadows to attack the wall. How Ravel and his sister grew their fangs and their claws.

And my mother—and Lux—

I turn to Ravel, who has followed close on my heels as I've gone down the corridor. It's all too easy to picture him here at a cruel past moment. With his cloak unfurled behind him like wings, his expression veiled by his mask. Hollow eyes and sharpened bones.

271

Lux in his arms, subdued and pliant as he takes her into one of the rooms, closes the door. As the vines begin to wrap around her. As the chapel devours her.

"Why didn't you tell me?" I ask, whispering, furious. His eyes follow mine, traveling along the rows of doors. "How could you hold this secret back after all I've shared with you?"

"Tell you *what*, Warden? That I'd fed your friend to my father for his experiments? I was at your mercy—do you think I wanted to give you more reason to cut my throat?" He gestures to himself, the light gleaming over his blunted claws. "I've never pretended to be anything other than this."

A monster.

"We made a truce, Ravel. I couldn't harm you even if I wanted to." My voice rises, halting and helpless as I move toward him. "And right now, I *do* want to—"

"Shh." He grabs for my hand, fingers curled around my wrist. He pulls me against his chest and lays his other hand over my mouth. Indicating the other end of the corridor, he murmurs, "Be quiet, or they'll come for us."

I follow the line of his gaze. There's only stillness, the cold hall, and the slithery feeling of magic. Then I hear footsteps, familiar now. Ravel tightens his hold on me, and we edge backward through the corridor. He leads me through an archway that's veiled by a curtain of leaves. Behind them is a door. He opens it slowly, guides me into the room.

A cold draft of air stirs past us, scented with ash and rot. I can hear the steady *drip, drip* of damp as it seeps down the stone walls. Ravel is behind me, his arm pressed solid across my chest, his hand still over my mouth. I peer through the scrolled iron grille, watch the vespertine emerge.

I've seen these creatures before, hunted them in the dark; I've carved them up and made armor from their bones. But here, lit plainly beneath the lanterns, all those adrenaline-blurred glimpses of claws and fangs are scored away, replaced by *this*—the unhidden wrongness of their forms.

The vespertine have countless eyes, with sclera like spilled oil, slick and shimmering. Gleaming bones spear from their furred backs, mantling their shoulders and spines in a gruesome simulacrum of armor. The frontmost one pads down the halls on gnarled feet with six claws. A row of oilslick eyes blinks discordantly along its jawbone.

The creatures pass us, and we're separated only by the shielding vines. Everything is choked by the bright stench of death. I start to shiver uncontrollably. Ravel holds me closer; his fingers press down, tightening our grasp on the shard between our hands. His power curls protectively around us. I swallow against my rising nausea, magic overwhelms my senses. I'm drenched in sweat, though I'm terribly cold. My heart is desperate, aching, as it beats against my ribs.

Ravel shifts slightly; then his hand draws away from my mouth, replaced by the press of his index finger—bitten and bloodied. My lips part, and I let him slide his finger into my mouth. My tongue chases the taste of his blood. I lap Ravel's finger with a wretched hunger. I ought to be exiled for this alone, no matter the other transgressions I've made.

The magic softens against me, over me, loosening its grip on my throat. Outside, the footsteps soften, then fade. The vespertine have passed the room. Ravel's arm is still around my waist, and I can feel the motion of his chest against my back as he breathes unsteadily. He slides his finger from my mouth, and I let out a ragged sigh.

Then my gaze catches on something near the farthermost wall. A wrought iron frame—perhaps once a bed—draped by the wreathing vines. Above is a row of candles, still burning, stuck in rivulets of ancient wax.

"It wasn't by chance that you brought me into this room," I say to Ravel. "Was it?"

He shakes his head, sorrowful. "No. It wasn't."

Slowly, falteringly, I step away from him. I am a child again, lost in a nightmare, powerless to do anything but walk toward the depths of the room with halting, unwilling footsteps. Toward . . . my mother.

I have longed for this with dread and wonder—knowing how the truth would ache, yet hoping that to find her would save me, absolve me. And now, here she is. In a tattered lace gown, with her loose waves of treacle-dark hair. Her face is a pale heart, her skin is stippled all over with freckles. Just like mine.

She's a creature drawn from my dreams, every haunting image made vivid. All the times I examined my own features and tried to puzzle an answer from them, as if I could find the key to the locked jewel box of my past. Every wretched moment where I thought the truth of her would be a vindication. Ila Blackthorn, frozen in time and timelessness, her long hair woven with vines, her lace dress covered by lichen and moss.

I go to stand beside my mother. She has been devoured just like the others, and beneath the lace and vines, most of her body is gone. I try to shut my mind to it, the image of her being carved apart like the creatures I've used to make my armor, but it's no good. All I can see is gleaming bones, vials of blood, the terrible price of power.

Ravel lays a cautious hand on my shoulder. "When you told me you were born on the border of the Thousandfold—when you said that my father had spoken her name—I knew, but I thought it better that you . . . saw for yourself." He pauses, takes a breath. Behind the mask, his gaze is dark with a mournful, sharpened guilt. "Everline, I'm sorry."

"It was her," I say, my eyes blurred with tears. "It was her your father used in the spells that changed you and Hazel, in the magic he tested on you both. Wasn't it?"

Ravel dips his head in a slow nod. His hand falls away from my shoulder, and he touches his wrist, fingers clenched as though in memory. "Yes. All the others here died long ago; their power was almost gone. To make Hazel and me strong enough to test his magic, he used your mother."

I let the truth of it cover me, smothering as a funeral shroud. Ravel, transformed into a monster as he was force-fed magic wrought from my mother's blood and bones.

I think again of the boy I envisaged—tender-hearted, desperate to grow claws. *He changed us*, Ravel had said of Nyx. And Fenn—he *knew*. Perhaps not the whole extent of these gruesome chambers, but he knew that Nyx persisted beyond these borders. That my mother had been claimed by him, claimed by the Thousandfold.

This is the inheritance Fenn tried to deny me, the truth for which I broke my vows.

I reach to Ravel. I feel so treacherous, seeking comfort from him. This boy who became a monster with my mother's blood. But still, I take his hand.

I think of cycles, of lives—my father, my mother, myself. Fenn fought so hard to spare me from this fate, yet I was drawn back here the way a river fills a floodplain each storm season. I ran to the monsters in the footsteps of my mother. I gave my promises and my blood to Ravel, let him work his ruinous power over me. I'm so afraid for how this will end—my sins, our unholy alliance. Furtive kisses in the dark, vows sworn to a boy who is my enemy.

But the path is already set. I can't turn back now. "Give me a moment," I whisper, wiping away my tears. "Please."

Ravel draws away from me and goes back toward the door. Head bowed, he casts a careful look through the iron grillwork. Keeping watch but also allowing me privacy, time alone with my mother.

Slowly, I lower myself to one knee, as though being closer to her will unveil all her secrets, soften my hurts. The Thousandfold has preserved her as she was at her death—at my birth—and she looks only the barest span of years older than me. As though I've peered through an enchanted mirror, into the past.

I touch her cheek. She is so cold. The vines rustle beneath my hand. I imagine all of her blood, her warmth, drawn out and absorbed by the eldritch power of this ruin. I want to speak to her, but when I open my mouth, no words come.

My gaze falls to her bared neck—unmarked and unadorned

beneath the darkened leaves. Wardens are always buried with their fiolae. I feel a sudden ache when I think of Briar and the stolen charms she's taken back to Fenn. I reach to my own fiola, the empty vial I've kept and worn, stubbornly, even though it would never be filled. I hold it until the glass is warmed by my hand; then I draw the chain over my head. It hangs, spinning gently with inertia. I wrap the chain around the vial and set the whole of it, carefully, at my mother's throat.

There's a brush against my shoulder. Ravel's hand, gentle, his thumb sliding beneath my hair to stroke the nape of my neck. It feels strangely bare without the hitch of the silver chain to catch against his fingers when he touches me.

"Everline," he says quietly, gently. "It's time to go."

CHAPTER TWENTY

I FOLLOW HIM BACK INTO THE CORRIDOR, FEELING AS THOUGH I am being led to an execution. I'm straining toward the sounds of the chapel—the muted rhythm of our footsteps over the wooden boards, the whisper of dead leaves brushed aside by the hem of my skirts—as I listen for the nearby vespertine. And all around us are endless rooms filled with the dead, gnawed away by the Thousandfold.

We go into the depths of the chapel, where the walls are completely covered by lush, snaring vines. At the very heart, we reach a door shrouded by a tangle of dark-leafed ivy. Ravel nods toward it, expression solemn behind his mask. I scrape the vines away from the iron lattice. My heartbeat rises; magic from the relics oozes syrup-slick through my veins.

Lux is inside the room, laid out on a wrought iron bed like the one that held my mother.

I grasp for the handle and pull, but the door won't open. None of the other rooms were locked—why would they be when the captives inside are long dead? I clench my teeth together as I bite back a cry, and pull again, uselessly, at the latch. "Here," I whisper to Ravel, drawing my smaller warden blade. "Break the lock the way you did in the attic."

He takes the unsheathed blade from me. Bending to the latch, he says, "Keep watch in the hall."

I stare into the heavy shadows of the corridor, listening to the scratch and scrape of my knife blade against the lock. It comes apart with a quiet *click*, the latch cleaved open like a cut fruit, the edge of my blade all notched and dulled.

Ravel offers it back to me; I shove it heedlessly into the sheath, then rush past him through the broken door and into the room. He follows close at my heels, his cloak a whisper of wool against the air.

The floor is flooded, a pool of fetid water with a sheen at the edges. A single candle burns on the windowsill, the dim light wavering against the rustling, glossy leaves that surround the casement frame. Swaths of vines cover the bed, snarled around Lux's throat and wrists and ankles. But her face is clear—and she is unchanged, not lost in death or turned to marbled stillness. I see, wreathed in ivy, her closed lashes, her petaled cheeks, the smudged traces of rouge on her mouth.

I bend to her, press my trembling fingers to her pulse. She's so terribly still, but after an agonizing pause, I feel the faint throb of her heartbeat. Her chest rises then falls with the shallow motion of her breath. I tear at the vines, at the tendrils that hold her trapped.

Ravel paces behind me, attention shifting between the bed and the open door. Magic seethes from the relics at my wrists. My claws dig into the roots of the vines. *Let her go—please—*

I clear the tendrils from Lux's throat, cup my hand against her cheek. Afraid she will feel as cold as my mother did. But her skin is soft, with the barest flush of heat. I'm overcome by emotion, too aching to be named relief. My fingers curl against her jaw.

"Lux," I murmur. "It's me; I'm here."

Her eyes flutter open. They're washed crimson—the color of a blood eclipse—her pupils blown wide. She stares at me without recognition. I think, helplessly, of Ravel with nightshade berries crushed between his teeth. The snare of magic and poison.

Her hand comes out, and she clutches my arm, her fingers digging bruisingly hard through my sleeve. A flare of power lights from the relics when she touches me. A wave of bright, hot pain tears across my skin, a sharp ache that spears my temples and splotches my vision.

"Lux." I let out her name as a jagged gasp. "Lux, please—it's *me*. It's Everline."

She blinks once. Her eyes clear—familiar hazel-gray replacing the bloodied hue. Her somnambulant breathing quickens. "Evie?"

I pull her into my arms, and it's all so *right* and so *wrong* at once. She's still Lux, even like this—poisoned by the Thousandfold. She feels the same—the same softness of her chest and her curved waist. Beneath the mud-and-decay scent that laces the air, she even smells the same—the lilac-and-elderflower perfume she wears, mixed with the honey she uses to cast her spells.

Her hand comes up, and her fingers comb shakily through my hair. "You're safe," I whisper raggedly. Tears spill down my cheeks. "You're safe."

I unwind the rest of the tendrils that cover her. Ravel is still pacing anxiously back and forth across the room, his boots splashing through the pooled water. Then he stops at the door, listening. "Hurry. They're coming back."

My fingers snag in the final tendril; it snaps, and Lux is free. She sits up, moving with the halting slowness of a sleepwalker. Her eyes have turned crimson again. I put my arm around her waist to steady her, help her to her feet. Lux steps away from the bed, and the vines snared against the walls start to twist and writhe. Beneath our feet, the water ripples and churns.

Ravel pulls Lux and me away from the center of the room. We stagger back, and I watch, horrified, as the branches rush past the empty bed frame, then uncoil and slither like a nest of snakes, stretching down into the murky water that covers the floor. Searching . . . they're searching for Lux. They know I have rescued her.

"Hurry," Ravel says again. He shoves us through the door; I stagger out into the hall with Lux held close against me. We turn toward the corridor, where the vine-covered stairs will lead us down into the dark, the hidden pathway out of the chapel. But I look back desperately, my eyes on the rows of closed doors. The other end of the corridor where my mother lies, dead and devoured by the magic of the Thousandfold. Entombed forever in this hideous place.

I can't bear the thought of running away and leaving her—and all the others—laid out, defiled, an eternal monument to Nyx's cruelty. "Wait—" I call to Ravel. "Please, I have to—"

He looks from me to the depths of the corridor, all of him is sharpened by protective anger; he's feral and frightening—the hollow-eyed specter who first spoke to me outside the ruins. Then he bows his head, solemn, and reaches into his satchel. He passes something to me. A small amber glass bottle, like the one filled with antiseptic. When I open it, the sharp scent is unmistakable. Lantern oil.

We exchange a glance, and I think of his sister, burned to ashes outside the hive fields. I think of the catacombs beneath the enclave chapel. I think of saltsprings and carved effigies, of monsters and gods, love and power. Ravel reaches for Lux, and I let him take her without hesitation. He lifts her into his arms, and she curls against his shoulder, lashes dipped closed over her bloodmoon gaze. I touch her cheek, my fingers shaking. Then, with my skirts gathered up, I run down the hall.

I open the vial as I run, letting the oil spill onto the floor. When I reach the archway to my mother's room, I press an oil-slicked palm against the wooden entranceway, dragging a streak across the timeworn palings. Then I grab the nearest lantern and smash it to the ground. The oil ignites with a *rush* that scalds my cheeks and steals my breath. It sounds like a sudden storm, like the roar of a flooded river.

Distantly, I hear Ravel call out my name—the sound of it from his mouth still strangely tender—and I turn as a trio of vespertine emerge from the shadows just past where I stand. The same one I saw outside my mother's cottage, with jutting horns and pallid fur, flanked by two smaller, sleeker creatures, all bone and claw.

I run back down the corridor toward Lux, toward Ravel, pulling down each lantern as I pass. The fire burns furiously, a haze of heat and clouding smoke. Beneath that is the sound of snarls and snapping teeth, the scrape of claws against stone as more vespertine rise from the depths of the chapel ruins.

I reach the end of the corridor and fall in beside Ravel, who still holds Lux. She curls closer against him, face pressed to the curve of his shoulder, and it's so like the night I saw him claim her. When she slipped, bespelled, into his arms. But I trust him now. I know he won't hurt her. He's sworn to me and I to him. He will see us safely from the chapel and back through the Thousandfold.

We run together, not to the stairwell that leads to the catacombs but toward the main doorway. All around us, vines uncoil as the fire consumes them, lashing at the air and at our feet. The vespertine howl and howl and howl—their otherworldly voices echoing against branch and stone. I catch glimpses of the monsters as we run, their hooked claws and their narrowed eyes, their bared teeth and their jutting bones. Their frantic, furious *hunger*.

Ravel works loose a shard from the depths of his cloak. He clutches it tightly, his knuckles blanched, and pierces his thumb. Blood spills through his fingers. The snaring vines flinch back from us, spiraling into the flames. The vespertine whimper and cringe away.

We reach the entrance, and Ravel flings open the enormous doors. We stumble out into the sharp, cold air, trailed by billowing smoke. I tear down the final lantern; it shatters across the threshold. Fire plumes behind us, turning the corridor to an inferno.

Inside the chapel, the cries of the vespertine become a higher, more frantic pitch that spirals out into the forest. Ravel swears beneath his breath. Strands of hair have plastered to his sweat-damp throat, and the bones of his mask are stained with smoke.

I take his hand. The bloodied shard lies between our palms like a promise. My skin turns sticky with his blood, burns with the flare of power. Magic spills between us, and I feel it simmer along my veins. My fingertips pulse; my claws are sharp, black as the depthless night. I let out a ragged, sobbing breath as we run toward the cover of the trees, let their leafless branches weave closed to hide us.

Once we're in the shadows, Ravel pauses, breathing heavily. Lux is motionless in his arms, her eyes closed, her face against his neck. He pushes back his mask, wiping smudged paint and perspiration from his eyes. We stare together at the chapel, now wreathed in flames. The spired roof is a silhouette against a tower of eager fire; tongues of smoke lick at the open maw of the entrance. "Your father—" I begin, but he shakes his head.

"I'll see you both past the border; then I'll deal with him."

Until this moment, I'd refused to face what would come next. We made our vow—Lux's life for his safety—and she is here, curled in his arms. I've found the secrets hidden in the depths of the Thousandfold—and now our truce will end. After I've crossed the border, I will never see him again.

I'm caught by a snare of incomprehensible emotions, but there's no time to loosen them, to lay them out into something that makes sense. There's only smoke and flames and the howls of monsters. The ashen scent of Ravel's magic as it spreads around me, over me. My mouth is bruised with the memory of his kisses, the coppery taste of his blood.

We run into the trees, and I don't look back. Not even when the chapel starts to collapse, the stones torn apart in the death throes of incinerated, dark-leafed vines. We retrace our path through the Thousandfold, our heads bowed beneath the shortening daylight. The sky is lilac-traced now, dusk spreading fingers across the clouds. Our breath is ragged; my throat is scored from smoke and my heart made wretched with adrenaline.

We pass the ruined cottage, hidden beneath its cloak of thorns. We go out into the fields where the trees are sparse and stretches of moorland creep in, trickles of gorse and heather, outcrops of lichen-covered stone. I can see the border marked by a line of slender trees, closer now, almost in reach.

Then a sound comes from behind us. It's an echo of the cries within the burning chapel but softer, more sibilant. A hiss, a whisper, the press of feet over decaying leaves and churned soil. The vespertine pour out from the trees and from the stones and from the ruins, surrounding us in an ever-shifting circle of claws and bones and snarling. Ravel draws to a stop. He lowers Lux to the ground, and she slumps against me. He slips his mask back on as he edges in front of us, his hand outstretched, his fingers trembling.

I wrap my arms around Lux and hold her close. One of the vespertine begins to howl. And the strange new sounds from before, that came from the depths of the Thousandfold, rise louder, draw nearer. Lux shivers. Her eyes roll back, and she lets out a low moan that comes in echo. As though . . . she's answering them.

I press my hand gently against her cheek, shushing her. "It's all right," I say, formless, useless words of comfort. I stroke her hair, careful not to scratch her with my claws. "I won't let them hurt you."

But we're trapped by a whole seething chaos of vespertine, too many to count. Row after row of them, mantled with jutting bones, their limbs wrapped by blackened vines, their eyes—black as a moonless night—fixed upon us. All narrowed and waiting as Ravel steps forward.

The wind whips back his cloak, and his horns pierce the sky like twin fanged teeth. "You cannot have them." He's fierce and wild as he faces down the monsters of the Thousandfold. Creatures that are, perhaps, as much his siblings as the girl whose throat we cut, who we burned in the hive fields. "You *cannot*."

In a sudden cascade, heavy mist spills across the ground, thick as the smoke that poured from the burning chapel. Bones spear up around our feet, torn from the earth like unburied wards. Everything is laden with the stench of grave dirt, of rot, of death. There's a far-off tremble, and all of the vespertine begin to howl.

Lux stirs. For a breath, she's lucid again, and her hand finds mine. Then her eyes cloud over, her pupils widening until her irises are pools of black. She turns to stare, rapturous, into the distance. To the mist-wreathed space among the trees where heavy footsteps now shudder across the ground. Where the vespertine writhe and cry and scream.

The footsteps grow heavier, nearer. A shape condenses against the mist, transparent at first, then rapidly becoming darker. My heart whines. My teeth ache; my bones hum. And Nyx Severin materializes from the shadows—solid and here and *real*.

He is everything and nothing like the image of him laid out in stone at the cliffside above the catacombs, in the obsidian glass of the chapel window. When I look at him, there's only an absence, as though my eyes can't comprehend the true horror of what stands before me. Pieces that won't fit into a whole: spiraled horns. Needle-sharp teeth. Rows of eyes that blink in a discordant rhythm. Long-fingered hands tipped by glimmering claws.

Where he walks, bones break through the ground. He comes closer, closer, closer. He is tall, endlessly tall, his sharpened horns piercing the canopy above. His mouth stretches wide, bearing cirriform fangs.

His gaze bores into me, a stare that hurts with how swift and deep it cuts, it *sees*. His eyes are vivid green—the same color as his son's.

Those eyes look through my flesh, my veins, my bones, and know the truth nestled there. That I was the child born at the edge of the lands which have been his prison. That my mother's blood was the blood he fed to his children to make them monsters. That I am the girl who bound his son in a vow of truce, sworn with holy words and unholy kisses.

Nyx reaches toward me. I open my mouth to speak, but my tongue is painted with ash; all I can do is release a soft, helpless cry. The world goes still. I sink to my knees, my arms still wrapped desperately around Lux. He touches my cheek; his hand is fever-hot. His sharp-clawed fingers trail gently through my hair.

"No." Ravel steps between us, shielding me from his father. He squares his shoulders, clenches his hands into blood-smeared fists. "Don't touch her."

Nyx stills, his attention diverted to his son. "Ravel." His voice is an ache. The sound of despair, of decay. Of things left abandoned to sink, forgotten, into the ground. "Take off that mask when you stand before me."

Head bowed, Ravel pulls off his mask with trembling fingers, banded by the markings laid there by his father as a gift, as a reward for shedding a layer of humanity when he grew his claws. He lets the mask drop to the mud, where it lies discarded beside the jutting bones. Uncovered, his face is smudged with corpsepaint. His loosened hair is snarled by the wind. The tattered hem of his mud-stained cloak snaps back and forth like a battle flag.

"Don't touch her," Ravel says again. His voice is low and terrible. "She's *mine*."

His words snake their way past tendrils and thorns, past the echoing space of horror where I kneel, clinging desperately to Lux. They pierce right into the center of my heart. I feel a pull, like there's a knot in my chest, a silken thread tied around each of my ribs, the other end of the thread anchored to Ravel. Our vows made real, our bond drawn tight.

She's mine.

Mine.

Mine.

Ravel stands between me and the monsters and his father who rules them all. He faces them down, and he claims me. *She's mine.* Wordless emotions surge up things that taste of want, of warmth, of heresy and broken vows.

I've fought and been ruined. My veins laced with magic and my fingers turned to claws. I think of my mother, now burned in the ashes of the chapel. Briar making the brave, dangerous journey alone back to the enclave. Fenn, who hid so many wretched secrets from me. The answers I've found, the questions I still need to ask.

I can't let this be the end. I refuse to submit; I won't accept a quiet death at the heart of the Thousandfold.

I pull Lux closer. At my wrists, the relics pulse and ache. A sharp, hard weight digs into my palm, and I realize I still have the shard Ravel used to draw his magic protectively around us. The end is all jagged, the bone sticky with his smeared blood. I nudge it into Lux's hand, my fingers pressed to hers. I shake her urgently, stir her awake. She shudders, her crimson eyes slowly focusing on me. Her attention goes to our clasped hands, the shard at the heart of our tangled fingers.

She gives me a soft, fleeting smile. "I missed you so much, Evie."

Then consecration flares up between us. It spills out across the ground and turns the rot and the mud to a wash of brightness, like the flames from a shattered lamp. Power spills in a wild rush, warden and vespertine, holy and unholy, the taste of honey and ash, life and death. This might be the last time I feel this. The last time I taste Ravel's magic, the last time I have the spark of consecration against my skin.

Around us, the jutting bones start to fracture, falling in pieces to the ground. My blood burns. The shard cuts into my palm as I clutch it tighter. I lean into the hurt as the world darkens.

The last thing I see, before the light blots out, is Ravel speaking rapidly to his father. And his face—there's no anger there, no knotted fury or teeth set in a fearful snarl. He's calm and earnest. Completely unafraid.

PART THREE

In blood and honey,
a warden swears eternal fealty.

—THIRD COMMANDMENT OF SAINT LENORE

CHAPTER TWENTY-ONE

I WAKE ON THE MOOR WITH LUX CURLED BESIDE ME; WE'RE laid out beneath a mist that covers the world in silvered silence—it could be morning or midnight or no time at all. My heart is pounding and my body trembling; I'm still caught by the panic of our flight from the Thousandfold. I sit up, look around anxiously for glimpses of vespertine, of the impossible eldritch form of Nyx Severin still reaching toward me.

But the air is still, and we are alone.

Ravel has gone. I knew he intended to leave, but the suddenness is an ache, a wound. I reach for Lux, who hasn't stirred. Her chest moves—she's breathing. And when I touch her, she awakens and sits up with a soft groan. She's pale and bewildered, but her eyes are clear—no longer the crimson-hued, blown-wide pupils that gazed raptly toward the approaching monsters.

"Evie?" She touches my hand, as though she isn't sure I'm real. Her breath sticks on a sound that's half-sob, half-laugh. "You saved me."

My eyes sting, and my vision blurs. *"Lux."*

Her name is all I can manage. A single, gasped-out note to encompass the time we've spent apart, the guilt that's chased me since I watched her vanish into the dark. And the image that lingers, persistent as a fresh bruise, of her laid out in the chapel with bones and vines and unholy magic snared all around her.

I cling to her, wishing I could somehow weave my entire soul with hers and never let her go. I want to take her back to the enclave where I can make her safe and warm, layer her in blankets and then, when she's recovered, dress her in polished armor with a sharpened blade at her hip. I will make sure the horrors we've escaped never find her or harm her again.

Lux starts to cry, pressing her face hard against my shoulder. I stroke her hair, soothing her, as fresh tears spill down my own cheeks. My new claws ache, and there's a welt at the heart of my palm left from when the shard I clutched pierced my skin. I feel as though I'm still in the Thousandfold, being devoured by the now-burned chapel, on my knees in the mud as Nyx Severin calls for me.

There's a stirring from the depths of the mist, the sound of footsteps. I glance up and see . . . Ravel. He stands at a measured distance away from us, his face turned against the wind. The sight of him—still here, when I expected him to have vanished—undoes something in me. I hold out my hand to him, my fingers trembling in the space between us. "You stayed."

He looks toward me. His mask is gone, and his face is bare, and without the horns and the corpsepaint, he's only *Ravel*—all concern and tenderness. The creature who held me in the dark and gentled my new claws. Who flushed when he kissed me, who stood up to his monstrous father in my defense.

He takes a step, sighs out a shuddering breath that plumes in the cold air. "Everline." His voice hitches. My name curls up on his tongue, silken and syrupy, like a heaped spoonful of honey. "Everline, you're safe."

Lux, still at my side, tenses as Ravel approaches us. Now she's free of the delirium of the Thousandfold, she sees him clearly for the first time. Her eyes widen, her cheeks are pallid beneath the wayward tears. She stares at him fearfully, and her hand goes to her waist in search of her absent blade. When her fingers close on nothing, she glances at me in confusion, her voice notched with fear. "Why is there a vespertine here with you?"

"This is Ravel. He—he helped me save you from the Thousandfold."

"He *saved* me? Evie, he *took* me there!" Lux stares at us both incredulously. The silence lengthens, a void filled by things I cannot say. A truth too complex to explain beneath the mist-draped sky with the dirt of the Thousandfold still clotted under my nails, with the lingering taste of magic on my tongue.

Then I notice Ravel has a cut on his throat: four jagged gashes—like claw marks—raked sharply across his flesh. Blood seeps over his skin, stains the open neckline of his shirt. "You're wounded."

He presses his hand to his neck. "It's nothing."

I get to my feet and move toward him, already tearing a strip of linen from my underdress. He tries to turn away, but I catch hold of his arm, drawing him to a stop. "Let me help you."

Lux watches as I tend to Ravel. I know she can see the familiarity in our movements. How he tilts back his head and goes pliant beneath my touch when I press the linen to his throat, how my hand doesn't tremble as I clean the blood from his wounds.

"What—" she begins, then falters, her voice turning haunted, the way she would sound when we whispered in the dark of our attic bedroom, when the memories of her sister pressed too close, and we would hold each other in the moonlight. "Everline Blackthorn, what have you done?"

Ravel takes the bloodied cloth from me, crumpling it inside his fist. He tightens the knot of his cloak, pushes a loosened snarl of hair back from his face. His mouth draws into a sharp, sorrowful frown. "Our arrangement is over now, Warden," he says quietly. "I've seen you both safely past the border of the Thousandfold. You owe me nothing more."

I take his hand, weave my fingers through his. This somehow feels like more of a danger than all we've done, all we've faced— the monsters and the burned-down chapel and the ire of his father. The press of our palms is agonizingly familiar, and even without a bone shard trapped between them, even without the snare of Thousandfold magic, there's a rightness to it, the way I feel when I'm close to him.

"Is that truly what you want?" I ask, soft and halting.

He traces his thumb across my claws, his eyes downcast. I take another step closer to him. Then—the ground flares alight. A line of wards has been sown through the grass. I falter back, confused, as the wards ignite one by one, until we're surrounded by a shimmering golden cage. In the distance, light flickers through the mist as though in answer to the wards; I hear my name caught up by the wind.

Lux gets unsteadily to her feet as two figures come into sight—Briar, with a lantern clutched in one hand, a string of bone beads in the other, and Fenn, his blade drawn, a halo of magic bright around his bloodied fist.

Briar gathers up her skirts when she sees us and begins to run, the light from her lantern throwing wild shadows against the ground as she comes closer. She stumbles to a halt when she reaches Lux. Then takes her by the shoulders and holds her at arm's length. Flushed and breathless, Briar examines Lux for signs of injury. "You're not hurt?"

"No," Lux says. "I'm not."

She looks again from me to Ravel. Her face crumples, and she starts to cry. Briar drags her into an embrace, and they cling to each other. Both sobbing uncontrollably, with the same raw woundedness I saw from Briar the night after Lux was taken.

Lux strokes her hands over Briar's hair, clutches at her waist, then buries herself against Briar's shoulder. It's a different grief, a different ache, than the way she cried when I held her. A mourning and a communion, the threads that were tied between them, that were severed by Lux's capture, now rewoven.

I'm lost to the sight of them, to the tangle of grief and guilt in my chest. I hardly notice when Fenn strides over to me, his hand on his blade, his gaze like blue fire.

"Everline," he says, and his voice has the same tenor as Nyx

Severin's did when he ordered Ravel to remove his mask. "Take your hands off that creature and get out of my way."

I look at my father. I look at Ravel, our hands that are still joined, our fingers woven together. Fenn draws his blade. I take a halting step forward, push myself in front of Ravel, shielding him. All I can see is the gleaming sharp edge of Fenn's weapon. The blade against Ravel's throat, a terrible repeat of his sister's death—blood and flames and ash, then nothingness. Tightening my hold on Ravel's hand, I shake my head. "No."

Fenn's brows drag together into a vehement scowl. "It wasn't a request."

He stares at me with the look of someone shown a captured image of the past. Here I am, repeating the same terrible steps my mother took when she betrayed her wardens for the love of a monster. But somehow, I can't regret this, any of it. I think of the rush of power that filled the room when Ravel fought back the vespertine surrounding my mother's cottage. How he stepped between his father and me at the edge of the Thousandfold. *She's mine.*

"We're vowsworn," I say to Fenn, sharp as a whetted blade. "He is *mine*. And I won't let you kill him."

Incandescent anger paints Fenn's features, as brilliant and furious as the fire that consumed the chapel. He sighs wretchedly and takes a leaden step toward us, teeth set, hand clutched tightly at his blade. He looks the way he did when he cut my palm that final time, when he last attempted to awaken my absent magic. Weary and desperate, a commander surveying the field of a losing battle.

He raises his blade, and I realize, helplessly, that he is crying. "Everline," he says again, fierce with grief. "Stand down."

With a blur of motion, Briar rushes forward and sets herself between us, her own blade drawn. Fenn falters back in blanched shock. He lowers his blade, so the honed edge points to the ground. Briar lowers her own weapon, too, but doesn't sheathe it. She raises a hand, her fingers trembling.

"Father—" she says raggedly, "please. Don't harm him. This creature—he helped us. He *saved* Lux."

Fenn stares at us wordlessly. Then, moving with the slow dread of someone caught in the depths of a nightmare, he turns toward Lux. He looks at her, with her white linen under-dress streaked by Thousandfold mud and the marks of snaring vines imprinted against her throat. The world turns still, all sound and motion suspended in a held-breath silence. Then, with a muttered curse, Fenn sheathes his blade.

He pulls the chain that connects the wards encircling Ravel and me from the ground. Drags it up in a confusion of silver and spark-lit shards and the trailing, dirt-clotted roots of torn-out grass. Teeth bared, he throws the mess of chains and bones at Briar's feet. "Bind him," he snaps, head tilted sharply toward Ravel. "Then all of you come with me."

Our return to the chapel is a grim mirror of the night when I first took Ravel captive. The same clink of chains snared tight around his wrists, the same bright song of unsheathed steel. Fenn holds the chain and keeps his blade set against Ravel's back, the point of it pressed neatly between his shoulders, just hard enough to be a warning.

Briar and I follow behind with Lux propped between us. Her fingers clutch tightly at my waist; her tears have dried to solemn salt tracks on her cheeks. Her other hand rests on Briar's shoulder, curled softly around the strap that holds her rib-cage armor in place. None of us speaks.

At first, there's only the undulating moorland grass and the clouded sky; then the veil of fog draws back and reveals the chapel, like an apparition. The scattered stones, the tangled ivy, the grove of citrus trees clustered beside the ruined kitchen.

Fenn waits beside the wrought iron fence while Briar takes down two of the wards. He drags Ravel through the gate, then motions for Briar to close it behind us. Grimly, she drops to one knee and pricks her finger as she pulls out fresh shards, resetting the barrier.

Inside, a fire burns in the brick hearth. More furniture has been brought into the room from the attic—a wooden bench and a table, the scarred top of which is covered by parchments and maps and a heavy book laid open, the pages weighted down by a ribbon-tied bundle of bone shards. It has the feel of Fenn's rooms at the enclave, except for the collapsed wall letting in a cold draft of air from outside.

Fenn turns toward Briar. "Take Warden Harwood upstairs and see to her wounds."

Lux casts a troubled glance toward me, her lip pinned between her teeth. Tightening her hold on my waist, she says, "I'm not so badly hurt, Commander."

Fenn glowers at her. Then, with effort, his expression softens. "Lux," he says, a note of gentleness laid over the cold steel of his voice. "Please do as I've asked."

She hesitates, then dips her head in a slow nod. She shifts her weight so she is leaning against Briar, who slips her arm around Lux's shoulders. Together, they make their way out of the room. I watch them go through the entrance to the main chapel, listening to the sound of their footsteps as Briar guides Lux up the stairs toward the barracks room.

Fenn winds up the clinking length of chain, then passes it to one hand. With his other hand, he reaches into the shard pouch at his belt and tugs loose a curved rib bone, sharpened at one end, and a vial of amber dark honey. He gives them both to me.

"Prepare the shard," he says. All the softness from when he spoke to Lux has gone.

With shaking hands, I open the vial and tilt it until a drip of honey spills onto the bone. When I've finished, Fenn takes the shard from me and pierces his thumb on the sharp edge. Blood wells brightly from his wound. He smears it down the edge of the bone, his blood mixed with honey and light gleaming up between his fingers, slow and guarded as a lantern flame. With the solemnity of a burial rite, Fenn presses the shard to my throat, where it curves against the purpled bruise left by Ravel's bite—the frank evidence of my treachery.

He begins to speak, gravely, words drawn out like an arcane spell. "Everline Blackthorn, I dissolve your vow to this creature. All you've promised to him is now undone. He is no longer beneath your protection."

I open my mouth to protest, but the force of his magic steals my breath. Fenn's power is heated and golden, and it pours down my throat like I've swallowed an entire bottle of tincture—it tastes of syrup and herbs, love and bitterness.

I clutch at my chest, as though there's a way to stop this, but the power has already begun to work through me, setting an ache against my ribs and a feverish heat inside my veins. It's like the fires we light in the flower fields to burn away the remnants of dead plants, to leave behind a scoured, clear earth.

Fenn notches the chains tighter around his fist. He drags Ravel toward him. With the blade still in his hands, he wordlessly directs him into the stillroom beside the kitchen hearth. I'm caught by the dying shudders of the torn-loose vow, my throat stopped with honey, my cheeks flushed with painful heat. I stretch out a shaking hand toward them both. "Wait."

But Ravel only shakes his head. He allows Fenn to lead him to the stillroom, his steps as slow and measured as if he's beneath the same spell that drew Lux from the ruins when he captured her. He refuses to meet my gaze, even as Fenn closes and locks the door behind him.

Fenn sheaths his blade, then looks down at his hands for a moment, as though they feel strange without the weight of the silver chain or the haft of his weapon. "Everline, I've spent your entire life teaching you to be a true warden. I can't believe how readily you've cast it all aside."

"All I ever wanted from you," I say quietly, "was the truth."

"The truth of the Thousandfold should be left buried."

A ragged laugh catches in my throat, threatening to become a sob. "Like my mother?"

As a child, I'd thought Fenn as wonderous as Saint Lenore—with his strength and his surety and his devotion to his vows. But now, beneath the proud commander of the enclave, I see the man who kept me at a distance when I wanted to be his daughter, to be loved unconditionally. Who lied to me about my past, who leavened me with guilt each time I questioned him.

Once, I would have done anything to win Fenn's approval. Once, his condemnation would have felt like a fatal wound. But now, as I stand before him with my bitten throat and the throb of Thousandfold magic in my veins, I refuse to be ashamed. After all I've seen and done—the broken vows and sacrosanct kisses, the way I let Ravel profane me on the altar—in the end, all that's left is this: myself, my father, and the past I fought so hard to uncover.

Fenn looks down at me. Fatigue cuts a deep shadow beneath his eye, and his hair has escaped its binding to fall loosely around his face. He glares at me, all challenge. Then, with a sigh, he tucks the strands of hair behind his ear with his chipped-polish fingers. "Yes, Everline. Like your mother."

Even now, my name on his lips makes my heart give a pained, treacherous hitch. I swallow, tasting crushed nightshade berries, the slickness of their dark juice. "You knew that she didn't just desert the wardens—she went to the Thousandfold. To Nyx Severin. You knew he was still alive."

Gently, Fenn puts his hand on my elbow and guides me out of the ruined kitchen, toward the main hall of the chapel. I look despairingly at the closed, locked stillroom door as we pass, thinking of the key Fenn holds, Ravel taken prisoner for a second time. All of this has the quicksand feel of a nightmare where I'm forced to repeat the same hopeless actions, until I'm fractured and ruined.

In the chapel, Fenn sits down on a wooden bench at the back of the room, as far as possible from the stained glass window. In the overcast light, the image of Nyx Severin is sullen and muted. Yet even this shadowy depiction—a silhouette in obsidian glass—is too much a reminder of the way he stood over me, reaching to me with his clawed eldritch hand.

I walk over to the bench, but I don't sit down. Instead, I stand in front of Fenn, the mud-stained toes of my boots lined with his. "You gave me a weapon and you taught me how to use it to kill the vespertine. You sent me out to fight them when they came from the dark. Yet you didn't think I was strong enough for the truth of my past?"

Fenn glances toward the window, staring at the leadlight form of Nyx for a long time. "When the vespertine broke through the wall, it wasn't at random—with unknown cause. The barrier didn't fail. Your mother let them through. It was sabotage."

"But—" I falter, trying to comprehend. "Why would she do such a thing?"

All the blood and ruin and death—Lux's sister, the lost wardens whose fiolae Ravel wore, all the people slaughtered in the

306

Hallowed Lands—it wasn't a chance occurrence. It was my mother's *fault*. Her deliberate choice.

Fenn spreads his hands wide, as though in supplication. "I loved Ila. It was a reckless love—it caught us both like a poison, like a fever. And as we grew closer, I failed in my duty. With Ila, I betrayed my vowsworn—Briar's mother—and I betrayed my wardens. There are truths I've had to bear, secrets each commander is entrusted to keep. Hiding Nyx Severin's existence is the most sacred of all my duties. But I was young, and it was a heavy burden. I . . . thought I could share that burden with Ila."

"You told her about Nyx Severin and she *went* to him?"

"There are some who cannot resist the allure of the Sanguine Saint. Even wardens are not immune."

I want to be horrified, shocked by the fact that among those who feared Nyx and all he'd wrought, there were others who were drawn to him. That my mother fell under the spell of such a monster. But is it so different from my own choices?

I bound myself to Ravel and used his magic for my own; I was *changed* by it. I learned his secrets and fed him my blood. I craved his touch. Even now, remembering the stolen closeness we shared in the hidden ruins sends a feverish tremor of heat through me.

"What—what did my mother do when she found him?"

Fenn lowers his head, releases a sorrowful breath. "Ila meant to offer herself to Nyx, and to offer you as well. I found her on the border of the Thousandfold with you in her arms. She had tried to cross and had been wounded by the vespertine magic. And Nyx Severin—he came for her. He came for you both. Your mother was dying, and I had no choice but to leave her behind, to save you and return to the wall."

Now the visions that plagued me as Ravel and I went through the Thousandfold make terrible sense. My mother in her white dress with her hair unbound, cradling me in her arms. The inhuman voice that called her name. It's always been my birthright—this betrayal, this unholiness. But I never knew how deeply it ran.

"I asked you," I say, my voice starting to choke. "So many times, I asked you. But you hid it from me, let me think I was ruined and powerless when my magic never came."

"I wanted to spare you from it all," Fenn insists. "You were already marked, and I thought to raise you at the enclave. That if all you knew was the warden vows, and that Nyx was dead, you'd be shielded from everything that had driven Ila to seek him out."

"And was part of that shielding to pretend I wasn't your daughter? How could I be a true warden, devoted to my vows, when my commander—my father—wouldn't even *look* at me?"

I fall to silence as tears rise, hot and sudden, behind my lashes. I swallow past the ache in my throat. With a blink, the tears fall loose, trailing over my cheeks.

Fenn shakes his head despairingly, his face carved into darkened lines of grief. "Because it was all I could think to do. It wasn't you I didn't trust. It was myself. I loved your mother. Enough to break my vows with her, to tell her the truth about Nyx. And she let the vespertine into the Hallowed Lands, used the distraction to flee the enclave, to go to him. I was her commander, and I failed her. I failed you, too, Everline. Just in a different way." He looks, stricken, toward the stained glass window. "But now we can finally end Nyx Severin's brutal reign."

My heart goes still. I picture Ravel in chains, the sharp point of a blade against his neck. Hazel with her throat cut, blood like garish lace on the front of her dress. The air in the hive fields clouded with funereal ash.

Nyx Severin, with his relentless craving for power, has cost the life of his daughter and has aimed a warden's blade at his son. And now my own father means to strike the final blow.

"No," I say fiercely. "Ravel had no choice in what he became. Nyx stole him away from the Hallowed Lands and made him into a monster. Ravel helped me to free Lux. He showed me the truth of my mother, stood with me as I mourned her. He protected me against the other vespertine. He doesn't have to be our enemy."

I lower myself down on the bench next to Fenn and lay my hand in the space between us, palm up, showing him the cut from where Ravel and I clutched the bone shard. The armor I made, tied at my wrists with crimson ribbons, the unholy relics still smeared with vespertine blood. Then I fold my fingers inward and let the faint lantern light gleam over my new onyx claws.

Fenn stares at me in silent horror. Painted clear across his features is all the love and guilt that he has for me, two emotions that bear equal weight. A broken vow, a secret shared, a daughter born at the border of the Thousandfold. A whole life spent trying to clean the blood from his hands, trying to atone for my mother's sins.

Quietly, he says, "Draw your blade, Everline." I hesitate, then draw the Vale Scythe and lay it across my knees. He looks at it solemnly. "Do you know why I gave this to you?"

I want to shake my head, but the answer is clear; it's the only thing he has ever asked of me. "So I could prove myself worthy of wielding it."

He nods, but my response only layers a further weight of despair on him. "You know what must be done, Everline. Take the relic blade and end that creature's life. This is the rightful choice, the best way to keep the Hallowed Lands—and the other wardens—safe. Without his son, Nyx Severin will be weakened, bound to the Thousandfold. We can strike against him with our full force."

"Ravel isn't our enemy," I say again, my voice fracturing. I taste blood and bitter honey and the ashen traces of Thousandfold magic. "Don't ask this of me. Please."

Fenn puts his hand over my hand, calloused fingers pressed to mine as we grip the relic blade in unison. "You have betrayed your vows, Everline. You've put the lives of your fellow wardens—including your own sister—in danger. You've drawn the fury of Nyx Severin, and bound yourself to his son. End that creature's life, tonight, and all will be forgiven. You'll make amends for not only your transgressions but those of your mother, too. We'll return to the enclave, and you'll have a place at my side as we prepare for the fight ahead."

I shake my head. "I can't."

"Then I will be forced to exile you to the Hallowed Lands. *After* I've seen that vespertine dead and burned."

"Father—" I choke, treacherous even now, more tears spilling over my cheeks.

There's a rustle from the stairs above, and I glance up to see Briar watching us in wide-eyed sorrow. Her cheeks are flushed, and her lip has been bitten raw; I know she's been there long enough to hear the entire truth of it—my blood-washed past, the depths of my mother's betrayal, and Fenn's ultimatum.

She comes down the stairs, her fingers tangled worriedly in the end of her braid. "Father," she says, and I shiver at the echo of it, of my own voice pleading to Fenn only moments before. "Some of Lux's wounds are worse than I thought. I need your help."

Fenn looks between us, his mouth drawn into a grim line. He takes the stillroom key from his pocket and presses it into my hand. "Everline, it's obvious you've grown close to that creature. But you can't forget what he is. Don't repeat the mistakes of your mother." He goes toward the stairs, then pauses with his hand on the banister to regard me levelly. "You have until I return to make your choice."

I stare up at him and Briar, the Vale Scythe an ominous weight across my lap. And then Briar looks at me for the briefest moment, her gaze full of unspoken things. She glances, meaningfully, toward the door that leads into the kitchen. Woven between us, like a tapestry of silken threads, comes delicate understanding.

This is the way she stood against Fenn out on the moors, when he held a blade to Ravel's throat. This is the way she held my hand and wore my armor, and we became truly sisters.

Briar and Fenn go into the rooms above the chapel hall. I get to my feet. I don't sheathe my blade. I curl my clawed fingers closed, tightly, around the key.

CHAPTER TWENTY-TWO

THE DOOR OPENS WITH THE SOFT *CLINK* OF KEY AGAINST lock. Ravel is sitting in the corner with the chains still wrapped around his wrists. His head is tipped back, his eyes are closed. The stillroom is dim, with only a sliver of illumination cutting down from where part of the ceiling has crumbled away, forming a makeshift skylight. All I can make out clearly is the glint of the silver chain, the pale column of his bared throat.

Seeing him this way, tired and wary, his face smudged by Thousandfold dirt and his hair tangled with dead leaves, I can almost forget what he is. And though he's never claimed to be anything *else*, I still don't know which is the truth: the monster or the boy. Perhaps it is both—a borderland where one eclipses the other. Horns and bones and claws, gentle fingers and soft breath and my name spoken like a secret.

Was this how it was for my mother, impossibly drawn to Nyx Severin? The horror of her betrayal, the destruction she wrought, is a fresh wound. Such violence and carnage, all those lives destroyed.

And for all that I've tried to distance myself from her legacy, right now I feel as though I'm at my own borderland, torn between duty and desire, faced with the suffering my choices will cause.

Ravel stirs at the sound of my footsteps. He turns to me with languid slowness. His eyes are blurred, shaded with fatigue.

"Come outside," I tell him, keeping my voice quiet. "We don't have long."

He gets to his feet, the chain clinking as it drags across the floor. His movements would be trusting if not for the way he watches me—his gaze is fixed, narrowed and wary.

When I gather up the chain, I feel the ghost of Fenn's touch, his fingers curled around mine. The solemn way he told me *I failed you* is imprinted on my heart like a scar.

I lead Ravel out of the ruin. At the wrought iron gate, I break the wards to let him pass. We slip through the overgrown garden, our heads bowed as we hurry beneath the storm-drenched citrus trees, rainwater dripping and dripping around us from their branches. The moorland is draped in fog; it swallows us as we leave the path behind. Swiftly, we walk away from the ruined chapel, and we're hidden by the shroud of silver.

Ravel casts a guarded look at me, tracing the line of the chains in my hands, the Vale Scythe at my hip. "Are you to be my executioner, Everline?"

I think of how I caught him and chained him and hated him. Held my blade to his throat, cut his claws, wounded him with the consecrated shard. The night he stole Lux away, I longed for his demise. And it hurts to know how easy it would be. The Scythe in my hand, the relic edge honed sharp.

I curl my fingers closed against my palm, my new claws pressed to the memory of a knife, a smear of honey, a vial. All those desperate, failed attempts to create a fiola, to make sense of my origins, to close the distance between myself and Fenn—my father. With Ravel's death, it could all be erased.

Here is a magic I could work: cut the throat of a monster and take the power from a god. I'd return to the enclave like a Saint, and this time, when I stand beside the wall at the gathering, I'd be there as an equal. A warden who has earned her place, proved her devotion. I could undo the wretched legacy of my mother, her betrayal and her broken vows.

I could undo the vows *I've* broken in my search for the truth about her life, her death.

But now, faced with this chance, all I can do is whisper, "I don't want to be your enemy."

The words feel too raw, too dangerous. Ravel's mouth crooks up in a hard, sad smile. Then he raises his hand, and bites at the edge of his thumb. The chain slackens in my grasp as he moves toward me, presses his thumb to my lips. I swallow, tasting his blood.

He leans close. The heat of his words casts over my skin like a caress. "Everline Blackthorn, I dissolve my vow to you. All I've promised is now undone. Our truce has ended." He bows his head in supplication. "I am entirely at your mercy."

I stare at him, struck wordless as the weight of his actions fall into coherence. Ravel has stripped away the vow sworn in blood that compelled us to protect each other. This is the moment when I stood at the altar and bared my throat to him, all the trust between

314

us—warden and vespertine, maiden and monster—laid out like bones on an ossuary. The rare and tender bond we've forged, the *we might*, is now distilled: We are bound not by force or magic, only our wills.

Ravel presses his lips to mine in a brief, tender kiss. The last strands of our bond dissolve with the feel of a silken ribbon drawn over my skin. There's none of the brutality with which Fenn tore loose our vows, no rush of holy fire. This is petals plucked from a flower, a handful of stones scattered into a mirror-still riverbed, clouds pared back from the moon on a darkened night.

I lean against Ravel, my face pressed to his shoulder as my eyes sink closed. I think of my mother beneath the snare of vines, the way my hands trembled when I placed my fiola against her throat. I think of a chapel outlined in flames, the howls of vespertine, the air filled with ash. All I am certain of right now is that Nyx Severin must be destroyed.

"It doesn't have to be this way," I murmur. "We worked together to make my armor with blood and magic. We rescued Lux. We don't have to be enemies."

My hair is still loose—a mess of waves and tangles that spills around my shoulders. He reaches to me, chains trailing, and tucks back a curl from my cheek. His claws linger, tracing delicately across my skin. "Then spare my life. Spare my life and set me free. I promise you: I will find a way to stop my father."

I pull him to me with the clink of chains. His mouth meets mine. He kisses me like I have a knife to his throat. He kisses me like he's condemned. His fangs are sharp against my lip. I taste my own blood mixed with the traces he smeared against my mouth when he unmade our vow. Tense heat uncoils from my belly, winds all through me. My want for him is too fierce, too hot. A poison spread too far through my veins.

We draw apart, our ragged breaths echoing loudly beneath the trees. Ravel's cheeks are flushed, a dark smear of blood stains the edge of his mouth. My hands are at his wrists, working loose the silver chains. They fall on the ground between us, and I let out a shuddering, wretched sob.

I look back in the direction of the chapel, now completely hidden by the mist. I wish . . . so many things. That Ravel was still my vowsworn. That I could stand beside Fenn and let him claim me as a true daughter. Instead, I'll go back to the chapel and set my betrayal down like an offering as I kneel at Fenn's feet, let him strip me of my place in the wardens and send me into exile.

I wrap my arms around Ravel, and we're swathed in his cloak; I can feel the heat of his chest and the shudder of his ribs. I run my hand down the line of his waist, thinking of the notched scar, the tender way he moved against me when I touched him in the ruins. "You have to go," I tell him, tears wet against my cheeks, my tongue tasting of salt.

Ravel traces his blunted claws from my nape to the base of my spine. Then his hand goes to my hip, his fingers curled against me. I can feel the feverish heat of his palm through the pale fabric of my dress. His mouth brushes my ear, my throat.

"I love you, Everline." His voice is soft—soft enough to go right through my skin and curl up beside my heart. He says it like a fact, like it doesn't matter if I love him or not, like he doesn't expect an answer either way. It's not a question, just words laid out like our footsteps across the moorland behind us, like rain over leaves, like clove-scented incense smoke trailing from a censer. "I love you."

Then his teeth scrape my neck, and he bites down.

I struggle against him, a confused, incredulous cry tangled in my mouth. "What are you doing?"

His tongue rasps my throat, licking at the wound; then he bites me again. Everything turns blurred and heated, my vision fading and my heartbeat faltering. Finally, with an aching slowness, he works his fangs free. He presses a sticky kiss against my ear, his breath sharp with the metallic scent of my blood. He's a wolf that has drawn back from a fresh kill, gore streaked over his fur.

My hand goes to my belt, fumbling and dizzy, as I try to draw my blade. But he starts to whisper against me, his voice low and lulling. Words sift into my ears: an eldritch prayer, grotesque poetry with the cadence of holy speech.

There's something in Ravel's hand. A bone shard. He twists it against his fingers, presses the sharp edge to his thumb. There's a sudden sting, a bright hurt, and his magic pours over me, through me. I feel as though I've been submerged in a too-hot bath, my skin streaked with sweat, my pulse turned slow, my blood like heated honey.

"Ravel—" I gasp; then my eyes sink closed, and I slump against him.

When he lifts me into his arms, my hand is still clutched around the hilt of my blade.

He holds me tightly, unyieldingly. He carries me away into the dark. I have been swept up by a feathered, fearsome beast who crosses night skies on onyx wings; I'm caught by a suddenly risen flood and swept beneath the current, my whole world lost to the lightless silence of the river depths.

We pass the ruins and the wind-bowed trees. The marshy tributaries of the Blackthorn River. We pass the cottage where my mother lived, where she gazed from the window and thought of Nyx Severin. We reach the border of the Thousandfold, and Ravel sets me down onto my feet.

I draw my blade, the motion all instinct—I'm caught by delirium, too unsteady to do anything but weakly struggle against his grasp. He lifts his hand, still clutching hold of the shard. His mouth moves, shaping arcane words. Mist spills past the skeletal trees with the hollow gasp of wind through an unlit fireplace. Beneath my boots, the ground turns to mud. Oozing, rippling, as Ravel drags me forward.

I will myself to struggle, to fight, but I'm lost beneath the force of his magic.

"No," I gasp. "Ravel, you can't do this. Please—"

I trusted him. I trusted him, I spared his life, and he has shown himself to be what I should never have forgotten. Treacherous, untamable. A monster.

We cross the border of the Thousandfold. Sharpened bones and dark-leaved vines and brutal thorns rise up, tearing through the earth. I stumble, faltering, trying to keep my balance. But Ravel hooks his foot around my ankle and shoves me forward. My knees hit the ground; I land beside the spired bones, the wild tangles of thorn.

He drops to one knee, crouched beside me, his fingers working through my loosened hair. He cups his hand over the back of my neck, where my warden mark throbs and throbs. He forces me to bow forward.

He holds me in place—supplicant—as his father comes toward us.

The world goes still. Everything tangles together, an indecipherable knot. And then, suddenly, I understand. The way Ravel stepped between Nyx and me after we escaped the burned-down chapel. His expression when he talked to his father, earnest and unafraid. How he claimed me—*mine*.

I thought it was the mix of Lux's magic and Ravel's power—the burn of holiness and decay, light and dark—that set us free from the Thousandfold. But I was wrong.

"We never escaped," I manage. "He—he let us go, because you promised him—"

"Yes." Ravel's fingers tighten against my neck, his blunted claws pressing harder into my skin. "I needed your warden returned safely to meet the terms of our promise so it could be undone. So I could offer you in her place—a holy girl who broke her vows, who corrupted herself with all the power of the Thousandfold."

"You betrayed me." My breath catches on the edge of a sob. "*Ravel*, I trusted you."

I am lost, lost, lost. I am devoured by a surge of hungering vespertine; I am inside the chapel as the walls ignite. I am snared by vines as the Thousandfold consumes me in a last, desperate swallow.

Nyx Severin rises out of the dark, an impossibility of shadows and horns and shimmering eyes. He stands above me, smiling widely. His mouth is endless teeth, a starveling gleam, as he reaches out with his cruel, pale hand; he has the same onyx claws as Ravel. His fingers are marked with the same pattern of lines, bands of blackened ink. It aches to look at him, but I'm held captive by my terror, unable to turn away.

He makes a sharp, displeased sound. His voice, cold and inhuman, scrapes like a blade against my skin. "You gave her your name."

"I did," Ravel says. There's a note in his voice—regret. But I can't tell if he's sorry for how he deceived me or if he hates to admit to our intimacy.

His hand slides away from my nape, and he takes a step back. My fingers clutch at the dirt. The Vale Scythe is half-buried in the mud beneath me. I should fight—I know I should fight—but Ravel's magic has turned me languid and syrup-soft, entranced by the familiar ache of vespertine power, his treasonous words placed with bloodstained kisses against my ears.

Nyx touches a claw beneath my chin. I stare up at him, helpless, as his face shifts and blurs. The hollowed gaze and horns and jagged teeth shimmer and soften; the eldritch brutality of his form coalesces into a new shape. He is no longer the inhuman creature I've seen carved in stone, paned in obsidian glass, the nightmare that appeared before me in visions, that has haunted me across the moorland.

Now, he looks human.

Nyx Severin looks like his son but with all the softness excised. The same silk-straight hair, the same golden skin, the same green eyes like multifaceted chips of malachite. His mouth tilts into a feral, familiar smile, and my heart falters.

"My son has found a way to prove his worth once and for all." His thumb skates along the line of my jaw as he examines me, a satisfied noise in the depths of his throat. "When he carves you open in the ashes of my chapel and spills your blood on my ruined altar, I will be unstoppable."

I try to pull away from his grasp, a frantic breath escaping my gritted teeth. Ravel didn't unmake our vows to prove his trust, to show we didn't need magic or promises to connect us. He needed me unbound, our truce broken, so my death will not harm him.

I'm a sacrifice, ready to be sliced apart, torn open, a replacement for his sister and my mother both. I clench my teeth until I taste blood. I swallow down the bitterness of Ravel's betrayal like it's a tincture. I tighten my hold on the Vale Scythe, and I let out a furious snarl as I push myself up from the ground.

My blade sings through the mist-wreathed air. Nyx feints easily out of reach, his laughter like the seethe of a storm cloud, the roll of thunder across barren ground. Magic rises around us in an endless haze, cold and brutal and wild. But I don't try to strike him again. Instead, I turn sharply to Ravel, shove him aside and run toward the line of trees.

I flee to the border of the Thousandfold, away from Ravel and his betrayal, away from Nyx Severin's reach.

"Stop her," Nyx snaps, biting down on the order like his teeth are piercing a vein.

Shadows rise around me, streaked against the heavy mist. My breath plumes out in clouds of frost. There are shapes painted against the darkness: sharp claws, snapping teeth, the gleam of narrowed eyes. Ravel comes toward me, borne on a sea of vespertine. A beat passes between us as his eyes search my face. I think of his gentleness, his uncertainty, the honeyed heat of his kisses, our tender words to each other in the dark.

Then I'm on him, frenzied, desperate. Everything moves in a blur—swift and brutal. Ravel's fingers curl to claws, and his bared teeth lengthen. I cut at his chest, slashing across his collarbones. His claws carve into my arm; his teeth snap closed in the air beside my throat. Blood spills down between us, copper-bright. As it falls to the ground, decay blooms from the earth. Sharp-tipped bones, snaring roots. Snakes that circle my feet—onyx eyes and gleaming ruby bellies, brilliant against the night.

We trade strike for strike. He is a monster, but I am a warden, raised to destroy creatures just like him. Raised to destroy the vespertine that circle us with bared fangs, snapping at my heels, sidling beneath the sweep of my blade.

"End this," cries Nyx Severin from beyond the line of trees. His voice is remorseless, harsh as a flood that means to drown the world. "Ravel, end this *now*."

The snakes at my feet turn to dark-leafed vines. The vespertine are a furious circle around me with no beginning or end—only fangs and claws and hunger. Ravel catches hold of the front of my dress, lace crushed to nothingness inside his fist, and drags me down into the mud as the vespertine howl and howl.

It's heart-wrenchingly intimate: his breath in my ear, my claws at his throat, the weight of him against my body. The way I can see myself reflected in his gaze, my tangled hair, my eyes spark-bright with rage, the Thousandfold mud smeared across my cheeks like a grotesque imitation of corpsepaint.

Ravel leans toward me, and everything is stained with despair and longing and flame-hot anger. "You're *mine*, Everline Blackthorn."

He raises his hand. I clench my fingers tight around my blade. Picture him torn to pieces, his throat cut open. Laid out on a pyre in the hive fields as I burn him to ash. I taste the force of it, my wish for his destruction, overlaid by the mournful bitterness of sorrow.

"And you're mine, Ravel Severin," I snap fiercely. "As much as I'm yours. I will not let you claim me."

We both move at the same time. My hand comes up; his comes down. He hits me at the center of my chest, his palm streaked with blood and pooled with writhing magic. It sends a shuddering, wretched ache through my ribs, and I gasp, tasting rust and poison. My claws rake across his face, and his blood spills over my fingers. A riot of power entangles him—the Thousandfold magic, caught up on my claws and my relics like a memory, like an aftershock.

Ravel looses a ragged cry. I slash at his throat with the Vale Scythe. The cuts on his face—left from my claws—turn black as poison. He crumples to his knees, his cloak around him like an oil spill, the wound on his cheek vivid and bloody against his shocked, pallid face.

Inside the Thousandfold, Nyx hisses and snarls. He strains against the border, one clawed hand outstretched, fingers hooked against the air. And on his cheek, four black marks rise raggedly—a mirror to the wound on his son. When I harmed Ravel, it harmed his father, too.

The vespertine surge forward, and I feel the heat of their panting breaths against my face. They form a line between Ravel and me, circling him protectively. The largest one steps forward, its pale coat like starlight. Ravel raises a shaking hand, then clutches the pale vespertine's fur. It bows toward him, and he whispers, desperately, his mouth beside its pointed, bone-studded ear.

The ground trembles beneath us, and more dark-leafed vines spear up through the soil. I stumble back, the single burst of furious adrenaline already dying from my limbs. Each time my heart beats, my whole body feels bruised, and my breath comes out aching. The other vespertine swarm around Ravel. They catch hold of him with their teeth—by his wrists, by his shoulders, by the trailing fabric of his cloak—and drag him back toward the border of the Thousandfold.

The sharp scent of decay and ash, the familiar scent of unholy magic, fills the air. Nyx folds himself around Ravel with a snarl. The world hazes over—blackness splotched with petalled red. I blink, and they are gone.

I blink again, and everything goes dark.

CHAPTER TWENTY-THREE

I'M LAID OUT ON THE MOORLAND BENEATH A COPSE OF TREES, their latticed branches sheltering me from the worst of the rain. Vague recollections of how I got here are marked on my body like a trail through a fabled forest: scrapes on my palms and mud on my knees, a tattered piece of lace bound to my throat like a bandage.

I sit up, disoriented. Everything is incoherent, the landscape lost beneath a heavy blanket of low-lying clouds.

Then, in the distance, I hear the telltale sound of the river, the chorus of currents drawing together. I get to my feet and stumble forward, my boots sinking into the mud. Hesitantly, I make my way through the mist with my hand outstretched and my gaze narrowed, trying to decipher the blurred shapes in the near distance.

I let the world condense, all my attention focused on the path ahead—my footsteps, the moor, the river. Thinking of anything but the pain in my chest or the wound at my throat. The persistent memory of Ravel's voice. It's not the words of his spell that linger but his other confession. *I love you, Everline.*

The taste of his confession fills my mouth like poison. I swallow it down with a shuddering sigh. When I look again at the moorland, a shape has arisen in the distance: dark stone, a moss-hemmed roof. I'm near the place where the river's tributaries weave over the ground, near the cottage where Ravel and I hid from the vespertine. My mother's cottage.

I bow my head against the rain and hurry toward it, drawn as though by an invisible thread.

Inside the cottage, everything is cold and unfamiliar. I shed my rain-drenched cloak and my mud-clotted boots, take off my armor. Without the relic bracers, my wrists feel strangely bare and vulnerable. I wish I could scour Ravel clear from my mind, but too many pieces of him are imprinted on me.

I press my hand to my bitten, lace-wrapped throat. Remembering his expression when he pushed me to my knees at the Thousandfold border. Like I was a lock and he heard the final click as he worked it loose.

I spared his life and learned his name. Kissed him. *Wanted* him. I searched out the softness around his edges. And I never should have forgotten that he was a monster. He never pretended otherwise; I deceived only myself. It's as though I cut a pattern from tailor's paper, then tried to make it into an entirely different garment; now I'm left with a mistake to unpick, and no idea where to begin anew.

I have to return to the chapel—to Fenn and Lux and Briar—and accept my fate. Just like my mother, I've entangled myself with a monster, and now everything the wardens are sworn to protect is at risk. I've become exactly what Fenn always feared—treacherous, foolish, my vows shattered like broken glass at my feet.

I cross the room on wavering footsteps, find a lantern on the shelves above the hearth. The oil is low, gritted at the bottom, but I coax alight a small, stuttering flame. There's a loose coil of rusted wire on the wall outside the door, and I hook the lantern there so the light can glimmer in the direction of the chapel like a beacon through the mist.

Then I go back inside the cottage. I tuck myself into the sleeping alcove, into the bed, wrapping my mother's tattered woolen blanket around me. Something sharp has tangled in the front of my dress, caught on a twist of ribbon. A shard of bone, sticky with dried blood and spiked at one end. The shard Ravel used to cast his magic when we fought.

I work it loose, the curved shape familiar against my palm. I turn it over and over, imagining my mother's last doomed days in this cottage. The Thousandfold a beckoning shadow at the horizon, her heart filled with equal parts fear and hope as the vespertine howled in the night. I close my eyes, give in to the fatigue pressing down on me. I wonder what she dreamed of on her final night alive.

Time drags out, vacant and formless, marked only by the ache of my wounds, the press of the shard against my palm. The rain falls with a drumbeat rhythm against the cottage roof, taps delicately against the window glass. Beyond, the moorland is cast by the low-pitched whine of wind, the endless rush of the river.

Then comes another, more human sound. A voice—calling my name.

I sit up, the shard still clutched in my hand. The voice comes again. I get to my feet, cross the room, and cautiously open the door. A light floats through the mist beyond the cottage, twin to the lantern I hung outside. It flickers, luminous, as the second lantern and its bearer come into sight. Lux appears like a creature from a dream, with her hair braided back and her lips painted dark, her blade drawn and her rib-cage armor buckled neatly over her dress.

She puts down her lantern and sheathes her blade, running toward me. I fall into her arms, my face buried against her shoulder as I start to cry. "Evie," she says, breathless, tearful. "Evie, what *happened* to you?"

I scrub at my eyes with my sleeve, fitfully wiping away my tears. "I thought I could change things, Lux. I thought Ravel wanted to change things, too. But I was wrong."

She draws back to look me over, tender and frightened, her hands trembling as she tucks my hair away from my face. She reaches to the makeshift bandage at my throat, peels aside the sodden fabric and inspects my wounds, hissing through clenched teeth at the sight of the ragged marks. Then, she leads me over to the bed. I sit down; she sits beside me and takes her field kit from her satchel.

As she draws out gauze and antiseptic, I tell her everything that happened while she was held captive in Nyx Severin's chapel. How I lured Ravel from the dark and made him my prisoner, how I saved his life, and we swore our vows. I tell her everything about the wretched, heretical nature of our agreement—my blood for his magic, the deepening bond that formed between us as he led me through the catacombs, then into the depths of the Thousandfold.

Lux shakes her head, her painted mouth tipped into a fond, mournful smile. "If anyone would try to make a feral wolf into a tame hound, it would be you."

I can't help but laugh. "Fenn was right, though—what he said when he found us, after we escaped. No true warden would ever make the choices I did. I should have cut Ravel's throat and burned him to ash long ago."

Her smile fading, Lux soaks the gauze with antiseptic and gently starts to clean my wounds. "Evie, don't condemn yourself because compassion stayed your hand."

I lean back as she blots the gauze over my skin, welcoming the sharp astringent hurt against the heated throb of the bite. "The wretched thing is—I can understand why Ravel betrayed me," I admit, my voice still heavy with tears. "Once, I'd have given anything for Fenn to see me wholly. Even tonight, when he told me I'd be forgiven if I executed Ravel—I was tempted. Ravel and I both wanted the same thing. To claim our birthright, to be recognized by our fathers. We were both offered that choice; only, we took different paths."

Lux takes out a smaller jar of honey salve. I breathe in the syrupy, herbal scent as she smears it on my cuts. "I won't let Fenn exile you. Neither will Briar. We'll stand by you when you come back."

I sit very still, clutching the bone shard, while Lux binds my throat with a fresh linen bandage. When my claws press against my palm, it's like a rediscovered memory. I think of Ravel, my fingers carving over his cheek. The way he flinched as the cuts turned black, like he'd been poisoned by my touch. And the way Nyx Severin hissed and writhed and bore an echoing wound.

Father and son, inexorably linked, both vulnerable to my attack.

The realization is a newly made set of armor, relic bones and ruined magic laced tight against my wrists. There's only one way this can end—and it isn't with my return to the chapel where Fenn waits to exile me.

Slowly, I stretch out my hand, show Lux the shard, which is still sticky with Ravel's blood. I show her my claws. She gasps, her cheeks turning petal-bright. "Oh," she says, raw and aching. "Oh, Evie."

"I was born at the border of the Thousandfold," I tell her. "I was marked for the wardens since that moment. I have no holy magic, but I can wear armor imbued with vespertine power, cross into their lands in a way that others can't. With my claws—with this shard—I could destroy him. I could destroy them both."

"And destroy yourself, too. You know how the story of Saint Lenore ends."

"But what they told us about her wasn't true. She sacrificed herself and weakened Nyx Severin's power, but she didn't kill him. He's always been there, alive. Waiting. Vulnerable. And now I can finish what Saint Lenore began."

Lux stares at me in wordless sorrow. Tears bead her lashes; she blinks them away. She takes my hands between her own. Her thumb drags over my claws, testing their sharpness. *You would make a beautiful monster.* Then, with a shuddering breath, she draws me close, presses her lips to mine in a desperate kiss. "Tell me," she whispers. "Tell me how I can help."

I wrap my arms around her, bury my face in her braided hair. "Give me your blood for the shard. Then go back to the chapel and tell Briar and Fenn you didn't find me."

She doesn't move. "I don't want to leave you."

We stay together on the bed, and I close my eyes, pretend we are back in the enclave in our attic room. Where Lux can soothe away my nightmares and my longing, and I can hear stories about her sister, her left-behind family, her hopes and grief. "Once this is finished, I'll come back. I promise. I walked from the ashes of the Thousandfold once; I will do it again."

Lux holds me for a moment longer, then takes the shard from my hand. Gaze downcast, she pricks her thumb and wipes a smear of blood across the bone. Her mouth moves, murmuring her spell with the softness of a lullaby.

The shard lights with a consecrated glow. I take it from Lux, slip it into my pocket. Then, taking me by the shoulders, she lays me gently down on the bed. "You should rest. Let that wound start to heal over, at least, before you leave."

I curl up on my side, let her tuck the blanket around my shoulders. She looks at me for a moment; then she unbuckles her armor—the rib-cage bodice I made for her—and places it next to my cloak and my bracers. "Thank you," I tell her.

In the doorway, she hesitates. Neither of us wants to say

goodbye, to acknowledge this might be our last moment together. She takes the lantern and walks out onto the moorland, sparing me one, final, yearning glance. Then the mist swallows her up.

As I sink into sleep, I feel the hum of magic in my bones, the throb of power at my wrists where the bracers were tied. And perhaps it's this snare of magic that makes my dreams betray me. They lead me to thorn-hemmed ruins, to vows sworn with bloodied kisses. To my name, whispered like a close-kept secret.

I feel the weight at the edge of the bed before I open my eyes. The lantern has burned out, and the cottage is all shadow. The figure beside me is a dreamscape silhouette—the silken fall of hair, the heavy fabric of an ink-dark cloak, the planed curve of a paint-smudged cheekbone.

"Ravel."

He is a creature from a lead-light window, carved on a cliffside above a saltspring. But when I stretch out my hand and touch him, he's solid beneath my fingertips.

My hand is on his wrist, my thumb against his pulse. He doesn't move, but his heartbeat is racing; he's wound tight with apprehension. "Everline," he says, voice as silvery as the mist. "I could kill you now, you know."

"Do you think your father would be proud if you did? You could go home and tell him, *I killed her when she was lonely, asleep in her bed*." I tighten my hold on him, claws pressed sharp against the tendons of his wrist. "I could just as easily kill you now, too."

He turns sharply to look at me. "Is that what you want?"

Our eyes meet, and all I intended to do—or say—is gone. Fresh corpsepaint marks his cheeks, but the right side of his face is raised, angry wounds. He's cleaned away the blood from the claw marks, painted them with some kind of salve to seal them closed. His eye is the color of a blood eclipse, crimson trapped beneath the sclera. His brow is notched by a cut, and it makes him look puzzled, even though his face is solemn.

I think of the shard tucked in my cloak, lit by Lux's consecration. No, I don't want him dead like this, in the cold anonymity of my mother's cottage. I want him on his knees, begging. My hand on his nape, pushing him down the way he pushed me into the Thousandfold mud. His face to the stone floor of the chapel ruins. The Vale Scythe sharp and singing as I draw it across his throat.

I loosen my hold on his wrist. I lift my hand to touch the edge of his ruined, beautiful face. "Was everything between us a lie, Ravel?"

He stares at me for a long time, expression filled with unreadable emotion. Then, haltingly, he says, "No. Not everything."

"I am going to kill you. And your father." My voice is a caress, as luring as the spell he cast on me. "Tomorrow, I'll kill you both. I'll find you in the Thousandfold and I'll destroy you; I'll destroy everything you've created."

Ravel lets out a tattered breath. My hand is still on his cheek, and he takes hold of it, capturing it between his own. He drags his thumb against the sharp tips of my new claws. The same way that Lux did. The similarity in how they've both touched me sends a shudder of longing through my body.

He presses down, just enough for my claws to leave a dimpled pinprick on his fingers. "Until then . . . what are your intentions?"

I force myself to keep still, but I'm already half-lost to the heat of his gaze, the electricity of his hand clasped to mine. "What are yours?"

"I want to keep our truce for a little longer."

Then he raises my hand to his mouth. He presses his lips to my palm. A sound escapes me, hitched and sharp, as his breath sears my skin. My wrists throb, and I feel the phantom weight of the relic bracers, now laid neatly on the floor beside my cloak and Lux's armor. I feel the remembered press of his magic in my veins, unspooled alongside some deeper current—tense and hot and deadly.

I curl my fingers against his jaw, and he kisses my palm again. This feeling—this longing—I should have banked it to ash. Buried it where I lay in the mud beside the Thousandfold. Ravel betrayed me, delivered me to Nyx Severin to earn his redemption. Tomorrow, I'll cut his throat while his father watches. And even with that inevitable truth, after everything that's passed between us . . . I answer him without hesitation.

"A truce," I echo. "For a little longer."

I knot my fingers into the fabric of his cloak, drag him close, and kiss him. His mouth is open, shocked and gasping, and he goes fearfully still—like he expects my claws sunk into his throat or my blade pressed to his heart. I draw him closer, coaxing him, my thumb beneath his jaw, feeling the riot of his pulse, the shiver that my touch has raised on his skin. He groans against me, catches hold of my waist, and bears me down onto the bed.

As we twine together, it draws loose a memory of our tryst in the ruins beneath the thorns. The way we unfolded, slow and tentative with each other, like we knew it should have been impossible, forbidden. But now, there is no softness in how I touch him or how he touches me. There's nothing tentative. This is a fight; it's cutting the skin to free the poison.

He struggles loose from his cloak and kicks off his boots. I untuck his shirt, rake my claws beneath the hem. His bare skin is feverish; his chest heaves with ragged, panting breaths. His claws pin my wrist. I set my blunt, unfanged teeth to his throat and bite him hard enough to bruise. He rasps out an eager sound, shakes himself free long enough to pull off his shirt in a single, fluid motion. Then he falls on me again.

My mouth grazes over the wounds on his cheek, wounds that I made with my claws. The coppery sharpness of his blood is on my tongue, mixed with something sticky and sweet—like he's used the same honeyed salve on his cuts as Lux used when she tended to me.

Ravel kisses me with the same desperation as when we made our vow, as though I have dragged him once more from the flooded river. He tastes of bitter coffee and despair.

I want this. All of this. No matter that it's reckless and terrible. No matter the betrayals he's served me and the lies we've told each other, that he offered me up to his father like a prize. I want him, but that doesn't mean I've forgiven him. Our fragile truce won't last, but now—right now—is an understanding, an acknowledgment that the way we've tangled ourselves up is owed adequate severance.

All that's passed between us could never finish with quiet death in a ruin on the moorland.

He presses closer and closer against me, the weight of him

between my parted thighs. My claws scrape his skin, mapping his ribs, the thorned scar on his side. His heart is wild when I lick my tongue over his pulse. His hands are in my hair, on my waist, tangled in my skirts as he pulls at the hem.

I sit back, sit up, and let him undress me.

I'm a ghost in the darkness. I'm relics laid into an ossuary. Ravel strokes my cheek, then trails his hand along my neck, across my collarbone. He waits—eyes on mine. "I want you," he says, gaze veiled, cheeks flushed.

My lashes dip as I nod once. As I give my permission.

His hands stroke over me. Lower, lower. Past the swell of my breasts, the curve of my waist, the softness of my belly. Lower. Want flares into star-bright desire. His fingers tremble against my skin, like he can't believe I'm real. Ravel leans over me, his forehead pressed to mine. He's shy and beautiful, and the way he slips his hand between my thighs is slow, reverent. He touches me like I'm something holy.

I lift myself against him. Run my fingers down the line of his ribs, his waist, his hip. The buckles at his waistband slide apart easily. I remember the way he guided my hands against him in the ruin, uncertain and boyish, so achingly new. He's laid bare in that same way now. I've learned how to touch him, learned exactly how to make him gasp.

"You're mine," I tell him. "You're mine."

"Yes," he breathes. "I'm yours."

He sinks into me. I'm unashamedly slick and needful, my back arched and my vision turned to a haze that's as bright as unveiled stars. There's a stark, delirious sensation at being so *near* to him—how there is no boundary left between us. The weight of him against me, the way his hair spills forward and brushes across my face.

He kisses me, and I think of magic made from blood, honey poured into a glass vial. I think of dark-leafed vines. I think of this cottage ringed by vespertine, the way they howled as we were here, hidden, protected by his magic.

With the rain pouring down outside and the wind crying past the window, it's scouring and cold, bereft as a moonless night. Even the bed is cold, but at the heart of it, snared together, we're a fever; we're a fire.

Neither of us says we're sorry, and I'm glad of it. We are vespertine and warden. We are enemies. So let that be resolute. It would hurt more, it would be worse, if we'd done this without conviction. There is no forgetting that our truce won't last. But when his hand slides up and clasps with mine, the space between our palms hums like a hive.

I close my eyes and see gold and dark—holiness and ruin—like strands of silk all snared up together.

CHAPTER TWENTY-FOUR

I WAKE IN A GOSSAMER HOUR—NOT QUITE SUNSET, THE SKY slowly fading as moonlight rises. I'm alone, and my truce with Ravel is over. We are enemies again, and my path forward is laid out as straight and neat as a row of running stitches.

I put on my cloak and my boots, use my mother's bone-handled comb to smooth the tangles from my hair. In my pocket is a vial of tincture; I draw up a stopper full and pour it onto my tongue. Swallow it down, sticky sweet, remembering how, when I had just begun my bleedings, Fenn—embarrassed but trying his best not to show it—had told me the tincture would work as a contraceptive.

When I put on my armor, I think of Lux, feel the presence of her hands beside mine as I tighten the buckles on my blade belt. I think of Briar, how her fingers pulled the crimson ribbons on my bracers into a doubled knot. I walk out of the cottage and feel them at my side—both of them—in the way they've worried for me and tended to me. They've loved me, and I love them fiercely in return.

I pick a clementine from the tree behind the cottage, eating as I walk out onto the moors. The fruit is sour and pithy; I spit out its seeds. It feels right, to begin this with my fingers all sticky and a bittersweet taste in my mouth.

A strange, dulled ache presses over my heart, deepening as I head farther through the whispering grass and past the susurrations of the river. I can't put a name to how I'm feeling. As the sun begins to set, the mist clears, letting the last strands of golden light filter over the low sway of the earth. The wind murmurs to me as I cross through swaths of heather, telling me ominous secrets.

This was the path my mother followed once.

When I see the Thousandfold in the distance—the line of slender, bone-strung trees, shadows laid heavily across the ground—the ache inside me sinks and settles. Magic slithers against my wrists beneath the press of the relic bracers. I flex my claws, run my tongue across my teeth. I'm not afraid, but alight with determination. As though my veins are flooded by holy fire, and consecration gleams beneath my feet.

My mother followed this path, and I am her daughter, but I am not *her*, not predestined to the same brutal fate or the same bloodied ruin.

At the edge of the tree line, the evidence of my fight with Ravel is still laid out on the ground—the churned mud where we struggled, the prints of claws against the earth, the tracks left where the vespertine dragged him to safety. I walk around the marks, careful not to disturb them. I want it to be preserved, this place where he betrayed me. To let it stay on the land until it slowly fades, eroded away by wind and rain and time.

I cross the border, my breath held. The relics hum against my wrists. I slip my hand into my pocket and take out the shard, the intermingled blood on it now the color of a dying rose. It lies against my palm like a memory, and when I curl my fingers into a fist with the magicked bone at the center, I think of Ravel. His lashes dipped, his breath on my skin as he pressed a kiss to my palm, the same place now marked by the shard.

The magic of the Thousandfold comes to me like the slow drift of incense smoke. Even the shadows have the same scent—ash and cloves—as the censers we burn in the chapel. It traces around me, curls questioningly against my skin. I lift the shard to my mouth and lick down the edge of the bone, tasting dust and grave dirt and the hint of faded blood. I swallow it down, swallow down memories of bitten, bloodied fingers pressed to my lips, my eager gasps as I consumed the offered gift.

The sky turns dark. Flakes of ash spill through the air like raindrops. The incense smell becomes stronger and stronger until I feel the smoke pour down my throat like a draft of honeyed wine. Beneath my boots, the ground is charred. A path of debris— burned wood and broken stones—leads to the ruined chapel.

And just like before, the magic holds me tenderly. The Thousandfold has known me since I drew my first breath on its border, and it knows me now as I return with relics and power, with my mouth bruised by a monster's kiss. Power swirls around me like an eddying current, like I have stepped into the Blackthorn

River and let myself drift as the water laps past my body and draws me deeper and deeper.

Nyx Severin's chapel silhouettes the horizon, dark on dark, the jagged shape of the broken spire like a hand outstretched, beckoning me closer. It is silent as a tomb.

When I rescued Lux and ran from these ruins, I left behind an inferno. Now, the skeletal outlines of the burned-down building are a hasty charcoal sketch—one smoke-stained wall strangled by traces of vines, a window like a blanked-out eye.

A flight of stairs leads to the entranceway. The doors are gone, now there's only an arch like a fanged, open mouth. A heavy thicket of brambles winds all around the foundation. A moat made of thorns.

As I reach the stairs, the thorns begin to blur and shiver. The magic tightens its hold, curls warningly around my neck, above my pulse. Beneath the bandage, the healing bite on my throat gives a deep, shuddering throb. I clasp the hilt of the Vale Scythe. I tighten my fingers around the bloodied shard.

The vespertine emerge from the shadows, led by the enormous, snow-white creature who came for Ravel when he was wounded. There's still a smudge from Ravel's bloodied, clutching hand on its shoulder. Others follow behind, with sabled fur and mantles of bone, with horns that are woven by strands of ivy. Their fangs are bared, their hackles raised. I falter to a stop, and, at the rear of the pack, a vespertine with triplicate, onyx eyes starts to growl. The sound reverberates beneath my feet.

Everything goes as still as an image captured in stained glass. The shadowed Thousandfold twilight picked out in shades of indigo and umber. Me, a small figure at the lower corner with garlands of crimson ribbons at my wrists and consecration leaking through my fingers where I hold the shard. The vespertine clustered together, unearthly and terrible, their attention fixed on me.

From inside the chapel comes a voice that is now hideously familiar. "Stand down," Nyx Severin tells the vespertine. "Let her approach."

The creatures all back away obediently, slunk low to the ground with their tails lashing, their teeth still bared. As I climb the stairs, I feel their gazes pinned to me, tracking my every movement. I walk past the monsters and the charred stones and the spiraled thorns. I go inside the chapel where Nyx rose as a god and fell as a monster. Following the same path he once walked with my mother's body in his arms.

He stands before the blackened remnants of an ossuary, one hand curled over a timeworn skull, stroking the occipital bone. He still wears his human guise, and his hair is smooth as raven feathers, his eyes like emerald glass. One side of his jaw is cut with four jagged lines—the marks of my claws, the echo of when I wounded Ravel. He looks at me for a long, silent moment, then raises his hand and crooks his clawed fingers.

The stone floor of the chapel begins to tremble. Bones spear up through the mortar, wreathed in tangles of ivy. They encircle me in a grim border, an eldritch cage. I force myself to be still, to keep hold of my blade and my shard. Standing at the center of the bones, I look toward the corridor beyond, where lanterns once hung, and cells housed devoured wardens. Where Lux was imprisoned and my mother lay, a marble statue, in her tomb. Now there is only ash-flecked darkness, shadows as plush as velvet.

Then—Ravel comes into sight; moving slowly, with careful, deliberate steps. We look at each other, and I hear the catch of his breath even with the distance between us. But when his eyes meet mine, he's resolute. "I wasn't certain you would come."

"Unlike you, I don't break my promises."

His mouth tilts into a hard-edged smile. At the ossuary, Nyx taps his fingers against the skull. "Ravel," he orders. "Bring her to me."

I clutch the bloodied shard. Ravel flexes his claws. For a breath, I remember all the things that I promised myself I'd forget. How he lay beside me in the tangled sheets last night and ribboned a wayward piece of my hair around his fingers. He drew me toward him, kissed a path from my mouth to my linen-wrapped throat.

Then it all fades. All that remains is the last thing I said to him before I fell asleep. *I'll kill you both. I'll destroy everything.*

This was inevitable from the moment I watched his sister die, from the moment he swept Lux into his arms like a winged nightmare. From the moment I took him prisoner and we exchanged our bloodied vows. I'm a warden, sworn to guard the Hallowed Lands against the horrors of the Thousandfold. Ravel and I, we've been caught up as if in floodwaters, tumbled and tangled and pressed sharply together. But there was no place else we could end up except for here.

We move at the same time. Claws meet claws; magic uncoils through my veins. I draw the Vale Scythe, and the relic bone sings.

I slash out—fierce and true—and my blade glances against Ravel's throat, leaving behind a slender crescent that wells with blood. He spirals back, feints beneath my arm, his claws raking across my shoulder. My heart is loud in my ears. He grabs hold of my wrist and drags me against him. His teeth are at my throat, sharp against the linen bandage.

I drive my fist into his ribs, the shard spearing his chest—just like it did before, when we fought in the attic of the ruined chapel. He reels back, gasping, a trickle of blood at the edge of his mouth. Nyx looses an echoing gasp. I slip away from Ravel, slash out again with my weapon. There's a *crack* as blade skims magicked bone, as it strikes his armor. Another thread of crimson wells at his chest, across his skin.

My heart is hungry. My claws are sharp. The shard glows inside my clenched fist, lit by consecration and sticky with freshly drawn blood. I'm a warden born at the border of this monstrous land, raised in the shadow of the enclave's bone-laced wall. I betrayed my vows and crossed forbidden reaches in search of my origins, so fearful that I was only retracing the ruinous path set by my mother.

But I have broken the circle. I am her daughter, and I am myself. I loved a monster, and now I will destroy him.

I raise the Vale Scythe, ready to deliver a final blow. Ravel goes still; then he dips to one knee and smears his bloodied palm against the bones that have speared up through the floor. A thorn-studded vine rushes from the foundations. It lashes against my skirts, then winds rapidly around my thighs. I falter, caught off-balance, and he strikes me hard at the center of my chest. My rib-cage armor cracks into splinters, piercing my skin. I gasp out a breath that tastes of blood. My blade slips from my hand and clatters to the floor.

Ravel grabs my arm, his hand clutched over my bracers, his fingers bruise-hard as he presses the relic bones. I writhe and twist against him, the delicate tendons in my wrist grinding painfully beneath his grasp. He snatches up the Vale Scythe and kicks my feet from under me. My knees fold, and I sink to the ground.

I turn to look at him, all my fury washed away, replaced by treacherous longing. The poison I couldn't excise. "*Ravel*," I cry, faltering. "Please—"

Nyx Severin begins to laugh. He stalks toward us with slow, ominous footsteps. "Ravel has waited a lifetime to prove himself to me, little warden. Did you truly think you could bind him and tame him with your promises, your vows? He is my blood and my life. I know his mind. He would never betray me."

Tenderly, Ravel strokes back my hair from my sweat-streaked face. Then he takes my weapon and shoves it into my hand, so hard that the hilt scrapes a welt on my skin. He forces my fingers closed, folds his hand around mine. The same way we held each other as we walked through the Thousandfold with a shard clutched between our palms. The same way we held each other in that last, stolen moment of our truce.

"Father," he says, voice turned low and feral. All bruises and rot, mud and decay. "If you come closer, you can look into her eyes when I cut her throat."

Nyx laughs again. He has the same tilted smile as Ravel, but his teeth are so much sharper. "I'd be honored."

The floor shudders as he comes to stand before me. The chapel is waiting for my blood to be spilled. It wants to devour me the way it did my mother.

Ravel holds the blade at my throat as I kneel at his father's feet. Nyx looks with pleasure at the sight of me caught and subjugated. He lays his inhuman hand against my cheek—knuckles flecked with unblinking eyes, fingers banded with dark tattoos. His claws are hard and cold as he slides his hand down the line of my jaw, my throat, and touches a fingertip to the blade that's pressed tight against my skin.

"This is the relic that Saint Lenore used to destroy you," Ravel tells him. "And now I will wield it to restore your rightful power."

I think of his voice in the darkened ruins as he gentled my new claws. How all his life, the signs of softness that crept through his sharp edges were seen as a weakness, something to be ashamed of. Nyx Severin made Ravel for power and power alone. How terrible—to wish up a child and raise him as a monster. The only love between them lies in this: approval at hard-won ruthlessness. Love on a knife's edge.

"Closer," Ravel says, a leashed-back wolf with bared fangs. "You'll have to kneel."

Nyx lowers himself to the floor. He's so tall that even kneeling, he towers over me. His sharp, pale face is so close that I can see how the edges of him shift and flicker, his true form seeping through his human edifice.

Ravel draws loose the ribbon that ties my hair, combs his fingers slowly through the strands. Then he curls it into a single length, wrapped around his fist. He pulls—gentle, insistent—until my head tips back and I'm looking up at him. His eyes meet mine. Virulent green, immutable. If I reached my hand into the air above, I'd feel the frayed threads of our vows tangled around my fingers like a cobweb.

There's a mark on his honeyed skin at the place where neck meets shoulder, a bite left by my blunt, human teeth where I kissed him last night—fervent and impassioned. I think of the words he spoke as he laid me down and drew me close. *I'm yours*. Like a vow, sworn anew.

Ravel's fingers flex around mine, tightening our joined grasp on the hilt of the Vale Scythe. He watches me, unblinking, as he sets the blade closer to my throat.

Then he bends to me, presses his mouth to my ear.

"You're mine." He strokes his thumb against my wrist. There's a pulse between our hands. The air sings with magic. And understanding settles on me—like I've followed a hidden trail through a wild forest and finally, finally found my way back home.

"You're mine," I repeat with the same heated note as when I whispered to him in the dark. "And I'm yours."

Together, we strike. The Vale Scythe goes out, a swift slice across Nyx's throat. Wide-eyed, he falls back, clutching at his neck. Blood spills through his clawed fingers like a torrent of floodwater that's swept over a riverbank. Ravel casts aside the blade and takes hold of my other hand, where the consecrated shard still lies curved inside my fist. I shove myself forward. With Ravel's fingers laced through mine, we plunge the shard into his father's heart.

Roots and rot and bones burst from the floor beneath him.

The walls of the ruined chapel begin to groan, filled with eager, desperate hunger—the bones sharp-tipped, the dark-leafed vines shivering with appetite. The air is heavy, laden with the stench of rust and copper. Nyx lets out a choking breath. Ravel bows over him with abject, painstaking tenderness.

He buries his teeth in his father's throat.

There is too much love in this to call it slaughter. He's gentle as he tears Nyx Severin apart, as he drinks down blood, strength, life. All that his father was, his fierceness and his cruelty, his greed and his hunger for power and power and power.

We're still holding on to each other. I don't let go. Our palms press together and the twinned, hollowed beat of our hearts is caught like a bone shard between our hands.

The strength of the Thousandfold spills loose from Nyx. It spills from his body; it spills from within him—from his slackened mouth, the wound in his throat. Ravel devours it all. He calls in the darkness, calls it to him the way he drew Lux from the ruins with a whispered spell. The way he spoke to me at the border of the Thousandfold—a command that's as lulling as a murmured promise.

Ash falls from the open ceiling like a rainstorm, flakes sticking to our hair and our skin. The vines that lace the walls begin to wither, their leaves stippling the ground, rotted before they've fallen. The bones that speared up at our feet start to crumble apart; soon they're nothing but grave dust in a ring around us, like a chalk circle drawn by a fable witch.

There's blood in my mouth; I've bitten down unknowingly,

cut my lip. I lick it away and watch as Ravel bows over his father like a penitent, as he curls closer, presses deeper, to Nyx's torn-out throat. The vespertine surround us, pacing back and forth outside the crumpled bones. They whine and snarl, then pause to tilt their faces up into the air as they breathe in the scent of blood, of power, of death.

Nyx flings his head back, and his features blur between his beautiful human face and the eldritch monster who was once the Sanguine Saint. Horns spear from his temples, wrapped with strands of his tangled hair. Endless rows of onyx eyes blink open at his brow bone, then roll back to slivers of white. His teeth snap tightly together, a fanged grimace.

Finally, his eyes sink closed. His claws slacken against the ground. Ravel wipes his mouth against his wrist, a smear of dark staining the sleeve of his cloak. The wound at his father's throat is bloodless and clean, like a carved piece of marble, lifeless as the weathered bones on the ash-streaked ossuary.

Ravel goes still; he's stunned, grief-struck. As if this were unexpected, that it's impossible for his father to be here: bled out, dethroned. Powerless.

With shaking fingers, he touches Nyx's cheek. "He told me loving was a weakness," Ravel says quietly. "And yet, I loved him still."

"I'm sorry," I tell him. And I am. I can see his grief marked plain across his features. I want to touch him, but even the small motion of my hand laid over his feels too immense.

Ravel sighs. His breath is heavy with held-back tears. "I didn't want it to end this way. For so long, I tried to believe what he did was right—the hurt, the hunger. I took the blood from your mother, and I let him make me a monster. I was glad of it. When Hazel died, all I thought of was vengeance. I would have torn your throat out, gladly, to please him."

"What made you change your mind?"

"You did, Everline. I should have hated you, been pleased to watch you suffer. Delivered you to these ruins and proved myself loyal. That was what I wanted at first. Then I only wanted—" He hesitates, his gaze sliding shyly away from me. "I wanted another way for this to end, for us to be something more than just a vespertine and a warden."

Carefully, I sit down beside Ravel, leaving a measured space between us. I look at his hand, still pressed tenderly to Nyx Severin's cheek. His blunted claws, the tattoos banded across his fingers. The stains of blood on his skin. "And to do that—you needed to destroy your father."

"I could never harm him on my own. He made it so when he created us. He wanted to avoid Hazel or me ever enacting something like this." Ravel looks solemnly to the prone form laid before us. "And no human could ever be strong enough to kill him, not even Saint Lenore. But you could wield the relic weapon of a warden and wear armor imbued with my power. When we first came into the Thousandfold, I began to wonder what might happen if we faced him together. If he could be destroyed."

"Who better to end the reign of Sanguine Saint than a warden born in the shadow of his stronghold?" I say, a laugh tangled sharp in my throat. It's the same conclusion that drove me here, the realization I had the power to strike this fatal blow. My breath catches, and I swallow back a sob. I press my face into my palms and fill the hollowed space with the slow, hot seep of my tears.

Ravel puts his hand, tentatively, on my shoulder. "I'm sorry I deceived you. He would have known if you came here with betrayal in your heart. I lied to myself, and I lied to you, and I hoped he would think himself safe enough to let us close."

It's the first time he's ever apologized to me—for anything. I feel like a thread pulled slowly from a length of cloth, unwoven inch by inch. "What will you do now?" I ask him, my voice thick and my words muffled. *What will we do?*

Everything beyond this moment is a blur. Ravel and I were thrown together in uneasy truce, then lies, then betrayal. I was born to destroy him, and he me. And we've ended in the remains of the Thousandfold with countless unknowns between us.

Ravel looks pensively to where the vespertine sit, circled and watchful, around us. "I'll never become the perfect monster Hazel would have been. I'm not my father remade. But I'm not the boy who was born on the other side of the wall, either. I'm both—I *want* to be both." He holds out a hand, and the largest, snow-pale vespertine creeps forward, head bowed, ears laid back. Cautiously, the creature licks Ravel's bloodied fingers. "I hope I will be a worthy heir to the Thousandfold."

"You will," I tell him. "I know you will."

He looks at me, his face carved deep in lines of anguish. "Everline," he says quietly. "There would be a place for you here, if you wanted to stay."

I press my lips together as new tears fill my eyes. I want to stay. But despite these reckless emotions I feel for Ravel, how can we possibly continue beyond this moment? With a shuddering breath, I manage, "I have to go back, to tell my father and the other wardens that Nyx Severin is dead."

Ravel lays his hands over his father's chest. His fingers curl. Slowly, I shift closer to him and place my hands beside his own. Nyx is cold and still, and when I shut my eyes, I feel as though I've pressed my hand to a streambed where the stones have been worn smooth by endless currents.

The air turns cold, and the dead leaves rustle around us, caught in an updraft that scatters them like a cloud of moths. Ravel starts to speak, whispering a spell in words as delicate as embroidery. I feel a tremor in the ground. The vespertine sit in their circled watchfulness as gradually, gradually, the remains of their creator begin to shift and shimmer. The darkness rises from the earth and, piece by piece, it takes him away.

All that remains is a blackened stain on the stone floor, fringed by a delicate tracery of moss. Ravel and I sit together in the space left behind. He picks up the Vale Scythe from where he cast it aside. Carefully, he cleans the blood from the blade with the hem of his cloak, then offers it back to me. Laid across his arm, head bowed in deference.

"If you wanted—" He breaks off, voice hitched, pausing a moment to gather himself before he goes on. "I would swear as many vows as you asked of me. Bind myself to you a hundred times over. I would keep our truce. But I will understand if you don't return."

I don't know what to say or how to answer; confusion weighs down on me, and I cannot speak. I take my weapon and slide it carefully into the sheath. Ravel holds out his hand to me. His fingers are slick with his father's blood. He's trembling. I reach to him, and he draws me into his arms. My head sinks against his shoulder.

The vespertine press close around us. We're enclosed in a wash of soot-soft shadows and gentle heat, their rasped breath, and their warm, furred sides.

CHAPTER TWENTY-FIVE

THE VESPERTINE ARE WITH ME AS I RETURN TO THE CHAPEL, all of us painted in moonlight as we cross the moor. They run alongside me, a swarming vanguard of ashen fur and jagged bones, and their quicksilver swiftness is thrilling, electric. Like I've stepped into the flooded river, and the slopes of earth beneath my feet are undulant waves, a rushing, windswept current that carries me along.

Two of the smaller vespertine, with onyx coats and bone-sharp horns, stay at my sides. They run with their fearsome heads lowered, their rows of night-dark eyes narrowed—as though accompanying me is a hallowed task that requires utmost deference and concentration. Perhaps it does. These monsters belong to Ravel now, their bloodlust quelled. Even though they would have torn me apart only hours earlier.

When the chapel comes into view, I slow, and the vespertine slow with me. The largest creature, with its snowy fur still printed with the mark of Ravel's grasping hand, gives me a careful look, regarding me with its myriad eyes. Another, farther back in the shadows, lets out a low, guarded bark. The two at my sides both place their fanged muzzles against my hand, gently; then all of them turn in unison, melting back into the shrouds of mist.

Without the creatures surging around me, everything feels strange and stilled. Slowly, I flex my hands open and closed, stand with my face tilted to the moon-scarred sky as I try to catch my breath. Then I gather up my skirts and run toward the chapel.

Lanterns blink in the distance. A row of ward lights is strung around the perimeter of the ruins like a circlet made of captive stars. Briar is outside, at watch—one hand on her blade hilt, a gleaming chain of bone beads wound tight around her other fist. She sees me approach, her black-painted mouth parts in shock; then she calls back through the overgrown garden, to a figure who stands in the shadowed depths of the building behind her.

Lux emerges from the arched doorway of the chapel like a wisp of silk, her dark hair and her pale dress haloed by the glowing wards. She takes a step forward, tentative, as though she isn't certain whether I am real or some mirage painted against the moorland night. Perhaps another luring spell cast by the vespertine, the same one that first drew her away from these ruins. Then she stirs, like someone woken from a restless sleep, and she runs toward me.

We meet at the ruined stones outside the chapel. I fall into her arms, breathless and gasping. The slow tears I cried earlier when I sat beside Ravel in the Thousandfold return, fiercer now, sobs tearing loose from where I've held them, trapped, beneath the curve of my ribs.

Lux drags me close. She's all in motion, stroking my hair away from my cheeks, checking the bandage at my throat. Then she catches my face in her hands and kisses me, fiercely. "You came back," she murmurs in my ear. "You came back."

I embrace her tenderly, mindful of the sharpness of my claws. "I promised that I would."

She wipes at my face with her folded sleeve, blotting away my tears as I sniffle and sigh. Her eyes narrow at my shattered armor, at my fingers, which are stained with dried blood. She takes me by the shoulders, her brow notching with concern. "Are you hurt?"

More tears spill over my cheeks, dripping past the corners of my mouth, over the line of my jaw. I swallow, tasting salt and the memories of vowsworn kisses. "No. It isn't— I didn't—" I start to shiver, the world turned suddenly cold. "We destroyed his father. Ravel and I, we killed Nyx Severin together."

Lux stares at me in startled confusion; her hands curl protectively around my shoulders. Briar comes toward us with a lantern. The light pools golden at our feet, as though the ground here has been consecrated. She unknots her cloak and offers it to me. I huddle beneath the fabric, grateful, shivering. Gently, Briar says, "Tell us what you've done, Evie."

And so, I tell them as we stand together in the shelter of the ruined stones where I first saw Ravel up close. Where I first heard his voice. I tell them how Ravel wanted to destroy his father, how he realized that I could tip the balance in his favor, how he deceived me so Nyx wouldn't know what he planned. That Ravel has now taken his father's place, become boy and monster both.

That he means to rule over the vespertine, that he wants peace between the Thousandfold, the enclave, and the Hallowed Lands.

A second lantern adds another wash of light to where we stand, circled. I look up to see Fenn, listening, his expression troubled and solemn, as I finish recounting what happened.

"Do you think it possible to have such a truce?" Briar asks, sending a tentative glance between our father and me.

Fenn shakes his head. "Everline, whatever you intended with this misguided, foolish mission, it won't be enough."

Briar takes my hand, squeezes my fingers. Her other arm slips around Lux's waist. "He hurt you both," she says, voice taut with emotion. "He helped you, Evie, but he stole Lux away, and he hurt you both. He betrayed you—even if it was a means to an end. After all that, do you trust him?"

We stand together, the four of us. I'm still crying, and I wish my tears could be like rain. That they would dissolve the truth the way our footprints are washed from the riverbank mud after a storm. Instead, everything that I experienced in the chapel stays vivid, even when I close my eyes. Ravel's teeth, buried in his father's throat. The hitch in his voice when he asked me to stay. The feel of the Vale Scythe against my throat.

I step out of the shelter of Lux's arms, move toward Fenn with my clawed hand extended like an offering. "Ravel had the chance to embrace the role he was destined for—the monster Nyx Severin raised him to become. But he chose me, chose to change *everything*, instead."

Fenn looks at me grimly; despair cast over his fatigue-lined face. "Do you truly believe the fate of the Hallowed Lands can be held so tenuously?"

I swallow back the lump that's built in my throat, the tightness in my chest that feels like a tangle of dark-leafed vines. "Saint Lenore gave her life for our safety. If there *is* a way to end this without more bloodshed, then we have to try. We owe it to the other wardens, to everyone in the Hallowed Lands. Which is why I want to return to the Thousandfold."

Lux turns sharply to look at me. Briar smothers a gasp with her hand. But neither of them speaks. The silence stretches out between us.

Fenn keeps his eyes on my bloodied palm. "And after you return, what then?"

"I will swear vows to Ravel Severin and he to me. I will stay with him and ensure his truce."

"Everline—" Fenn begins; then he exhales a weary sigh that carves all the jagged edges from him. His shoulders are less sharpened, his gaze less remote, as he looks at me anew. "I thought I'd lost you to the Thousandfold, just like I'd lost your mother. All I've ever wanted was to spare you from her fate."

"I am not her, and this is not fated. This is my choice. I've spent my whole life trying to keep my vows, to be a true warden." I take a breath. My voice has turned as wavering as the lantern's light. "I care for Ravel, the boy and the monster. And I know that together, we can keep this truce."

"Is that really what you want?" Fenn asks, his words stilted.

"Yes, it is. The Thousandfold has been in my blood, a part of my being, since I drew breath. This is my choice. I want to go back;

I want to stay. And I'm asking your blessing as my commander—as my father."

His expression falters at the sound of the epithet. Then he nods, face turned solemn. With careful, chipped-polish fingers, he takes off the insignia that is fastened to his shoulder. "Everline Blackthorn, I name you ambassador to the Thousandfold. You will stay beyond the borders and ensure the truce remains between the vespertine and the citizens in the Hallowed Lands."

"And," adds Briar, "you will report to us at the enclave every year after the gathering."

Lux nods agreement, tears glimmering in her eyes. She sniffles, and tries to blink the tears away, wiping a hand across her matted lashes. Briar, gaze solemn, draws Lux against her. They stand with their arms wrapped around each other's waists, their cheeks flushed with sorrow.

Fenn places his hand on my arm. His touch is achingly familiar, an echo of the night in the watchtower when this all began with a slaughtered girl and a blood-red moon.

I reach to my chest, to the place an empty glass vial was once strung from a chain. Palm pressed to a memory, I bow my head. "I accept."

Fenn pins the insignia above my heart. His hands are trembling, and mine are, too. I press my fingers against his own, and I look at him, at Briar, at Lux. As though I can capture this moment in panes of colored glass to set in a chapel window, all of us here in the depths of the moorland, feeling more like a family than ever.

I start to cry again. Fenn hesitates, then guides me into his arms. He rubs my back, his touch uncertain, fingers shaking as they stroke between my shoulder blades. There's an aching care-fulness to how he holds me, a featherlight touch, and he trem-bles as though he's afraid. But I don't hold back. I wrap my arms around him, my bowed head notched into the curve of his neck. His chin rests against my hair. He sighs out a heavy, relenting breath. His arms tighten around me, holding me close.

As my father embraces me, I lean against his chest and listen to the rhythm of his heart. The night stretches on around us, the clouds pared back to reveal a clear sky, watched over by a bone-pale moon.

CHAPTER TWENTY-SIX

W E GO TO THE THOUSANDFOLD AT SUNRISE: LUX, BRIAR, and I. The latest storm has left the sky a liquid silver, just shading into light as daybreak gathers at the horizon like folded silk. The moorland is a wonder, all shimmering frost and lavender hues. Our breath sends clouds like incense smoke into the frigid air.

In another time, in another world, we might have just set out to walk the line of wards. It all feels so familiar—the three of us with our armor and our blades, the whisper of rain-streaked grass against our skirts, the way we instinctively fall into step with one another. This isn't the last time I'll cross the moorland, but I know that when I next return to the enclave, I will have changed. Everything will have changed.

I've spent so long believing my path was preordained—a fable of monsters and Saints, betrayal and fealty, written long before I ever drew breath. Now, with Lux and Briar, I've stepped outside this legacy. This isn't time spun back, my mother alive and safe, her vows unbroken, while Fenn claims me as true and magic fills my fiola. I am still the daughter of Ila Blackthorn, who betrayed the wardens and sacrificed the lives of those she was sworn to protect, all for the love of a monster.

But I am not destined to repeat her choices. Mine is a new life, a circle broken. I will forge my own way, wherever it takes me. I'm no longer bound in a cycle of guilt and secrets and hidden truths. Now there is only the relics at my wrists, my blade that killed a god, and my new insignia pinned above my heart.

As we reach the border of the Thousandfold, I notice that the trees have fresh leaves budded along their branches. The ground beneath them is carpeted by new blooms of asphodel flowers. Even the shadows within seem softer, paler—a lilac haze to their shrouded depths. But the wind that whispers through the branches still sends a shiver over me.

Briar clasps my hand. "You're sure of this?"

"I am."

We all look past the trees, beyond the border, to the path that will lead me to the ruined chapel. There's a faint scent of wood-smoke in the air, as if someone has lit a fire in a hearth nearby. Lux slips her arm around my waist. She tries to smile, but her face stays serious, her gaze troubled.

"I don't want to have to rescue *you*." Her voice is hemmed with worry. "If you get lost or trapped . . ."

I lean my chin on her shoulder, snuggling my face into her hair. "I won't be lost. I could never be lost here."

The Thousandfold doesn't feel like home. Not yet. But as I

stand in the shadow of the whispering trees, a strange feeling rises from the magic imbued in my armor, from the relic bones. It's like calling to like. I am a warden, and this is my legacy: to be a girl and to be a monster. I curl my fingers against my palms and feel the prickle of my claws.

I press closer to Lux as discomforted silence falls around us. It hurts, knowing that in a few moments, our paths will divide. I'll go onward while Lux and Briar return to the enclave for the gathering, to use their magic to strengthen the wall. This was my choice, and I don't regret it, but it hurts all the same. "I'll miss you," I say, stroking my fingers through Lux's hair.

She takes a step back and turns to face me, standing at arm's length as she inspects my armor. She checks the buckles on my bodice, tightens the fastenings at my wrists. Solemnly, she starts to tend to my hair, smoothing down the wayward strands and retying the silken ribbon at the end of my braid.

She gives me a careful look. "Do you really trust Ravel?"

"I love him." It makes me blush to admit it, but the truth comes simply, as though the words have always been in my mouth like a spoonful of honey that has slowly dissolved across my tongue. "I love him, but I don't trust him. Not yet."

"Strange how love can come easier than trust," Briar says, but she's gentle about it—almost teasing.

I manage to laugh. She smiles at me fondly, then reaches out and hitches the strap of my satchel higher on my shoulder. It's packed so full the buckles could barely fasten, and alongside the practical items like clean dresses and field kit supplies are more personal treasures—a jar of honey, a parcel of coffee, a bottle of black nail varnish. Pieces of the enclave brought to my new life.

"It's *because* I don't trust him that I'm going," I explain, still feeling shy. "It's a way to be sure he keeps the truce. And he and I . . . whatever else lies between us, I believe we might trust each other with time."

What I feel for Ravel is as dim and incoherent as the moorland when the shadows lie thick, and mist hazes the air: hard to see clearly even as it surrounds me. Our love is interwoven from the tangled threads of raw betrayal, furious longing, tentative hope. But I know we can lay down our weapons, sheathe our claws, and find a way to be soft with each other.

Lux takes out a pot of rouge and touches up my lips with paint dabbed on the edge of her finger. When she's finished, she closes the glass jar and slips it into my pocket. She takes my hand, her thumb tracing softly across the sharpness of my claws. I wrap my arms around her neck, draw her close, and kiss her. Then I reach out to pull Briar into our embrace. I curl between them both, allowing myself one last moment of stillness, of closeness, before we draw apart.

"I'll see you both after the gathering," I tell them.

We don't say goodbye but instead part in silence. I watch Lux and Briar as they walk away, their arms around each other, their heads bowed close with aching tenderness. It makes me glad, among the hurt of leaving them, to know they'll be together.

I watch until they disappear behind the slopes of the moorland, swept up in waves of heather and gorse. Then I cross the border of the Thousandfold. As I slip past the trees, the scent of smoke grows heavier. Shadows wend around my feet, beckoning to me. Before long, I see the ruined chapel—sharp against the sky, like the skeletal remains of some enormous fallen beast. From here, it looks vacant and still, as untouched as a wind-carved cliffside.

But a path to the entrance has been cleared through the mud, lined with more of the pale, new-grown asphodels. I climb the stairs to the arched doorway, and for the first time since I crossed the border, I catch glimpses of vespertine in the shadows. Curled against the jagged stones, they watch me with their new moon eyes, their ears flickering back and forth as they follow the sound of my footsteps.

When I draw close, the snow-pale vespertine rises and comes toward me. In the clear light, I see each shimmering fragment of its gaze, the honed edges of its horns, the bones mantling its powerful shoulders. A quaver of fear spikes in my chest, but I push it aside. Slowly, I extend my hand to the creature. It gives me a cautious glance, then dips its head to my fingers and licks, gently, at my palm. Its tongue is whetstone rough, its breath casts against my skin like a candle flame. Tentatively, I stroke my hand along the vespertine's back, tracing my fingers through the weft of its fur. The creature leans into my touch, then nudges against my thigh, urging me forward.

Inside the chapel nave, a fire has been lit in an iron grate. Two carve-backed chairs are pulled close to the hearth. A moka pot is set above the coals, steam drifting up in a plume from the spout. Vines wreath the windows and the walls in gentle lacework, as though the dark-leafed tendrils are trying to knit the ruined stones back together. More of the asphodel flowers grow here, clustered in the corners, their petals gleaming like bonewrought constellations.

Ravel is sitting in one of the chairs, the two onyx-furred vespertine who ran alongside me when I crossed the moors are stretched at his feet. His hand strokes idly at the nearest creature, petting its ears as it nuzzles against him. My footsteps echo quietly over the stone floor. At the sound, Ravel stands quickly and turns toward me. He is barefoot and without his cloak, and the sleeves of his thin knit shirt are pushed back past his elbows. A bracelet of leather and bone is tied around one wrist, but he is otherwise unarmored.

He looks so different from the night I met him, that wolflike mask and armor of bones, his painted features. Now, there's a new easefulness to him, a quiet confidence. He isn't Nyx Severin remade, but his own being. He bears the power of the Thousandfold in a way that is completely his own.

"Everline," he says, his voice unsteady, all hope and longing.

I smile at him, feeling strangely shy. "Ravel."

He draws a trembling hand through his hair as he looks me over, taking in the Vale Scythe hilted at my waist, my armor—the relics tied in place with their crimson ribbons—and my painted lips. His gaze lingers at the insignia pinned to my chest.

His mouth tilts, a guarded smile. "I wasn't sure you'd come."

I move toward him, passing the ossuary where his father stood with his hand curled over a skull. The bones are covered with the same vines that have started to mend the walls, the leaves rustling softly. A tremor of apprehension goes through me. This chapel devoured my mother, it held Lux prisoner with thorns and bones. It meant to devour me, too, hungering for my blood as Ravel held the Vale Scythe to my throat.

But I am not afraid—of anything. I stand before Ravel and know the Thousandfold is ours, is *mine*, the same way my blade hilt fits to my hand, the way the relic magic slips quietly through my veins. "This is where I belong," I tell him. "This is where I want to be."

Ravel closes the distance between us with careful, measured steps. A flush paints over his cheeks—perhaps from the heat of the fire, perhaps not. We meet at the center of the ruins. I lay my satchel down. Everything is laden with the heavy, solemn sense of a ritual. When I take a breath, the scent of clove incense is mixed with brewing coffee, with smoke from the fire.

I reach for Ravel and take hold of his hand, with the memory of a shard caught between our clasped palms. He moves tentatively, like he's afraid I'll vanish. His fingers trace over my cheek, claws careful as they follow the line of my jaw. He's still trembling. I rest my hand over his and he bends to me—yielding, his gaze veiled by inky lashes. Our foreheads touch, and I let out a shaky breath that feathers against his lips.

We stand together as the fire crackles and the vespertine sigh in the dancing light of the flames. Ravel casts me a tentative look. "Will you give me your vow, Everline? I—I want you to be mine again. And I want to be yours."

I place my hand against his chest, feeling the rising beat of his heart. "Yes," I tell him softly. "I will be yours. And I will have you as mine."

Bowing his head, he offers me a pleased, unguarded smile. Then, slowly, he bites his thumb and smears a line of blood across his mouth. I turn my face upward; he cradles my jaw tenderly between his hands.

I think of the enclave chapel where I pressed my lips to the effigy of Saint Lenore and promised my loyalty. I take Ravel's hand and lay it over the insignia pinned to my heart. I draw him closer. His mouth brushes mine, a kiss of vows and trust and deference.

I sigh against him, sinking closer. He draws me toward him, deepening our vow-kiss. There's a slow delight in the way our bodies knit together, the familiarity of his hands on my waist, the ashen scent of Thousandfold on his skin. This is a communion, a fealty, a new beginning that marks the end of death, of violence.

I kiss Ravel Severin, and taste blood and magic and promises.

We seal our truce in the heart of the Thousandfold.

ᴀCKNOWLEDGMENTS

Unholy Terrors is my ode to the stories I loved as a misfit teenage girl who, much like Everline, often felt adrift in the world. I am so glad to have the opportunity to share this—my third book—with readers, and I am endlessly grateful to everyone who has made this possible.

To my agent, Jill Grinberg—thank you for your support, wisdom, and patience. Your insightful advice, both on matters of craft and career, have made the chaos of author life so much calmer. And to Denise Page and Sam Farkas, thank you for providing such excellent notes on this book when it was little more than moodboards and daydreams.

To my editor, Kat Brzozowski—it has been such a delight to work with you on *Unholy Terrors* from start to finish. Your editorial eye has been invaluable in finding the true heart of this story. Thank you for your flawless organization, for answering my countless questions, and for loving Everline's fierceness from the very first draft.

To the exceptional team at Fierce Reads, who have made such a welcoming home for me and my books—thank you to Katie Quinn, Naheid Shahsamand, and Morgan Rath, whose magic with marketing and publicity rival the strongest warden spells; to art director

Rich Deas for once again creating the most *beautiful* cover; to Ann Marie Wong, and the entire team at Holt BYR and MCPG.

To Welder Wings, for capturing the soul of my story in your illustration—having your artwork on the cover of *Unholy Terrors* is a dream come true.

To the team at Penguin Young Readers—Amy Thomas, Lisa Riley, Tijana Aronson, Rebecca Diep, and everyone at PRH—thank you so much for welcoming me and my book to our new Australian home.

To the generous booksellers and authors who provided such lovely blurbs—Lauren Abesames, Kelly Andrew, Alexandra Christo, Ashley Dang, Kylie Ann Freeman, Rachel Gillig, M. K. Lobb, Victoria Mier, Bridey Morris, Amy Poirier, Monica Robinson, Kel Russell, Mara Rutherford, Brittany Smith, Kailey Steward, Dana Swift, Erica Waters, and Cass Webb—thank you for your time, your support, and your unending kindness.

To the earliest readers of *Unholy Terrors*—Riss Neilson, Cyla Panin, and Jess Rubinkowski. Thank you for your encouragement through multiple drafts and existential crises and bookish milestones. I'm so glad we're on this author journey together.

To Kat Delacorte, I cannot express how lucky I am to have you; thank you for being the Lux to my Evie, and for loving this weird, goth book about sad monster boys and fierce bone girls so wholeheartedly.

To my family for their unending support and encouragement. And especially to B., none of this would have been possible without you. I love you endlessly, and would break countless holy vows for you.

ABOUT THE AUTHOR

Lyndall Clipstone writes about monsters and the girls who like to kiss them. A former youth librarian who grew up running wild in the Barossa Ranges of South Australia, she currently lives in Adelaide, in a hundred-year-old cottage with her partner, two children, and a shy black cat. When she isn't writing, she dreams of secret adventures beneath the moorland mist. She has a bachelor's in creative writing and a graduate diploma in library and information management. She is the author of the World at the Lake's Edge duology—*Lakesedge* and *Forestfall*—which have been published in over four territories, including multiple translations.